Dear Readers,

Many years ago, when I was a kid, my father said to me,
"Bill, it doesn't really matter what you do in life. What's important is to be the *best* William Johnstone you can be."

I've never forgotten those words. And now, many years and
almost 200 books later, I like to think that I am still trying to
be the best William Johnstone I can be. Whether it's Ben
Raines in the Ashes series, or Frank Morgan, the last gunfighter, or Smoke Jensen, our intrepid mountain man, or John
Barrone and his hard-working crew keeping America safe
from terrorist low lifes in the Code Name series, I want to
make each new book better than the last and deliver powerful storytelling.

Equally important, I try to create the kinds of believable
characters that we can all identify with, real people who face
tough challenges. When one of my creations blasts an enemy
into the middle of next week, you can be damn sure he had a
good reason.

As a storyteller, my job is to entertain you, my readers, and
to make sure that you get plenty of enjoyment from my books
for your hard-earned money. This is not a job I take lightly.
And I greatly appreciate your feedback—you are my gold,
and your opinions *do* count. So please keep the letters and
e-mails coming.

Respectfully yours,

WILLIAM W. JOHNSTONE

THE FIRST MOUNTAIN MAN: ABSAROKA AMBUSH

COURAGE OF THE MOUNTAIN MAN

PINNACLE BOOKS
Kensington Publishing Corp.
http://www.kensingtonbooks.com

PINNACLE BOOKS are published by

Kensington Publishing Corp.
850 Third Avenue
New York, NY 10022

All Kensington Titles, Imprints, and Distributed Lines are available
at special quantity discounts for bulk purchases for sales promo-
tions, premiums, fund-raising, and educational or institutional use.
Special book excerpts or customized printings can also be created
to fit specific needs. For details, write or phone the office of the Kensington special sales manager: Kensington Publishing Corp., 850
Third Avenue, New York, NY 10022, attn: Special Sales Department,
Phone: 1-800-221-2647.

Pinnacle and the P logo Reg. U.S. Pat. & TM Off.

ISBN-13: 978-0-7860-1900-7
ISBN-10: 0-7860-1900-X

First Pinnacle Books Printing: June 2007

10 9 8 7 6 5 4 3 2 1

Printed in the United States of America

THE FIRST
MOUNTAIN MAN:
ABSAROKA AMBUSH

AUTHOR'S NOTE

The various Indian tribes who knew him called him Ghost Walker, White Wolf, Killing Ghost, and a dozen other names, all attesting to the man's ability as a fighting man who had no equal. The other mountain men called him Preacher. He had walked and ridden into the high mountains as a mere boy, and had not been west of the Mississippi since then. His home was the High Lonesome. The Big Empty. Preacher was a lean-hipped, wide-shouldered, heavily muscled man of average height for the time. Many women thought him ruggedly handsome. Preacher was a man to ride the river with. He liked his coffee hot, black, and strong, his whiskey raw, and his women lively.

He thought he was about thirty-five years or so, but he wasn't real sure about that. And while the mountain man known as Preacher was by no means the first mountain man ever to ride the High Lonesome. He was there during the good ol', wild ol' times, and he rode with the best of them. Preacher lasted long after the final chapter was written about the breed called Mountain Man, continuing to gain fame as an army scout, a warrior, a leader of wagon trains, and an Indian fighter. Preacher named creeks and rivers that still bear the names he gave them.

Many modern-day campers and hikers return from the high mountains with wild tales of seeing a ghost rider ambling along. Some say he sings old songs; others say they have awakened to find this old mountain man squatting beside the dying embers of their fire, drinking coffee right out of the pot. They say that he smiles at them, stands up silently, and then disappears into the night. Still others have said they have seen a man dressed all in buckskin playing with wolves and cougars.

One camper awakened in the dead of night to the sight of an old man standing over him, and when he recovered from his shock, asked the ghostly old mountain man his name.

"Preacher," the apparition replied.

BOOK ONE

No matter how thin you slice it, it's still baloney.
                                    —Alfred E. Smith

1

It was still winter in the high country when the man called Preacher packed up his few possessions and stood for a moment before pulling out.

"Horse," he said, "I think you and me have done agreed to a bad deal."

His horse, named Hammer, turned his head and rolled his eyes, as if saying that he didn't have a damn thing to do with any deal Preacher might have made.

Preacher looked at Hammer. "All right, all right. Stop lookin' at me that-away. I'll make a deal with you. You don't give me no trouble on this run, and with the money I was promised, when we get back I'll put you out to pasture in a pretty little valley and you can live out the rest of your days with a whole herd of mares. How about that?"

Hammer stared at him for a moment, and then snorted.

"I'll take that as a yes," Preacher said, then gathered up the lead rope of his packhorse and swung into the saddle. He pointed Hammer's nose east.

It was not uncommon for solitary-riding men to talk to their horses, and Preacher was no exception. A mountain man's life was a self-imposed lonely one, and he had not seen a white man all winter; spotting only the occasional Indian during the long winter months. The Indians had left him alone, and he'd returned the favor. Preacher was not a hunter of trouble, but he damn sure wouldn't back away from it if trouble came calling. And the Indians knew that only too well.

Preacher topped a rise and stopped for a moment, knowing he was sky-lining himself, but not terribly worried about it. Hammer was relaxed, and Hammer was a better watchdog than any canine that Preacher had ever seen. If there had been any Injuns about, Hammer would have let him know.

Near as Preacher could figure it, he had near'abouts seven hundred and fifty miles to go to the jump-off place in Missouri. And while the government had agreed to pay him more money than he had ever seen in his whole life, Preacher damn sure had misgivings about this job.

If them men out yonder in the northwest had such a cravin' for womenfolk to marry up with, seemed to Preacher like they could do their own fetchin'.

But they hadn't, and the government man had handed the job to him.

Preacher figured he might just retire after this job was over and done. Providin' he got it done, that is.

He walked Hammer on down the slope to the valley below. The government man had said there would be between a hundred and twenty-five and a hundred and fifty women ready to move west across the mountains.

Preacher shuddered at the thought.

He'd spent all winter trying to figure out a way to hand the job to someone else. But he hadn't come up with anybody he'd felt was dumb enough to take it. Besides, he'd given his word, and Preacher had never broken his word to anybody in his life. The government man had also said there'd be fifty wagons. Preacher would make a bet it would be more like seventy-five or eighty wagons.

First thing he'd have to do is dress up about half of them women in men's britches to fool the Injuns. If the Injuns ever found out there wasn't no more than a handful of menfolks with the wagons, they'd attack. And before they pulled out, Preacher would have to find out how many of the women knew how to shoot, and how well.

"Boy," he said to the lonesome beauty of the wilderness around him, "you can damn sure get yourself into some pickles. And this is about the sourest barrel you ever dropped into."

As soon as the other mountain men within a two-hundred-mile radius had learned of the agreement Preacher had made with the government, they had immediately left the area, knowing that Preacher would be sure to ask them to help him out, and not wanting any part of it.

"Cowards," Preacher muttered, for the thousandth time that winter. "A-leavin' me to do this by myself." But he knew there wasn't none of them that were cowards. They was just showin' a whole lot of uncommon good sense.

"Probably a lot more sense than I got," Preacher muttered. "Come on, Hammer. Let's make tracks."

A very uneventful week later, Preacher had put the High Lonesome of the Rockies behind him and was on the flats. He had not seen a living human soul and that suited him just fine. He angled south for a day and then once more cut east toward Missouri. As he rode, he tried to figure out what year it was. He thought it must be 1839. Someone had told him it was '38 last year, so it stood to reason. Providin' the person who told him it was 1838 knew what the hell he was talkin' about, that is.

In his mind, Preacher was going over the trail that lay behind him—the trail that some folks had taken to calling the Oregon Trail. But that was not official yet.

Since there was no way to talk the women out of this fool's mission, Preacher was working out in his head the best way to lead these female types, with marryin' on the mind, to the coast. The Injuns were getting some worked up about all the people with a sudden urge to move west, and for sure there was going to be trouble with them.

All in all, Preacher thought glumly, *I have got myself into a mess.*

Then he saw the smoke and reined up short. He hopped off Hammer, ground reined him, and with Hawken rifle in hand, edged up closer for a look-see. Preacher grinned. It was Blackjack Perkins, live and in the flesh. If there was a surlier man anywheres to be found than Blackjack, Preacher didn't know of him. But Blackjack was a man to ride the river with, and if he gave his word, it was the same as chiseled in stone.

Preacher knew Hammer and the packhorse would stay right where he left them, come hell or high winds, so he wasn't worried about them. He began Injunin' up on Blackjack, the devilment fairly popping out of his eyes.

Blackjack was hummin' to himself, as he was boilin' coffee and fryin' bacon and stirrin' up a pot of beans. Blackjack had himself a regular feast a-goin'.

Preacher had worked in close and Blackjack's horses were beginning to get a little skittish. Blackjack cut his eyes toward them and, without giving anything away, reached for his rifle with one hand and kept on stirrin' the beans with the other. Preacher grinned and decided the game was up; Blackjack's horses was near'bouts as good at watchin' as his own.

"Steady now, Blackjack," Preacher called, still on his belly in case Blackjack wanted to shoot first and feel sorry about it later. "It's me, Preacher."

The big buckskin-clad and bearded mountain man relaxed and said, "Show yourself, you damn reprobate. I'd recognize you anywhere. You be so ugly you frighten the flight right out of birds. I believe the last time I caught a glimpse of you was back in '35 on Horse Crick."

"You be right on one point, Blackjack," Preacher said, rising to his feet in one fluid movement. "But if I was you, I wouldn't be talkin' none 'bout 'ugly.' Even your dogs run away from home. I'll fetch my horses and then partake of your grub."

"You got any salt, Preacher?"

"I do for a fact."

"I run out. I found me a lick a few days ago, but I didn't feel like fightin' no puma over it. He'd nailed him a deer and I never liked to disturb no man nor beast whilst they's feastin'."

"That's right considerate of you. But I'm fixin' to disturb you."

"You ain't gonna get me to hep you lead them petticoats to the coast," Blackjack called. "You can put that slap out of what good sense you got left."

"It never entered my mind," Preacher said, leading his horses into camp. "How'd you hear about that anyways?"

"Ever'body from the Missouri to the Pacific knows about that," Blackjack said, pointing to the coffeepot. "That's why you ain't seen nobody for the past week—and you hasn't seen nobody, has you?"

"For a fact it's been sorta lonesome," Preacher admitted.

Blackjack grunted. "It's gonna get worser, too." He shook his shaggy head. "A hundred and fifty or so wimmen headin' into the big lonesome. I never heared of such a thing in all my borned days. Foolish, is what it is."

"Yeah, it's gonna be a real challenge," Preacher said with a straight face. "That's for a fact. It's gonna take a real special kind of man to get this done. Most men I know just don't have the sand to do it."

Blackjack's eyes cut to Preacher. "What the hell do you mean by that, Preacher?"

Preacher poured him a tin cup of coffee and shrugged his muscular shoulders. "Just what I said, Blackjack."

"Are you suggestin' that I ain't got the wherewithal to see it done?"

Preacher looked hurt. "Now, Blackjack . . . did you hear me say that?"

"You better not say it, neither." He tossed Preacher a plate. "Eat. Grub's done." While Preacher was filling his plate, Blackjack eyeballed the pistols strapped around Preacher's waist. "What the hellfire is them things? I ain't never seen nothin' like that in my life."

"They take some gettin' used to, but once a body gets the hang of 'em, they give you eight times the firepower. And I been practicin', too. I can shuck these outta leather faster than you can blink."

"So I heared. You might be on to something with them terrible-lookin' pistols, Preacher. I heared ol' Duckworth call you a gunfighter. He was at the fort when you plugged them three men last year. 'Gunfighter' . . ." He tasted the word. "Has a ring to it, don't it?"

Preacher nodded his head and chewed for a time. "I best be headin' out, Blackjack. I got to head past the Mississippi to find me some men with the backbone to help me take them women west."

Blackjack threw his fork to the ground and glared at Preacher. *"Easterners!"* he shouted. "No damn easterner could find his butt with both hands and a trained dog."

Preacher sopped up the juice in his plate with a hunk of panbread. Blackjack was a good cook and set out a mighty fine meal. "I ain't got no choice in the matter, Blackjack. 'Pears to me like the men I been knowin' all these years just ain't got the stomach for it . . . the way they been runnin' and hidin'."

"Do you see me runnin' and hidin'?" Blackjack roared, rattling the leaves of the trees along the little creek.

"No," Preacher said carefully, ducking his head to hide his smile. "But you done said you wasn't gonna help me."

"Well . . . mayhaps I got more important things to do."

"What? You ain't totin' no traps. You don't 'ppear to be huntin' gold. Maybe it's true what I heard about you?"

"What?"

"That you was gonna take up farmin'."

Blackjack dropped his plate to the ground and his mouth fell open. *"Farmin'?"*

"Yep. That's what I heard," Preacher said sorrowfully. "Man that told me said: 'Poor ol' Blackjack. Done gone and lost his nerve.' That's what he said."

Blackjack was approximately the size of a grizzly bear, but very agile for his bulk. He jumped to his feet. "I ain't lost nothin'!" he shouted. "And, by God, you don't have to look no further for a man to hep you with them wagons. I'll show you, by God, a man who can get them wagons through."

"Why, Blackjack, that's plumb kindly of you. I knowed all them rumors wasn't true. But Ned, now, I reckon what I heard 'bout him was true."

"Ned Mason?"

"That's him."

"I ain't heared nothin' 'bout him." Blackjack sat back down and filled his coffee cup. "Hell, his camp ain't thirty miles from here. Over on the Badger. Are you tellin' me that Ned has lost his nerve?"

"Yep. That's what I heard."

"We can be there this time tomorrow if we leave now."

"You ready?"

"I will be in five minutes."

After Ned Mason heard the rumor about his supposed loss of courage, he jumped up and down and roared and cussed. He uprooted a small tree and threw it into the creek. Then he picked up a boulder that would have herniated a lesser man and it followed the tree. He faced Preacher and Blackjack. "I just been a-waitin' for you to ax me to hep you with them wagons, Preacher." It was a lie and Preacher knew it. "I didn't know how to get in touch with you." Another lie. "And Charlie Burke is 'pposed to meet me here. He's over-due now. He'll come along."

"Don't you think Charlie's a little long in the tooth?" Preacher asked innocently.

"Long in the tooth?" Ned bellered.

"Yeah. This is gonna be a right arduous journey."

"What do arduous mean?"

"Difficult. This is gonna be a lot of work and Charlie ain't no young man, you know?"

That started Ned off on another round of hollerin' and cussin' and jumpin' around. He and Charlie had been friends for years. Ned finally settled down and glared at Preacher. "I double-dee-damn-darr you to say that to Charlie's face."

Preacher held up his hands and shook his head. "Don't get mad at me, now, ol' hoss. I'm just repeatin' what I heard is all, Ned."

"Well, there ain't none of it true. It's a damn lie. Come on." He kicked dirt over the fire and began grabbing up a few possessions, tossing them into a pile. "Let's go find Charlie. I know where he is."

Standing by Hammer, out of earshot of the others, Preacher grinned, stroked Hammer's nose, and whispered, "It's workin' out better than I thought, Hammer. Time them boys figure out that I suckered them, it'll be too late to turn back. And they ain't even asked me how much the job pays." He laughed softly and Hammer rolled his eyes.

"If you all through talkin' to your horse," Blackjack hollered, "let's us go find Charlie. Time's a-wastin'."

Preacher swung into the saddle. "Lead on, Blackjack," he called, again hiding a smile. "I want to get there 'fore Charlie falls over from old age."

2

Charlie Burke was no spring chicken, but neither was he likely to fall over from old age anytime soon. Preacher just wanted to play the game as long as possible. He might be able to come up with several more if he kept this sham up long enough.

"Old age!" Charlie fumed at him. "If I didn't like you so much I'd flatten your snoot, you damn whippersnapper. Let's go lead these poor pilgrims 'crost the plains and the mountains."

Preacher grinned at him. "Don't get all worked up, Charlie. You liable to have a seizure, or something."

Charlie glared at the younger man, and then a slow grin creased his lips. "These others," he said, jerking a thumb toward Blackjack and Ned, "they don't know what you're up to. But I do, you connivin' horse thief."

"What's he up to?" Ned demanded. "What's he talkin' 'bout, Preacher?"

"I ain't got no idee," Preacher said innocently.

"Say!" Blackjack said. "How about ol' Snake?"

"I thought he was dead!" Preacher blurted.

"Naw. He just looks dead. He's 'bout as old as dirt."

"You know where he is?"

"Shore. He's got him a cabin 'bout two days south of here."

"What's Preacher up to, Charlie."

"You boys try to figure it out," Charlie told the pair. "While we ride."

The old mountain man known as Snake was ancient. He could have been anywhere between seventy and ninety. Not even he knew. But what Snake did know was every trail between the Missouri River and the Pacific Ocean, and for his age, he was almighty spry and as tough as a boot. He still had enough of his teeth to gnaw with, and was no man to try to push around. Snake would either cut you or shoot you faster than a striking rattler. Hence, his name.

"I ain't never in my life been around a hundred and fifty females," Snake said. "And I ain't right sure I wanna be now. But you boys is friends, and a friend is a valuable thing. So count me in."

They were gone within the hour, heading east toward what would someday be called Kansas. Days later, they rode into a sea of waving grass and rolling hills and hostile Indians. And the men knew they were very likely to run into any number of tribes: Kiowa, Comanche, Pawnee, Osage, Shawnee, Arapaho, Wichita, and Kansa. None of whom would be terribly thrilled to see a hundred wagons come lumbering across their land. But a war party would be delighted to spot five men alone with no place to run.

"Been years since I been this far east," Charlie said, waiting for the coffee to boil over a hat-sized fire. "Ten years, at least."

"Longer than that for me," Snake said, gnawing on a piece of jerky. "I had me a runnin' battle with a war party of young bucks not too far from right where we's sittin'. That

must have been, oh, 1820 or so. I think they was a raidin'
party from down south that had just got whupped and they
decided to take it out on me. They fought me pretty good and
I still got a piece of arrowhead in my back from that skir-
mish. They chased me for miles, but my good horse carried
me safe. I finally lost 'em up past the Little Beaver."

"What tribe?" Preacher asked.

"I never knowed. I gleaned right off that they didn't appear to be in no mood for genteel conversation. As a matter
of fact, they was right unfriendly."

Blackjack said, "Preacher, there ain't no way the five of
us is gonna be near enough. Have you give that any thought?"

"Practically every hour on the hour," Preacher replied,
dumping cold water into the coffeepot to settle the grounds.
"I'm hopin' they'll be some ol' boys we know around the
stagin' area that'll be willin' to throw in with us.

"And if they ain't?" Ned asked.

"We hire some pilgrims, I reckon."

Snake shook his head. "We're gonna need at least twelve
to fifteen more men to see to the needs of all these heifers.
And that ain't takin' into consideration them that might feel
the need for some servicin'." He lifted wise old eyes to
Preacher. "And that's gonna create problems, Preacher."

"I been givin' that some thought, too. I'm just gonna have
to lay the law down to the men and the ladies. I can't keep
men and women from doin' what comes natural, but I can
damn sure warn them that something like that could tear this
wagon train apart. Well, we got about three hundred miles to
go 'fore we have to do much worryin'. I think it's the first week
in March. We're s'pposed to be there in three weeks. Give or
take a day or two. I figure a week or ten days to sort things
out and hire men. Then, boys, our troubles really begin." His
eyes cut around as Hammer's ears pricked up. "Look sharp.
We got company."

The men had picked up rifles and taken up positions before Preacher's words had stopped echoing in the cool air.

"Relax," Charlie said, standing up. "It's Ring and Steals Pony."

No one knew if Ring was the man's first or last name, and he never volunteered any explanation. Ring had come west about the same time as Preacher and was a man with no backup in him. Steals Pony was a Delaware Indian who had been taken in as a child by a white family and educated back east until he was about thirteen. He'd then said, "To hell with it," and took off for the far western mountains. He had never been back. He was the finest horse thief Preacher had ever seen and he had a wicked sense of humor.

"What the hell are you two doin' comin' in from the north?" Charlie asked, as the men rode in and dismounted.

"Runnin' from the goddamn Pawnee," Steals Pony said, walking to the coffeepot.

"I think we lost 'em," Ring added.

"You *think?*" Preacher said.

"They might show up," Steals Pony replied, pouring a cup of the hot, black brew. "I told Ring not to mess around with that girl. She was a chief's favorite daughter."

Ring grinned. "I can't help it if I'm so handsome women just naturally throw themselves at me."

"The girl's name was Stands Like Dog," Steals Pony told them. "That ought to tell you something about how attractive she was."

"How many Pawnee is there?" Snake asked.

"Oh, 'bout fifty or so," Ring said casually.

"Fifty!"

"How far behind you and how long have they been chasin' you?" Ned asked.

"They've been chasin' us for a week," Steals Pony said. "And I think they're about two hours behind us."

Ten minutes later, the mountain men had packed up and were moving east. Rapidly.

*   *   *

The days passed as the men left the rolling sea of grass, the endlessly blowing wind, and entered the flint hills section of what would someday be called Kansas; that gave way to the rolling hills and forested eastern one-third of the region. A half a day's ride from the Missouri border, the men stopped at a clear-running little creek and took turns bathing while some others watched for trouble. They then shook out their best duds—mostly buckskins—and let them air some.

"This town we're s'pposed to meet the wagons at," Snake said. "How big you reckon it is?"

"I was told about five hundred or so people live there," Preacher replied.

"Why?" Charlie asked.

Preacher shook his head. "I sure can't give you no answer to that, Snake. Takes all kinds to make up this old world, I reckon."

"Fools," Steals Pony said. "I lived like that for years in my youth. All jammed up like pickles in a barrel. No good way to live."

The same man who had approached Preacher with the envelope from President Van Buren last fall was waiting for them on the trail, accompanied by a half dozen other men, who, while dressed in civilian clothing, all bore the stamp of cavalrymen. Those men stared openmouthed at the seven mountain men.

Even though they had bathed and either shaved clean or trimmed their beards and mustaches, they were still a wild-looking bunch—faces burned dark by years of sun and wind, hats that had lost their shape months back. All carried at least two pistols at their waists, and four or five more hung on their saddles in addition to at least one rifle, which they carried across the saddle horn; another rifle was in a boot. Each man carried at least one war-axe and a long-bladed knife, either in a sheath or jammed behind a waist sash. They all had bows and quivers of arrows on their pack animals.

"Howdy, Mister Government Man," Preacher said, swinging down from the saddle. "I'm here like I said I'd be. Where's all the females?"

"Ah . . . in Missouri. Just a few miles away. I take it these are to be your assistants?" He waved at the others.

"No, they ain't my assistants," Preacher told him. "I brung 'em along 'cause they's first class fightin' men, hunters, scouts, trailblazers, liars, drunkards, card-cheats, and for the moment, clean. Although I can't guarantee they'll stay that way for very long. I also trust 'em with my life, and a man can't say that about very many other folks. I told 'em what this here job would pay, and they agreed to that. If you don't, we all just get back in the saddle and head west and you can push this gaggle of hens to the coast yourself."

"Oh, I'm sure the sum is agreeable, Preacher. As I told you last fall, I would leave that entirely up to you. I have taken the liberty of hiring on a dozen or so other men—subject to your approval, of course."

"Let's go look this mess over," Preacher said, and turned toward his horse.

A hand fell on his shoulder and spun him around. Preacher faced a young man who carried himself like some army officers Preacher had known over the years. Very arrogant ones.

"Git your goddamn hand off me, pup," Preacher told the young man.

"I take exception to your surly attitude and your very cavalier approach to this important historical undertaking, sir," the stuffed shirt said.

Preacher smiled while his friends rolled their eyes and elbowed one another, all knowing that Preacher was about two heartbeats away from knocking the young man on his butt.

"I'll tell you one more time, sonny-boy," Preacher said. "Git your goddamn hand off me."

The young man's hand tightened on Preacher's shoulder. "I am Lieutenant Rupert Worthington, sir. United States Army. I will be in command of the small detachment of troops accompanying this train. All in civilian clothing, for obvious reasons. At least to those of us with some formal education. I might have to explain that to you and your . . . assistants. But one thing we shall straighten out right now is this: *You* will take orders from *me."*

Preacher hit him with a left that crossed the lieutenant's eyes and set him down on the ground, on his U.S. Army butt.

Then Preacher turned and stepped into the saddle, the other mountain men following suit. The president's man's eyes were amused. Preacher looked down at the young officer, being helped to his feet by two of his men.

"I figure, boy, that you just got out of some sort of high-falutin' military school and you're still pretty wet behind the ears. I also figure you ain't never heard a shot fired in anger. I figure, too, that you got all sorts of ideas about fair play and rules of war and that sort of crap. Leave them here. They don't work in the wilderness. And don't you ever speak down to me again, young feller. Not to me, not to none of us. Mayhaps we don't have no fancy de-gree from some university. But what we do have is about three hundred years of experience in stayin' alive in hostile country. When one of us tells you the trail is wrong, you leave it. When we say don't drink the water, don't drink it. And when one of us tells you to get ready for an Injun attack, you damn well better get ready. And then you might stay alive out here."

Preacher and the others swung their horses and rode off at a trot.

"Savage!" Rupert said, holding a dampened handkerchief—handed to him by one of his men—to his swollen jaw.

"Son," the president's man said. "Preacher might be wild and woolly and uncurried, but he and those men with him opened up this country. Neither you, nor I, can even come close to understanding the hardships and mind-numbing deprivations they have stoically endured over the years. There is no law past this point, Lieutenant. None except what powder and shot the individual carries with him. There are no courts of law. Past this point, it is a hard and violent land, where life is cheap and death can be either quick or terribly long and painful. You don't know the breed of men called mountain man. And I scarcely know much about them. But I do know this: crowd them and they'll hurt you. The best advice I can give you all is to keep your mouths shut and your ears wide open."

The president's man swung into the saddle and rode after Preacher and the others.

"It's going to be a very interesting journey," a young soldier said.

"Sergeant Scott," Lieutenant Worthington said, after rendering the young man silent with a hard look, "mount the men."

3

Preacher and his friends sat their horses in a line on a ridge and stared openmouthed at the scene before them. None of them had ever seen anything like it, and had nothing with which to compare it. Before them there were more women than any of the men had ever seen gathered in one place. And when the mountain men came into view, all the women fell silent and heads turned to look at the mountain men on the rise above them.

"I think," Steals Pony said as he broke the silence, his voice mirroring his inner shock at the sight of so many women, "that I should prefer to be elsewhere."

"Well, you ain't," Preacher told him. "But I do know what you're talkin' about."

"There must be a thousand females down yonder," Snake said.

"One hundred and thirty-five," the president's man said, riding up behind the mountain men. "With fifteen more due in sometime today or tomorrow."

"How many wagons?" Charlie Burke asked.

"Sixty-five."

"God have mercy on us all," Blackjack muttered.

"There is a female journalist among the ladies, coming along to chronicle the event, the president's man said."

"A journal-whichilist to do what?" Ned asked.

"A writer to keep a diary."

"Oh. Why?"

"It will be printed in newspapers back east." He smiled. "You gentlemen are about to be famous."

Preacher grunted. "Stay here," he told his friends. He flipped the lead rope to his packhorse to Snake. "Hold on to that for me, Snake."

"What are you gonna do?" Snake asked.

"I'm gonna go down there."

"You be careful, Preacher," Charlie told him. "Them females look man-hungry to me. They grab you, you'll disappear amongst all them petticoats and paint and powder and they'll wear you down to a shedder. There won't be enough of you left to bury."

"You want me to tie you into the saddle?" Steals Pony asked.

"Now, gentlemen," the president's man said with a smile. "Those are ladies down there. They were all carefully chosen from hundreds of applicants. Many of those ladies come from fine old respectable families."

"And some of 'em are bound to have come from whorehouses," Preacher added. "But that don't make no difference to me. I got to eyeball 'em all up close."

"I'll pray for you," Blackjack said.

Snake looked at the huge mountain man. "You—pray?"

"I prayed a-plenty when them goddamn Utes had me back in '31. You can bet on that."

Lieutenant Worthington and his detachment had ridden up. "You probably antagonized them," Rupert said. "I was taught that the Utes were very friendly toward the white man."

"You shore have a lot to learn, sonny-boy," Snake told him. "Utes is like any other Injun tribe. They're all notional. Some good, some bad. But an Injun don't think like so-called civilized white folks do." Snake looked at the young officer. "You been around many Injuns, sonny?"

"I have studied them extensively," Rupert said stiffly.

"Uh-huh," was Snake's reply.

Preacher rode down the ridge and walked Hammer up to a group of women. The women stared at him, none of them ever having seen anything quite like Preacher.

"He's a savage," one whispered.

"I think he's cute," another said.

Soon there were women of all descriptions, sizes, and shapes surrounding Preacher. Even Hammer got a little nervous. Some of the ladies were beautiful, others were so ugly that they could stop a rampaging herd of buffalo with one look. There were ladies who were slim and trim and others of more than considerable heft. But Preacher was looking for the boss lady, and he knew there had to be one. Or two.

"You there!" a woman's voice bellered out from the crowd. "Up there on that wild-eyed looking horse."

Preacher cut his eyes to a tall and full-figured female all decked out in a black dress. She was comin' stridin' through the crowd of women and they was partin' the way like Moses done the Red Sea. The woman wasn't no real looker—to Preacher's eye—but she had her a commanding manner that he liked, and he knew he'd found one of the ramrods of the petticoat train.

Hammer turned his head to stare at the woman and Preacher tightened up on the reins. If Hammer didn't like somebody, he didn't draw any distinctions about gender. He'd just as soon bite or kick a woman as he would a man.

"Are you the famous mountain man everybody's been bragging about?" the woman demanded, staring up at him, hands on her hips. "The one who is going to lead us across the wilderness?"

"I don't know about famous, lady," Preacher matched her stare. "But I'll get most of you across to the blue waters."

"My name is Eudora Hempstead. And what do you mean by 'most of us'?"

"I mean that not all of you ladies is gonna make it. And the whole kit and caboodle of you damn well better understand that now. Now gather around and hear what I got to say. But stay out of bitin' and kickin' distance from Hammer here. He's like me; he ain't the most cordial thing in the world. Now listen up: some of you will quit and try to find your way back. But you won't make it back; Injuns will grab you and tote you back to their camp. That is, if you don't give them too much trouble. You aggravate 'em and they'll just rape you, kill you, and scalp you where you happen to be. If they make slaves of you, well, that ain't such a terrible life. They'll work you hard and only beat you occasional. Some of you are gonna die out yonder on the trail from stupid fool accidents, Injun attacks, snakebite, hydrophobic skunks, drownin'. One or two will go crazy in the head and wander off and get et up by a bear. And don't think I'm funnin' you, 'cause I ain't. I'm just tellin' you like it is."

A group of men had gathered around at the edge of the crowd of women. Preacher figured they were the ones the president's man had hired. Preacher picked out two that he was going to unhire right off. One he knew slightly and the other had a shifty look to him. He pointed at the one he knew.

"You, Jack Hayes. Get gone from here and take that ratty-eyed friend of yours with you."

"I wasn't hired by you, Preacher," Jack said.

"No. But you're gettin' fired by me. Now hit the trail. If I see you in an hour, I'll either shoot you or stomp you. Move."

Jack and his buddy left, but from the look in their eyes, Preacher sensed he'd not seen the last of them. "Jack Hayes is a murderer and a thief," he told the large group of women. "He's wanted back in Virginia."

"He told us his name was Wilbert Dunlap," Eudora said.

"That proves he's a liar too."

"We only have your word for that, Mister Preacher what-ever-your-name-is," a voice sprang from Preacher's other side.

Preacher turned his head. "Preacher'll do. Who you be?"

"Faith Crump. I am a journalist."

And a damn pretty one, too, Preacher thought. Red-headed and green-eyed. A shape that'd cause young men to act silly and old men to weep in remembrance of better days. Them duds she had on was handsewn for her, and fine material they was, too. Preacher knew a little something about ladies and their clothes.

Eudora stepped close and whacked Preacher on the leg, startling him. "Well, I like you, Mister Mountain Man," she thundered. "You don't priss around and honey-coat your words. I like that in a person. But don't you get the wrong idea about me. My man's waiting for me by the blue waters. You lead, and we'll follow, right, ladies?" she roared.

The women gave Preacher a loud hip, hip, and a hooray and Hammer just about came unhinged. Preacher had to fight to keep a hold on the reins. The president's man came riding to his rescue.

"There will be a meeting right after lunch tomorrow afternoon, ladies," he said. "Any and all questions will be answered then. Shall we go, Preacher?"

"With pleasure," Preacher muttered.

The president's man tried to put Preacher and his friends up at an inn, but the mountain men would have no part of that. The feather ticks were always too soft and the rooms too small. The men preferred to sleep out under the skies and stars.

Later that afternoon, Preacher went strolling amid the wagons and the women. There were some kids, but not many—

something that Preacher was profoundly grateful for. He smiled and spoke to the women as he walked, but did not stop to talk. That would come in a day or two. He wanted to personally talk with every female there, to spot the strong as well as the weak.

Quick as a sneaky snake, Faith Crump was by his side, tablet and pencils at hand. "So what do you think about this venture, Mister, ah, Preacher?"

"I ain't paid to think, lady. I'm paid to get you people through."

"Do you always carry that big gun wherever you go?"

"Yes."

"Why?"

"Because if I run into Jack Hayes, I might take a notion to shoot him."

"Why don't you leave Mister Hayes to the proper authorities?"

"What proper authorities, Lady? He's been loose and free for years after all the bad he done back east. Don't seem to me like anybody's doin' anything to grab him and string him up. And this is the last chance for anybody to do something legal-like." He stopped, turned, and pointed west. A dozen other women had stopped what they were doing and gathered around, listening. "A few miles yonder, Missy, the laws that you live under stop. For hundreds of miles the only law is that which a man carries in his heart and mind and what comes out of the barrel of a gun. Missy, you ain't never seen nothing like what you're a-fixin' to see in a few days. None of you. You're all a-thinkin' this is some sort of grand adventure. But I'll tell you what it is right now. It's dirt and sweat and pain and grief. It's bein' so tired you can't even think. It's pushin' and tuggin' and heavin' and jerkin' 'til your hands bleed. You ever seen a person die, Missy? No? I thought so. You're goin' to. You're goin' to see painted up Injuns who, rightly or wrongly, don't like people comin' through lands they been callin' their own for hundreds of years. You folks back east, now, you think the Injun is dumb and savage. He ain't dumb. Far from it. He's just got a way of life that suits him just fine and he's prepared to fight and die to keep it that way. And who are we to say that he's wrong and we're right? Missy, you better stock up on writin' tablets and quills and ink, 'cause you're gonna have a lot to write about. And you all had better reach down deep inside you and find all the strength you can muster up. Because you're damn sure goin' to need it." Preacher turned and walked away from the group.

"He's just trying to scare us off this journey." Faith finally broke the silence after Preacher had gone.

"No, he isn't," Eudora said. "I think we've finally found a person who is telling it straight. And I think we all had better remember every word."

"Nonsense!" Faith scoffed. "The man is no more than an uneducated lout and a bully."

Eudora looked at the fast-fading back of Preacher, striding through the camp. She was thoughtful for a moment. She came from a long line of seafaring stock, and was quite familiar with the type of man called adventurer. She knew that while they were among the best at spinning tall tales and great yarns, when they became serious, it behooved a body to listen and pay close attention. And she believed every word she'd heard from Preacher.

"Gales are going to blow," she muttered. "And the seas will be running high before we finally make port."

"Beg pardon?" a lady asked.

"Nothing, Madeline," Eudora said. "Nothing at all."

On the morning of the second day, Preacher eyeballed the ten men who'd volunteered to accompany the wagon train to the coast. There had been fourteen originally. Preacher had now kicked out Jack Hayes and three others. There would be eight soldier boys, including Sergeant Scott and Lieutenant Worthington.

Bad thing about it, Preacher thought, is that none of these men have ever been more than a few miles past the Missouri line. There ain't an Injun fighter in the lot.

"Get 'em outfitted," Preacher said to Blackjack. "Plenty of powder and shot and spare molds. I done looked over the spare mounts. They'll do. You boys take a look at them, too. See what you think. I got to go see . . . what is that damn feller's name from Washington?"

"He never said," Snake replied.

"Smart. This thing goes bad, nobody can blame him. I'll see you boys this afternoon at the meetin'." Preacher went in search of the mysterious man from Washington and found him at a pub, having him a drink of whiskey. He was sitting alone at a corner table. Just him and the jug. Preacher fetched a cup from the bar and joined him.

"You lay in them britches and shirts like I told you?" Preacher asked quietly, filling his cup.

"That I did. And I approve of your plan. But whether the ladies will, remains to be seen."

"They ain't gonna have nothin' to say about it. After we pull out, am I gonna see you again?"

"Doubtful." He pushed a wax-sealed envelope toward Preacher. "Your money will be waiting on the coast. This venture is backed by the government of the United States and there are payment on demand vouchers in there. Open it and look for yourself if you doubt my word."

"I don't have to do that. 'Cause if I get out there and find that you've cheated me, I'll track you through the gates of Hell and kill you personal."

The man nodded his head. "I am fully aware of that, Arthur."

Preacher cut his eyes to the man. First time he'd heard his Christian name spoke aloud in years. "Done some checkin' on me, did you?"

"As much as we could. We had to be sure you were the right man for this assignment. You are. Your parents are alive and very well and living comfortably in retirement. They have moved up into southern Ohio. Near your mother's relatives. You have several brothers and sisters still living. They didn't seem to be particularly interested in your whereabouts or well-being."

"I left home when I was about the size of a tadpole, Mister. I wouldn't know none of them if they was to walk through that door right now. They went their ways, I went mine."

"You haven't communicated with them at all over the long years?"

"No. Well, that ain't rightly true. I posted a letter to ma and pa some years back. I never knowed if it got through to them. Then I heard they had died. I sorta lost interest in going back."

"They know you are alive and doing well and they've been reading about you. They are both very proud of you."

"Mayhaps I'll go back east after this is over and visit with them some. Might be the last chance I'll ever get. They sure as hell ain't gettin' no younger. You gonna be here when we pull out?"

"Oh, yes. I shall leave for the east as soon as I see you off."

"I'm probably off, all right, for taking this job. Off in the head."

The man from Washington smiled. "Oh, I think not." He splashed some more whiskey into Preacher's cup. He lifted his own cup. "Shall we drink to the success of this journey?"

The mountain man and the bureaucrat—circa 1839—smiled at one another and clinked their cups.

"You gonna be at the meetin' this afternoon?"

"Oh, yes. I'll be there. You might get some questions thrown at you that you can't answer. That'll be my job."

Snake stuck his head inside the tavern. "They's some yahoo in town lookin' for you, Preach. Says you kilt a friend of hisn last year and he's gonna pin your ears back."

"He got a name?"

"Didn't say. But he's a shore 'nuff big 'un."

Preacher pushed back his chair and stood up, hitching at his pistols. "You want to come along, Mystery Man?"

The man from Washington smiled. "I hate violence."

Preacher laughed. "Somehow I doubt that, friend. I surely do."

4

Preacher stepped out of the tavern and almost knocked Faith Crump off the steps. He grabbed her just in time or she would have landed on her bustle in the muddy street.

"Missy, what the hell are you doin' hangin' around a place like this?"

She struggled free of his grasp and said, "I wanted a sip of whiskey. That's why!"

"Woman, you can't go in no tavern! That ain't no fittin' place for a lady."

"Who says I can't?"

"Well . . . it's the law, I think."

"And who makes the laws?"

"Men does!"

"Men have no right to tell a woman what she can or cannot do."

"The hell you say! And a woman ain't supposed to partake of strong drink, neither."

"Who says so?"

"I don't know who says so! It just ain't right."

"Well, I think it would be perfectly all right if I want to do it!"

"Good Lord, lady, I ain't got the time to stand here and argue this silly stuff with you. I got to go hunt up a man and whup up on his head some."

"What?"

"You there, Preacher!" The harsh shout came from across the muddy and rutted street.

Preacher turned and faced the man across the muddy expanse. He didn't think he'd ever seen the fellow before. But Snake had sure been right: the guy was big, for a fact.

"You know him, Preach?" Snake asked.

"I don't think so. What the hell do you want?" Preacher shouted.

"To put some knots on your head, Preacher!"

"Why?"

" 'Cause you kilt a friend of mine up the mountains last year. He was ridin' with the Pardees."

"He deserved killin', then," Preacher replied.

The man cussed Preacher loud and long, while a crowd began gathering on both sides of the street. A man with a large badge pinned to his shirt came running up.

"Here now!" the badge-toter shouted. "I won't have any of this in my town."

"Shut your mouth and get out of the way 'fore you get yourself hurt accidental," Preacher told him. "This ain't none of your affair." And while the town marshal stood with his mouth hanging open at such an affront to his authority, Preacher yelled to the oaf across the mud: "Do you have a name or are you all mouth?"

"Tom Cushing, you mangy bastard."

"Somebody call the police!" Faith yelled.

"I am the police!" the marshal told her.

"Well . . . stop them!"

Preacher looked at the marshal. "You go in the tavern

there and have yourself a drink on me. Just stay the hell out of this. I stomp on my own rats."

Preacher handed Snake his Hawken rifle, then he and Tom Cushing started across the street.

"Guns or fists, Preacher," Tom said. "It don't make a damn to me."

Preacher answered that with a crashing right fist to Tom's jaw that sent the taller and heavier man slopping into the mud, flat on his back.

"Stop them, stop them!" Faith yelled, jumping up and down.

"Tear his mainsail down, Preacher!" Eudora Hempstead hollered, having just walked up to see what the shouting was all about. "But watch that port fist. He's a lefty."

Other ladies from the wagon train had gathered, most of them standing silently, some smiling, ready to enjoy a good fight.

Preacher let Tom get to his feet and with a curse, the big man charged him. Preacher sidestepped him and stuck out a foot, tripping the man. Tom once more landed in the mud, wallowing around like a big hog.

"Oink, oink," Preacher said, a smile on his tanned face.

"Stand still and fight like a man!" Tom roared, climbing to his feet. He was covered head to toe with mud.

"All right," Preacher said, and drove a right fist to the man's mouth, pulping his lips and loosening his front teeth. Tom's boots flew out from under him and he hit the ground, stirring up another parcel of Missouri mud.

"Stop this barbaric behavior immediately!" Faith shouted.

"Tear his meathouse down, Preacher!" a lady yelled from the crowd.

"I command you both to stop in the name of the law!" the town marshal hollered, pulling out a huge pistol and waving it in the air.

"Ah, hell, Matthew!" a local said. "Put that damn thing

away and let them fight. We ain't had a good fight in a month
or more."

"Oh, the devil take them," Matthew said, and stowed his
pistol. He walked into the tavern, took a seat by the window,
and ordered a drink.

Tom Cushing again got to his feet and stood swaying,
glaring at Preacher. The man had lost his pistols while wallowing around in the mud. He suddenly spread wide both
arms like a bear and roared, charging Preacher. Preacher knew
better than to let the man get him inside those huge and powerful arms. Tom could easily break his back. Preacher jumped
to one side and slammed a fist against the side of Tom's
head. Tom grunted with pain and turned. Preacher hit him
with a test combination of blows to the belly and face. Tom's
face went white with pain and he went down to his knees.
Preacher stepped forward, grabbed Tom's head with both hands,
and put a knee into the man's face. Tom's nose was suddenly
flattened all over the center of his face and the blood flew. He
fell backward onto the street and lay still for a moment, his
chest heaving.

"It's over," Preacher told him. "You called me out and I
came. It's over."

"I'll kill you, you son of a bitch." Tom lay on his back in
the mud and pushed the words past bloody lips. "We'll meet
again, Preacher, bet on that. And when we do, I'll leave you
for the ants and the buzzards."

"You best just go on back to where you come from and
forget it," Preacher told the man. "I was just playin' with you
this time around. If there's ever a next time, you'll find that
playtime is all over."

"Magnificent, mate!" Eudora hollered from the sidelines,
while most of the other women clapped their hands.

Faith looked disgusted.

"Write this here little fracas down in your journal, Missy,"
Preacher told her, scraping the mud off his moccasins and
leggings.

"You . . . you . . . *brute!*" she told him.

"I think she likes you, Preacher," Blackjack said, as Snake handed Preacher back his Hawken.

"Oh!" Faith said, tossing her head and flouncing off toward the encampment.

Preacher eyeballed her as she left. Mighty pleasin' sight to the eyes. Mighty pleasin'.

Preacher stood on the lowered tailgate of a wagon and looked out over the sea of females; Faith Crump and Eudora Hempstead were in the front row.

"The man who put all this together tells me you all know how to hitch up a team and handle the reins—for them of you who chose mules and them that preferred oxen, you best know what to do with a yoke and proddin' stick. You all better know. I ain't runnin' no baby school here. I'll let you all know how I feel about this mess right off. I personal think it's probably the most ignorant plan that was ever conceived. But I give my word that I'd see it through, and I will."

Preacher looked out onto the bonneted heads of the ladies; beneath the bonnets were grim and determined faces, showing some fear, but that was good, Preacher thought. When a body stops being afraid in the wilderness, the next move is death.

"Me and the men I brung with me will personal go over every wagon and every animal, commencing right after this meetin'. And it's gonna be a short one. Bet on that. And I'll tell you the reason why: 'cause I could stand up here and talk about the wilderness and the plains 'til I fell over from lack of breath, and my words would mean nothin' till you all see it and taste it. So there ain't no point in askin' a bunch of damn fool questions. The trail will answer them soon enough, believe you me." Preacher paused for a few seconds.

"Ladies, I ain't tryin' to be difficult, and I don't mean to belittle y'all's headin' west. Some folks say the country needs settlin'. I got mixed feelin's about that. Howsomever, it ain't up to me to make them decisions. My job is to get as many of you through as I possible can. We're gonna pull out three days from now. We're gonna travel for two days, and then we'll have us some rifle and pistol practice for a couple of days." He noticed the women exchanging glances. "That's right, ladies. 'Cause when the Injuns attack, and they will, y'all got to fight right alongside us men, and you got to know how to load and fire. I've laid in ample stocks of lead and powder and molds for the balls. When I'm satisfied that y'all can more or less hit what you're aimin' at, we'll stretch out for a week. Then we'll stop and do some shufflin' around. By that time you ladies will have had some squabbles and made friends and enemies and you'll know who you want to travel with for the next four or five months. Now then, I want you all to get back to your wagons for inspection. Right now! Dismissed. Haul your bustles!"

The ladies scampered back to their wagons and Preacher hopped down and came face to face with Lieutenant Worthington.

"I was trying to get your attention . . ."

"I seen you out there hoppin' up and down like a bee-stung bear," Preacher said. "I figured you had to pee, way you was actin'."

"Now see here, Preacher. I represent the United States Army. I . . ."

"I got to go, boy. I got wagons to inspect. You go sharpen your saber or something. We'll talk 'fore we stretch 'em out. I can't see no way to avoid it."

Preacher left him standing with his mouth open, momentarily speechless. Which for Lt. Rupert Worthington, of the Virginia Worthingtons, was a very distressing experience.

"They look pretty good to me," Blackjack said.

It was the evening before the wagons would roll out from

the last large pocket of civilization for hundreds of miles. The men were lounging around a fire, drinking coffee and talking. All the men were there, including Lieutenant Worthington and his small troop. Of the civilians hired to accompany the wagons, there was Nick, Sam, Jake, Dan, Frank, Barnaby, Teale, Gabe, Hugh, and Upton. They ranged in age from about forty to fifty. Preacher had wanted no young studs along; not with this many females. There would have sure been trouble with young men along.

"Yeah, they do," Upton said, then smiled. "Twenty-five men and a hundred and fifty odd women, settin' out to do something that ain't never been done 'fore. You think the history books will write about this a hundred years from now?"

"What difference will it make to us then?" Charlie asked lazily, his head on his saddle. "We won't be nothin' but dust in the ground. Providin' we're lucky enough to get a proper buryin', that is."

"You do have a point," Preacher said. "Rupert, what do you think?"

The question startled Rupert; he was so accustomed to Preacher ignoring him. "Why . . . yes, I do believe history will record this journey. After all, we do have Miss Crump along. And I'm fair bursting with excitement myself at just the thought of it. It's going to be quite the grand adventure indeed."

The mountain men had decided to try to be as nice to the young lieutenant as possible, so they hid their smiles and did not look at one another after his remark.

"Well, Rupert," Preacher said as civilly as possible. "You damn sure right about that."

It was going to be an adventure all right. With mosquitoes in some places as big as bats, rattlesnakes and scorpions, swollen rivers, hostile Indians, gangs of thugs and murderers, heat and dust and boredom, mud and rockslides, and the seemingly never-ending western horizon that they all had seen drive some men into raving lunatics. Not to mention driving rains that would slow them down to a crawl, or sometimes to a complete halt. For the next three or four hundred miles, Pawnee, considered to be the best horse thieves in the world, would be slipping around trying to steal their livestock. There would be guns going off accidentally, blowing holes in people. Axes slipping and causing hideous wounds. People with twisted ankles, fevers, busted fingers and toes, tempers flaring as the trail got longer.

Oh, yeah. It was going to be quite the grand adventure.

Rupert got up to go check on something or other. He was always checking on something and writing things down in a book, and his men left with him. Ring cut his eyes to Preacher.

"A grand adventure, Preach?"

Preacher tossed the dregs of his coffee onto the ground. "Yeah," he said with a sigh. "Ain't that what they all say, startin' out?"

5

In the years to come, the methods of pushing wagons west would change, little of it for the better. Wagon masters would have sentries firing guns at four in the morning to awaken the sleeping pioneers—a rather stupid practice in Indian country when, in the very next minute, every grain of powder and lead might be needed in a fight for life. They would have bugles blowing to form the line and many wagon trains would stretch out for several miles.

But Preacher and those few other mountain men who would agree to lead wagons west would have none of that nonsense. In the years ahead, the danger of Indian attacks would lessen to near zero, but for those first few movers West—about which little had been written until now—Indian attacks were the norm, rather than the exception.

Preacher had gone over the supplies—not just the list of what every wagon should contain, but personally checking over each wagon's contents. On foodstuffs he checked everything from eggs and molasses to sugar and hardtack. He made certain the wagons contained extra augers, shovels, oxbows, linchpins, and gimlets. He ordered the man from

Washington to provide additional wagons and drivers, the extra wagons containing barrels of axle grease, spare ox-yokes, tents and blankets, powder and shot, hammers and nails, and rope and trading goods to placate the Indians. Oscar, Sid, and Felix were the new drivers, all seasoned hands with reins. Preacher put some of the older kids in charge of the spare mounts, mules, and cattle . . . but always with adult supervision.

The day before they pulled out, starting well before dawn, Preacher rousted out the sleepy-eyed women and went through each wagon with a fast but unrelenting vengeance, ordering heavy chest of drawers, iron stoves, and huge grandfather clocks to be left behind. That move didn't endear him to the hearts of some of the women, but he told the ladies to either get rid of the crap or stay behind.

They all got rid of it.

The wagons were all new and well-made of hardwoods, each wagon four feet wide by twelve feet long. Each wagon carried spare canvas and spare parts such as iron tires, spokes, and tongues.

If there was anything Preacher missed, he didn't know what it was.

On the morning of the pullout, Lieutenant Worthington rode about the camp singing, "Oh my darlin', to the West we go," to the melody from "My Darling Clementine," until Preacher told him if he sang it one more time, he'd jerk him off his horse and stuff a rag in his mouth.

A bit crestfallen, Rupert shut up.

At 5:00 A.M., after breakfast and after everything was packed up, Preacher rode up to the lead wagon—which he had personally chosen—being driven by Eudora Hempstead and Cornelia Biggers. The third person, in the bed of the wagon, was a woman named Anne.

"We have a fair wind blowing, Eudora?" he asked the woman with a smile.

"She'll puff the mainsails and move us right along, Captain," the tall and handsome woman replied, also with a smile on her lips in the predawn hours.

"Be you excited, Eudora?"

"I'd be telling a big whacker if I said no."

"I'll set an easy pace for the next two days. That'll work the kinks out and settle everybody in. I don't figure to make more than twenty miles 'fore we stop for some rifle and pistol practice. That close to the fort, I don't expect any Injun trouble. But you just never know." He rode on, pausing every now and then to stop and talk to the ladies on the wagon seats.

Faith Crump was riding with Gayle Hawkins and a lady named Wallis.

"It's a barbaric hour," Faith complained. "Why, the sun isn't even up."

"It'll rise," Preacher told her. "It always does." He smiled at Gayle and rode on.

Over the past few days Preacher had learned from the president's man that Faith came from a very wealthy family—her father owned ships, railroads, newspapers, banks, and the like—and that Faith was known as a very head-strong, opinionated, and outspoken young lady (Preacher had already known that), and that her father had agreed to her coming on this trip just to get her out of the house and give him some relief. Faith had started her own monthly magazine back East and was very strong in the women's right-to-vote movement. She and many of her friends and coworkers had been arrested several times for bellying up to the bar and demanding service in various saloons in Boston, New York City, and Philadelphia. Faith had also been arrested once for telling the mayor of New York City to "Go suck an egg!"

"Lash that canvas down tighter on the left side and secure it, Maude," Preacher told a lady. "They's winds out on the plains that you just won't believe."

"You can't drive oxen sittin' on the damn wagon seat,

Orabella," he told another lady. "Get out here and walk. You know better."

As the first faint rays of light began streaking the eastern skies, Preacher rode back to the head of the column. "Scouts out?" he asked Charlie.

"Snake and Blackjack left an hour ago, Preach. The local gospel shouter is here to say a prayer for us."

"Good. We need all the help we can get."

A minister intoned a short prayer for their safety and then stepped aside.

Preacher nodded his head. "I guess we got it to do," he muttered. He twisted in the saddle and shouted, "Stretch 'em out, ladies. Let's go!"

Preacher sat his saddle on the south side of the train and watched it slowly rumble past. Because of the mixture of oxen and mules, he figured on any good day of doing no more than twelve miles. Mules could do twenty, but oxen averaged fifteen. So he split the difference. When conditions worsened, either on the trail or because of bad weather, they'd be lucky to do eight in a day. It was a nearly two-thousand-mile, five-and-a-half-month trip any way you wanted to cut it.

These wagons were called prairie schooners—they were not Conestogas. The Conestogas—which weighed one and a half tons, empty, were developed by Germans in Pennsylvania and used primarily on developed eastern roads, which could be graded from time to time, taking six to eight mules to pull the loaded wagons. They were far too heavy for the early roadless west.

When the last wagon had passed and the livestock had been driven by where Preacher sat, the lights of the town on the Missouri border could no longer be seen by Eudora in the lead wagon.

"Get up there, now. Haw!" Eudora hollered to her team of mules, then muttered, "We have done it now, ladies. May God smile on this venture."

* * *

For two days the wagons rolled, from first light to one hour before the sun set. Preacher set an easy pace and, at the end of the second day, figured they had covered about twenty-five miles. They had seen no other human beings except their companions on the wagon train. He let the women sleep late the next morning, until 7:00 A.M., and then Preacher rolled them out.

After breakfast, he pointed to a wagon he'd had pulled in close. "Men's britches, men's shirts, and men's hats," he told them. "From this point on, half of you are gonna be dressed like men."

"Hot damn!" Eudora shouted. "We're throwing convention to the wind and to hell with what other people think."

"That's for me!" Faith said.

Preacher had expected a tremendous hue and cry of outrage from the ladies. He got none.

"Well, I'll just be damned," Preacher said to Snake. "How do a man ever figure a woman?"

"You don't," Charlie told him. "Don't ever try to second-guess no female person. It can't be done. My daddy tole me that right before I left home, and he shore was right."

Eudora took charge and began assigning clothes to the ladies. None of them argued with her, and Preacher knew he'd made a wise choice in naming her wagon boss.

"Captain," Eudora called to Preacher; she would call him nothing else, for the moment. After a few months on the trail, they all would be calling him many things, usually under their breath.

"Wagon boss," Preacher said, walking up to her.

"We can't have the make-believe men having long curls. How about we whack them off? It'll all grow back, time we get to the blue waters."

"Good idea. But save the curls and tie them to the barrels of your rifles so's the Injuns will think it's scalps."

"I do like the way you think, Captain," Eudora said with a smile. "If I wasn't bespoken for, you'd be in trouble."

"You right sure that feller a-waitin' for you is man enough to handle you?"

"If he isn't, you better keep a sharp eye out on the seas behind you, Captain."

The women all roared at that and Preacher laughed and walked away.

It got deadly serious in a few hours, when Preacher lined them all up for weapons' practice. It turned out that about half of the women had come from towns and cities and had no idea how to handle any type of weapon.

"I think we're gonna be here longer than we furst thought," Blackjack opined. "Some of them gals don't even know which end the ball comes out of."

"But ain't they attractive in them men's britches?" Ned said.

"Well, we brung more than ample shot and powder," Preacher replied. "Let's get to it. But for God's sake, let's don't have no one blowin' somebody else's head off accidental."

The wagon train stayed where it was for three days, the rolling, seemingly empty, and constantly windblown sea of grass reverberating with the roaring and cracking sounds of gunfire. Some of the ladies took to the guns like they was born to it, others, even after three days of practice, couldn't hit a barn if they was standin' inside it.

Preacher and the other men decided that just about a third of the women would handle the guns; the rest would reload and stand by to put out fires caused by fire-arrows and tend to the kids, livestock, and, in case of Indian attack, the wounded, which, the mountain men knew, would need help somewhere up the line. Eudora, to no one's surprise, turned out to be a crack shot. Faith couldn't hit a bull in the ass with a bass fiddle.

"There ain't no point in wastin' no more shot and pow-

der," Preacher said. "We pull out in the mornin'." A dozen or
so women had gathered around him, and Preacher squatted
down and brushed a grassless area clean with his hand. With
a stick, he started a rough map. "Lookie here, ladies. A couple more days on the trail, and we head northwest. We'll
cross the Kansas and keep headin' north by northwest until
we reach the Platte. We'll follow that, on the south side of it,
until we reach the South Platte. We'll cross that, and follow
the North Platte until we reach this tradin' post here"——he
jabbed at the earth—"that some has taken to callin' Fort
Laramie. From there, we follow the Sweetwater to South
Pass, then south to another tradin' post. From there, we cross
the Tetons up to a Hudson's Bay Company post on the
Snake. Next stop is a tradin' post up here on the Boise—providin' the Injuns ain't killed everybody and burned the damn
place down. Which they had done more than once. Then we
head north through the Blues up to the Whitman Mission.
Then west followin' the Columbia over to the Dalles. Past
that, we're home free and y'all can hitch up with your men
and live happy ever after." He smiled up at them. "Looks
easy, don't it?"

The women, including Eudora and Faith, did not return
his smile. Even after only twenty or so miles, most of the
women had discovered that this journey was going to be
rough.

They had no idea how rough.

The women got their first taste of river crossings at the
Kansas. It was running slightly high due to spring rains, and
the crossing was rough and for a few, very wet. Some of the
women fell off the wagons and into the drink.

"What the hell are you doin', Preacher?" Steals Pony
asked, riding up. "There is fine crossing only a few miles
south of here."

"I know it," Preacher replied. "But I want any quitters to
start hollerin' now, whilst they can give it up and still get
back to Missouri."

"But we'll have to cross the Soldier and the Vermillion on this route," Snake said.

"Damn sure will." Preacher's tone was firm. "I want to shake down this train right off. If they all can stick it out over the next few days, we'll know what we've got."

"You're a hard man, Preacher," one of the locals he had hired back in Missouri said. "But I see why you're doin' this. I better get over there and help with the ropes."

"No, you won't," Preacher stopped him. "This crossin' ain't nothin'. The water ain't even hub deep. Let the women handle it. We showed 'em how. Now it's up to them. I want their muscles hardened up whilst we're still in more or less friendly country. You local boys ain't never seen no mountains like we're gonna have to cross. I want these women tough 'fore we hit 'em."

The women began to toughen up, and many of them also got mad. They stood on the bank and watched the men sit in their saddles, staring at them, not lifting a finger to help. Those women who had been raised on farms, or, in Eudora's case, on the coast, and were used to hard work chuckled at the other ladies, smiled at each other, and simply went to work.

Many of the women would not cook for the men that evening, much less speak to them. But other women held no hard feelings, so the men got fed. Eudora smiled across the fire at Preacher as he ladled out stew into his pan.

"You didn't win any popularity contests this day, Captain," she said.

"I didn't plan on winnin' no prizes. What I plan on doin' is gettin' you ladies through to the coast. We ain't hit nothin' yet, Eudora. It's been a cakewalk so far. But these gals will be a hell of a lot tougher when we get there than when we left. Bet on that."

"I have no doubts about that, Captain. None whatsoever." She tossed him a huge chunk of bread. "Just baked. Enjoy."

The following days plodded on and passed uneventfully.

By the time the women had crossed the Soldier and then the Vermillion, they knew how to cross rivers—at least small ones—and asked no help from the men. It became a matter of pride to the ladies. And that was what Preacher had been hoping they'd develop.

Despite himself, knowing that the awful, terrible worst was yet to come, he began to feel proud of these women. These women wasn't no shrinkin' violets. They were women wanting a new start in a new land, and they were willing to work for it.

They were about three days south of the Little Blue when Steals Pony came galloping back to the train and up to Preacher.

"Indians! Sauk, Fox, and some Winnebagos, Preacher. They've come down from the north for their annual spring hunt on the plains."

There were only very minor differences between the Algonquin tribes such as the Fox, Sauk, Winnebagos, Ojibwa, Ottawa, Illinois, and Miami. Sometimes several tribes would band together for the great spring hunt on the plains. Only a few tribes did not make the trek southward for buffalo, among them the Potawatomi and the Ottawa. They really didn't have to, for their own country was abundant with moose and deer and bear. Most of those northern tribes combined the planting of crops with hunting.

"Are they friendly?" Preacher asked, not yet halting the wagons.

"Well . . . they were not unfriendly. But we have to remember that this is their great religious time, too."

"Yeah," Preacher agreed. "Manitou. And Manitou can make them unpredictable as a tornader."

To many Indian tribes, Manitou was all the forces that were present in things—men, rocks, trees, the wind . . . everything. Manitou also was the controlling hand in their destinies, and if they felt the power of Manitou within them, the Indians' temperament could be violent.

"Pass the word, Steals Pony. Tell the gals to haul out them

rifles and shotguns. Make sure that hair is danglin'. We're gonna circle for the afternoon and put on a show of force for them."

Preacher rode up to the lead wagon.

"Savages, Captain?" Eudora asked calmly, no fear evident in her voice.

"Yep. And a bunch of 'em, too. Begin the circle, Eudora."

"Aye, aye, Captain. If the savages want a fight, we'll give them one."

Preacher smiled. For a fact, he'd damn sure hate to tangle with Eudora Hempstead.

6

Preacher sent scouts out to keep an eye on the Indians while he sat his saddle and watched the wagons slowly circle the driven livestock. He'd had the women practice this move, and they did it perfectly, without panic. He rode up to the wagon that had Faith, Gayle, and Wallis in it.

"Don't worry too much about this bunch," he told the women. "They're not gonna risk gettin' killed and leavin' their families without no means of food. If they do come close to us, Miss Faith, what you're gonna see is all that's left of the Great Lakes tribes. And I mean this is it. They really ain't been a force to reckon with since Black Hawk and his Sauks and Foxes was cut down back in '32 as they tried to swim the Mississippi."

"Then why are we doing this?"

" 'Cause you just don't never know about an Indian. They don't think like we do. Their values ain't the same. I'm not sayin' they're right or wrong; they're just different. I 'spect once they see how big a force we are, they'll ride on. But they might come back tonight and try to steal horses or oxen, or maybe take a scalp or two. You just never really know."

Faith was scribbling furiously on a tablet.

"Y'all fetch your weapons and get behind cover. I'm goin' out to confer with them."

"Pretty sorry-lookin' bunch," Ring remarked, when Preacher rode up.

Preacher looked at the gathering of Indians about a quarter of a mile away. And as he watched them, he knew this bunch would give them no trouble. Even at this distance, he could tell that many of the men were old by the way they sat their ponies. "Get all the men up here," Preacher told Ring. "Rifles in hand. Line up along this ridge. I think that'll be all we have to do. And put that damn Rupert Worthington right here next to me. I don't want him startin' nothin'."

The twenty-five men, all carrying rifles, lined up in a single line on the ridge, each man about five feet from the next.

"Are they hostile?" Lieutenant Worthington asked, his eagerness for battle obvious in the question.

"No, boy," Preacher told him. "They ain't hostile. They're just old and tired and beat down in spirit and wore out. That's all. And I ain't gonna take what pride they have left away from 'em. Stay here. Steals Pony, Snake, let's ride."

The three mountain men rode up to the mixed band of Indians. Preacher lifted one hand, palm out, to a man who wore the headdress of a chief. The chief hesitated, then returned the gesture of friendship, peace, and welcome.

"We apologize if we have interrupted your hunt," Preacher said. "We are only passing through. We will be gone in the morning."

"That is good," the chief replied. "Would that be so with all white men?"

"All white men are not the same," Preacher said. "Like all Indians are not the same. There are good and bad among us all."

"You speak the truth. It is good to hear it from the lips of a white man. It is a rare thing. You will not be bothered by us. Come and go in peace." He turned his horse and rode away, the large band of Sauk and Fox following.

"There are a few mean-eyed young bucks among that band," Steals Pony said. "I think we'd best double the guard tonight."

"I think you're right," Snake said. "Do you know what that was you was talkin' to, Preach?"

"No."

"That was Chief Chekuskuk. The head honcho of the Fox."

"And one of those young braves was Wind Runner," Steals Pony added very, very dryly. "With fresh scalps on his horse's mane."

"Keep the young'uns in the center of the circle," Preacher instructed the women with kids. "They'll be a few Sauk or Fox trying to slip inside tonight to take scalps. By now they've broke away from the main band and are circlin' the train. But they're miles out."

"But you said the chief promised us safe passage," a woman named Claire Goodfellow said.

"The chief don't always speak for everybody," Preacher told the women. "What color you are don't make no difference. Young people is the same everywhere. Some of them have respect for their elders, some don't. They'll be a dozen or so paying us a visit tonight."

Eudora had done a bang-up job of circling the wagons. She had pulled them in tight, angling them close with tongues pointed inward so the mules and oxen could be unhitched inside the protective circle. The tall, handsome woman was definitely an asset and Preacher vowed to stay on her good side. She had never said why she was going west, and Preacher would never ask. He'd heard rumors that Eudora had been jilted by a beau back east and was heartbroken. But he didn't believe that rumor. The one he believed was the one that she'd caught her intended with another woman and had jerked out a pepperbox and drilled him through the brisket. Her father, a fairly wealthy shipowner, had gotten her out of Boston a half a step ahead of the law, who had a noose ready for her shapely neck.

And Eudora Hempstead was not her real name. But it would be from now on.

Steals Pony, the Delaware, slipped back into the camp like a ghost and almost caused one of the drivers to soil his underwear when he tapped him on the shoulder. "You will die unless you open your ears to the night," he told the Missouri man. "You stand and shuffle around instead of squatting and being silent. You also smell bad." He walked on, chuckling softly.

He found Preacher. "They come."

"How many?"

"Ten. Maybe twelve."

Lieutenant Worthington walked up. "What do you want me to do, Preacher?" he asked nervously.

"Get back to your post and stay there," Preacher told him shortly. "And don't be firin' at shadders. You'll have the whole damn camp shootin' at the wind."

Rupert walked off, muttering to himself.

The first young buck made the fatal mistake of going after Eudora Hempstead. He thought the tall "man" would prove to be a formidable foe and that once he had "his" scalp, he would show it proudly and songs would be sung about his bravery.

The only song that would be sung about that young Fox would be the death song, sung by his relatives.

Eudora uttered a very unfemininelike oath and flipped him off her back and smashed the butt of her rifle into his face, then ruined his throat with another savage butt-smash. She was a very strong woman. The brave died horribly, thrashing about on the ground.

"You want his scalp?" Snake called out.

"Heavens, no!" Eudora said.

Faith turned green.

"Then I'll jerk it off," Snake said, kneeling down with a knife in his hand.

Faith belched, as ladylike as possible.

Snake whacked off the hair and hung it on his belt. Then he and Steals Pony tossed the carcass outside the circle of wagons.

Faith turned her head and lost her supper, as did several other women standing close by.

"Must have been something they et that didn't agree with 'em," Snake said.

"Of course," the Delaware agreed, his eyes twinkling. "Probably the venison."

"I'm shore that's it."

"Wipe your mouth," Eudora told Faith, as she removed the blood from her rifle by rubbing the butt-plate on the ground.

Faith wiped her mouth with a dainty little hanky and gave the tall woman a very dirty look. The look bounced off Eudora with a laugh. Eudora cradled her rifle and turned her attention to the blackness outside of the circle.

Preacher's eyes picked up a flitting shadow and he cocked his Hawken.

There was no moon; the skies were overcast and the air heavy with moisture. They'd have rain in a few hours.

The shadow flitted again and Preacher lifted his rifle. If the Indian held to his course, he was heading for a tangle of old brush, about fifty yards from the train.

The brave jumped and Preacher fired, the ball taking him in the side and blowing out the other side. The buck screamed once and fell to the ground. He lay still.

"Good shooting, Captain," Eudora said. Then she lifted

her rifle and blasted into the night. A brave let out a mighty yowl of pain and the sound of running feet was heard—feet running away.

"Where the hell did you shoot that buck, Eudora?" Preacher called.

"In the sternum," she replied. "Dead center."

Across the way, old Snake chuckled. "He'll not be sittin' on no horse for some time to come. She's firin' a Whitney military .69 rifle. Their new model. It's a dandy, too. That buck probably ain't got but one back cheek left. If you ladies will pardon my unseemly talk."

In the distance, faint sounds of squalling from the buck who'd been shot could still be heard.

Preacher grimaced in the night. There was no doubt in his mind that Eudora's shot was deliberately placed. He wondered where she had plugged that feller back in Boston? He thought he could guess. Probably shot it off. Preacher shuddered.

Preacher and the others waited for a long and silent ten minutes.

"They go," the Delaware called, lying on his belly with his ear to the ground. "They will not return."

"Their medicine turned sour on them," Charlie Burke said, walking up. "That shootin' by Miss Eudora done it. You'll do, lady," the old mountain man said. "You'll do just fine."

"Don't bother cranin' your necks to see the bodies," Preacher told a few of the ladies the next morning just before the wagon train's dawn pullout. "They're long gone. Injuns tote their dead off. Y'all done just fine last night. That was just to get you ready for when a real war party comes at us. And they will."

"Worse than last night?" Faith asked. "How could that possibly be?"

Preacher just looked at her, disgust in his eyes.

"Oh, you're just trying to frighten us." Faith dismissed his remark with a toss of her strawberry curls.

After a couple of weeks out, Faith had been horrified to discover that there really was no road, just a trail, of sorts but the Eastern socialite and sometime writer had toughened up, despite herself. Her face and forearms had turned red from the sun, blistered, and then begun the tanning process. Her muscles, which had ached fiercely the first week, had grown stronger from the pushing, shoving, hauling, and hours at the reins handling the big mules. Of course Faith still complained all the time, but now no one paid any attention to it.

So far none of the women had voiced any desire to turn back. And the men had been surprised at that, for they had been watching about a dozen of the ladies whom they felt were the weak ones, not necessarily in body, but in spirit. But even those women had toughened up and were enduring the trail.

They saw no signs of the Sauk or Fox as they rolled out. Preacher knew they had killed at least three of the attacking Indians and wounded at least two more. To an Indian's mind, those losses were too great to continue the battle. They had failed, but perhaps there would be another day.

Preacher headed the wagons for the Platte.

In about seven years, when the flow of westward pioneers would number in the thousands, the U.S. Army would establish a fort on the south side of the Platte, and it would be one of the most important forts on what would soon be called the Oregon Trail. But for now, Preacher, his friends, and the ladies on the wagons, were alone in hostile country. Should it be needed, there was no one they could turn to for help. If something were to happen to them, it might be months before a patrol was mounted to look for them. And by then it was doubtful any trace of them would be found. There are no accurate records as to the number of men, women, and children who just vanished—disappeared from the face of the earth, with wagons, mules or oxen, and equipment, forever—on their way west. Some place the numbers in the hundreds, others say it was in the thousands. No one really knows because many wagon trains were hastily thrown together and headed west without U.S. Army permission. Many foolhardy folks headed west in small trains—three or four wagons—and were never seen again. Once the wagons left the edge of civilization and hit the Great Plains, they were adrift in a sea—a vast sea—of silence, void of all the amenities they were accustomed to. Danger lay all about them. The horizon seemed to stretch forever.

They were alone.

Totally alone.

7

Steals Pony had been gone for two days. Something had been troubling the Delaware and he had pulled out, heading toward the wagons' backtrail. On the afternoon of the third day of his absence, he reappeared and swung down from the saddle. The wagons had completed their circle, cookfires were blazing, and the coffee was ready when Steals Pony rode in.

Preacher took one look at the Delaware's worried face and asked, "What's wrong?"

"A large band of white men are following us. They carry supplies for a long journey and are well-armed. They are being careful to stay two days' ride behind us. We are in trouble," he ominously ended it. He poured a cup of hot, strong coffee and took a big gulp.

"Did you recognize any of the men?" Snake asked.

"Jack Hayes," Steals Pony said, refilling his cup. "Tom Cushing. Rat Face. I could not recognize any of the others, but a tall, well-dressed man appears to be in command."

Preacher waved Lieutenant Worthington over to the fire and told him what Steals Pony had just reported.

For the last several days, Rupert and his small troop had

been very quiet and reflective. Preacher and the other mountain men knew what had happened. They'd seen it many times over the years. The vastness of the land had numbed Worthington and his men. This was what Preacher had tried to explain back in Missouri. But the plains could not be described. It was simply impossible to do that. They had to be seen and tasted personally. And for most, it was a very humbling experience. Their next humbling experience would be when they hit the Rockies.

"Is it possible, Preacher," the young soldier said after a few seconds' pause, "that these men are heading west on legitimate business?"

"I wouldn't think so, Rupert. I got me a hunch—'cause I run into this very same thing last year—that Jack and Rat Face was supposed to be the inside men. Once we got several weeks from the jump-off point, them others in the gang would ambush and take over the train. Hell, folks have been doin' this ever since men and women left the colonies and headed west. It ain't nothin' new."

"But . . . but this is, well, dastardly! Well! We'll just alert the authorities and let them . . ." He slowly trailed that idea off, suddenly remembering that there were no authorities out here. The nearest law was days to the east and almost two thousand miles to the west.

Preacher took a sip of coffee and smiled. "Now you're beginnin' to understand what we been tryin' to tell you, Rupert. There ain't no law 'ceptin' the pistols buckled around your waist and the rifle in your saddle boot. We'll find us a good ambush spot up ahead and you and your men will take the wagons on. Me and my friends will take care of Jack Hayes and his bunch of no-counts."

"Ambush spot?" Lieutenant Worthington said.

"Yeah."

"You'll lay in wait and . . . ambush those men coming up behind us?"

"Yeah. You got a better idea?"

"But . . . but . . . you can't do that!"

"Why not?" Snake demanded.

"Because those men haven't *done* anything. That's why."

"But they're *gonna* do something!" Preacher said.

"You don't know that for sure."

"I know Jack Hayes. He's a murderin', stealin', rapin' no-good, and has been that all his miserable life. And anyone who rides with him is just as bad."

Rupert shook his head vigorously. "Sir, I have studied the law at a very fine university. I know something about the law. And what you are proposing just won't do. There is such a thing as due process. Every accused person is entitled, under the constitution, to a fair trial. You can't just *kill* somebody because you *think* they might be planning some evil deed."

The mountain men exchanged glances. "Why not?" Blackjack asked. "We've all done it before."

Lt. Rupert Worthington had supper with Eudora Hempstead, Cornelia, and Anne. He confessed to them his worry about Preacher and what he might do.

"I can't leave the train," Rupert said. "None of us can. I mean the men in my command. We are under strict orders to stay with the train at all costs—even if it means my life and the lives of my men. Otherwise I would send a runner back to alert the Army at Fort Leavenworth." He sighed. "I am certainly impaled upon the horns of a dilemma."

Eudora sopped out her plate with a hunk of bread. "I agree with Preacher," she said. "Ambush the murdering scum." She popped the bread into her mouth and chewed.

"Miss Hempstead!" Rupert said, horrified. "I cannot believe you said that."

"Why not? I come from seafaring stock, Lieutenant. For over a hundred and fifty years my people have answered the siren's song of the sea. Ships' captains all. And they worked their way before the mast, from cabin boy to master. Do you know much about the sea, Lieutenant?"

Rupert shook his head no.

"Ships signal with flags. They talk with flags. They have flags for every conceivable occasion and threat. Ships that sail under no flag do so at considerable risk to themselves. Many a ship has been blown out of the water for refusing to show their colors. Or to strike them," she added without a smile.

"This is not the sea, Miss Hempstead," Rupert replied softly.

"Same as," she told him. "It's a vast, ever changing, constantly windswept, landlocked sea. Those men behind us are deliberately staying behind us—out of sight. Like pirates until they make their move to shoot and board. We can't let them get ahead of us, Rupert. Preacher can't take that chance. They'll ambush us at their leisure. I see Preacher's methodology."

"What he is suggesting is murder, Miss Hempstead."

"When there is no one in the woods when a tree falls, does it make a sound?" she asked with a smile.

"What? Oh. Yes. I see your analogy. There is no law out here."

"Except for survival," Eudora said gently.

Rupert thought about that for a moment. "It comes down to whose life is more important, theirs or ours."

"I suppose it does," Eudora said.

"You should have studied for the law, Miss Hempstead. It might have altered your views."

"Women aren't allowed to do that, Lieutenant." She smiled. "Yet."

Across the wide inner circle formed by the wagons, the mountain men sat, drinking coffee and talking quietly. "I'd forgot how strange the laws is back in the States," Ned said. "Plumb goofy, I say."

"I sure hope that way of thinkin' never gets past Missouri," Ring offered.

"It will," Steals Pony said sourly. "And in our lifetime, too."

"We been out here too long, boys," Snake said, stretching out on his blankets with a contented sigh. "We should have gone back from time to time to polish our manners, I reckon. Most of our kind did, you know?"

"Most of our kind will be gone in a few more years," Preacher said. "Quite a few has done hung up their buckskins and donned fancy pants and is makin' their way pretty good in California. Rubbin' elbows with the genteel and livin' in houses and workin' in stores and the like. No thank you."

"What are we gonna do about all that trash followin' us, Preacher?" Blackjack asked.

"I don't know," Preacher admitted. "Way Rupert acted to my suggestion, I reckon we're just gonna have to let them attack us 'fore we do anything."

"That's foolish," Charlie said.

"So is haulin' a hundred and fifty women 'crost the damn wilderness," Preacher countered. "I reckon we all done won the grand prize for foolish. So I'll apologize now for gettin' you boys in this mess."

"We came along because we wanted to, Preacher," Steals Pony said. "Besides, what else did any of us have planned?"

"Yeah," Blackjack said. He looked over at Preacher and smiled. "I knowed what you was doin' back yonder in my camp. I just played along with you. I think we all done earned the right to act foolish if we want to."

"I personal think we're doin' the right thing," Snake said. "Hell, I helped open up this country. It'll be fun to see it all again." He was thoughtful for a moment. "Cause I ain't gonna git another chance," he added mysteriously.

"All this talk ain't givin' us no answers 'bout what to do with them followin' us," Charlie said. "And I shore don't like the idee of waitin' for them to attack us. That purely cuts agin the grain far as I'm concerned."

Preacher drained his coffee cup and tossed the dregs to one side. "Well, boys, I think I'm sorta in a jam. In one way

I'm in charge of this fool's parade, but on the other hand, the army is in charge."

"Now we are in trouble," Blackjack grumbled.

Preacher smiled. "How old was you when you first come out to the wilderness, Blackjack?"

The big man grunted. "You do have a point. A lot younger than Rupert, that's for sure. Surely he ain't as dumb as he sounds 'bout half the time. You know, it sure seemed back then like we knew a lot more about livin' than he appears to."

"We did," Charlie agreed. "These young folks nowadays . . . I don't know about 'em. Seems like they ain't got no respect for their elders. You can't tell 'em a damn thing. They know it all. Country's goin' to hell in a handbasket, way I see it. Why, I heard from my sister back home two, three years ago, and she told me the kids are a-sparkin' each other at a mighty young age nowadays." He shook his head sorrowfully. "It's pitiful. Morals has gone to hell."

"You mighty right 'bout that," Snake said.

Blackjack grinned. "I come out just 'fore you did, Preacher. Wasn't it grand?"

"It was, for a fact." And that got the men off spinning tall tales far into the night. Why, it was at least 8:00 P.M. before they wound down and hit the blankets.

Preacher heard the first drops of rain begin falling just about midnight, he figured, and pulled his robe over him more snugly. The Delaware had said before the men retired that it was going to rain for two or three days. Up to this point there had been only a few brief showers that didn't last too long. Now the ladies were going to see a mighty soggy trail.

"Walk!" Faith said, standing in the downpour, hands on her shapely hips. "Have you taken leave of your senses?"

"Probably," Preacher told her. "I'm here, ain't I? But you still gonna walk."

"Why?"

" 'Cause I ain't gonna put no more strain on them mules and oxen than needs to be, that's why. Look at them ruts yonder, Missy. They're deep and gonna be a lot deeper 'fore the day's done. The ground's already soaked. Look at them clouds behind us. This is one of them storms that's comin' out of the east. And they're always bad. We're gonna have rain for about three days."

"Who says so?"

"Steals Pony. That's who."

"That's ridiculous! Nobody can predict the weather with any degree of accuracy."

"The Delaware can."

"Poppycock and balderdash!" She stamped her little booted foot and it sank about ankle deep.

"It's rainin', ain't it? You can't deny that. Just like he said it would."

"We will all catch pneumonia and perish out here!"

"Naw. It's unnatural warm for this time of year. You'll just get wet, is all. You'll dry out." He grinned. "Get a bar of soap and take a bath. I'll hold the canvas so's nobody can see you."

"You are a vile and evil man, Preacher," Faith flared at him. "Your thoughts alone will surely guarantee you a place in the Hellfires."

Preacher laughed at her and that made her madder than ever. She flounced around and tossed her strawberry curls and jumped up and down in the mud and sank a little deeper. She sure was cute when she was all flustered up.

"Pass the word, Eudora," Preacher called. "Everybody who's drivin' oxen will walk, and only the driver will stay on the box behind the mules. The rest of you—walk!"

"You are a perfectly *horrid* man!"

"Walk, Missy, Walk!" He looked down at her feet, which were out of sight in the mud. "Providin' you can pull your boots out of that mess."

In a downpour that reduced visibility to only a few hundred feet, the wagons rolled out, with the women slogging along beside them. Long before the nooning period, most of the women had removed their slickers and tossed them into the wagons; they were just too hot.

Preacher—as did the other mountain men—had him a hunch this unnaturally warm weather was only a fluke. It was not yet mid-April, and the weather could, and probably would, abruptly shift and turn very cold. Here on the plains, this warm rain could just as easily have been sleet slashing at them.

About an hour before the nooning, Preacher made up his mind. "Find us a place to hole up," Preacher told Steals Pony, his mouth only a few inches from the Delaware's ear, because of the howling winds. "There ain't no point in goin' on through all this crap. They'll be a bad accident if we keep on like this."

"Have already found one, Preacher," Steals Pony said. "Just up ahead. Maybe a half an hour. No more than that."

"Lead us to it." Preacher rode over to Eudora's wagon. "Follow Steals Pony. We're gonna sit it out."

She nodded and lifted the reins, hollering at her big mules, which were just as unhappy with the weather as the women.

The place Steals Pony had found was a thin stand of trees. The women circled the wagons and climbed under the canvas to change into dry clothing. Preacher rode around the wagons several times, seemingly oblivious to the raging elements. Something was wrong, but he couldn't put a finger on it.

"What's wrong, Captain?" Eudora shouted, during Preacher's third passing.

He rode over to her wagon. "I don't know. But something is. Get a head count, Eudora. I got a bad feelin'."

One wagon and three women were missing.

8

"Nora Simms, Betty Rutherford, and Phyllis Reed," Eudora told the men, who had strung up a sheet of canvas and were crouched under it. "But they were in the center of the column. How could they just disappear?"

"Easy, in this weather," Blackjack said. "I'll wager it was during that real bad spell when couldn't none of us see nothin'."

"Eudora," the soft southern voice came from the edge of the group. They all turned to face April Johnson, a slim and attractive young woman from Georgia.

"I overheard Nora and her group talkin' the other night. I thought they were only funnin'. They were talkin' about turnin' back. Then they saw me and all of them laughed. I . . . should have reported it. I'm sorry."

"It isn't your fault," Eudora said, putting an arm around the smaller woman's shoulders. She looked at Preacher and he jerked his head toward the wagons. Eudora led the young woman away, back to her wagon.

"We wasn't a mile out when that bad storm hit," Preacher said. "I figure we've come five miles. So if they kept on and didn't stop, they're a good eight to ten miles back." He waved at a Missouri man. "Saddle us some fresh mounts, Felix. The best in the herd." Felix took off at a run. "Snake, you and Charlie stay with the women. Let's go, boys. We got to find them women 'fore Indians or that trash that's followin' us does."

Lieutenant Worthington burst onto the scene. "Is it true about the women?"

"Yeah. It's true," Preacher told him. "Stay with the wagons and be sure to post extra guards this night. The goddamn Pawnee love to strike in this kind of weather. And in this part of the country, them goddamn Pawnee are liable to be right over the next rise."

Preacher rarely spoke of the Pawnee without putting some sort of oath before them. Preacher and the Pawnee just did not like one another. Never had. But he never underestimated them. The Pawnee were sly, slick, and the best horse thieves on the plains. The story goes that a Crow warrior decided to rest during the heat of the day. He tied his horse's reins to his wrist and stretched out and went to sleep in the shade of trees. A Pawnee came along, looked at the scene, and smiled. When the Crow awakened, the reins had been removed from his wrist and his horse was gone.

That's why Preacher never underestimated the Pawnee.

"We're gonna have to be ridin' with lady luck beside us, Preacher," Ned remarked. "You know we've had Injuns all around us for several days."

"Yep," Preacher said, swinging into the saddle of a tough-looking, long-limbed roan. "Keep your powder dry, boys. Let's go."

The women stood silently and watched the men ride out into the drenching rain, heading east. The men did not push their mounts, but left at a steady gait. They would alternately trot and walk their horses to save them.

About a mile from the wagon train, the men split up, left

and right, staying about a hundred yards apart, to better spot where the errant wagon had left the train.

Ned had summed up the feelings of all the men on this ride. None of them expected to see the women again. At least not alive. If Indians had found them, anything might happen. They might be taken as slaves and treated reasonably well, after they were repeatedly raped. If it was a war party looking for scalps, they would be raped and then killed. If they were lucky. If the Indians were in a bad mood, the women might be tortured. There was simply no way of telling about Indians. Some would not harm them at all. They would just look at them and ride off, leaving the women be, to fend for themselves. But the plains Indians were warriors, fierce fighters; killing a woman meant no more to many of them than killing a poisonous snake, and no Indian held to the same moral code as the so-called civilized white people. The Indian was neither evil nor morally wrong—not to their way of thinking; to them it was the white people who were terribly cruel and unfeeling. Indians respected the land and most of the creatures who inhabited it with them. Not so the white man. The white man raped the land and cut down all the trees. He diverted the flow of water to suit his needs and to hell with what others thought. He killed off all the game, left nothing, and would not share. The Indian never killed more than he needed. White men would kill game for something they called sport and take only the best cuts, leaving the rest to rot. That was a sin to an Indian. And the white man lied. Every time he opened his mouth he told great lies. You just could not trust most white men to keep their promises. Many people believed the western Indian knew nothing of how the eastern Indians were treated by the whites. That was a ridiculous theory and showed the arrogance and ignorance of the whites. As the tribes were pushed west, they brought their tales with them, and they were told over and over again. It was no wonder the Indians distrusted the white

man. And the Indians knew that many whites believed that
the only good Indian was a dead one. It was no wonder that
many Indians soon believed the same to be true about whites.

The Indians were not necessarily wrong in their beliefs
and way of life. They were just different.

After a few miles, the men reined up in a ragged group of
trees to rest their horses and talk.

"We got to be gettin' close now," Blackjack said. "And
the hair on the back of my neck is standin' up, boys."

"They're all around us," Steals Pony said. "Pawnee. I
sense them." He shook his head and his eyes touched those
looking at him. "And I think they are Bearmen."

"Damn!" Ring said. "That would be our luck."

The Bear Society was a very elite one among the Omaha
and the Pawnee. And they were feared by all. They were
fierce fighters, like bears, unpredictable and dangerous.

"If they took the women, we'll not never get them back,"
Ned said.

"No," Preacher agreed. "We sure won't. We'll be lucky to
stay alive. The Pawnee hate me worser than they do the
Assiniboins. And that includes anyone who rides with me.
Goddamn Pawnee," he added, as all the men knew he would.
Preacher stood up from his squat and gathered the reins.
"Well, this ain't doin' nothing but gettin' us wet. Let's ride."

The men mounted up and headed out, but riding much
more slowly now. To a man they knew they were in trouble.
They had spent all their adult lives in hostile country, and all
could sense the danger that lay around them, lurking silently
behind the silver shield of the hard-pouring rain.

The men carried their pistols under their buckskin shirts
and in covered holsters on their saddles; the rifles were carried in hardened skin cases that could be discarded in a second. And a second might be all the time they would have if
the Bearmen of the Pawnee attacked out of the storm. Long-
bladed knives and war-axes were readily at hand.

Steals Pony reined up and, with a wave of his hand, signaled to the others. He had found where the women's wagon had left the train. The men gathered around and looked. The rutted tracks were still clear.

"Headin' straight back, following the trail," Ned remarked. "Foolish, foolish ladies."

A few hundred yards later, the fears of the men were silently confirmed. The tracks left by a dozen unshod ponies were clearly visible. And the Pawnee were closing on the wagon very quickly.

"How many you make it, Steals Pony?" Blackjack asked, staring at the churned-up earth.

"At least twelve," the Delaware said. "Maybe as many as fifteen."

The rain continued to come down in torrents. But the men knew it could not last much longer. It would slacken as the storm moved on.

The mountain men rode for another hour, following the wagon tracks. The rain began to abate, finally dwindling down to no more than a drizzle. Preacher stood up in his stirrups and pointed.

"There it is," he said, his voice flat.

Ned took a spyglass from his saddlebags and opened it full. He peered through the lenses for a moment, then silently handed the spyglass to Preacher. The hard look in his eyes told the entire story.

Blackjack, Steals Pony, and Ring had turned their horses, to cover the other directions. All had a hunch the war party had not gone far, knowing that someone from the train would come looking for the women.

Preacher's face hardened as he viewed the scene. Two of the three women were clearly visible through the magnification. They were naked, of course. And they were dead. Both had been scalped. The Indians had taken the mules, although many Indians disliked the fractious animals. Preacher handed the spyglass to Ned without a word.

The men cautiously walked their horses up to the savage

scene. Nora Simms had been the youngest and the prettiest of the three women. She was gone. They had taken her.

Betty Rutherford had been used badly and the back of her head bashed in by a stone war-axe. She had then been scalped. Phyllis Reed probably had broken free sometime during the struggle and tried to run away. She had gotten only a few yards before an arrow in her back brought her down. She lay facedown and naked on the wet prairie grass, her inner thighs bruised.

Steals Pony dismounted, covered the lower part of Phyllis's body with a discarded blanket, then broke off the arrow and looked at it. "Pawnee," he said, then threw the arrow to the ground in disgust.

"Yonder's two of the mules," Ned said, pointing toward the southeast. "Draggin' their harness."

"Stay where you are," Steals Pony said. "I will look to see if it is a trap while you bury the women. If it is safe, do you want the mules, Preacher?"

"Yeah," Preacher said, rummaging around in the clothing-strewn bed of the wagon for a shovel. "We'll take the wagon back and tear it down for spare parts. You watch your butt out yonder, Steals Pony. It ain't like them goddamn Pawnee to go off very far. With them knowin' somebody would come lookin'."

It was easy digging in the soaked earth, and the men worked swiftly, digging down as far as they dared, constantly looking over their shoulders. The women were wrapped in blankets and buried. Then the men went looking for stones to cover the mounds, to keep animals from digging up the bodies and eating them.

Blackjack found a Bible in a trunk and handed it to Preacher. Preacher opened it at random and read a few verses while they stood over the lonely graves. Two small fresh mounds of earth on the vastness of an untamed land.

"That sounded strange, Preacher," Blackjack said. "What did you just read?"

"I don't know." He looked down at the page. "It's from Romans. I thought it sounded pretty good."

"What do intercession mean?" Ring asked. "That sounds kinda vulgar to me."

"I ain't got no idea," Preacher replied, closing the Good Book. "I ain't no student of the gospel. But it's in the damn Bible. So it can't be bad, can it?"

"I reckon not," Blackjack conceded.

" 'Sides," Preacher said, "I thought that part about 'groanings which cannot be uttered' sounded about right."

"Amen," Ned said, looking around him. "Let's get the hell outta here."

Steals Pony had found all four mules and brought them back to the wagon. "The Pawnee are gone. They left in a big hurry for some reason. One horse is carrying double, so they took Nora with them for sure."

"She'll soon wish she had died with these others," Preacher said ominously.

"For a fact," Steals Pony said. "I do not envy her existence from this moment on."

The men stood around the graves and looked at one another for a few seconds.

"Well, hell!" Blackjack said.

"Now what do we do?" Ned asked.

Preacher kicked at a clump of dirt. Then he sighed heavily. "What say you boys?" he asked, looking around him. "Do we go after her?"

"By the Lord, I couldn't live with myself if we didn't at least try to fetch her back," Ring said. "I think we got to at least try."

"I say we go after her," Steals Pony said.

"Count me in," Blackjack and Ned said together.

"All right. Let's do it," Preacher said. "We'll brush-corral the mules over yonder by that thicket and come back for them. If we don't, well, they'll bust out of it when they get hungry. Somebody take that shovel yonder with them. If

Nora kicked up too much of a fuss, they'll just knock her in the head and dump her. Personal, I hope they do. We've all seen what a war party can do to a woman."

"I'll bring along that Bible I found," Blackjack said. "Just in case."

"If we need it, let me read the passages," Steals Pony said, looking over at Preacher. "I know a more appropriate verse or two."

"Which one?" Preacher demanded.

"The Twenty-third Psalm," the Delaware said gently.

"How do that go?" Ring asked.

"It starts: 'The Lord is my shepherd; I shall not want.' "

"Give him the Good Book, Blackjack. He's got me bested, this time."

9

The mountain men found Nora Simms less than three miles from the new twin graves on the prairie. The Indians had bashed her head in, scalped her, and dumped her. She was a pitiful sight, lying naked and bloody on the ground. Ring had brought along a blanket and he wrapped her up, and all together the men took the body back to where they had buried the others and laid Nora to rest beside Betty and Phyllis.

Steals Pony read the Twenty-third Psalm and the men stood for a moment over the graves. The initial storm had blown itself out and for a brief moment, while the Delaware was reading from the Bible, the sun broke through. But already, dark storm clouds were beginning to gather, and the men knew they were in for a couple more days of terrible weather.

Just like Steals Pony had predicted.

The mules were hitched up and Ned tied the reins of his horse to the rear of the wagon and took the seat. The men started back for the wagon train. They were a silent bunch for most of the way. Ever vigilant, for that was a way of life, but not talking much. It was not that they were unaccustomed to death; they'd been around violent death for all of their adult lives. Violent, and in this case, the needless death of innocents.

Ring broke the silence. "We're being trailed, boys."

"Yes," Steals Pony said. "Pawnee Bearmen. But they are holding back. I think they have bigger plans and don't want to waste them on us."

"The wagon train?" Blackjack asked.

"Probably," Preacher said. "But they're fools if they attack. We could hold off one hell of a war party. But did y'all notice the torture marks on the Rutherford woman? She might have broke and told them about the wagon train bein' mostly women. That might have got them all excited. That may be why they bashed in Nora's head and dumped her."

"I never thought of that," Ned called from the wagon seat. "But you might be right. If that's the case, they've sent for more bucks."

"That'd be my guess," Preacher said.

"We're in for a long night," Ring opined.

It was dark when the men arrived back at the wagon train. Preacher gathered the women around and leveled with them about the fate of Nora, Betty, and Phyllis. His words were brutally hard, deliberately so, for he wanted the women to know every detail. It just might save their lives in the future. He spared them nothing. Then he told them about the Pawnee war party trailing them.

"We've got a good defensive spot here," Preacher said, speaking to the group. The other mountain men were standing guard, with some of the Missouri men. "And before you ask, put everything you ever heard or read about Indians never attackin' at night out of your heads. Sometimes they do, sometimes they don't. It all depends on how strong they believe their medicine is at the time. Now let's get supper cooked and eat and get everybody in place. I think we're gonna have us a wet and wild night."

Faith sidled up to him when he was alone. "I have noticed, Mister Preacher, that your quaint manner of speaking sometimes vanishes and you do seem to be able to speak proper English. Why is that?"

"I ain't got no idee, Missy."

"There you go again. Do you wish people to believe that you are nothing but an ignorant buffoon?"

"I don't give a damn what people believe me to be, Missy. What other folk think ain't no concern of mine. It's what they do that I pay heed to."

"What are you running from, Mister Preacher?"

"Huh?"

"It's obvious to me that you are hiding out here in this desolate place because of something terrible that occurred in your past."

"Is that right?"

"Yes. It is. Did some lady break your heart years back and you had to run away to ease the pain of love lost?"

Preacher stood in the light rain and blinked. "What are you talking about, Missy?"

Old Snake had slipped up and was standing a few feet away, behind Faith. He was listening and struggling to contain his laughter.

"You can tell me, Preacher," Faith said, stepping closer. He could feel the heat from her body. "I want to be your friend. I really, really do."

"Uh-huh." Preacher resisted an urge to grab her and run off under a wagon with her. Faith was ripe in all the right spots and even with a dark floppy hat covering her cut-off strawberry curls, she was lovely to look at and quite desirable. Faith was pushing hard to get bedded down. However, with anywhere from twenty to two hundred Pawnee, or more, prowling around the encirclement, Preacher concluded that this was a poor time to be thinking about romance.

"Yes," she whispered, stepping closer still. Another two inches and she'd be crawling inside his buckskins.

Steals Pony unknowingly saved Preacher from what was fast becoming a very awkward moment. "They come, Preacher!" the Delaware called.

"Get back to your wagon, Faith," Preacher said. "This night's about to blow up in our faces."

Preacher turned and was gone, old Snake right behind him. "How many?" Preacher asked Steals Pony.

"Too many," the Delaware said softly. "We're not that far from the Platte, and they must have just broken their winter camp there. This would be quite a prize for them."

"I can smell war paint," Snake said. "My God, there must be hundreds of them."

"Several hundred, at least," Steals Pony agreed. "I think they know about the women."

"I got the women under the wagons and behind boxes and the like," Blackjack said, striding up, big as a bear. "They're scared, but game."

"I don't understand this," Preacher said. "Something's got 'em all stirred up and we ain't it. We're just bearin' the brunt of whatever it is."

"You reckon Jack Hayes and that trash with him somehow is mixed up in all this?" Ned asked.

"It wouldn't surprise me none. I just can't figure out what it might be." He turned his face skyward. The rain had stopped for the moment. "They'll be hittin' us right about now," he said. "Get in place."

The first wave of the war party came at the westward women and their few men in a silent surge of painted-up fury. "Now!" Preacher shouted, and nearly a hundred rifles smashed the wet night, turning it into a bloody, pain-shrieking darkness.

Whatever the Pawnee expected, it certainly was not this. The only white women they had ever encountered were all cowering, trembling types, and that is what they believed they would encounter on this train. They were wrong. The heavy balls from the rifles tore their flesh and bloodied the ground. The Pawnee lost nearly fifty men in the first few seconds, and that was quite enough for this night, thank you.

They gathered up their wounded and their dead and pulled back to talk this over. They looked with contempt at their medicine men, who had promised them that their medicine was good. The medicine men shrugged and took the hostile looks stoically. Sometimes it worked, sometimes it didn't, the shrugs seemed to imply. Sometimes the thrown bones lied.

Those women whose jobs it was to reload the rifles and pistols worked fast, and within seconds, the women behind the rifles were ready for another charge.

But it did not materialize. The night grew steadily quieter as the Pawnee pulled back, well out of range. Some of their dead were too close to the wagons for them to recover, and the mountain men were quick to take advantage of that.

Most of the women and many of the Missouri men looked on, horrified, as Preacher and his friends pulled out knives and began mutilating the bodies.

"Stop that!" Faith shouted.

"Shut up," Preacher told her. "We ain't likin' this no more than you all. But it's got to be done."

"Why, for God's sake?"

"Cut out the eyes so's they can't see their way to the Great Beyond. Cut off their hands so's they can't fight any enemies they might come up on. Now they'll be forever lost in the darkness. To wander forever."

"That's the most unchristian thing I have ever witnessed!" Miss Claire Goodfellow said.

"You shoulda seen Nora Simms, Betty Rutherford, and Phyllis Reed," Ring called over his shoulder, his long-bladed knife flashing bloody in the night. "Then mayhaps you wouldn't be so aghast at this."

Steals Pony let out a blood-chilling, wild war cry and held up two severed hands. He called out loud in Pawnee, heaping insults on the dead. Faith shuddered. Eudora smiled.

"Every other person get some rest for a few hours, then take your partner's place," Preacher called. "Work it out, ladies. It's gonna be a long night."

"I thought you said they wouldn't return?" Faith's voice cut into the damp night.

"I said they *probably* wouldn't be back," Preacher replied. Under his breath he muttered, "I wish I hadn't said nothin'."

"What's that?" Faith called.

"Nothin'," Preacher said. "Just nothin' at all."

"Are you going to leave those disgusting bodies right there?" she called.

"No, Missy," Preacher replied wearily, for it had been a long day. "We're gonna pick 'em up and tote 'em over to where the Pawnee have made camp and dump the bodies there."

That shut her up for about five seconds. "Well, you don't have to be sarcastic about it."

"Hush up," Preacher told her, wiping his hands on the wet grass to remove the Pawnee blood.

It was the wrong thing to say to Faith. Whatever ardor they might have experienced a few moments ago suddenly cooled and evaporated into the night air. She told him to absolutely, positively never again tell her to hush up. Of course she was quite vocal about it and it took considerably longer to express her thoughts, but that was the sum of it.

Blackjack looked at her in awe. He shook his head. "That woman can shore string words together, can't she?"

"If Preacher don't give her what she's a-cravin' pretty soon," Snake whispered, "we're in for a long trip."

"Have mercy on us," Steals Pony replied.

About that time, a lady named Madeline Hornbuckle found a very large rattlesnake curled up in her blankets and she let out a war whoop that brought the whole camp running. The snake disappeared, but no one got into blankets for the rest of the night.

* * *

It poured from the skies the next day, and Preacher told the ladies to rest—and shake out their blankets for the umpteenth time.

"Go kill a rattler and bring it back here," he told Steals Pony. "That's the only thing that'll calm these women down. Damn bunch of city women anyways."

"I have a better suggestion," the Delaware said.

"Oh?"

"Yes. *You* go kill a rattlesnake and bring it back here. And good luck finding one in this rain."

"And watch out for them Pawnee," Blackjack added with a smile. "Way I see it, most of them hightailed back to camp. But I figure they's maybe fifty or so who stayed behind with revenge on their minds. And they'd just love to find you ridin' out there alone."

"What a bunch of friends I got," Preacher muttered, making another walk-around of the circled wagons, slopping through the muddy and churned-up ground, the rain beating down on his hat. "Smart alecks, all of them." Then he grinned, knowing that a man could not have better friends than those who accompanied him on this journey.

He stopped by a wagon when he heard a hard, wracking cough. Squatting down, he looked at the three women huddled on the ground under the wagon bed. "Get that woman inside the wagon and get her warm," Preacher ordered. "If you got any ginger root, make some tea. She's on the verge of pneumonia. Strip 'er down to the buff and rub her good; get that blood to the surface and keep her warm. Pneumonia's a killer out here. Oncest you get her dry, warm, and full of ginger tea, add some clove to it and she'll go right to sleep. She's got to rest."

When the men who were to be called mountain men had first arrived in the west, they had discovered that the "poor ignorant savages," as whites called the Indians, knew a hell of a lot about medicine and healing of the body.

Perhaps one of the reasons the breed of men called mountain men were considered so tough is that they just simply would not succumb to illness. No matter how they felt, they just kept on going.

Rain continued to pound the pioneers during all that wet and gray day. The only bright spot was that the Pawnee had chosen not to launch another attack. Charlie and Steals Pony rode out about noon and completed a wide circle around the area. The Pawnee were indeed gone.

"They headed north," Charlie said, huddled under a canvas, his hands clutching a tin cup full of hot coffee. "Then they cut west. I reckon they figured the rain would cover their tracks, and it would have in another hour or so. That bunch of revenge-seekers will be hittin' us somewheres along the Platte."

"I most certainly will not do that!" a woman's voice declared across the muddy circle to the men.

"Suit yourself, lady," Steals Pony said, and came walking over to the small group of men.

"What was all that about?" Preacher asked, as the Delaware poured a cup of coffee.

"The woman said her child had gotten into poison ivy and asked me what to do about it. I told her to strip the child and dunk her into a mud puddle. That would help relieve the irritation. She refused."

"It works," Snake said.

"Of course it does," Steals Pony said. "But I will find some goldenseal when the rain ends and that works better. Even though I was raised by whites back east, I have always felt that whites are sadly lacking in basic knowledge. It's amazing to me that the white people have progressed as far as they have. Present company not included, of course."

"Folks got things too easy back east," Snake opined. "I was told about something called a train. Runs on steel tracks.

Carries people at fantastic speeds. Ain't no horse in the world can keep up with it. Makes my mind boggle to think about goin' that fast. What's the point in it?"

"If it goes that fast, how do they stop the damn thing?" Charlie asked.

"I ain't got no idea," Snake replied. "Drag something behind it, I reckon. I don't even know how they make it go noplace. I hope I don't never see one of them things. I might decide to shoot it." He was thoughtful for a moment. "If I could figure out where its vital organs was."

"It runs on steam," Eudora said, walking up with Faith beside her. "Burning wood heats the water and the water produces steam which turns the wheels. It's quite the coming thing. Someday the trains will be out here, too."

"You actual ride on one?" Ring asked her.

"Oh, yes," Faith said. "It's quite an exhilarating experience."

"Faster than a horse?" Charlie asked.

"Oh, my, yes! Ten times faster." It was a slight exaggeration on her part.

"Ten times!" Snake said. "Why, that'd suck the breath right out of you."

"It is a thrilling ride," Eudora said; then the ladies walked away.

"Do you believe all that?" Charlie asked.

"Yeah," Preacher said. "Woman told me about it a couple years ago." He didn't bring up the story about a man over in France who flew through the air hanging in a basket under a balloon. That would have been just a bit too much for anybody to believe.

Preacher wasn't even so sure he believed that one himself.

10

Preacher awakened long before the others and looked up into a brilliant star-filled sky. He lay in his blankets and smiled. The storms were past and they could move on. Under the hot sun, the plains would dry faster than a man unfamiliar with it would believe. In two days they'd be choking with dust and bitching about the heat.

Preacher had no way of knowing it, but in the spring of 1839, back in Peoria, Illinois, Thomas Farnham and thirteen other men were just leaving with a pack train, heading for the Willamette Valley in Oregon Territory. Both Preacher and Farnham were riding into destiny. That spring, the population of the United States was sixteen million people. Ninety-nine percent of it was east of the Mississippi River.

The people had to move west. The east was getting too crowded. And the Indians would be caught up in the middle. Later in the year of 1839, the horrible Trail of Tears would take place, when the U.S. government would force many thousands of Indians from their homes in Alabama, Georgia, Florida, and Tennessee, to the Indian country in what would someday be called Oklahoma. Several thousand men, women, and children, of the Cherokee, Choctaw, Chickasaw, Creek, and Seminole—the Five Civilized tribes—would die on the forced march.

"The women are up to something." Steals Pony whispered the caution to Preacher at the cookfire.

Preacher got a plate of food and a cup of coffee and he and the Delaware sat down on a log to eat. "What?"

"Don't know. But I think it has something to do with the dead women."

Charlie Burke and Snake came up, both carrying plates piled high with food. One thing could be said with absolute certainty about the mountain men: they could all eat enough for two or three men.

"The women is puttin' together a choir," Snake said, then filled his mouth with food.

"A choir?" Preacher looked up. "What the hell for?"

Ring, Blackjack, and Ned, strolled up, their plates filled to overflowing. "At first light," Blackjack said, "the women is gonna have a tribute to them three dead ladies. Singin' and readin' from the Bible."

"Damnit, I already read from the Good Book!" Preacher said. "Me and Steals Pony both done it."

"You tell them they can't do it." Blackjack settled that point quick.

Preacher grunted, ignoring the smile on the big mountain man's face. "Oh, hell. I ain't gonna interfere with no Bible thumpin' and praisin' the Lord in song. I ain't no heathen. But whilst that's goin' on, I'll saddle up and scout ahead for a few miles. You wanna come along, Steals Pony?"

"Actually, I find the sound of feminine voices blending together in song quite moving. I shall stay and perhaps join in song with them."

Snake looked at him. "I know you got you a hellacious good education. Seventh grade, I think I heard. But I wish just once you'd talk like a damn dumb Injun."

Steals Pony nodded his head and grunted, "Grub heap good." He smiled. "Are you satisfied now, Snake?"

Snake took his plate of food and his coffee and walked off, muttering about smart-aleck Injuns. Fifteen minutes later, he had his horse and Preacher's horse saddled and was ready to go, 'fore them females started singin' and preachin' and got all emotional and started blubberin' all over the place. Snake didn't think he could stand that.

As soon as the women started tunin' up their vocal cords, Preacher and Snake rode out to the west. The sun was beginning to color the east with dawn's silver hue.

"Snake," Preacher said, after the camp was behind them and the voices of the women were faint in the early light and cool air of the plains. "I been knowin' you ever since I come out here. And I been out here since I was knee-high to a grasshopper. You ain't changed none. How old are you?"

"I don't rightly know, Preacher. I think I'm some'eres 'tween seventy and eighty. I know I was years out here 'fore Lewis and Clark come a-traipsin' through. You see, I killed me two men in Vermont back in '85."

"Seventeen eighty-five?" Preacher blurted. That was about seventeen or eighteen years before he was even *born!*

"Yep. I fit with Washington in the Revolution. And a mighty cruel time that was, too. Anyway, I lit a shuck for the far western lands and never looked back. Not one time has I looked back further than St. Louie."

"Never heard another word from kith and kin?"

"Nary a peep. I reckon they're all gone now. I've lived more 'un I ever figured I would. There ain't no place west of the Mississippi that I ain't seen, neither . . . well, you know what I mean. Cain't no man see it all, but I reckon I've crossed ever' crick and river there is out here. Preacher, can I ask you a favor?"

"You know you can."

"If you're clost by when it comes my time to check out, you bury me high, will you? You wrap me up real good and tight so's the smell won't make you puke, and tote me up to the highest peak you can find. Plant me there."

"I'll do 'er, Snake." He cut his eyes to the old man. "You figurin' on cashin' in this trip, are you?"

"You never know, son. You just never know. But I got a feelin', I do. I'll be honest with you. I'm tired. Almighty tired. It ain't so much that I'm tired in my body as it is I'm tired in my mind. I've rid all the trails there is to ride, seen all the sights—some of them a dozen times over—and I've buried more friends than I care to think about. They're callin' to me, Preach. I swear to you they is. I hear 'em in my sleep. You reckon I'm losin' my mind?"

Preacher shook his head. "No," he said slowly. "I don't think that at all, Snake. But I do believe a man knows when it comes his time to go. I'll plant you high, Snake. You got my word on it."

The old mountain man nodded his head. " 'ppreciate it. Takes a load off my mind, it do."

The voices of the ladies could no longer be heard, and with one hundred and forty-seven of them shoutin' to the Heavens, that meant the men had ridden about two miles, more or less.

"You want to stop?" Snake asked.

"Hell, no! I want to put some distance 'tween us and them females. Blackjack knows the way. I want to see what the Platte looks like."

"It's wet," Snake said with a straight face.

"Thank you. I remember that much about it."

"We gonna cross it just north of here?"

"I ain't made up my mind yet. What worries me is why Washington wanted us to leave Missouri so soon. Ain't no way they could have predicted this early spring with plenty of graze."

"That's why them extra wagons of feed was put on, Preach. At the last minute," he added.

"But why?"

"So we stand a better chance of coverin' two thousand miles 'fore the snows fall."

"Maybe. Maybe."

"You got something stuck in your craw?"

"Yeah. Plenty. All of it worrisome. You and me and the others, we've seen buffalo stampede, and we was lucky enough to get out of the way. You know what's gonna happen to the women and the wagons if they get caught up in one?"

"I can make a fair guess."

"Yeah. And on top of that, we got alkali water and Injuns to worry about. We're gonna lose livestock and lives crossin' rivers and run off by Injuns. These women are gonna have to boil water 'fore they drink it to keep from gettin' sick. We was lucky back yonder that no lightnin' was with that storm. But we'll face it in the months ahead. We're gonna be humpin' it to keep this train in fresh meat. We're gonna have to wind-lash these wagons down the grades up ahead. And I mean we. Them ladies won't be able to do it alone. You noticed these big bastard wagons don't have no brakes? That's why I raised so much hell back yonder about additional heavy rope."

Snake cut his eyes to Preacher. "You're just a barrel of laughs today, ain't you, Preach?"

"Hell, Snake, I ain't even got goin' good yet."

"I was afraid of that."

"I laid in a good stock of dried apples. But it won't last the trip."

"Scurvy?"

"You bet."

"And the last of it?" Snake pressed. "I hope."

"We're gonna face dust storms, wind storms, busted wagon wheels . . . and the lonelies."

"We can deal with all them things 'ceptin' the last," Snake said, his eyes never stopping their scanning of the country-side. "Over the last fifty-odd years, I seen big, strong men fall under the vastness of it all. I mean, go stark, ravin' mad. You've seen it, too."

Preacher nodded in silent agreement. He'd seen men succumb to the silent horizon that seemed to have no end; to the
enormity of it all that reduced man to a tiny nothing. Most
men just shrugged it away and accepted it. A few others lost
their minds.

One or two, or more, of these women would not be able to
cope with it. And then they'd have a raving lunatic on their
hands.

Preacher had seen that, too.

"And let's don't forget them men on our backtrail," Snake
said. "They shore ain't up to no good."

Again, Preacher nodded. The past night, alone under one
of the supply wagons, Preacher had carefully gone over the
documents given him by the government man back in Missouri. Preacher was convinced the papers were genuine and
that the man from Washington was up to no skullduggery.
He did not believe the government man was in any way
mixed up with that band of scallywags who were following
them.

So what were they up to?

He didn't know.

Who was the tall, well-dressed man who appeared to be
leading the group?

He didn't know that either.

But Preacher had him a hunch he'd know the answers to
his questions pretty damn quick.

The going was slow that first day after the torrential rains,
and the train made only a few miles. But under the blistering
sun, the land dried out quickly and on the second day after
the passage of the storm, the wagons made a good fifteen
miles. The westward women had said and sung their goodbyes to the three ladies who had become discouraged, and no
more was said about them, at least not to Preacher.

Preacher told Blackjack and the other mountain men to

take over for a few days. He was going to lag behind and get him an eyeball full of the men following them. He had a place all picked out, and he had his good spyglass. Then Preacher decided he'd best tell Lieutenant Worthington of his plan.

"You're not going to ambush them, are you?" Rupert asked, a worried look on his face.

"Me? Against forty or fifty armed men? Hell, no!"

"I had to ask, Preacher. Your exploits of daring-do are well known."

"Uh-huh." Preacher had no intention of telling the young lieutenant that he did plan—if possible—to grab one of the bunch and get the truth from him.

"In case you are not back when we reach the Platte, do we cross it when we come to it?"

"No. Stay on the south side of it. But you won't reach it 'fore I return. I'll be back 'fore you know it."

"You will be careful?"

Preacher grunted. Careful? Every time Preacher thought Rupert might be showing some sense, the lieutenant had to go and mouth some stupid remark. Out here, a body best be careful twenty-five hours a day.

Preacher left within the hour. Hammer was getting on in years, but he was still twice the horse of anything that could be found in the train's herd. And Hammer loved the trail and loved to run. But Preacher had made a promise to Hammer, and when this journey was over, he planned to keep that promise. He'd turn the big horse loose with a bunch of mares and let him enjoy the rest of his life. He knew just the valley, too. Isolated and lovely. Preacher had staked that valley out for himself. He had him a young Appaloosa horse there that he'd been training, as big as Hammer and just as mean and strong.

And that animal was as loyal to Preacher as a good watchdog too, probably because Preacher broke a horse in gentle ways. He had no use for a man who would mistreat a dog or a horse.

Preacher headed for a series of bluffs he'd checked out a few days past, an upthrusting of rocky-faced cliffs that had torn out of the earth hundreds of thousands of years back. Sandstone, Preacher thought. But they had a good stand of timber on top which would offer plenty of cover. From up-top he could see for miles and there were plenty of spots where water gathered and held.

He gave Hammer his head and let him set his own pace. The big horse would trot for a while, then slow to a walk. Hammer could sense no urgency in his master, so when he tired, he stopped and rested. Had his master wanted it, Hammer would have run until his heart burst.

Preacher reached the bluffs about an hour before dark and quickly found the trail up to the top. He wiped the tracks clean and scattered handfuls of dirt over his work. It would not fool anyone who knew tracking and was carefully looking, but it would be dark soon and Preacher would go back over his work come the morning. He picketed Hammer and then spent a full twenty minutes on the bluffs with his spyglass, carefully scanning in all directions. He could see no smoke, no movement other than animals, and could detect no danger within miles of his location. That didn't, of course, mean there were no Indians about, just that Preacher could not see them. When you couldn't see an Injun, Preacher had always opined, that was when you best start worryin' and see to your powder and shot.

There was no way Preacher was going to risk a fire this night, so he ate a cold supper of bread and meat he'd taken from the wagon train, took him a long drink of cold water that had gathered in the rocks, then rolled up in his blankets and went to sleep.

He was up long before dark, once more on the bluffs with his spyglass. He still could see no glow of fires anywhere.

He went back to a rock depression where he had gathered up and laid out twigs and dry wood the night before, and built a tiny fire for coffee. When his coffee had boiled and his bacon cooked, he put out the fire and ate his bacon, sopped out the grease in the pan with a hunk of bread, lit up his pipe, and enjoyed his coffee. The whole potful.

At first light he was again on the bluffs, carefully hidden in brush, with his spyglass. He used the glass north, south, and west, but not east. The rays of the sun might reflect off the lens.

He saw no signs of Indians nor of the large party of heavily armed white men he was expecting. When the sun was overhead, he began using the glass toward the east. After an hour had passed, he caught the first sight of the men. When they drew nearer, he began his count, and when he had finished, he was really worried.

Fifty men, all heavily armed, with plenty of packhorses and provisions. And Preacher knew the man out in front of the loose column. Personally.

Victor Bedell. Victor had been a very successful merchant in St. Louis up until a few years back. He had dealt in furs and in gold and precious gems. He had owned saloons and sporting houses and other businesses. And he had also loaned money and grubstaked trappers. The gold and precious gems had all been stolen in far-off places, and Vic cheated the trappers out of everything they brought back. When they complained, he showed the authorities (usually the army), the papers the always uneducated (Bedell made sure of that beforehand) trappers had signed. It was all legal. Bedell made sure of that, for he was a lawyer as well.

The last time Preacher had traveled to St. Louis, Bedell had mistaken him for being unable to read or write, and tried to get him to sign with his fur company. Preacher carefully read the wordy document, then wadded it up and tossed it aside, telling Bedell to go commit an impossible act upon his person.

Bedell got hostile. Bad thing to do with Preacher. Preacher whipped him up one side of a street and then down the other side, thoroughly humiliating the fancy-pants liar, cheat, whoremaster, and all around scoundrel.

Bedell swore he'd someday kill Preacher. Preacher had laughed at him and headed back west. The very next year, so Preacher had heard, the law caught up with Bedell and he barely escaped the hangman's noose, fleeing St. Louis with his gang. He'd shown up in New Orleans, and Preacher had thought he was still down there, with his whores and dirty deals.

Now here he was, big and bold as brass.

Preacher watched the gang of cutthroats ride on until they were out of sight.

"Well, now," Preacher said aloud. "That wagon train is surely in trouble. That's got to be the reason for Bedell followin' and layin' back. Now, what do I do about that?"

He decided that for the moment, until Bedell and his men got long out of sight, the best thing he could do was to take a nap.

So he did.

11

Preacher napped for about thirty minutes, then saddled up and broke camp. He was uncertain as to what he should do. Steals Pony had said only that it was a large band of men. But *fifty?* And why did Bedell want the wagon train? There had to be more to this than meets the eye, Preacher thought.

But what?

He didn't know.

Preacher had always felt that the story about the men out on the coast wanting wives was a bit thin in spots. He didn't doubt some of it. The government was trying to settle that area. He'd read in a newspaper that there were millions and millions of people back east of the Mississippi. Preacher couldn't begin to fathom millions and millions of folks. Why, they must be fallin' all over each other back yonder. He sure didn't have any desire to see something as terrible as that.

So what other reason would bring Bedell all the way from New Orleans clear up to the wilderness? For a fact, the wagons were all new, and the man from Washington had said they were specially made just for this trip. But Preacher, a suspicious man by nature, had gone over the wagons personally, looking for secret hiding places where gold might be hidden. There were no specially built hiding places. They were good, strong, sturdy wagons and that's all they were.

The Army had scouted out some of the wilderness, and reported back that there was no gold to be found west of the Mississippi. Preacher knew that was a crock of crap. He'd found him a vein years back and kept a small pouch filled with nuggets on him at all times. But not being a money-hungry man, Preacher had no special interest in the precious yellow metal.

But Victor Bedell was a money-hungry man—the thought came to Preacher abruptly.

He whoaed Hammer and slid out of the saddle, to sit on the ground and think. Maybe that was it. Maybe Bedell wasn't after the wagons, but had some information about gold and was going after it. The mules, oxen, and the wagons, filled with supplies, would just be the cherry on top of the cake— not to mention the women. Use up the women, trade them off to the Injuns as a token of friendship, and with the additional supplies, Bedell and his men would be set for months.

"I think you may have it, old son," Preacher said aloud.

Preacher put it out of his mind and concentrated on the hoofprints that stretched out ahead of him. Fifty men, he thought, shaking his head. Up to what?

Tonight, if at all possible, he'd find out something.

Preacher left Hammer safely hidden and Injuned the remaining two miles to Bedell's camp. The first thing he learned was that the men with Bedell were not a bunch of greenhorns. They had a carefully staggered circle of guards out and they knew their business. He figured them for a bunch of ridge-runners from Missouri, Arkansas, Kentucky, and Tennessee, with maybe a few from Mississippi and Louisiana.

They were good, all right. But Preacher figured that he

was better. And he knew he was when he managed to steal one of their horses and lead him into a shallow ravine and picket him quiet.

Shortly after he returned to the camp, the second shift took over, and Preacher picked out his man. The man moved around too much, and had a bad habit of turning his back to the darkness outside the circle. Preacher laid the flat side of his war-axe to the man's noggin and dragged him off to the ravine.

Preacher didn't tarry. He tied the unconscious man belly down across the bare back of the stolen horse and got the hell gone from there. He was betting Bedell and his men would think Injuns grabbed the fellow and would not follow in the darkness.

Preacher rode for over an hour, choosing his route carefully. He followed creeks, staying in the water much of the time to throw off and slow down any of Bedell's men who might follow him—but he did not think any would.

Finally, miles from Bedell's camp, Preacher swung down and let the prisoner fall to the ground. The man had been awake for quite some time, but had the good sense to keep his mouth shut, since his belly-down position on the bare back of the horse prevented him from seeing just who had grabbed him. Relief showed on his face when he realized a white man had taken him.

But that relief was short-lived when Preacher pulled out his bone-handled, long-bladed Bowie knife and touched the point of the blade to the man's cheek. "You ever seen a man skinned alive?"

"N . . . n . . . no, sir," the man stammered.

"You want to witness it firsthand?"

"H . . . hell, no!"

"You got a name?"

"Woford. Woford Lewis."

"You ever heard of a mountain man called Preacher?"

"Yes, sir."

"What have you heard about him?"

"That's he's mean, vicious, and a killer. That he's lived with the savages for so long, he's become one. There was a newspaper story on him back home. It said that Preacher has done gone and kilt more'un a thousand men . . . red savages and white men. That he fought grizzly bears and won. That he lives in a cave with a mountain lion. You know Preacher?"

"I am Preacher."

Woford fainted.

"Shod horse," one of Bedell's men said, rising from his squat where he'd been studying the tracks, now hours old. "But from what I learned back in Missouri, that don't necessary mean it was a white man. Injuns steal lots of horses."

Victor Bedell stood silent and thoughtful for a few seconds. For the time and the place, he was very elegantly dressed. Compared to those standing around him, he was a regular dandy. "Woford was a fool. Most of you thought so and told me you did. I won't risk lives by going after him. If this was the work of red savages, perhaps that's what they want us to do and are waiting for us. The tracks head north. We'll continue on west. Personally, I think we're better off without Woford. It was a mistake to bring him."

That was a relief even to his motley band of surly cutthroats, thugs, rapists, thieves, and ne'er-do-wells. Woford had been generally disliked. Back in Kentucky Woford had killed his mother and father in a dispute over money, and, over the ensuing years, had left a bloody trail of rape, murder, and mayhem. Not that the men riding with Bedell were any better—they weren't—they just liked to think they were.

Bedell and his pack of two-legged hyenas mounted up and pulled out.

* * *

Woford didn't know much, but when he awakened from his faint, tied head down from a limb, looking at Preacher about to light a fire only inches from his hair, he was more than happy to share his limited knowledge with the legendary man. Woford was so scared he peed in his longhandles. Preacher disgustedly cut him down and bodily threw him into a creek to cut the smell and then hauled him out and slapped more piss out of him. It only took about five minutes to reduce Woford to a trembling, crying shell, huddled on the ground, begging for his life.

Bedell had him a map, supposedly showing where a large deposit of gold was, and he and his gang were heading there. Once they had the gold, they were going to stake out, claim, and then rule a large portion of the northwest. A king and his soldiers, was the way Woford put it.

And Preacher had guessed right about the wagon train. When Bedell had learned about it, they had hastened their departure in order to fall in behind the train. Later on up the trail, they planned to attack the train, have their way with the women, then kill or trade them to the red savages, and take the supplies.

The men with Bedell were terrible people, Woford said, a sly look in his eyes. "Me, I was shorely duped," he said. "I thought they was really swell guys going on a grand adventure. I would never have come along if I'd a known what kind of criminals they really was."

"You're a liar," Preacher told him. "And a damn bad one, at that. Shut your mouth while I figure out just what I'm goin' to do with you."

"Please, sir," Woford begged. "I have my aged mother and poor crippled sister back home to support."

Preacher looked at him in disgust. Woford wisely shut his mouth and said no more.

"Where are your friends gonna hit the wagons?" Preacher asked.

"Please, sir. They are not my friends. I told you, I was hoodwinked. I'm a good man. I . . ."

Preacher popped him in the mouth with a hard fist that bloodied Woford's lips. "Liar!"

"What are you going to do with me?" Woford whined.

"I ain't made up my mind about that, yet. Now shut up."

At first light, Preacher tossed the unlucky hooligan onto his horse and stood glaring up at him. "I ought to kill you. I know that. But I can't kill no unarmed man, 'specially one that's as yellow as you. But hear me well, Woford Lewis. If I ever see you again, no matter where it is, I'll kill you on the spot. Do you understand that?"

"Yes, sir, Mister Preacher. Are you gonna give me a gun?"

"No."

"Dear God in the Heavens!" Woford wailed. "I'm surrounded by red savages and unarmed. I won't stand a chance out here."

Preacher had had enough; he slapped Woford's horse sharply on the rump and the animal jumped out into a run, with bareback-riding Woford hanging on to the mane, his butt bouncing up and down, and hollering for dear life.

On his return trip Preacher stayed north of Bedell and his men and swung wide, hooking up with the wagon train just as they were making camp for the evening. Preacher said not a word to anybody until he'd poured himself a cup of coffee and grabbed up a hunk of bread and some bacon from the pan. Lieutenant Worthington, Eudora, Faith, and a few other women had gathered around Preacher and his friends.

"There was fifty of 'em," he said, after chewing and swallowing a mouthful of the bread and bacon. "I snatched one out of camp, read to him from the scriptures, and he was right glad to tell me everything he knew. Which wasn't much, by the way. Now they's forty-nine of 'em."

"You *killed* that man?" Faith blurted.

"Nope. I just slapped him around some and then turned

him loose." He told the crowd everything that he had learned from Woford, then poured him another cup of coffee, and sat down on the ground.

"You know this Bedell person, Captain?" Eudora asked. It irked Lieutenant Worthington to hear her call Preacher "Captain," and she knew it.

"I know him. He's a bad one. And that scum he's got with him is just as bad. And they ain't amateurs, neither. They're mean and low-down, but they're all game to the end."

"Ain't Bedell the one you whupped in St. Louie, Preacher?" Blackjack asked.

"One and the same. He's a cheat, a murderer, a liar, a whoremaster—beggin' you ladies' pardon, but he is—and anything else mean and low-down you can think of. Army run him out of St. Louis; had a noose waitin' for him, they did. The man will do anything. He's as poison mean as a copperhead."

"You have a plan, Captain?" Eudora asked.

Preacher shook his head. "I surely don't. But startin' tomorrow, we'll have more outriders roamin' a couple miles from the train. In all directions. And y'all ain't gonna be seein' much of me. I'm gonna be doggin' Bedell and his men." He cut his eyes to Blackjack and the huge mountain man smiled. Blackjack knew that doggin' Bedell's gang wasn't all that Preacher would be doing.

He'd be head-hunting, too.

Lieutenant Worthington came to Preacher later on that evening and asked if he could sit and talk.

"Sure," Preacher said. "The ground's free."

"I think I shall disobey orders and have my men unpack and wear their uniforms from this point on."

"Oh?"

"Yes. I have discussed it with my sergeant and I believe that merely the sight of the United States Army would deter

Mister Bedell from any acts of violence against the wagon train."

The mountain man paused in his lifting of the coffee cup. "All eight of you?" Preacher asked softly, pouring the young officer a cup of coffee.

Rupert looked over the small fire at him, frowned for a moment, and then grinned boyishly. He shook his head. "I see what you mean, Preacher. Yes. Thank you for not letting me make a fool of myself."

"We all get to do that bunches of times over the years, Rupert. You boys stay in civilian clothing. That's my thinkin' on it. Them pretty uniforms make dandy targets."

The young officer was silent for a moment, sipping his coffee. When he spoke, his voice was soft. "I love this country, Preacher. What's it like further on?"

"The most inspirin' thing you'll ever see. Exceptin' the second comin' of Christ, I reckon. It'll grab you, son. When you get in the middle of what we call the Rockies, it'll fling something fierce all over you. And if you're lucky, it'll never turn you loose. I ain't got the words to describe it. It'd take a man with a poet's heart to put it in words. You'll feel like you're so close to God, you can just reach right out and touch his face."

"That is lovely, Preacher," Faith said. Neither man had heard her walk up.

Rupert immediately sprang to his feet and whipped off his hat. Preacher sat where he was and grunted his greeting. But he did snag another coffee cup, fill it up, and wave the woman to a ground sheet.

"Thank you," Faith said, sitting down and accepting the cup of coffee. She smiled at Preacher. "You have the soul of a poet and don't realize it, Preacher."

"Just don't let it get around. Something like that would ruin my reputation."

Then Sergeant Scott called for the lieutenant, and Rupert excused himself and vanished into the shadowy darkness.

"You're leaving in the morning?" Faith asked.

"Long before dawnin', Missy."

"Aren't you ever afraid, Preacher? I mean, out here?"

"Hell, yes! Man who says he ain't never been afraid is either a fool or a liar. You just got to overcome it, live with it, and go on about your business."

"You think we're really in trouble, don't you? You believe that this Bedell person and his thugs will actually attempt to harm us."

"Yes, I do, Missy. And I ain't a man to deliberately cause a person undue alarm. I ain't no see-er into the future. I can't tell you where or when Bedell will strike. But strike he will. Y'all got to be extra careful. I got to convince you of that. He'll come on like a real gentleman. He can do that. I 'spect that what him and his men has planned is to get all mixed up with the members of the train and then strike like lightnin' when your guard is down. That's what I think."

Blackjack and the other mountain men were staying away from Preacher and the lady on this night. The wagon train was quieting down as the women were preparing for their night's rest. Guards had been doubled. Slowly, the fires were being extinguished within the huge circle.

"You best get on back to your wagon, Missy," Preacher told her. "People will talk."

"You care about things like that, Preacher?" she asked, standing up.

"Not one twit."

"Neither do I," she whispered.

Their eyes met and held for a moment. Faith smiled at Preacher and then walked away into the gloom of the pale canvas-ringed circle. She stopped, turned around, and stared at him for a moment.

Preacher lay back on his blankets, his head on his saddle, and looked up at the diamond-pocked heavens far above him. After a moment, he sighed heavily. "That woman's gonna get you in trouble," he muttered.

"Hee-hee-hee," Blackjack giggled from a few yards away, and Ned, Steals Pony, and the other mountain men joined in the snickering.

"Oh, shut up!" Preacher told them.

Charlie Burke then stepped out of the shadows and went swishing across the clearing like a fop, both hands on his hips. He sashayed about. Soon Blackjack and the others stepped out and began mincing about like fops, with the huge Blackjack closely resembling a drunken grizzly bear. Preacher just lay on his blankets and let them have their fun.

Preacher had to stick his fist in his mouth to keep from laughing when he spotted Eudora, Faith, and about twenty other ladies all hunkered down on the ground, peering intently through the wheel spokes at the foppish dancing and other strange antics of the mountain men.

He figured Blackjack and the others would have some tall explainin' to do come the dawnin'.

12

Preacher was a good five miles from the wagon train when the eastern sky began splitting into color. He'd had him several cups of strong coffee 'fore he left the circle—he stopped a woman just in time to keep her from throwing it out; told her he didn't give a damn if it was hours old, it was still hot, wasn't it, so turn the pot a-loose, you crazy female! And when he reached a clear running creek, he swung down from Hammer to eat some cold biscuits and salt meat he'd snitched from an oven.

He ruminated as he chewed. Preacher figured that Bedell and his trashy bunch would be starting to close the distance now, maybe laying no more than a day's ride behind. In two or three days, the wagons would have reached the Platte and be heading west along its southern banks.

"That's where they'll hit 'em," Preacher said, finishing off his breakfast. He took a long drink of water from the creek, and tightened the cinch on Hammer. Hammer pulled his usual stunt and puffed up. If Preacher didn't catch it, when he tried to step into the saddle, Hammer would exhale, loosening the cinch strap, and Preacher would hit the ground.

Hammer would then roll his eyes and show his big teeth. Preacher always swore the damn horse was laughing at him.

"Caught you that time, didn't I?" Preacher said to Hammer. The big horse tried to step on Preacher's foot but the mountain man was too quick for him. Preacher knew all of Hammer's tricks. But ever' now and then Hammer would catch him.

To listen to Preacher cuss his horse, a stranger might have thought the two hated each other. But exactly the opposite was true. Hammer would kill anyone who tried to harm his master, and Preacher would kill anyone who tried to do harm to his horse.

Preacher rode another six or seven miles, then reined up before he topped a fairly high ridge. He picketed Hammer and, taking his spyglass, bellied up to the top of the ridge and began scanning. It didn't take him long to spot the riders. They were closing fast now, riding at a distance-consuming pace, but not a punishing one for their horses. And their horses, Preacher had noticed the other night, were all top quality mounts. Preacher had never seen so many fine horses in one bunch.

"Definitely closin' the gap," Preacher muttered, lowering the spyglass. He stayed where he was until the band of men were out of sight. Then he sat for a time and thought a few things out.

As to what Bedell and the men might be up to, he had only the word of Woford Lewis to go on. And even though Preacher knew for a fact that Victor Bedell was a no-good, capable of doing anything mean and nasty, and that good men don't ride with no-goods, he was at a loss as to just what he should do to cut the odds down some. Preacher didn't think one man tackling forty-nine would be real smart. That is, providing the men were after the wagon train and the women. Preacher was 100% sure they were, but so far they had not made a move against the train.

Then Preacher's eyes narrowed as a thought came to him. A very disturbing thought. The bunch he'd watched through his spyglass had been a few men short. About five or six short. He was sure of that.

What had happened? Where had the five or six men gone? Had the men quit Bedell and turned back? Preacher didn't believe that. Not for a second. Their absence could only mean one thing. Bedell had become suspicious and had ordered the men to lag behind, keeping a sharp lookout on the party's backtrail. Bedell was as wily as a fox. Preacher silently admonished himself for forgetting that. And he just as silently realized that he was in a lot of danger.

Preacher took a slow, careful eyeballing of his surroundings. The land looked peaceful. Empty. A slight breeze was blowing. But this part of the country was very deceptive. A whole bunch of people could be hiding anywhere within a hundred yards of his location. His eyes cut to Hammer. The horse's ears were pricked and he was tense.

"You done it stupid this time, ol' son," Preacher muttered. "Them men of Bedell's is out there and workin' in close to you. Damn!"

Preacher carefully checked his pair of awesome pistols. He then checked his rifle just as carefully. Hammer blew softly. Preacher cocked his rifle. The very softest of sounds reached him. He whirled around, came up on one knee, and fired just as a man topped the ridge. The big ball caught the man in the center of his chest and stopped him cold for an instant, then he was flung backward as if hit with a giant fist. Preacher ran toward Hammer and leaped into the saddle just as a bullet slammed into his back, almost knocking him out of the saddle. Hammer leaped into motion as rifles boomed all around him. Preacher pulled a pistol and fired nearly point-blank into the bearded face of a man who had jumped up out of the tall grass. The face erupted into a terrible mess of blood as the ball hit him dead center. Another man appeared in front of Preacher and Preacher fired, the ball striking the man in the shoulder. He heard the horrible screams as Hammer's hooves pounded the man's flesh and shattered his face. Hammer was running all out now. And there was not a horse around that could outdistance Hammer in a flat out run. Another rifle sounded, and Preacher's head exploded into a blinding mass of pain. He threw his arms around Hammer's neck and held on. Then he remembered nothing.

It was nearly dark when Preacher forced his eyes to open. He was flat on his back on the ground, and he was cold. His head hurt something fierce. Slowly, his mind started working and he recalled the gunfight back on the ridge. He'd been shot. More than once. He felt around him. His arms and hands worked. He found a pistol and pulled it to him. He felt his left side holster. That pistol was still in place. He turned his head and sorrow struck him hard. Hammer was down, lying on his side, his pain-filled eyes open and looking at the man he loved. Preacher could see pink foam coming from the faithful horse's nose and mouth. Hammer had been lung shot.

"Oh, no," Preacher said. "Oh, Sweet Baby Jesus, no." Summoning his massive strength, Preacher forced himself to his knees, then to his feet. He swayed for a moment, conscious of a pain in his back and side. He ignored it. He staggered over to Hammer and looked down at the horse. Hammer was finished. He'd been shot four times, but had still managed to carry his master to safety.

Preacher was openly, unashamedly weeping as he put a merciful, pain-relieving bullet into Hammer's brain. Then he fell down to his knees and wept some more. He collapsed beside the big, faithful horse and the pain took him. Preacher fought it hard, but it was a losing battle. He was taken into blackness.

* * *

It was light when he awakened. He looked overhead and saw buzzards circling ever closer. He clawed for the rifle in the saddle boot and blew one buzzard out of the sky. He reloaded and knocked another spinning. The remaining buzzards seemed to get the message and soared higher.

Preacher fought the swimming pain in his head and rose to his feet. He found his other rifle and reloaded both, then checked his pistols, reloading them fully. One buzzard made a bad mistake by landing and staring with his evil eyes at Preacher. The mountain man blew his head off.

He stripped saddle and saddlebags from Hammer's stiffening carcass, having to dig under the horse with his big knife to finally get the saddle free. Exhausted, Preacher rested for a time, fighting pain and nausea. He dampened a kerchief and held it against his aching head, near the back where he figured the ball had clipped him. It seemed to help. He pulled up his buckskin shirt and looked at the hole in his side, close to the outside. He felt around to his back. The ball had entered in his back and exited out the front. Preacher figured if the ball had hit anything vital, he'd a been dead by now. He cleaned the wounds as best he could, and then found some moss and placed it over the holes, tying them in place with pieces of cloth he tore from his only spare shirt.

He built a small fire and boiled coffee, chewing on jerky while making his coffee. Then, ignoring his pain, he worked for hours covering Hammer with rocks, until he had a pile nearly as tall as his chest. Animals might get to his faithful companion of many years, but if they did, they'd have to work like hell to do it.

"I broke my promise to you, Hammer," he said. "I'm sorry. I truly am."

Preacher then turned his face toward the west. "Bedell," he said, his voice low and full of menace, "you sorry pile of coyote shit. You better catch you a whaler ship to China and slant your eyes, yeller your skin, and belly up in a rice paddy. 'Cause I'm comin' after you, you son of a bitch. And I'll find you. I don't care how long it takes me, or how many miles I got to travel. You are dead, Bedell, and anyone who rides with you is dead. And that there is a cold promise, you low-life bastard."

Preacher patted the pile of rocks. "Rest easy, now, old friend. You carried me many a mile, and we rode some trails, we did. You earned your rest. You ride the skies now, Hammer. And I promise I'll avenge you. I swear to God Almighty I'll do that."

Preacher had deliberately put all thoughts of the wagon train out of his mind. For he did not know how long he'd been unconscious. He figured he'd drifted in and out of consciousness for two days, maybe three. He'd ridden a full day from the wagons, so he was sure that whatever evil Bedell had planned, the deed was done.

Dragging his saddle, Preacher made it to a creek and rested in the cool shade. For several days he drank often and ate up his meager supplies, managing to catch some fish to supplement his diet. He dug up tubers and ate them, and tended to his wounds by making poultices. When he started walking west, he knew he wasn't 100%, but he was strong enough to get going. On the second day after leaving the creek, he found himself looking at three Kansa braves, sitting on their horses and staring at him.

Of the tribes in this area, the Kansa, Mandan, Osage, and the Missouri all spoke basically the same language, and so did Preacher.

"I am Preacher," he told them.

They looked at one another. "We know," one finally said. "That's a fine-lookin' spare horse you got. I want it."

"Perhaps we do not wish to trade," another Kansa said.

But Preacher could detect nervousness in his words. The Kansa were only armed with bows and arrows, and one carried a lance. Preacher knew they had not missed how heavily armed he was. And the ferocity of the man called Ghost Walker, White Wolf, and other names was known from the

Pacific to the Mississippi. The Kansa clearly did not wish to tangle with Preacher.

"I think you'll change your mind. How is the horse called?"

"We just caught him. He has no name.

The horse was shod, and Preacher figured it had belonged to one of Bedell's group who ambushed him. Preacher pulled his spare Hawken from the boot and tossed it to the Kansa holding the reins of the horse. As soon as he caught up with Bedell's group, he'd have him another rifle right quick. He tossed a bag of shot and powder horn to the Indian.

"Fair trade?" Preacher asked.

The Kansa nodded and dropped the reins. "Fair," he said, and he and his companions were gone.

Preacher petted and spoke to the big brown. He had him gentled down and taking grass from his hand in a matter of minutes. Preacher liked horses and most seemed to like him. Preacher was in the saddle and riding west within the hour.

"You're a dead man, Bedell," he said to the wind. "And that's a promise."

A half a dozen Pawnee spied Preacher and with gleeful shouts of killing anticipation—there wasn't a Pawnee in the tribe who liked Preacher—they rode to block his way. But Preacher wasn't about to be intimidated by the Pawnee. He didn't like them any more than they liked him. Preacher had discovered that whoever trained this horse had done a fine job of it. He looped the reins loosely around the saddle horn, filled both hands with those terrible pistols of his, let out a war whoop, and charged.

Scared the hell out of those Pawnee.

Preacher rode right in amongst them and blew three of them straight to the arms of whatever or whoever they believed in after death. The other three took off like their asses were on fire and didn't look back. Preacher watched them until they were nothing but dark dots on the vastness of the land.

They'd be back, for sure, and Preacher knew that. But he

had him a little time to inspect the dead 'fore they returned . . .
with more warriors, he was sure of that, too. He first reloaded his pistols, then began the grisly job of checking out
the dead.

One of the dead Pawnee had a rifle beside his body that
Preacher recognized. Ring had carried it. With a sigh, Preacher
picked up the plains rifle and checked it, then tore the shot
pouch, powder horn, and caps bag from the dead Indian. He
tried at first not to look at the hair on the Pawnee's war-axe.
It was Ring's. But something else about the scalp troubled
Preacher.

He jerked the scalp loose and felt it. It was dry. Even the
underside was nearly dry. No Pawnee had killed Ring. They'd
just come along after the bodies had stiffened and done their
knife work.

Preacher did some fancy cussin' for a time. Made him
feel a little bit better.

He took all the powder, shot, and caps—the percussion
caps told him the Pawnee had more than likely taken the
rifles from the train for every rifle there had been of the latest
model—and left the bodies where they lay. He swung into
the saddle and headed out. When he made camp that evening,
he buried Ring's hair.

He found where the battle had taken place. Bedell had
split his people. One group had swung wide and gotten in
front of the wagons and another had hit them from the rear
while the wagons were strung out and on the move. It had
been one hell of a running battle, and the last wagon had
been halted some five miles from the ambush site. Preacher
found lots of signs of dried blood, but he could not find one
body. So where the hell had the Pawnee come up on Ring?
He'd probably never know. Some animals may have dragged
off the body, or bodies, by now.

He backtracked. There was no point in getting into a

hurry now. The deed was done and he couldn't undo it. Every few hundred yards he'd stop and sniff the air. Preacher knew Bedell and his thugs wouldn't have taken the bodies far. They had to be buried somewhere close by. Finally he smelled it: the unmistakable odor of death.

Four of the drivers hired back in Missouri were buried in a shallow grave. Animals had uncovered them and had been eating on the bodies. Preacher covered them again, piling rocks over the dirt, and went looking for more bodies.

He found the body of a woman he'd known only as Ros, buried in a hastily dug grave with a woman he'd heard called Marylou. Their heads had been bashed in. Neither of the women was real lookers, so Bedell and his gang figured they wouldn't bring much in trade, or to sell to slavers, so they killed them.

Preacher found the other drivers. They'd been shot and part of a creek bank caved in on them. One hand, curled into a fist, was protruding from the earth. Preacher left them in peace where they lay. He walked a short distance and found two of Lieutenant Worthington's soldiers next. And good ol' Ring was lying dead with them. All had been scalped.

Casting about, Preacher could see plain the wagon ruts. It looked like Bedell and his men were going to follow the ill-defined trail all the way. Even though to Preacher's mind that was risky. Once on the coast some of the women might talk and that would bring a hangman's noose to Bedell and the outlaws.

"Black-hearted heathens," Preacher muttered. "Filth and trash."

Walking on, he found Charlie Burke dead and uncovered in the brush. Ol' Charlie must have put up one hell of a fight, for he had been shot half a dozen times and had still managed to get away, to die alone. Preacher had found a shovel and he buried his friend, and his weapons with him.

"Sorrowful day," Preacher said to the blue sky. "And folks call the Injuns savages."

Fifteen minutes later, he found Ned. The mountain man had been shot 'bout as many times as Charlie but had still gotten away from the terrible fight and he had propped himself up against a tree and was smoking his pipe for the last time when he died. His pipe was still in his cold hand. Preacher buried him.

Then he found some of the young children and was taken by a savage, terrible rage that was almost blinding in its fury. The boys had been tortured and the girls used horribly. Preacher choked back his outrage and carefully buried the young'uns, boys with boys and girls with girls. He couldn't find enough of their clothing to cover them proper, and that seemed like a sin to Preacher.

Then he found Sergeant Scott and the rest of Rupert's soldiers. They had sought cover in a short ravine and had died like soldiers, fighting to the last man.

Preacher laid them out in the shallow ravine and caved earth and rocks over them. Bedell's men had gone through their pockets, removing all papers and money.

When he could find no more bodies, Preacher began casting about for bloodstains that might have been left by any wounded. He found plenty of that. It looked like Steals Pony, Snake, and Blackjack had taken lead but had managed to get away. It was getting too dark to track, so Preacher made camp and cooked a rabbit he'd caught in a snare.

His thoughts were as dark as the night as he rolled up in his blankets. Old Satan himself would have tiptoed light around what Preacher was thinking.

13

At first light, Preacher was tracking with the skill and tenacity of a bloodhound. He soon found what he'd hoped to find. A small group of women had gotten away, and they had done so on horseback. Eudora had a foot size that was equal to her height, and she had led the group of females out and away from the attack. Obviously, Bedell and his men had decided not to pursue the women, thinking they'd probably die out here anyway. It took Preacher most of the day to find them. He spotted them through his spyglass and he noted with satisfaction that they had picked good cover in which to rest. He didn't want to spook them, and as jumpy as he knowed they was, he might get shot right off the mark if he showed himself plain, so he commenced to hollerin' while he was out of rifle range.

"My stars and garters, Captain!" Eudora exclaimed. "It's good to see you."

There were seven women. Eudora, Faith, Cornelia, April, Lisette, Madeline, and Claire. They all hugged him, with Faith doin' a bit of rubbin', too; then Preacher took the cup of coffee Eudora handed him and sat down to hear their story.

"It appears that Bedell had women loyal to him on the train," Eudora said. "About twenty or so of them. Whores from out of New Orleans and Natchez. They turned out to be meaner and crueler than the men with Bedell. They tortured poor Anna to death while some of the men were busy raping and others gathering up the stock and wagons."

"I seen the young girls and boys," Preacher said, his words hard-edged. "I buried ever'body I found. I reckon they took the girls that was of age. I didn't see none of them. Do you know what happened to Steals Pony, Snake, and Blackjack?"

"The Delaware and Blackjack were both wounded, I know that much," Madeline said. "I witnessed that. I don't know what happened to the old man."

"You don't look well, Preacher," Claire said. "Are you all right?"

"I was shot a couple of times," Preacher said. "But it ain't serious. They're healin' up proper. I just ain't got all my strength back yet. It'll come soon."

"That's a terrible gash on your head," Eudora said, peering at the wound. "But it seems to be healing."

"I been treatin' it with poultices. Same with the bullet hole in my side and back. It's still some sore. But the bleedin's long stopped and it's closin' up. I just need two/three days to take it easy."

"We can take the time," Eudora said firmly.

"But the ladies . . ." Madeline said.

"What's happened to them has happened," Eudora said. "They're not going to die from being raped."

"I'd rather die!" Madeline Hornbuckle said, closing her eyes and pressing the back of one hand to her forehead dramatically.

"Then you're a damn fool," Eudora told her bluntly. "And

I don't want to hear anymore such talk." She looked at Preacher. "What are we going to do, Captain?"

"We're going to attack," Preacher said.

Preacher moved everyone back close to the trail and then he ate, slept, ate again, then slept again for three days. He knew there was no point in his jumping right out after Bedell when just shoveling a few spades of dirt over the dead had damn near tuckered him out total. While he rested and got his strength back, he had the ladies over at the ambush site going over the weapons he'd took from the dead.

Food was a problem, but it wouldn't be for long. Just long enough to catch up with the wagons. Bedell and his bunch liked to terrorize people. Preacher would soon see how he liked it when the tables got turned around.

"How about Rupert?" Preacher asked, on the morning they were saddling up to pull out.

"None of us saw him," Faith said. The city woman had toughened, both mentally and physically. Her face and forearms were tanned now, and while her tongue could still be as sharp as a rapier, she had softened it quite a bit. All the women knew they were in a real pickle; Preacher had laid that out strong to them. There was little joking now. The women and Preacher were quite alone in a vast and terribly inhospitable wilderness . . . as Faith had put it.

"And it's gonna get vaster, a lot more inhorsetable, and wilder'an hell," Preacher added.

"In*hospitable,*" Faith gently corrected.

"Whatever, Missy."

In the chilly gray light of morning, Preacher looked at the ladies. They were all dressed in men's clothing. They had chopped their hair off even shorter than before. Each carried a rifle in one hand and another in a saddle boot. They had pistols hung everywhere and each woman carried two buckled around her waist.

"We got it to do, ladies," Preacher said, stepping into the saddle. His side and back still bothered him a little, but the head wound was very nearly healed. Neither wound had been serious, just painful. Preacher had been shot before, and knew how fast he would heal. By the time they caught up with the wagons, he'd be 100%. "Let's ride."

About six or seven miles from the ambush site, Preacher called a rest period along a little creek shaded by cottonwoods. He'd seen something glittering brightly and wanted to check it out. While the ladies rested, he found the source of the twinkling. Rupert Worthington's cavalry saber. Had his name engraved right on the blade. He showed it to the women.

"I seen some tracks leadin' toward that ridge yonder. I'm goin' on foot. Stay here."

He found the young lieutenant. He was lying on his belly in a clump of brush just off the crest of the small ridge. He was sound asleep.

Preacher took the officer's rifle and slipped his pistols from their holsters. Then he squatted down beside the sleeping young man. He tickled his nose with a long stem of grass. Rupert brushed at his nose. Preacher tickled the man's ear. Rupert grunted and opened one eye. Then both eyes opened wide.

"My God!" Rupert said. Preacher then noticed the front of Rupert's shirt was covered with dried blood.

"No, it ain't. It's just me. You hurt bad, boy?" Preacher looked at the bump on his head and the split skin.

"I thought I was." Rupert sat up and then noticed that Preacher was holding his rifle and his pistols. "You're quite the expert at sneaking up on people, Preacher."

"Tolerable, boy. Tolerable. Are you hurt?"

"Not badly. I thought I was mortally wounded at first. The ball struck a watch I'd been carrying in my shirt pocket. My father gave it to me. I was proud of that watch. I don't know how I'll break the news to him . . ."

Preacher sighed and waited.

". . . Anyway, the shot knocked me off my horse and I struck the back of my head on a rock and fell into unconsciousness. When I awakened, I found that fragments of the watch had penetrated my flesh and the wound had bled quite profusely for a time."

Preacher looked at the back of the young man's head. Had himself a pretty good bump there, too. "What happened to the front of your noggin?"

"I tried to catch up with a frightened horse and got kicked in the head. I feel like an idiot. When I came out of that, I was discombobulated. I wandered lost for several hours in a daze. I remember I was waving my saber and ranting like a wild man. But I don't recall ever going to the wagon for my saber. Then my next conscious thought was that I was burning up with fever. I don't remember coming here. But I lost my saber."

"I found it. I left it with the ladies down by the crick."

"The ladies! They're alive?"

"Seven of 'em with me. The others was took prisoner by Bedell and his trash. A few was killed outright. So was the kids. And your command," he added as gently as he could.

Rupert put his face in his hands and wept. Preacher couldn't fault him for that. He'd bawled himself over Hammer.

Whilst the lieutenant was clearin' his emotions, Preacher looked out over the land. No smoke. No signs of Injuns—not that that meant a whole lot. He stepped to the crest and called down to the ladies.

"Build a fire and boil some water. And save some to clean up Rupert's wounds. He ain't hurt terrible bad. We'll be down directly."

Preacher knelt down beside the young army man. "It all right to cry, Rupert. Damn people who say a man ain't s'pposed to weep. Them rotten sons of bitches kilt my good horse Hammer, and I squalled something fierce, I did. So you go right on and get it clear of your system. When you feel up to it, we'll head on down to the crick and get you tended to. We got spare mounts, so don't worry about that."

"You are an understanding man, Preacher." Rupert blew his nose on a rag.

"I wouldn't know about that. You ready to head on down to the crick?"

"Yes. I have composed myself."

The women fussed over Rupert and made a big deal of his wounds, which Preacher considered very minor. But the young officer needed the attention. His morale was very low.

Preacher climbed back up the ridge to keep watch while the women worked on Rupert. He decided to leave the still ill-defined wagon trail and stay to the south of the stolen wagons and kidnapped ladies, who would be following close to the Platte. Preacher had a plan, sort of, but it was a chancy one. He had his bow and quiver of arrows, and planned on some silent killing. He planned to retake the wagons . . . one at a time.

"You can't be serious, Preacher?" Rupert questioned him as they rode along, heading slightly south for a few miles before cutting west.

"I'm as serious as death, Rupert. It's the only way. Once we get twenty or so women freed from them damn trash, we'll have us a force large enough to mount some sort of attack."

"But this Bedell person might challenge that by saying if we attack, he'll start killing the women he still holds."

"Could be. But do you have a plan that's better than mine?"

He did not.

"Thought so."

Rupert looked back at the women, all dressed in men's britches and riding astride in single file. In just a few short weeks they had undergone a drastic change. They looked . . .

he struggled for the right word . . . *capable;* he finally found what he considered to be an apt description. Their shirts were loose-fitting and their hats floppy. Even at a reasonably close distance, unless one made a very careful inspection, they would pass for men.

"My men, Preacher," Rupert said. "How did they die? I mean . . ."

"I know what you mean. They died like soldiers, boy. They dug in and fought to the finish. When you make your report, you can say that."

Rupert gave the mountain man an odd look. He shook his head and tried a small smile. "You really believe that we'll come out of this alive, don't you?"

"Hell, yes, I do. This time tomorrow, I'll start cuttin' down the odds some."

"Suppose . . . just suppose, that the last wagon is driven by one of the women who was in this with Bedell?"

"What about it?"

"Would you kill her?"

"As fast as I would a man. Trash is trash."

"I don't know that I could kill a woman," the young officer admitted.

"Them whory women who tossed in their lot with Bedell and his scum tortured Anna to death, Rupert. They laughed and helped the trashy bastards to do unnatural things to the boys 'fore they killed 'em. I seen what was left of them young boys. And I ain't goin' into no details about it. Use your imagination. Them with Bedell is twisted, boy. In the head. And don't give me no eastern crap about due process and feelin' sorry for scum. I don't want to hear it. And get this straight, Rupert: I ain't takin' no prisoners. And I ain't gonna let a damn one of Bedell's people reach the coast— male or female. Them sorry white trash killed my friends and killed my good horse, Hammer. This is personal, now. And it ought to be for you, too. They're cold-blooded murderers all. They killed your command. You better make up your mind whether you're with me all the way. 'Cause in this situation, halfway won't do it."

"Amen to that," Eudora called, riding just behind the two men. "You just let me get that damn Ruby in gunsights. I'll gut shoot her so fast it'll billow your mainsail."

"My word!" Rupert muttered.

"I want that damn Cindy Lou," Cornelia Biggers called out. "I never did trust her."

"I got my mind set on Allene," Claire said, her words containing a hard, bitter edge. "I saw what she did. I see it every night in my dreams. And I'll not rest easy until she's rotting in the grave . . . not that she deserves a grave."

"Hate is not a good thing," Rupert said. " 'Vengeance is mine, sayeth the Lord.' "

"Stick your platitudes where the sun doesn't shine," Faith told him.

That widened Rupert's eyes. "There is no need to be coarse, Miss Faith."

"So how do you think you'd like it if one of Bedell's men bent you over a wagon tongue and sailed up your stern?" Eudora asked him.

Preacher shook his head at the bluntness of the lady's words. But she was right in saying it.

"My heavens!" Rupert blurted.

"Now you know what they done to some of them young boys, Rupert," Preacher told him. "So shut up and get your mind set for killin'. We got to be just as cold-blooded and hard as them we fight. If we're not, then we'll lose. And that's all there is to it, boy. That's the sum total."

"I think my overall education has been sadly lacking in some respects," Rupert admitted.

"Before this is all over," Preacher told him, "I figure you'll have earned several more diplomas.

"I'm very afraid you are going to be correct," Rupert said, his tone quite dry. "Although the subject matter might be a bit suspect."

"The Army's liable to make you one of them highfalutin' generals after all this is over, Rupert."

"What I'll probably get is a courts-martial," Rupert muttered.

"Cheer up, Rupert," Eudora called. "You can always transfer over to the navy. . . . After the army lets you out of jail."

14

"Just like I figured," Preacher muttered. He had left the others well-hidden about two miles south while he headed for the Platte. "Stayin' right on the trail." He had not been too worried about Bedell putting outriders very far from the wagons. With the supplies on hand, they really didn't have to hunt, except occasionally, when they wanted a taste of fresh meat.

Preacher waited until the last wagon had passed, then he hightailed it back to the others. "Let's go, people. This time tomorrow, we'll have spilled some of their blood . . . for a change," he added, a grim note to the words.

The party took off, heading west for some ten miles, then cutting straight north. They reached the Platte River—which would later be dubbed as "too thick to drink and too thin to plow" by the westward-bound flow of settlers—and Preacher selected his ambush site.

He fixed a small fire out of dry, virtually smokeless wood, and venison steaks, but from a deer that Preacher had killed with an arrow that day, were soon cooking.

Rupert watched Preacher carefully going over his arrows. "What in the world are you doing?"

"I got to make the first shot count, boy. I can't let him or her scream. Gurgle or moan is all right, but screamin' is definitely out."

"Where do you plan on shooting the person?"

"Right through the throat. All they can do is moan soft and gurgle some."

Rupert swallowed hard at just the thought.

"Or," Preacher said, "I might take a chance and get on the wagon through the rear and cut his throat. Or her throat. Whatever. I'll just have to see what it looks like. Them steaks is done. Let's eat."

Preacher had dug up some tubers and wild onions and with the meat, he considered the meal quite a feast. Most of the others were less than exhilarated over the meal but ate it down without complaint.

"I have seen tubers that weighed as much as thirty pounds," Preacher said. "That'd feed us all for a week, wouldn't it?"

"A thirty-pound potato?" Rupert asked. "Now, come on, Preacher!"

"Oh, it's true. Injuns call the tater from the wild 'tater vine man of the earth.' Staple food for lots of tribes." Preacher dug in his bag and handed them all what looked like thin, dried roots. "After supper, chew some of these. They're right good."

"What is it?" Faith eyed the stuff suspiciously.

"Wild licorice. Injuns been dryin' it and chewin' it for centuries. That's where I learned about it. The earth is always pregnant, people. Always. Even under cover of snow, something is growin'. The earth will feed you, if you'll learn from it and use it proper. In this area where we are, stretching way down into Mexico, is a tuber called hog potatoes. They ain't the tastiest things I ever put in my mouth, but they'll keep you alive. They's all kinds of eatable things all around us. They's wild cabbages, squashes, and punkins. Injuns use the goosefoot herb in several ways. They can cook it up like greens and grind the seeds into a flour. In the deserts, the Injuns use the pulp of the cholla cactus to make candy and syrup. Hell, I could talk half the night on things to eat that's growin' wild right out yonder." He jerked his thumb. "I've eat my weight in pond lily roots and dried 'em and made tasty flour." He smiled and winked. "But you got to know *which* pond lily. That there's the trick. They's all kinds of plants that'll kill you deader than hell if you eat 'em raw, but cook 'em up, and they're lip-smackin' good. And some of them will kill you deader than hell raw or cooked. Lemmie tell y'all something about the wilderness. It ain't agin you. It really ain't. The wilderness is neutral. But if you try to fight it, it'll kill you. You got to learn to live with it. Now go to sleep. We got some killin' to do come tomorrow."

The ambush site was in the eastern bend of a long curve. It was a rocky section of the trail, and the going was tortuously slow. Preacher figured the stock would be driven on ahead and he had figured right, because that's what he would have done. The man who was driving the last wagon was a hard-faced, sour-looking man, whose face bore several deep scratches. He'd had his way with some woman, but she had damn sure marked him up good 'fore he got her britches off.

Preacher'd left Rupert to guard the women, telling him that he was needed there, and telling him that he was really depending on him. And that he was taking Eudora in case some of the women in the wagon wasn't in proper dress and needed a woman's touch.

Rupert bought it. He was really a good lad; Preacher just needed someone with him who would not hesitate to cut a throat if need be. And he knew that Eudora would not hesitate one second.

"You can be diplomatic when you try, Captain," the tall, handsome woman whispered to Preacher as they crouched in the thicket along the river. "That was kind of you to soothe Rupert's feelings at being left with the women. Even though I know it was a crock of stinking fish."

Preacher grinned at the woman. They were only a few yards from the trail; if spotted, it would almost certainly mean instant death, and the lady could still make small talk as if nothing was wrong. "Just as soon as I let the arrow fly, I'm out of here and on the wagon seat, Eudora. When I signal, you come hoppin'. I figure we got three to four minutes at the most to get it done. We take supplies and any prisoners that might be ridin' in the wagon bed. They got to think it's Injuns. You ready?"

"As I'll ever be."

When the next to last wagon had rounded the bend and was out of sight, Preacher stood up and let his arrow fly. It was true to the mark. The driver threw up his hands and toppled backward into the covered bed of the wagon. No sound came from the bed, so Preacher figured there were no prisoners there. He leaped from the brush and hopped onto the seat, grabbing up the reins and stopping the wagon. The dying outlaw thrashed and jerked on the floor of the wagon. Preacher paid him no mind. Eudora quickly gathered up sugar, flour, beans, and bacon, while Preacher picked up blankets and coffee and as many other items as he felt he could carry. The outlaw's horse was tied to the rear and Preacher took the animal, after quickly lashing the supplies to the saddle and behind it. Then he and Eudora were gone, racing back to their hidden horses.

Preacher did not expect any pursuit, and none came. Bedell was too smart to send men into what might be an Indian ambush. Long after the wagons were out of sight, Preacher and Rupert rode back to the ambush site. The wagon had been abandoned, but the mules had been taken. It looked like Bedell didn't have any spare drivers. Preacher grinned at that. The bastard was going to have less drivers come the dawnin'.

"Take the canvas, Rupert," he told the young officer, "and the rope. I'll see what they left in the bed."

"What about him?" Rupert asked, pointing to the dead man hanging half out of the tail of the wagon.

"That ought to tell you what kind of people we're dealin' with. They didn't even take the time to bury him. Sorry bunch of bastards. Leave him."

"But . . ."

"Shut up, Rupert. Do what I tell you to do. I warned you about arguin' with me."

Rupert closed his mouth and turned his head as Preacher carefully removed his arrow from the dead man's neck. "It's a good arrow," he said.

Bedell's people had not even bothered to inspect what contents remained in the bed of the wagon. Much of it was useful to Preacher and his small group. Preacher took the dead man's pistols to give to the ladies, and fine pistols they was, too. He started to take the dead man's hat, for it was a good one, until he saw lice crawlin'. He decided to forego the hat.

"I still think we should bury the poor wretch," Rupert said again.

"Stop thinkin', Rupert. I'll tell you when to think. Let's get gone."

Bedell didn't believe for one second that Indians had been responsible for the ambush of the wagon. The handsome, well-dressed man sat drinking coffee and staring morosely into the dying flames of the fire. The sounds of weeping women were all around him as the outlaws continued their raping and defiling, but Bedell paid no attention to it.

The man who ambushed the wagon—and it was one man; Bedell was sure of that—was Preacher. His men had said that they'd seen Preacher take at least two balls into him days back, one of them to the head. The wounds must have been slight, Bedell concluded. But no matter. Preacher would be dealt with in due time. He had more men waiting to join up with the group when the wagons cut north some days ahead. They would more than make up for the men Preacher had killed thus far.

But Preacher was still the fly in the ointment. He had to be killed, and so did those who were with him.

Damn the luck! Bedell thought. Faith Crump had gotten away and that was the card Bedell had counted on to play. Old Man Crump would have paid a fortune to get his daughter back. With that money, plus the money the gold brought—and the gold was there, all right, Bedell knew that—he could live like a king for the rest of his life.

Damn Preacher's eyes! Bedell thought. Goddamn the man to hell! When the wagons linked up with the men from California, Bedell would assign all the new men to kill Preacher and grab Faith Crump. It had to be. It was the only way. He had already promised the women to some of the men, and they would be taken to California and sold into brothels . . .

"Oh, God, no more!" a woman pleaded with an outlaw. "Please, God, no!" Her pleadings ended with a scream of pain and several other women laughed in the night.

Bedell paid no attention to it. Neither did one of the guards stationed around the protective circle. He couldn't because he was dead, his throat cut from one side to the other. Preacher had then lashed him to a wagon wheel so's he'd look like he was standing up, and then made his way to the horses. He moved quietly, whispering to the animals and petting them. Preacher had a way with horses, and none of them so much as blew. He led several away from the wagons and picketed them. Then he returned to the wagons.

He passed up several wagons, for the outlaws were busying themselves with the ladies in them, until he came to a wagon that was silent. He peeped in. Gayle Hawkins, Brigitte Wilson, and Bertha Macklin were all trussed up like hogs, with gags in their mouths. Preacher slipped into the darkened wagon.

"Don't make a sound, ladies," he whispered. "Not one sound or we're all dead."

The women, wide-eyed in shock, surprise, and relief, nodded their heads in understanding. Even in the darkened bed of the wagon, Preacher could see that the women had been savagely beaten. They were all naked and had been used badly. Preacher cursed silently at the brutality of the outlaws and tried to keep his eyes from the bareness of breasts and the whiteness of bruised thighs. He slashed the ropes and the women quickly slipped into britches and shirts and boots.

"One at a time, gals," Preacher whispered. "It gets real chancy from here on. Follow me and don't trip on nothin'. Don't make a sound."

They almost made it without incident. They had just reached the horses when a guard found the dead man and sounded the alarm. The camp was instantly alert.

"Rider!" Preacher told the women. "Ride like the devil and his demons is after you."

"They are," Brigitte said bitterly, and bit her lips against the pain as she settled into the saddle.

Shots were fired from the circle, but Bedell would not allow pursuit.

"No!" Bedell shouted the camp into silence. "We stay right where we are for the night and we'll mount a party come the dawn. Blundering around in the dark, in unfamiliar country, will just get more of our people killed. Stand down for the night, but double the guards."

After a moment of hugging and rejoicing among the women, Preacher put a halt to it. "Pack it up and let's get gone. Bedell will have men out come the mornin' lookin' for us. We'll swing wide around the wagons, then follow the river for a time."

"For how long a time?" Gayle asked, fatigue in her voice.

"Till I say we stop. Let's go."

Preacher pushed the tired group hard for several hours. Then he let them sleep for a few hours, and then rolled them out and pushed them hard for several more hours. Just at dawn, he finally allowed them to stop and make camp.

"Fix something to eat and get some rest," Preacher told the exhausted group. "I'll stand first watch and then wake you up, Rupert. It's not only Bedell and his people we got to look out for, it's the Injuns as well. We been real lucky so far. But the further west we travel, the more likely that is to change . . . at any moment. Eat and rest."

Preacher let them rest for four hours. A slight noise made him quickly turn around. Eudora was up and pouring a cup of hot black coffee. "Get some rest, Captain," she told him, picking up her rifle. "I'll stand the next watch."

Preacher smiled at her and nodded. So complete was his trust in the New Englander that he went right off to sleep and didn't wake up until the middle of the afternoon.

He opened his eyes and without moving, looked around him as much as he could while lying on his side. Rupert was on guard, and keeping a low profile of it. Madeline was cooking, the small fire built under branches to break up the smoke, and she was using wood that was nearly smokeless. It hadn't taken these women long to learn. Eudora was sitting with her back to a large rock, a rifle across her knees. Preacher had the thought that Eudora would be one hell of a fine wife . . . as long as her man stayed true to her. But God help him if he ever strayed.

Preacher stirred and Eudora cut her eyes to him. "All quiet as far as we can see, Captain."

Preacher nodded and accepted the cup of coffee from Madeline. The women he'd taken from the train the night before had washed up and changed into cleaner britches and shirts. None of the group, including Preacher, were real sanitary and sparklin' clean at the moment, but they were trying to stay alive, not set records for cleanliness.

Preacher ate some bacon and beans that was flavored with molasses, and some pan bread. The hot food hit the spot. He polished off his meal with another cup of coffee, pulled out his pipe and stuffed it, then lit it up. "Everybody et?" he asked.

Eudora nodded her head and smiled at him. "All except Bertha, Gayle, and Brigitte. I wanted them to rest as long as possible. They had a bad time of it, Captain." In spite of his ample use of mountain slang, she knew that Preacher had more than the average amount of education for the time and certainly for the place, and could read and write and do sums as well as most. And he could speak better English than he usually did, for he had done so with her. He used what most would consider terribly bad grammar because he could get the same thing said in far less words.

"They's a better place I recall about five miles further on. It ain't a bad ride, neither." He smiled, but the humor did not reach his eyes. "And it's a hell of an ambush spot."

Bertha and the others had awakened, and were stretching the kinks out and getting coffee and food. "Y'all eat," Preacher said. "Then we'll move to a better spot. But attackin' the last wagon is out for the time bein'. They'll now be wise to that trick and cautious."

"So what will you do?" Bertha asked. "Or rather, what will we do?"

Preacher smiled again. These gals had their dander up now. They were out for blood. God help any of those outlaws who fell into their hands. The outlaw's death, Preacher thought, would be a slow and painful one. He'd seen personal what Indian women did with prisoners. It wasn't an experience Preacher had any desire to go through.

"We kill some outlaws."

"Good," Brigitte said. She pulled a hunting knife out of a sheath and went to work sharpening it on a rock.

Preacher had him a thought about what she had in mind. He shuddered.

15

Knowing that Bedell and his people would be doubly cautious after Preacher's raid, he let them alone for this night. It was probably for the best, 'cause the women needed the rest and, Preacher admitted to himself, so did he. He was still not 100%, but he knew he would be in a few more days.

Just before the fire was doused for the night, Preacher ruminated awhile and then stared hard at Faith, a thoughtful expression on his face. "Faith?"

She looked up. "Yes?"

"Your pa is worth considerable, ain't he?"

"Oh, yes. He's quite wealthy."

"Like in thousands of dollars?"

Faith smiled. "Like in *millions* of dollars, Preacher."

"Your ma?"

"She came into quite a vulgar sum of money when her parents died a few years ago."

Preacher nodded his head. "Part of it is comin' together now." He cut his eyes to Eudora. "I figure Hempstead ain't your real name, Eudora. But it'll do far as I'm concerned. You got in a mite of trouble back east and your daddy bailed you out in the nick of time and sent you west. You reckon they's any way that Bedell might know who you really are?"

"If he reads the newspapers, yes," Eudora admitted. "And I see what you're driving at. I think you're right. My father is a prosperous man, but not wealthy like Faith's parents. But both would pay a lot of money to get us back."

"But only Bedell and Jack Hayes would be in on it. Maybe one or two more. The rest of them scum would be kept in the dark. Bedell promised the women to the trash to do with as they pleased. He wanted the supplies and the mules to use in his quest for gold, and Faith and Eudora for ransom. The men would be more likely to stay with him for the long haul if they had women to use along the way. Bedell planned this out long and hard, and it has damn near worked. So in his mind, we all got to die. Bertha, ladies, did any of you see what happened to Steals Pony, Snake, and Black-jack?"

The new trio all shook their heads. Brigitte said, "No. It was all so confusing and it happened so fast."

"I got to think they made it out," Preacher said. "I have to keep thinkin' that."

Preacher rolled up in his blankets and lay for a time before drifting off to sleep. There probably would be no more chances to grab any women from the train. If they had any sense, the outlaws would be placing the women in the center of the circle now. Of course, Preacher thought, if they had any sense, they wouldn't be outlaws.

He had to keep cutting down the odds. Had to keep nib-bling away at Bedell's men. And Preacher knew that he was the only one to do that. Rupert had courage and would stand and fight. But the young officer was not a frontiersman. The ladies would also fight, but they wouldn't be much good at sneakin' in and out.

Preacher tried to figure how many women were captive. About a hundred, he concluded. That was too damn many for Bedell's men to guard effectively. Then he opened his eyes wide as another thought came to him: there would be women escaping. All odds pointed to that. And if Preacher and his group stayed in front of the wagons, the women would be escaping from one terrible fate right smack into another one. Alone and unarmed in a hostile environment.

"Damn!" Preacher muttered. "Double damn," he added.

"What are you damning now?" Faith whispered from a few feet away.

"Go to sleep," Preacher told her.

Maybe it wouldn't be such a bad thing after all, Preacher ruminated. Attacks from the rear would mean Bedell would have to switch more men from the front and the flanks. And after a couple of hit and run attacks on the rear, Preacher could change tactics and strike from the front. Yeah. The more he thought about that, the better he liked it. And he'd hit them just as they were ending the day on the trail, and the men would be tired and not terribly alert; maybe he'd hit them just as they were all waking up, grumbling and sleepy. "Yeah!"

"Now what?" Faith asked.

"Go to sleep," Preacher replied, and closed his eyes.

The group unanimously agreed to Preacher's plan.

"Of course some of the ladies will be getting away," Eudora said. "I didn't even think of that."

"I didn't either 'til last night," Preacher said, rolling up his blanket and canvas ground sheet. "Let's hit the trail and come in behind 'em."

That afternoon, as the group swung in behind the wagons, staying back about five miles, they came upon a body sprawled beside the trail. The woman was naked and she had been savagely horsewhipped.

"Leigh Maxwell," Brigitte said. "She always fought her attackers until they beat her to the ground."

Eudora covered the lady with a ragged blanket. Preacher rolled her up in the blanket and tied it securely with rope.

"They done this to set an example," Preacher said. "Try to keep the other ladies in line. Fetch the shovel, Rupert."

Preacher cut his eyes to the ladies. They were angry and it showed. This single act of viciousness had knotted the group together even more firmly. If there had been any reluctance on anyone's part, it was gone now. Even Rupert was cussing under his breath. Quite ungentlemanly-like, too. The young man had some really terrible things to say about Bedell and his men.

"You got anything else to say about codes of conduct, fair trials, and lawyers and such, boy?" Preacher asked him, taking his turn with the shovel.

"Not a thing," Rupert replied tersely.

"Think you can shoot one of them bastards or their lowlife bitches down in cold blood, now, do you?"

The look Lt. Rupert Worthington gave Preacher was savage. "Without hesitation."

"Good. You just might survive out here, then."

Preacher stood away from the group as the ladies lifted their voices in a Christian song and Eudora spoke a few words over the lonely grave.

Be hundreds, maybe thousands more graves like that one, Preacher thought, as the ladies sang a final song over the remains of Leigh Maxwell. When easterners start scratchin' the itch to move west, and the floodgates open, folks will be turnin' this route into a regular graveyard.

We damn shore got a good start on it with this run, he concluded to himself.

The group tagged along behind the wagons for two more days after the burying of Leigh. Preacher made no moves against the outlaws.

"I want them to get a little careless," he told Eudora. He'd already spotted the two figures stumbling along, far in the distance, and knew he'd been right in his decision to swing in behind the wagons. Two women had managed to escape their cruel captors. If this kept up, Preacher would have to steal some more horses.

Rupert galloped. "You see them, Preacher?" he asked, excitement in his voice.

"I been seein' them, Rupert. But you're gettin' better at takin' in what's around you. See the ladies, Eudora?"

"Now I do."

They were Maude and Agnes, sisters from Baltimore. And they was worn to a frazzle.

"They'll come after us," Agnes said, after a long drink of water and a bite of food. "They told us all the other evening that if anyone escaped, they'd track us down and kill us slow. They can't be more than an hour or so behind."

"Good," Preacher said with a smile. "We'll not only cut the odds down some, but we'll have us spare mounts, too." He looked around. "Right over there," he said, pointing. "Let's get into position."

This was perfect ambush country, and Preacher was an expert at picking the right spot from which to launch one at Bedell's men. He positioned the ladies and warned them not to move anything except their eyes. Agnes and Maude were left to rest, for the two women were running on only a slim reserve of strength. They both had been badly used and beaten more than once.

Preacher found the highest spot around and started scanning the terrain. The outlaws showed up quicker than he anticipated. Six of them, riding those fine mounts and keeping their eyes on the trail left by the escaping women. Preacher worked his way back to the group and smiled.

"They're ridin' right into it," he told the group. "Let them get close in enough to see their eyes. Fire on my command. Get set."

Bedell's outlaws never knew what happened. Twelve rifles roared suddenly as one and the men were literally torn from their saddles and hurled to the ground, great bloody holes in all of their chests.

Preacher and Rupert jumped into the saddle to gather up the spooked horses of the dead trash while Eudora and the others made damn sure the outlaws were dead. One wasn't quite dead. Brigitte cut his throat with no more emotion than in scalin' a fish.

"Son of a bitch!" She spoke the only eulogy the man would ever get.

The ambush netted the group six fine horses and more supplies, blankets, and ground sheets. They had powder, shot, lead, and molds. They also now had more weapons than they could possibly use. Preacher checked them all carefully and used part of the canvas taken from the abandoned wagon to wrap them and lash the guns on a packhorse.

"When we finally make our stand," he told the women, all gathered around, "we'll load 'em all up and have more firepower than Bedell. I hope. But I can't help but believe he's got more men a-waitin' up ahead."

"He does." Maude confirmed Preacher's suspicions. "I overheard men talking about that more than once. But the second group is days ahead of the wagon."

"Where?" Preacher asked.

"I don't know the precise spot. Just that they would be waiting at the spot where the wagons cut north."

"That's a long way from here," Preacher said. "I know 'xactly where it is. We got time to cut the odds plenty more before then."

"I can hardly wait," Brigitte said, wiping her knife clean on her britches.

When his men had not returned by dusk, Victor Bedell felt the first seed of doubt enter his mind. He had now lost eleven men to Preacher, and they were still days away from the rendezvous point. Including Jack Hayes and the two thugs with him, Bedell was down to forty men and the twenty women he'd personally recruited for this journey. Savage bitches, he thought. In many ways, they had blacker hearts than most of the men who rode with him. They were vicious, coarse, and cheap . . . but what did you expect? Angels?

Bedell made up his mind. They would have to abandon some of the wagons. He just didn't have the men and women to drive them all and still keep outriders looking for hostiles. And they would have to abandon some of the mules. Bedell hated mules anyway. He'd hated them since the time one had kicked him clear over a fence when he was a boy. And they would have to abandon some of the supplies; Bedell had sense enough to know that he couldn't afford to overload the wagons, for he'd heard that this trail turned into a hard one later on.

He hated to leave the barrels of flour, salt pork, and sugar, but he would be more than happy to leave the feed for those goddamn mules. He hated mules.

Preacher sat his saddle and stared at the dozen wagons sitting motionless on the trail. The mules were still hitched up to them. He couldn't figure that. If Bedell had abandoned the wagons—and it sure looked like that's what he done—the least the sorry bastard could have done was unhitch the poor critters and let them fend off the land. It was late in the afternoon and had turned hot. The wind was kicking up a lot of dust.

"Stay put until I scout this out," Preacher told the group, stowing away his spyglass. "Them damn wagons might be filled with riflemen. But the way them mules are fidgetin' and sufferin' down there, I doubt it. They smell that river and want a drink bad."

Preacher slipped down to the unexposed side of his horse and circled the wagons a couple of times, studying the strange scene by looking under his horse's neck. The mules sure appeared glad to see another living creature, even if it was nothing more than a damn horse.

Preacher slid off his horse at a run and rolled under the rear wagon, his pistols at the ready. But he could tell the wagons were void of human life. He quickly inspected them all and waved for the group to come on.

He was unhooking the mules when they rode up. "Take these poor critters to water," he told them. "Haul back on 'em now, they're some thirsty."

He and Eudora and Faith inspected the wagons and found fodder for the mules and plenty of food and spare clothing for them all.

"I don't understand this," Faith said.

"We cut them down so thin, Bedell doesn't have the men to drive the wagons," Eudora explained. "Right, Captain?"

"That's it. But he must be more of a black-hearted son than I thought to leave those poor mules to suffer in harness."

"I drove mules as a boy," Rupert said, the statement surprising the hell out of Preacher. "I can fix these harnesses to increase the team size. We can hook the tongues of the spare wagons to the underpinning of the front wagon and only have to use six drivers instead of twelve. That way we'll still have ample guards out. But I've first got to determine which mules are the leaders."

"Well . . . you just go right ahead there, Rupert," Preacher said. "You get them rigged up and we'll all be back in business, by God."

"They're right behind us!" a scout reported to Bedell.

"Who?" Bedell demanded.

"Preacher and a bunch of men!" the excited scout said. "I

seen 'em with my own eyes. They've hitched up the wagons we left behind and are comin' on. The wagons are double-teamed."

"You saw Preacher, probably," Bedell replied. "But the others are women dressed as men. Preacher double-teamed those goddamn mules because he didn't have enough people to drive single wagons—just like us."

"What are we gonna do?" Rat Face asked. Preacher had accurately pegged the name back in Missouri. Everyone called the man Rat Face. He looked like a two-legged rat, and was just as vicious and sneaky.

"We'll not ambush Preacher again," Jack Hayes said, riding up. "I say we attack."

"Yeah," a thug called Tater said. "Just ride right over 'em. We can do it."

Bedell looked at Tater. The man was not known for his intelligence. For that matter, neither was Jack Hayes. Bedell shook his head. "Our losses would be too great. Even if we managed to succeed, which I doubt we could, our numbers would be cut in half. And then where would we be?" Before anyone else could answer, he said, "I'll tell you where we'd be. In the middle of hostile country with not enough men to fight off an Indian attack. You want that?"

No one did.

Bedell sat his saddle in silence. He really didn't know what to do about Preacher. To launch an attack against those behind would be folly. Bedell guessed, and guessed accurately, that Preacher had armed the women well. Each one of them would have six or seven, or more, loaded weapons available. To charge into that would be the end of Bedell's plans.

No, they would have to hold out until the rendezvous point; then they could deal with Preacher and the women. Bedell twisted in the saddle and looked behind him.

He'd be doing a lot of that before his game was played out.

* * *

"Why don't they attack?" Faith asked. Supper was over and the fire put out before darkness fell. This close to Bedell, there would be no night fires. "I would."

"I think," Rupert said, "Bedell has calculated the odds of conducting a successful attack and found them not to his liking."

"You're learnin', Rupert," Preacher said, lying on his blankets, his head on his saddle. "I took a terrible chance by pullin' us this close to that trash, but it looks like it worked. Bedell's worried, and I intend to keep him that way for a few days." He drank the last of his coffee and tossed out the grounds that remained at the bottom of his cup. "It would still be too risky for me to try anything for a few days. Them outlaws will be shootin' at the wind."

"What do we do now?" Brigitte asked.

Preacher rolled up in his blankets. "Go to sleep." And he did.

16

At the end of the second day after learning that Preacher and the others were tagging along behind them, a thoroughly disgusted Bedell glared at the scout for that day. "Well?"

"They's still back yonder," the man reported. "Just a-ploddin' along."

"Did you let yourself be seen as I told you?"

"Yes, sir, Mister Bedell. I showed myself up no more than five hundred yards from the wagons."

"What did Preacher do?"

"He waved at me."

"He did *what?*"

"Waved at me."

Bedell cussed, loud and long. He'd been doing quite a lot of that the past couple of days. He'd also been toying with the idea of meeting with Preacher and trying to work something out between them. He kept vacillating on the thought, finally giving it up and putting it out of his mind. Having firsthand and quite painful knowledge of Preacher's volatile temper, Bedell reached the conclusion that even if he called for a gentleman's agreement, and met the mountain man un-armed, Preacher would probably just shoot him on the spot.

Preacher was little better than a damn savage himself, Bedell thought. Breeding always tells.

"We'll just push on," Bedell told his men and women. "And stay alert. If Preacher waits much longer, we'll have him where we want him."

Just after dusk, Preacher was belly down in the grass, not a hundred yards from Bedell's circle of wagons. He had not come to attack, although he would if the opportunity pre-sented itself, but to observe. Just as he had guessed, Bedell had put the women in the center of the camp. No way in hell he could help them while they were located there.

Preacher sensed, more than heard, movement behind him and to his right. He moved only his eyes. Indians. Kiowa or Cheyenne, probably, and they were moving in closer.

Preacher, he said to himself, now you have really gotten your butt in the pickle barrel.

Preacher waited, motionless. The night had turned cloudy, the stars and moon not visible, and it smelled like rain. Which was why Preacher had decided to visit Bedell's camp. He now wished he had stayed back in his own camp. He very slowly turned his head to the left. Indians over there, too. Crap!

He wondered if there were any behind him. He surely hoped not. If one of them crawled on top of him, it was going to be one hell of a surprise for both of them.

Not to mention damned unpleasant for one of them.

Preacher had left his horse about a mile back, in a deep ravine. He had switched horses for this ride, but nevertheless did not want the fine mount to be stolen.

Preacher remembered a slight depression about fifty yards behind him. Fifty yards, he thought. Might as well be fifty damn miles with scalp-huntin' bucks all around him. But he sure couldn't stay here. He started making like a crawdad; a very slow-moving one.

Come on rain, Preacher urged the elements. Start comin'
down in sheets.

Then the clouds shifted and faint moonlight began to illu-
minate the area.

Son of a bitch! Preacher thought. My medicine sure ain't
no good this night. He kept backing up and, much to his surprise, reached the protective depression in the earth. He slid
down and landed right on top of the biggest and meanest-
looking Kiowa brave he had ever seen.

They both jumped back and for about two seconds,
Preacher and the brave looked at each other in shock and
surprise.

Then Preacher hauled off and hit that Injun just as hard as
he could with his fist, right on the side of the jaw.

Didn't faze that brave. That Kiowa just crouched there on
his knees in that big hole in the earth and grinned an evil
curving of the lips at Preacher, pure murder in his eyes.

"Oh, hell," Preacher muttered, just as shots roared from
the circled wagons and Preacher reached for his knife.

The Kiowa opened his mouth to scream victoriously and
raised his war-axe at the same time. Preacher cut him wide
open, from one side of his belly to the other, with his big
bone-handled knife and then came around again and damn
near took the brave's head off with the next swipe.

Preacher was out of that hole in the ground and moving
like he had bees in his drawers. He had always liked to run,
and most always won the footraces at the rendezvous. He
beat his best record this night. He figured he made that mile
to his horse in about six minutes. He was really pickin' 'em
up and puttin' 'em down. Behind him, Bedell's men were
filling the air with lead balls as fast as they could and probably not hitting a damn thing—Kiowa being what they are.

He got gone from there swiftly. Back in camp, he had
things organized in two minutes flat, with every rifle and pistol they had out and loaded and everybody in position.

But the attack never came. The Kiowa probably had their

eyes on the larger train and failed to notice the small group of wagons, miles behind. Whatever the reason, Preacher decided his medicine had changed to the good.

Preacher delayed the morning pullout until he had made a wide circle of about two miles all around his camp. There was no smoke from the west, so he reckoned the Kiowa attack had failed. He led the wagons on, making good time, but being very cautious.

The Kiowa had taken their dead with them, of course, but Bedell hadn't even bothered to take the time to bury his dead men, "his dead" not being really accurate. The only dead were four women from the original group.

"That's Judy Barnes," Eudora said, standing over one woman with an arrow still in her chest. "I never did learn the names of those two," she pointed, "but that's Rosanna there. I don't know her last name—sorry."

"Fetch some shovels," Preacher said, suddenly very weary of it all. These women had come west to start over and make a new life for themselves. Their intentions were good and they'd proved to be a stouthearted bunch of ladies. "Damnit!" Preacher kicked at the ground. "Damnit to hell, anyways!"

The others let him cuss, rant, rave, and stomp around. They knew what was bothering him.

"I ain't never known it to fail," Preacher said, winding down. "Ever' time the damn government tries to do something, they foul it up. Those nincompoops can't do nothin' right. And it just keeps on gettin' worser and worser. They could have checked them women out better. But they didn't. Hell, I seen right off we had a bunch of whores in the group. Them people in Washington must breathe different air than the rest of us. I read in the newspapers about how people change when they go off up there." He snatched the shovel out of Rupert's hand and started jabbing at the earth. "Go find you another one and start diggin'."

"Yes, sir," the startled young officer said.

"Don't call me 'sir.' I ain't your daddy. Damn politicians

must go total deaf, dumb, and blind when they get elected. They lose all common sense. I was in St. Louie one time and had the misfortune to wander in a meeting hall where a senator or representative or somebody trying to be one of them fools was a-talkin'. I swear to God Almighty, that pompous jackass talked longer, used the biggest words, and didn't say a goddamn thing that made no sense to me a-tall. Somebody would ask him a simple yes-or-no question and he'd take ten minutes to answer it and when he was through, ever'body was more confused than they was before. And the fool still hadn't answered the question. But he'd talked so damn long that nobody could remember what the question was in the first place."

The women had busied themselves digging graves, and even though it was a solemn time, most could not hide the smiles on their lips, for having just come from the settled east, they knew far better than Preacher just how accurate his words really were.

"Goddamn politicians," Preacher said, flinging dirt every which way. "I started to go for my gun to shoot that loud-mouth. Wish I had now." Preacher paused in his digging. "Come to think of it, I believe that fool was elected President and somebody *did* shoot him! Or shot at him. Maybe it was a duel. I disremember. News is usually two or three years old, time it gets out here. Who the hell is this Martin Van Buren, anyways?"

"He's a good man," Eudora said. "For a lawyer."

"A lawyer?" Preacher looked up, horrified. "A damn lawyer is president? That's disgustin'."

"He is responsible for creating the true and separate Democratic Party," Rupert said.

"The what?" Preacher asked.

"It's a political party. Like the Whigs. As a matter of fact, William Henry Harrison is a Whig and he'll probably be the next president. Van Buren is becoming increasingly unpopular among the people."

"Why?" Preacher asked.

"Why are you so interested, Preacher?" Cornelia asked. "Do you vote?"

"Kinda hard to find a place to vote out here, Missy. But I have voted a time or two when I was in a village here or there. And then I've had other opportunities to vote, but when I seen the caliber of men runnin' for office I opted not to. Be right interestin' to see what Congress is like a hundred or so years from now. Be more brayin' jackasses runnin' around there than a body could count. Ever'one of them talkin' out of both sides of their mouth a-tryin' to please ever'body and even a damn fool knows that's impossible. So they all end up pleasin' nobody."

No one offered to argue that because they all felt it was a valid statement.

For the rest of the time the group worked in silence burying the dead. When that was done, Eudora read from the Bible and the ladies sang a sad song.

"Group sure is gettin' thinner and thinner," Preacher said to his horse.

Bedell sent three men out to scout their backtrail. But since Preacher had decided on a late start, and then stopped to bury the women, the scouts did not ride far enough to spot Preacher and the wagons. Instead they mistook a dust cloud for smoke, and raced back to Bedell with the erroneous news.

"You're sure it was smoke?" Bedell asked, his spirits lifting.

"Positive. Them savages must have hit them after we run 'em off. Preacher and them women is buzzard bait now."

Bedell smiled. "Excellent. Very good, boys." Bedell happily put Preacher out of his thoughts. He gathered the prisoners and told them what his scouts had found. "So there is no point in trying to escape," he warned them. "You'd be committing suicide. So my advice to you all is just settle down and accept your fate. You cannot change it."

The shoulders of the women sagged in defeat. That evening, Bedell selected a very young and very pretty woman to satisfy his perverse desires. Her screaming shattered the night for hours.

BOOK TWO

One man with courage makes a majority.
                                    Popular saying.

1

Lt. Rupert Worthington lost his breakfast, and only Eudora Hempstead and Faith Crump had the iron in them to stand with Preacher and look upon the body of the young woman. The other ladies fled the scene and returned to the wagons.

"Bedell's work," Preacher said, covering the battered body with a blanket. "Doin' things like this pleases him. He's a twisted man. There was all kinds of talk around St. Louie about him. Somebody get a shovel."

Eudora's face was pale and her eyes were furious. "It would take a madman to do something this hideous," she said.

"No," Preacher disagreed. "Just a man who won't control himself. Any man that can function, speak proper, dress themselves, work, and step out of the way of carriages, and so forth, ain't crazy. And I don't give a damn what these so-called smart people say. Men like Bedell, and anyone who rides with him and stands by and watches something like what was done to this poor child and don't do nothin' about it deserve a bullet or a rope. They sure as hell don't deserve no sympathy."

"This journey has changed me considerably," Faith said. "I shall never be the same. I used to deplore the conditions of prisons and jails and the treatment of criminals. I will never again editorialize on that subject."

"Then you'd be wrong," Preacher surprised her. "They's innocent men in prison, Missy. They'd be men behind bars who couldn't pay their debts because of one good reason or another. Just because a man falls on hard times don't mean that man should be locked up like a murderer or horse thief or the like. They's men in prison for defendin' hearth and home, and that's wrong. Man has a right to protect kith and kin. I'll go to my grave believin' that."

"I certainly agree with you, Preacher," Rupert said. "I wouldn't have a few weeks ago, but I damn sure do now. Like Miss Crump, this journey has changed me immeasurably. I will never be the same."

"None of us will," Claire said, walking up. "None of us."

You can count me in there, too, I reckon, Preacher thought. But I'm afraid ain't none of you seen nothin' yet. "Let's get this child buried, people."

By the time they finished burying the young girl, with Eudora once more reading words from the Bible and then the ladies singing some sweet church songs, they could only make a few more miles before it was time to prepare for the night's camp. But Bedell was using every moment of daylight to push on westward. What Bedell didn't know was that three tough, very angry, and determined mountain men were paralleling him on the north side of the Platte.

Snake, Steals Pony, and Blackjack.

The three had not been back to the site of the attack and they all presumed Preacher had been killed along with Ring, Charlie, and Ned, for they had all seen the others take a lot of lead. The trio of mountain men would have their revenge against Bedell and all those with him. But they would wait until the wagons hit the mountains.

"I'm gonna miss Preacher," Blackjack said. "As I know you'll miss Ring, Steals Pony."

"I will have my revenge," the Delaware said.

All three men had been wounded, but none seriously. By the time they had found each other, the fight was over and there was nothing they could do except save themselves and see to their wounds.

"I'm glad we're goin' back to the high country," Snake said. "I got me a feelin' this is gonna be my last ride."

Steals Pony glanced at him. The Delaware did not make light of such predictions. He had seen too many of his own kind predict nearly to the minute when they were going to leave this world to walk over to the Other Side.

Blackjack said nothing about it. The mountain man had lived with Indians and knew when it was a man's time to go; a lot of men could predict it . . . or will it to happen, he silently added. But ol' Snake had lived a good long life. A hell of a lot longer than most.

Snake told them the agreement he'd had with Preacher, and both Steals Pony and Blackjack agreed that they'd bury him high up.

"We got company," Snake said. "Ponca. They're not lookin' for trouble; they got their families and belongings with them."

The three men rode over to the small band of migrating Indians and greeted them as friends. An old man peered closely at Snake. "I know you," he said. "You shared my tepee many, many winters ago. My wife and family were sick and you hunted meat for us. I have never forgotten you. I have news that might interest you. My old friend Preacher has taken up the blood hunt for those who attacked him. I do not know what happened, but it must have been terrible for Preacher to swear such vengeance."

"When did you hear this?" Steals Pony asked.

"Two days ago. Preacher is leading a small band of women-less people through to the shining waters across the mountains. I always wanted to see the shining waters," he added wistfully.

"Did you learn where Preacher is?" Snake asked.

"South of the river," the Ponca said, pointing in the direction of the Platte. "On the trail. East of a huge line of wagons that are driven by very unfriendly men. Stay away from them."

After the Ponca had moved on, Blackjack looked at his friends. "Well?"

"Well, what, you lard-butt?" Snake asked, knowing full well what his friend was asking.

Blackjack grinned, not taking umbrage at the friendly insult. "Which direction do we head?"

Steals Pony said nothing. He just turned his horse south and rode off. Blackjack and Snake galloped after him, wide grins on their faces.

"Riders coming," Rupert called out. "Three men, coming from the north."

The boy is gettin' good, Preacher thought. He seen them 'fore I did. Preacher squinted his eyes and immediately grinned. That elephant in the middle couldn't be nobody 'ceptin' Blackjack.

"Hell, Preacher!" Blackjack boomed as the trio drew near. "We done sang death songs for you, flung praises to the Lord about you, and made up lies to tell about you. Now here you show up alive. Ain't you got no consideration for your friends a-tall?"

"I purely am sorry you found me alive, Blackjack," Preacher called. "I do apologize for not dyin'. But on the other hand, I done buried you three in my mind. Now I got to adjust myself to look upon your ugly faces agin. At least you and Steals Pony, that is. Snake's looked dead for years. It's gonna be kinda hard to tell when he do pass."

"If'n I don't move nor eat for several hours," Snake said,

"you come over and take a long sniff. If'n I'm ripe, then you can plant me, you heathen."

Steals Pony looked at the old man. "If that is the case, we should have buried you years ago. You haven't taken a bath in all the time I've known you."

The men dismounted and hugged each other and danced around, whooping, hollering, and filling the air with profane insults. While the mountain men sated their appetites of jubilation, Eudora halted the wagons and started a fire for coffee and food. Preacher told his friends what had transpired.

"That's about it, I reckon," Preacher said. "Them no-count trash killed Hammer, and I aim to avenge my good horse."

The men nodded solemnly. They knew how deeply a man could feel about the loss of a good horse or dog. Since the domestication of animals, more men have probably been killed over horses and dogs than have been killed over women. Leaving a man alone and without a horse in hostile country was just about the same as signing his death warrant.

The mountain men then sat, drank, and ate and listened to the women tell of what had happened to them . . . and to those they had buried.

"They got to be kilt then," Snake opined when the women had finished. "It offends me to have to breathe the same air as men who done things like that."

The women then sat wide-eyed and open-mouthed (Rupert included), and listened to the suggestions the mountain men had as to what should be done to Bedell and his followers. Some of the suggestions were quite inventive. The women were learning quickly that the mountain men, while oftentimes unshaven and shaggy, and certainly hard, crude, and lewd to the eyes and ears of so-called civilized easterners, operated under a strict code of conduct. Step across their invisible line, and one faced death at their hands.

"So they're linkin' up with another party of outlaws up the trail, hey, Preacher?" Blackjack asked.

"Yep."

"How many?" Steals Pony asked.

"I don't know. Twenty-five or so, I'd guess. And I don't know whether Bedell's headin' for California or the northwest. Mayhaps he had plans to split up. But now . . . I'd take me a guess that he's gonna stay together and head for the gold he claims he's found."

"Then we got to hit them 'fore he links up with them others," Snake said. "We let him get too strong, and we ain't gonna be able to do nothin'."

Preacher nodded his head in agreement. "That's right. But I don't see no way of gettin' ahead of Bedell. We can't leave the wagons. They'd be looted and burned 'fore we got ten miles."

"Then he must be slowed down or stopped for a day or so," Rupert said. "Allowing us time to catch up."

"Good thought, boy," Snake said. "You got a plan?"

"Unfortunately, no."

"Just below where the rivers split," Steals Pony said, "there is a place where three men could stall the wagons for as long as need be. You have dozens of weapons here, Preacher. You give us extra rifles and caps, shot and powder, and we'll ride on ahead and buy you the time to close the gap."

"Sounds good to me," Preacher said.

"When do we leave?" Snake asked.

Blackjack stood up. "Right now."

Bedell sat on the ground drinking a cup of coffee. He still had trouble believing Preacher was really dead. He wanted desperately to believe it . . . but try as he might, something deep within him would not let the doubts fade.

Later on, after he'd had time to think over what his scouts had reported, he'd wanted to scream at them, asking them why they had not worked their way closer to the smoke and made certain that the damn meddling mountain man was dead.

But, it was too late now.

After that one successful attack by the savages, the wagons had encountered no trouble at all. The trip could now be called monotonous. And hot, Bedell thought, looking up at the sun, now just beginning its westward dip. It was time to end the rest and food break and get moving.

Tom Cushing approached him. "The women have requested they be allowed to bathe, sir. And to tell the truth, we all need a good wash and scrub. Ain't a one of us that ain't gettin' right gamey."

Except me, you oaf! Bedell thought. Well, why not? They certainly weren't in any imminent danger. "Very well. Post the guards and take your baths."

Several thousand miles away, in the nation's capital, the man who had recruited Preacher and seen to the gathering of the women who wanted to move west and start a new life sat in his office and stared out at the rain. He took a sip of coffee and spat it out. The coffee had turned cold.

"Miserable weather," he muttered. He could never understand why anyone would want to build a city in the middle of a damn swamp. He wished he could have gone along with the wagon train, for he truly loved the western frontier. He'd been along when the Iowa Territory had been formed in '38 and had traveled with the Army up to the border of Canada. What a grand adventure that had been. But the President would not post him for long outside of Washington. He had asked so many times, and had been turned down an equal number, that it had now become something of a joke.

He stared out at the rain and the ominous storm clouds that were continuing to build over the capital city. He sure wished he was out on the plains with Preacher and those other characters he'd gathered around him. The man from Washington felt he was missing the time of his life.

Yes, he concluded, Preacher and the ladies must be having the adventure of their lives.

He turned back to his paperwork with a sigh.

* * *

Preacher rode about a mile from the lead wagon. The Great Plains had opened her vastness to summer and it was hot. The wagons were making good time—better time than Preacher had expected—but they were still many days away from the agreed-upon ambush point. Only days if the weather stayed good, a few weeks if it turned sour.

He twisted in the saddle and looked back at the wagons, then slowly scanned the plains that lay all around him. This country could crack a man's brain-box wide open. He knew. He'd seen it happen. It was just miles and miles of nothing but more miles and miles. Some folks called it the Big Lonesome. When the buffalo started moving, Preacher had felt the ground actually tremble under the impact of thousands of hooves. The herd might be miles away, but a body's feet could register the deadly awesomeness of a thundering herd of the shaggy beasts. If a man was to get caught afoot with a stampeding herd of buffalo comin' dead at him . . . well, Preacher had seen that, too. There wasn't enough left of the man to bury.

The ladies had been unusually quiet for the past couple of days, and Preacher knew the country was getting to them. It was the awful aloneness of it all. The endless rolling plains, the horizon that just never seemed to quit. Even Rupert had stopped his vocal flights of prose in describing the journey. Well, almost stopped.

But Preacher had seen the young man toughen, mentally and physically, almost right before his eyes. And the journey had really just begun, for what lay ahead of them was ten times rougher than what they'd traveled over since leaving the jump-off point back in Missouri. If Rupert stayed in the army, which he'd said he was going to do, he'd be a fine officer. And this trip would be the steel that would reenforce his backbone. He had courage a-plenty, Preacher had seen that. The young man would do to ride the river with. And there wasn't no finer compliment a mountain man could give than that one.

Preacher dismounted and let the lead wagon catch up with him.

"Trouble, Captain?" Eudora asked, pulling up beside where he stood.

"Naw. Just takin' a rest. We're makin' good time. You handle this long team of mules like you was born to it, Eudora."

"We understand each other," the New Englander said with a smile. "I knew to get their attention right off and I did. They know I won't take any guff from them."

Preacher swung back into the saddle. He was beginning to feel the hair on the back of his neck bristle. Something was wrong. "Just keep headin' west, lady." He rode back to the last wagon, where the sisters, Maude and Agnes, were handling the double-teams. Maude held the reins, Agnes cradled the rifle.

"We're all right, Preacher," Agnes assured him. "We're just fairly aching to get Bedell and his men in rifle-sights."

"Aching in more ways than one," Maude added drily.

Preacher smiled at that. Many a prim and proper Eastern lady would have hidden her face in shame and disgrace after enduring what these ladies had been through. They'd have been to bed for weeks or months, considered themselves soiled for life, and some might have actually killed themselves. But these women were made of sterner stuff. They'd faced assault, rape, and degradation at the hands of white trash and overcome it. Preacher was just as proud of them as could be. These gals were pioneers, by God, and they'd made a man the right kind of wife. The kind of wife who'd stand by her man, shoulder to shoulder. And God help the husband who tried to demean them or worse yet, slap these women around. That husband just might find himself gelded in the morning. Or stone dead.

Preacher nodded at the sisters just as goosebumps were beginning to rise on his flesh. He rode back to the drag, where Rupert was.

"It's too quiet, Preacher," Rupert said. "I may be over-reacting, but it's too quiet to suit me."

"I know what you mean. You're learnin' fast. Yeah. I started feelin' the same thing 'bout fifteen minutes ago. It's doubtful the attack will come from the north, but with Injuns you never know. I think they're up here on a raidin' party."

"The Kiowa again?"

"I'd bet on it. But it could be Cheyenne or even Comanch or Dakota. Might even be Pawnee. Doubtful it'll be Northern Cheyenne. I get on well with them. Course that don't make no difference if it's a bunch of young bucks lookin' for hair to impress the gals." He tensed. "Get ready, boy. It ain't long in comin'."

Preacher slowly rode up to the lead wagon, and, as he passed each wagon, told the driver to get ready to circle and told the other woman on the seat to get in the back and start loading rifles.

When he reached Eudora, he slowed and said, "Get ready to circle at my holler, lady. We are about to be set upon. Cornelia, get in the back and start loadin' up them spare rifles."

"Savages, Captain?" Eudora asked, her strong hands filled with reins.

"I 'magine. I 'spect it's the same bunch that hit Bedell the other night. They was plenty sore about that and it was our bad luck they found our tracks and know we're a hell of a lot smaller bunch."

"I'm ready at your signal, Captain," Eudora replied calmly.

Preacher spotted just the faintest of movement to his left and shouted out, "Circle!"

The Indians came on foot at first, the second wave on horseback, rising out of the deceptive country.

"Jesus!" Preacher said. A second's look was all it took to tell him they were in big trouble. This was no small war party. This looked to Preacher like the whole goddamn tribe!

2

A big, screaming brave came straight at Preacher. Preacher stopped him cold by firing his Hawken one-handed into the Kiowa's chest at almost point-blank range. The big ball slammed the Indian backward and into another brave. Both of them hit the ground and Preacher whirled his horse and jumped him into the circle of wagons. He left the saddle and jerked out both pistols, running to the side of Faith and Gayle. Then he began firing his pistols just as fast as he could cock and work the complicated triggers. That first thunderous volley, and how quickly the second and third volleys followed, must have frightened the Indians, for they broke and ran for cover. Preacher, his pistols empty, grabbed up a rifle and very nearly took the head off of a brave just as he was heading for cover, a good two hundred yards away.

"Good shooting, sir!" Rupert said.

"Not really," Preacher replied without looking up, as he was quickly reloading. "I was aimin' for the middle of his back, not his head."

"What tribe, Preacher?" Faith asked, looking at the dead

through cool eyes. She had toughened just like the rest of the ladies.

"Kiowa. And they're just a tad off of where they usually hunt and fight. Something's got them stirred up. See that dead brave there. That long thin mustache. I had been told the Kiowa of a long time ago wore face hair like that. So he's probably a chief or sub-chief or some other important man in the tribe. That's good for us . . . for a time. Now they got to mourn, dance and sing, and elect a new man to replace him. Well, we're here for a spell, so break out the food and coffee. We might as well be full and comfortable. We're gonna have a wait."

Preacher took that time to have half the women start un-hooking the mules and getting them into the center of the small circle, while the other women stayed on guard. The animals were watered and fed. Preacher made sure that every available rifle and pistol was loaded, and he double-shotted many of the pistols. For he knew that it was a certainty some of the Kiowa would get inside the circle of wagons and, by using double-shot, he increased the chances of a killing shot.

Preacher also knew that there was no way such a small band could withstand a determined charge by the Indians. They were outnumbered ten or twelve to one and they only had one thing going for them: lots of weapons.

Preacher took a look around him. The circle of wagons was so small in area, the backs of the people were only a few yards from pushing up against the butts of the mules.

"It's bad, isn't it, Captain?" Eudora asked softly.

"I won't kid you, lady," he replied. "It's real bad. We was damn lucky the first time around. We got ample weapons agin their arrows, and that's about the only good thing about this whole shebang, 'ceptin' our location, which couldn't be much better. At this point on the trail, we're practically sit-tin' in the river, so they can't come at us from the rear. The country's wide open all around us. Our water barrels is full and there ain't nobody hurt . . . yet," he added sourly.

"I've heard the savages use fire arrows."

"For a fact. And they'll do it, too. That's why I had y'all doin' all that practicin' weeks back. We hurt them during that first charge. They'll have to think about that for a time. If we can hurt them that bad the next time, they just might say to hell with it and pull out. An Injun is not goin' to fight no losin' battle."

"We are too few in number to fight both the savages and a burning wagon," Eudora pointed out.

"For a fact," was all Preacher had to say.

The air was suddenly filled with arrows, seemingly coming out of nowhere, for not a single Kiowa could be seen. Two mules were hit, one seriously and the other hurt only slightly. When the barrage of arrows stopped, Preacher put the badly wounded mule out of its pain while Eudora applied salve to the other mule's slight wound.

"You make war against defenseless animals!" Preacher shouted out in Kiowa. "You are nothing but cowards, fops, and old trembly women. You are not braves. You sleep with boys. No woman would have anything to do with you." He shouted out insult after insult on the warriors.

When he had finished, a voice called out from the prairie. "Who are you who knows our language?"

"I am Ghost Walker. The man called White Wolf. And I will kill you. I will gouge out your eyes so you cannot find your way after death. I will cut off your hands and feet and leave you helpless against your enemies. I will tear out your tongue so you will be mute for eternity."

"Preacher is dead. We heard the men from the long wagons talking the other night."

"Did you find a Kiowa with his throat cut?" Preacher yelled. "I did that. So if I am dead, I am a ghost." He moaned, loud and long. It was so realistic, most of the women shuddered.

"How can you fight a ghost?" Preacher shouted. "Come on, you old women. Let me show you my powers; powers that I now have after death. My guns will fire ten times more than those in the hands of the living." To Eudora: "When I fire my pistols, you reload them just as fast as you can."

She nodded her head. "You think it will work?"

"You never know with Injuns. They're notional."

"You convinced me of your ghostly abilities," Rupert called softly.

"You lie," the Kiowa spokesman said. "You are not a ghost. You do not have magic guns."

"Faith, you, Eudora, and Gayle get you double handfuls of dirt. Just as soon as I finish actin' the fool, you hurl that dirt high into the air and keep pickin' up dirt and tossin' it. Whilst you're doin' that, each of you start squallin' like a bunch of pumas. You got it?"

They smiled through the grime on their faces and filled their hands with earth.

"I will summon friends from the dark side of life!" Preacher shouted. "You will be able to see their evil coming like a whirlwind. Listen and watch! But if you stay here, you will die!" Preacher cut loose with another ghostly sound, the women tossed the dirt into the air, and then screamed like a pack of wounded animals. Preacher moaned long and loud and fired his pistols faster than he ever had.

He tossed his pistols to Eudora and began jumping around, throwing dirt into the air and whirling around, darting in and out of the open space between the wagons. The women began hurling more dirt into the air until it looked like a sandstorm.

"Your guns are empty now, White Wolf," the Kiowa called. "They boom no more."

Eudora tossed the recharged pistols to Preacher and he cut loose with another barrage.

There was a moment of shocked silence from the other side, then the sounds of galloping horses.

"They fell for it," Preacher said, and looked over at the ladies and started laughing. All of them were covered with dirt. Soon the entire contingent of the wagon train was howling with laughter.

A lone Kiowa brave who had hung back, albeit with much fear in his heart, listened to the wild howling coming from the circled wagons. He rolled his eyes and looked toward the heavens. Then he drummed his heels against his horse and got the hell gone from there.

After the group had settled down, Preacher ordered the teams hooked up. "Let's get gone from here whilst we got the chance to do it."

The ladies didn't need a second urging.

Preacher picked the most easily defended place he could find for that evening's camp.

"Will we see those Indians again, Preacher?" Agnes asked, handing him a cup of coffee.

"Doubtful. That bunch was some ways from home. We might not see another Indian on the warpath for the rest of the journey. But don't count on that. In their own way, ladies, the Indian is a good person. Now, that sounds funny, seein' as how we just killed a few back up the trail, but if you stop and think about it, their way of life makes sense. For them at least, if not for us. They respect the land and use it well. Can't say that for the white man. And how would you like it if somebody was to come driving a bunch of wagons across your yard back home? Indian feels the same way. This is his yard." He waved a hand at the prairie. "It's been his for centuries. I don't feel hard toward the Indian. I've lived with 'em. Now the Pawnee just flat out don't like me and I don't like them. Never have and never will. They been tryin' to kill me since the first day out here when I was just a boy. Ever' time they try they lose one or two or three more. Seems like they'd learn after a time, don't it?"

"Do you know why they dislike you so?" Faith asked.

"Nope. And neither do they. If either of us ever did, it's

been lost durin' the years. I'm the type of man who would get along with ever' one of God's children and creatures if they'd just let me. Bears, snakes, scorpions, and all. Even a buzzard, and the Good Lord knows I can't hardly abide a buzzard. But they've a place in things. They're nature's garbage collectors, I reckon. But I still don't like 'em.".

"Why don't the savages stop fighting the whites?" Maude asked. "If they would do that, then we could all get along."

Preacher smiled. "Listenin' 'tween your words, lady, I hear: 'If they'd just be like us!' But they ain't like us. You're you, I'm me, and they's them. I couldn't survive back east. And it ain't that I *wouldn't* survive, I couldn't. I been free too long. Really free. The only law I have to worry about is the laws I set on myself. I'm like the Indian, I reckon. I don't like people tellin' me what to do and where to go and where I can't go and what I have to do oncest I'm there."

"But any productive society has to have laws, Captain," Eudora said.

"Sure. I know that. And the Indian tribes all have their own laws. It's just that they ain't like the white man's laws, that's all. And the laws them fancy-pants lawyers and swelled-up judges and goofy-actin' politicians force people to live under ain't my laws, neither. I don't want any part of it."

"There is a great hue and cry back east for people to move west, Preacher," Faith said. "Soon this part of America will be abounding with humanity. Considering how you feel about that, what will happen to you?"

Preacher's smile was a slow and sad one. "I reckon I'll suffer pretty much like the Injuns is gonna suffer. Not as much, 'cause I ain't got no thousand-year-old way of life behind me that's gonna have to be pitted agin another thousand-year-old way of life. White man says his way is the only way, Injuns say their way is the only way. And pretty soon, if I'm readin' the newspapers right, the black folks all over the country is gonna have freedom. And when that happens that'll mean another way of life will be challenged. I figure the next twenty to thirty years is gonna be right interestin'. With the white man always endin' up havin' his way, of course."

"All the savages have to do is to adopt Christian ethics and we can all get along," Bertha Macklin opined. "Everything is spelled out quite clearly in the Bible."

"Is that right?" Preacher said. "I read the Good Book from time to time. It's contradictory to me. One line reads an eye for an eye and a tooth for a tooth, another line says don't kill nobody. Some of them folks in there took all sorts of wives to bed down with, begettin' sons and daughters all over the place. But now it's agin the law to have more than one wife. Certain parts of the Good Book is right comfortin'. Other parts just don't make no sense to me. Now if it don't make no sense to me, who was raised up readin' the Bible and goin' to church on Sundays and prayin' over grub, how in the hell do you expect an Injun to understand it?"

"After all the times the savages have tried to kill you," April Johnson said, "I find it hard to believe that you are defending them."

"Well, Missy, I reckon it's because like can be said about the white people, they's a hell of a lot more good Injuns than there is bad ones. Injuns got their own code they live by, and it ain't like ours. Now I don't agree with all the codes the Injun lives by, but then, I don't agree with all the laws the whites live by, neither. So I reckon I'm closer to the Injuns than I am to the whites."

"But you know right from wrong!" Lisette protested.

"I know the white man's definition of right and wrong, Missy. The Injun's version is different. And it ain't up to me to say which one is the correct one. 'Sides, it don't make no difference. It won't be many more years—in our lifetime, probably—when the Injuns will be killed off or herded onto reservations like animals in a cage. And then the white man will say, 'There now, we've done it. We've destroyed a way of life so's ours can thrive. Let's all be right proud of what we done.' Well, you be proud. I ain't so damn sure it'll be anything to boast about."

"Anyone who stands in the way of progress is apt to get hurt, Preacher," Rupert injected. "Progress is the natural order of things."

"That's right," Faith said. "We cannot stand still. We must go forward or we'll stagnate."

"Ain't that a fact," Preacher replied. "With no regard to whether it's men, women, or kids."

"It certainly doesn't appear to me that that makes any difference to the savages," Cornelia said. "They've been butchering women and children for years. Certainly you won't argue that fact."

Preacher shook his head. "No. I can't argue with that. The Injuns earned the name of savages. I sure won't be the one to deny that."

"I can't feel much sorrow for a people who won't change for the better," Gayle said.

"Nor can I," Faith agreed, as the other women gathered around nodded their heads in agreement.

Preacher smiled at those statements, but held back the words he wanted to say. He drained his coffee cup and stood up. "Oh, 'fore you misunderstand, I don't blame the white man for pushin' west. Hell, I come west. And I understand what has happened and what is gonna happen. The Injun has just run out of time, that's all. That's been happenin' to various folks since God picked up the clay and flung humans on this earth." Preacher stood up and picked up his rifle and looked out over the terrain outside the small circle. He looked around at the small gathering of people in the waning moments of daylight.

"I ain't no highfalutin', fancy-talkin' man from Washington," Preacher said. "And they ain't nobody gonna ask me nothin', 'cause them nitwits back in Washington think they know the answer to everything. But here's how I would do this settlin' the west thing: First off, I'd put me together a whole bunch of soldier boys. Thousands of 'em . . ."

"At least a division," Rupert said, his eyes shining with excitement at just the thought.

"Whatever," Preacher said. "I'd have cannons, wagons, and troops that would stretch for fifty miles across the plains. They'd be flags a-wavin', bands a-playin', buglers a-tootin', and drummers just a whackin' away. It would be the grandest sight red or white had ever seen. I'd gather the chiefs, tribe by tribe, and invite them to sit down and talk. And they would. Once they seen that many fightin' men, and seen the cannon boom and the rifles roar, they'd talk. Injuns is far from stupid. In their own way, they got more sense than them damn fools that claim to be runnin' the country." Preacher thought about that for a moment. Then he shook his head. *"Anybody's* got more sense than them ninnies.

"Anyway, I'd tell the chiefs that the white folks are comin'. Then I'd show them pictures of the eastern cities and how many people there are back there. You'd have to do that slow; 'cause an Injun really don't grasp a whole lot of numbers. But it could be done with patience. And that's the trick, folks. Patience. And I ain't puttin' down the Injun when I say that. They're just different from us, that's all.

"Then I'd tell the chiefs that the white people who are comin' through don't want no trouble. They're just gonna be travelin' a few of the trails on their way west and doin' some huntin' for food along the way. Some of them are gonna be stayin'. But they ain't gonna bother no one. And if they do, the government soldiers will come and punish them, just like the government soldiers will punish the Injuns if they bother the white settlers.

"Then I'd seal the borders from Canada down to the Gulf of Mexico. Nobody would move west across the Red River or the Missouri or the Mississippi without permission of the government. Now this wouldn't be no sudden thing, folks. This would take years. Years of educatin' the Injuns to the white man's ways and of linin' out boundaries as to who belongs to what. This is *their* land, people. There ain't no markers or signposts or the like, but it's theirs! And we ain't got the right to come in here like lords and kings and push them off of it or get mad when they fight to keep what they consider to be theirs.

"Any promises made have to be kept. You can't tell the Injuns one thing and then turn around and do the other. People, the plains Injuns' life depends on the buffalo. Their whole bein' revolves around the buffalo. Most of 'em are hunters, not farmers. The buffalo herds is their life and they've got to be kept strictly for them."

Preacher paused and shook his head. "Ahh," he said disgustedly. "Why am I flappin' my mouth anyways? It ain't gonna happen that way nohow. The white man is too impatient to give the red man time to get ready for the flood. They're just gonna come bustin' through here tearin' up ever'thing and killin' off the buffalo and callin' ever'thing they do progress. And the Injuns will fight. What else can they do? I seen what our diseases have done to whole tribes already. Damn near wiped them out. I seen that with my own eyes. Pitiful sight." He leaned up against a wagon wheel, cradling his Hawken.

The women looked at him, rugged and handsome, his face burned dark by the sun and the wind, standing there in his buckskins, a pensive look on his face—although Preacher wouldn't have known what that word meant.

"Why don't you go to Washington and make that speech to a joint gathering of the House and Senate?" Faith asked. "It was very eloquent."

" 'Cause them peckerwoods wouldn't hear the real meanin', Faith. They'd hear the words but they wouldn't know what they meant. Oh, they'd pat their soft powdered hands together in applause, but it would all come to naught. Common man can't tell a politician nothin'. You say good mornin' to one and they'll look out the window to see."

Preacher walked off to make his rounds, muttering to himself about politicians.

"I am very hesitant to tell him that my father has been very active in politics for years and is thinking about running for governor back home," Rupert said.

"Keep that knowledge to yourself," Eudora told him. "Preacher might recall that apples don't fall far from the tree and shoot you."

3

Each day became as the day just past as the wagons rolled and rumbled westward. Preacher had left the trail that morning and had found a place that would be perfect for the wagons and the mules. It had plenty of concealment and good water and grazing a-plenty for no longer than he'd be gone. He had to leave the wagons and go on ahead to be sure that Steals Pony, Blackjack, and Snake had made it and were in place for their ambushing and holding up of Bedell and his men.

Their plans had been very loosely laid and discussed, subject to sudden change.

Preacher rode back to the wagons and halted the train. "Cut south here, Eudora. I found y'all a place to hide, rest up, and take baths and all that whilst I'm gone."

Eudora nodded, lifted the reins, and called out to the leader mule. Preacher rode back to Rupert.

"I got to go, Rupert. Just as soon as I get the ladies settled in. You're in charge."

"I won't fail you, Preacher."

"I know it." Preacher grinned at the young officer. "I seen the way Brigitte is a-battin' them blues at you, boy. You bes' be careful. She's liable to snatch you under a wagon some dark night and show you somethin' that'll put a curl in your hair and pep in your step."

Rupert blushed a deep crimson, from his neck to his forehead. Even his ears were red.

Preacher laughed and rode back to the head of the column. Getting to the place he'd found was tricky, for it wound through a short series of ravines and was protected on three sides by high broken bluffs.

"What a marvelous place!" Eudora exclaimed, when the valley suddenly sprang into view.

"And lookie yonder at that crick," Preacher said, pointing. "Plenty of cover for you gals to bathe and hide from Rupert whilst you're in the raw."

"Preacher!" Rupert said, riding up. "I'll have you know I am a Virginia gentlemen."

"Men and women still spark back there, don't they?"

"Well, of course, they do."

Preacher grinned at him. " 'Nuff said."

He waited until the mules were unhitched and put to pasture and Rupert and the ladies fully understood what they could and could not do—then Preacher pulled out. He rode until just before dark and made a cold camp. He rolled out of his blankets before dawn. The morning was chilly, so Preacher warmed the bit under his jacket before he bridled the horse. He rinsed out his mouth with water and chewed some jerky for his morning's meal. Then the mountain man checked his guns and rode out before the first rays of sun reached the plains.

That afternoon he topped a rise and grinned when he saw the canvas of Bedell's wagons stretching out a couple of miles away. They would reach the ambush point just in time to make camp, Preacher guessed. Bedell's scouts would have already seen the spot and, if they had any sense at all, would see it as a natural campgrounds.

Preacher stayed well back and was both amazed and

amused that Bedell did not have men trailing the wagons. Showed how arrogant the man was, he thought.

There was no way Preacher could be sure that his three friends were in place in the rocks. He wouldn't know that until they opened fire. When Bedell reached the natural camp-grounds and halted the wagons, Preacher quickly stripped saddle and bridle from his horse and filled his hat full of water to let him have a long drink before picketing him on good grass. He took both rifles and began working his way toward the camp. The terrain was perfect for concealment and creepin' up on a body, and Preacher had spent years perfecting that deadly art. He was just getting into position when three rifles barked out death from the rocks just west and slightly above the almost circled wagons and three men on horseback tumbled to the ground. Two of the fallen did not move. The third man crawled a short distance and then collapsed in the dirt, leaving a trail of blood behind him.

Bedell's men panicked, just like Preacher figured they would do. The rifles in the hands of the mountain men roared again, and three more men went down. Preacher lined up an outlaw and squeezed the trigger. The Hawken thundered and the man went down like a rag doll, the big ball splitting his spine. Preacher snatched up his other rifle and drilled a man clean through the brisket, doubling him over and sending him to the grass. He lay kicking and hollering and squalling for the Lord Jesus to come help him out of his pain.

"You a little late to be askin' Him for help, you rotten turd," Preacher grimaced and muttered, quickly reloading both rifles.

Within the span of a minute, Bedell had lost eight men. Three or four more and the backbone of his strength would be broken.

Preacher was only about a hundred and fifty yards from the wagons; just about the same distance as his friends up in the rocks. He watched as a man with a rifle knelt by the rear of a wagon and took a look all around him, trying to spot the

ambushers. Preacher grinned as he saw a woman lean out of
the wagon and bash the top of the man's head flat as the bottom of an iron with a heavy skillet. Then she hopped out and
grabbed up the man's rifle and pistols and jumped back into
the wagon. Blood was streaming from the top of the outlaw's
mushed-in head, so if anyone did notice him, they'd think
first that he'd been shot.

Bedell and Jack Hayes tried to rally their men, shouting
and cussing at them, but with the wagons so wide apart, the
oxen fighting their harness, horses rearing and screaming in
fright, and unknown attackers dropping men with every volley, chaos reigned among the outlaws. Wounded men were
crying out for help, dust was swirling everywhere, and that
only added to the confusion. Bedell's men were shooting
wildly, not knowing really where the enemy was or who it
might be.

Preacher made up his mind and left his cover and went
running to the scattered wagons. He hopped into the back of
one wagon and the three women there started crying and
hollering when they saw who it was.

"Hush up!" Preacher told them, slashing at their bonds.
"This ain't the time for no waterfalls."

A wide-eyed and scared man jumped onto the wagon seat
and just had the time to stare at Preacher for a heartbeat and
grab for a pistol in his belt. Preacher took the front top of his
head off with one swing from his heavy-bladed knife. The
blade sliced through the man's skull and it was not a real
pretty sight to behold.

"Every man for himself!" Preacher caught the faint
shout. He thought it was Bedell's voice, but couldn't be sure.
"Ride, ride! You know where the rendezvous point is. Abandon the wagons and ride for your lives."

Preacher jumped out of the wagon and jerked out his
awesome pistols. He leveled them at a knot of horsemen and
started letting the balls fly. Men were knocked from the saddle, most of them grievously wounded at this close range.

A screaming outlaw charged Preacher, swinging his rifle like a club. Preacher's pistols were empty, so he ducked the rifle butt and kicked the man in the groin. The outlaw hollered, his dirty face turned white, and he hit the ground. The three women that Preacher had just freed jumped out of the wagon and trussed the man up with the same ropes that had just seconds before bound them. They did not handle the man with gentle hands. He was screaming in pain long before they finished hog-tying him.

"You in big trouble," Preacher told the moaning outlaw. "If I was you, I'd start prayin'."

Bedell and his men were gone. Like most basically simple plans, this one had worked. Preacher always knew that the more elaborate a plan, the more likely that it would fail.

"Free the other women," Preacher told the trio of women, just as Steals Pony, Blackjack, and Snake came strolling into the area, a dozen men and women marching ahead of them, hands in the air, prodded along by rifle barrels. "Move quickly 'fore they regroup and return."

"By God, she worked, Preacher!" Blackjack roared.

"I've never seen such a beautiful sight in all my life," a lady named Rexana said. Her face was bruised from beatings, but she was smiling.

"I love you all," Odella McNutt said, smiling through her swollen lips.

"Get armed first," Preacher told the ladies, as they were freed. "Then in small groups, you can bathe and fix yourselves up. We'll wait 'til my group joins us, then we'll try the prisoners."

"This ain't no court of law!" a whore called Cindy Lou hollered.

Odella walked over to her and busted her right in the mouth with a balled fist. Cindy Lou hit the ground, blood pouring from her mashed lips. "You twisted bitch!" Odella said. "You sorry white trash. I'll see you hang and take great satisfaction in watching it."

"Punish them in the ways of my people," Steals Pony said. "Lasts much longer than hanging."

"Truss 'em up tight," Preacher told the group. "I'll be back tomorrow afternoon with the others. See you folks."

It was a grand reunion between the ladies. Fewer in number now, but ever so much stronger and wiser to the ways of the world, especially of a certain type who inhabited the said planet.

"Lord, Lord," one rescued lady said, after hugging Eudora. "Heaven could not be any more beautiful than the sight of Preacher and his friends yesterday."

The women had all bathed, most several times, and fixed themselves up as much as they could. They had spent hours washing shirts and britches and undergarments and seeing to their various injuries.

On the morning of the third day following their rescue, the women's greatest fears had narrowed down to only one: were any of them with child?

Preacher and the other mountain men, Rupert right along with them, ran off and hid in the rocks when the ladies started talking about that!

"What a disgusting thought," Rupert said. "To be with a child fathered by one of those swine."

"What do you reckon they'll do if they is with child?" Blackjack asked.

"Women are much smarter than men in such matters," Steals Pony said. "They know what to do. I think we shall see a lot of walking, running, and other vigorous forms of behavior among the ladies."

"But that can't be!" Rupert said. "They must rest and . . ." He stopped and nodded his head. "Oh!" he had got it.

"I got to talk to them men about something," Preacher said. "I'll be back."

He went to the trussed-up prisoners. "Any of you boys

diseased? And you all know what kind of diseases I'm talkin' about."

"Go to hell!" a man called Vince said.

Preacher laid the muzzle of his Hawken on the man's forehead. "If you think I won't kill you, think again. Now answer my question."

Vince told him to go commit an impossible act upon his person. Bluntly.

Preacher pulled the trigger. Afterward, there was not much left of the upper part of Vince's head. The whores all started squalling and several of the men peed in their already dirty drawers.

Preacher moved to another man. He stood over him, reloading his rifle. "You get the same question, toadface."

The women had gathered around, as did the other men. They stood silently, after looking at the mess that was once Vince's head. There was not one note of pity in anyone's eye.

"Lord God Jesus and Mary!" the bound man yelled. "I'll answer it."

"Then answer it," Preacher said savagely.

"As far as I know, nobody was havin' no problems peein'. Do that answer your question?"

"Probably as good as I'll get. What's your name?"

"Louis."

"Name them that killed the women."

"You son of a bitch! You keep your mouth shut up tight!" one of the men hollered.

Preacher lifted his Hawken and one-handed, shot that man between the eyes.

"He was one of them," Louis said, his voice breaking with fear. His face was covered with sweat; it dripped off his chin and onto the ground. "Handsome Dan over there was another one."

Handsome Dan cussed Louis, loud and long.

"Hang him," Preacher told Blackjack.

"Now see here!" Rupert said.

Preacher only gave him one look and that was enough to make him decide to shut his mouth and to keep it shut for the duration.

Preacher looked up at the sky. The sun was directly overhead. "Let's get this here trial over with," he said. "We got more'un a thousand miles to go."

4

"This ain't legal, you ugly bastard!" one of the "soiled doves" yelled at Preacher.

"She's one of them who helped Bedell torture poor Caroline to death," a lady named Yvonne Knight said from the crowd. "Her name is Frida."

"How do you women find her?"

"Guilty," they called out.

"Any nays?"

There were none.

Orabella, Cecilia, Nancy, and Rexana led the women to the hanging tree and did the deed. The Bedell confederate checked out with a curse on her lips. One of the outlaws fell to his knees and started praying.

"That one who is calling on the Lord did unnatural things to the boys," a woman named Vesta said. "Horrible, filthy things."

"How do you find him?"

The verdict was unanimous.

The man was still praying when the noose was slipped around his neck. The praying stopped quite abruptly.

Six women and eight men were hanged that sunshiny afternoon along the Platte River. They were buried in a common grave, dug by those few the women decided, for one reason or another, to let live.

Louis, as it turned out, and that was verified by the whores and outlaws, had taken no part in the raping, had not killed anyone back at the ambush, and had been belittled by his older brother into coming along with Bedell. His brother was one of the dead that was killed during the first volley of shots from the mountain men.

He was sixteen years old, but looked some older, as did many people of that era.

"You can come with us, Louis," Eudora told him. "All you need is some mothering and salvation." She pursed her lips. "And maybe a lanyard laid across your stern every now and then for good measure."

"Yes, ma'am," Louis said meekly. "Whatever you say, ma'am." He was ever so grateful to be away from Bedell and what remained of his gang.

Preacher turned to the few whom the women had let live. "I'd a-hanged you right along with the rest of your friends. But the women ran this trial. Now I'm gonna tell you how the cow ate the cabbage. A full report of everything that happened on the trail is going to be sent to Washington, D.C., when we reach the coast. That'll take some months, so's you all got time to change your names and live quietlike . . . for the rest of your lives. 'Cause you can bet the government is gonna put federal arrest warrants out for all of you. Now, you each got a horse and some food. I put your weapons in the saddle boot and bags. You got shot and powder, lead and molds, and caps enough to get you back to wherever the hell it is you've decided to go. And it better be far, far away. And you better live real quiet and decent. Don't you ever let me cast my eyes upon you. Ever! If you follow us, or try to swing around to join up with Bedell, I'll know it and I'll kill you personal. I won't say howdy or good evenin', or top of the mornin' to none of you. I'll just ambush you and then I'll take your hair and leave you for the buzzards, the coyotes, and the wolves. Rupert?"

"Yes, sir!"

"Start countin'. Loud. When you get to sixty, if any of this trash is still within range, me and the boys here is gonna start shooting. Now, *git!*"

They got.

Bedell looked at what remained of his gang. Nine men and ten women. He knew that more had escaped the ambush, but they had gotten separated and only the devil knew where they were now. But Bedell knew, too, that the nine men and ten women were the foulest, most evil, and ruthless of the lot. There was nothing they had not done or would not do. To Bedell's twisted mind, that was a very big plus.

So they had lost a battle. That did not in any way mean the war was lost. Bedell had twenty-odd of the hardest men he could find waiting up the trail, with supplies, guns, and everything else they would need. And the wagons had a long way to go before they reached the coast. Bedell had lots and lots of time and country to once more seize the wagons and the women.

He smiled, sighed, and stretched out on the ground. He needed a bath, a shave, and a change of clothing, but all that could wait. He fell asleep and dreamed of torturing Preacher to death. In his mind, he could hear the man screaming as his life ebbed away.

Just the thought of Bedell making Preacher scream out in pain under torture was something that would have given many an Indian a good laugh. Some of them had tried it. None had succeeded.

* * *

The teams were rearranged, the supplies redistributed among the wagons, and on a gray morning, the skies threatening rain, the wagon train, minus a good many of its original passengers, rolled westward. Some of the wagons were left behind due to the sudden decline of occupants.

The women took turns driving and walking alongside the wagons. They wanted a great deal of exercise and absolutely no help in lifting heavy and bulky objects.

Preacher sat his horse off to one side and watched the wagons roll by. Blackjack had taken the point, Snake and Rupert the flanks, and Steals Pony was far out in front, scouting. Preacher wanted to hang back a ways, just to see who might be trying to sneak up or following from a distance.

By mid-afternoon, he was fairly certain those they had set free were not following, and he'd bet that Bedell and his mangy crew had gone on west to link up with his other men.

Preacher knew that he'd meet up with Bedell again. And he also knew that these women would never allow themselves to be taken alive. He had had more than one tell him they never really knew what the phrase "Shoot first and ask questions later" meant. They did now. And any band of Indians who felt this train would be an easy mark were going to be in for a very brutal, and for many, a very fatal surprise.

In a few days, the trail was going to get leaner and meaner and in many spots, the going would be slowed.

Preacher sat his saddle for several minutes, just content to look at the land that rose and fell all around him. A feeling, sort of a sadness, came over him that after this journey, it would never be the same. Oh, the land would be here for thousands of years after his bones had turned to dust, he knew that. But . . . in a strange way, it would not. With the coming of the white man, it would all change. Already it was changing. Although Preacher did not know it, he was already fast becoming an anachronism. As were Steals Pony, Snake, and Blackjack. Their time had come, and it had gone.

Preacher took off his hat and ran his fingers through his

thick shock of hair. He wondered what this country would be like fifty years down the trail. Houses, farms, fences, probably. The buffalo would be gone, and so would the free-roaming Indians. Back east, they'd already been put in reservations and left to rot.

"Wait 'til the Army tries to do that with the Plains' Injuns," he muttered. "They'll find that's easier to say than do."

He turned his horse and headed back to the wagons, reaching them just as they had finished circling for the night's camp and were seeing to the mules, horses, and oxen.

Blackjack and the other mountain men, Rupert included, had them a little fire going off to one side and the coffee was near to boilin'. Steals Pony had killed a buffalo that afternoon and they would have fresh steaks and the tongue for their evening meal. Since the kill had been made close to the wagons, he had been able to salvage all parts of the buffalo and had even given the hide to a lady to scrape.

She had promptly given it right back.

"Behaved as though it insulted her," Steals Pony groused. "It's a fine skin and would make a wonderful robe. I thought I was doing her a favor. I have discovered that white women are very strange."

"Where's the skin?" Preacher asked, a twinkle in his eyes.

"Right over there," Steals Pony pointed.

Blackjack looked at him. "What are you gonna do, Preacher? You got a funny twink in your eyes."

"Have me some fun."

Preacher got the dullest knife he had out of his pack and then shouldered the heavy skin and located Faith, sitting with Eudora and Wallis. He plopped the skin down beside her and she immediately wrinkled her pretty little nose.

"Get that disgusting thing away from me!"

"Scrape it," Preacher told her.

"I beg your pardon?"

"I said scrape it for me. Make me a fine robe. It'll be cold time we get to the mountains. You might want to snuggle up in there with me."

"What!" she shrieked.

"You heard me." He tossed the knife on the ground beside her. "Use that an' be careful. Don't punch through the hide."

Eudora had to turn her head away to hide her laughter. She knew there was something building between Faith and Preacher. She'd seen that way back in Missouri.

"Scrape all the scraps of meat and fat offen that and then I'll be back and show you what to do next. It'll take you about a week, I 'magine."

"This thing still has *fleas* on it!" Faith yelled, kicking at the robe.

"They'll leave. They just ain't realized their home is dead. Get to work, woman."

"I most certainly will not! Scrape your own damn buffalo hide."

"I thought you liked me." Preacher did his best to look hurt.

Faith picked up the knife and slowly rose to her feet. She advanced menacingly toward Preacher. He beat a hasty retreat, calling over his shoulder, "I'll be back for my robe in about a week, dear."

"Dear!" Faith shrieked. She threw the knife at him and just missed a laughing Steals Pony. Faith took a step backward and her foot snagged on the buffalo hide. She sat down right in the middle of the hide and did a fairly respectable job of cussing.

Back at their fire, Steals Pony speared himself a hunk of buffalo steak and said, "I say again, white women are very, very strange."

"Somebody help me drag this stinking damn thing off and burn it!" The voice of Faith could be clearly heard throughout the circled wagons.

* * *

The wagons rolled on, now taking a northwesterly route, and still following the Platte. Indians were spotted several times, but they made no hostile moves and the westward movers did the same.

"Dakota," Blackjack said to the women driving the wagon beside which he was riding. "Sioux to you. All kinds of Sioux."

"I've read they are fierce," Maude said.

"You read right. The Sioux, the Cheyenne, the Blackfoot, the Arapaho . . . they can be right hostile if they take a mind to it."

"Why don't they attack?"

"That's a question that only an Injun could answer. They's been times when I rid right past an Injun village and they didn't do nothin' 'cept look at me. Other times they've chased me for miles, hollerin' and yellin' and shootin' arrows at me. They's a notional bunch for a fact. Them over yonder might be lookin' for Crow. They don't like each other much."

"Why?"

"Damned if I know. Probably goes back five hundred years. I've heared a dozen different reasons for the feud.

"If the white man would treat them with respect, they could reason with and live with these Plains Injuns. But the white man won't treat an Injun as equal. White man is arrogant. To a white man, if it's different, it's wrong. And that's why all the trouble. It's got to be the white man's way, or no way."

Blackjack rode on ahead and Steals Pony rode up. "Is it difficult being a part of two cultures, Steals Pony?" Agnes asked the Deláware.

"Not for me," the Indian replied. "I just take the best of both worlds and reject what's left."

"But you're educated. That makes a difference."

"True. In many cases. But you would be surprised at the number of whites who don't even know me, but resent, fear, and reject me just because I am Indian."

"Well, you will have to admit, there aren't that many Indians living in Boston or New York."

Steals Pony smiled and cut his eyes to her. "You would be surprised how many are there, lady. They just cut their hair and adopt the language, dress, and customs of the white man. It is a white man's world. It doesn't make a bit of difference if, as in this situation, where you are few and the Indian is many, it is still a white man's world and it always will be. Whether you be a red man or a black man or a yellow man, if you wish to get along, you must adopt the white man's ways, or there will always be trouble. That is something the Indian must accept, or the whites will destroy him."

"You don't sound at all bitter about that."

"Oh, I'm not. Often amused, but never bitter. One changes with the whims of the white man. That is the way it shall be. Resist that, and one becomes an outsider and is shunned."

"Will the savages ever learn that?" Maude asked.

The Delaware smiled at the term "savages," but knew she meant no disrespect toward him. "No." He frowned. "Well, doubtful, at best. And in an ever-changing climate, to cling to old ways that are suspicious, out-of-step, or seemingly hostile to those in power is a very stupid thing to do. One must constantly adapt. There will be much blood spilled before the white man settles the west."

"The blood of both the Indians and the whites," Agnes said.

"Yes. But much more red blood than white blood. One of the reasons so many tribes hate the Crow is because the Crow learned very quickly that to fight the white man was foolish. The Crow decided to work with the white man. A very smart move on their part. But you wait and see. The white man will still stick the Crow on reservations. They will not allow them to become a part of their society. My words will be truth. You wait and see."

"There is talk back east of freeing the slaves held in the south."

"They will be freed. Someday. Slavery is wrong. No man has the right to own another human being. But unless the black people adopt the white man's ways, they will be like the Indians, free to a point. But never totally free, never totally accepted."

"You are quite the philosopher, Steals Pony," Agnes said.

"I am a realist, lady. I do not stand in a meadow and shout at the lightning or curse at the wind and the rain. If I chose to live back east, I would cut my hair, dress in a suit, speak the white man's language, and be polite to those around me. I would be accepted. I have done so before. That does not mean I would lose my heritage. That would be impossible. A red man is a red man and a black man is a black man and a white man is . . . well, who knows what a white man is? The whites don't even know who they are. But they know *what* they are. They make the laws and they rule. They always will."

The Delaware smiled. "I know how to sit properly and balance a teacup on my knee without spilling a drop and eat little cakes and cookies and wipe my mouth with a napkin. I also know how to stalk and kill a man, take scalps, skin a deer or a buffalo, and survive out here. I have not lost my heritage. I shall never lose my heritage. How can you lose what you are born to be? But I shall always adapt and therefore I shall always be accepted by those whose opinions matter."

"When in Rome, do as the Romans do."

"Exactly," Steals Pony said. "The alternative—as the Indians and any other racial group who chooses to violently confront the whites will discover—is being fed to the lions."

5

The wagons rolled sixty miles over the next four days with not a single mishap. When they bedded down for the night, many of the women were complaining of nausea, restlessness, and aching in their bones.

"Do you suppose? . . ." Rupert trailed that off.

"No," Preacher said. "Some of the women who were not touched by the trash are sick, too. I don't know what it is. But I got a bad feeling about this."

Steals Pony walked up. "Linda Parsons and Katie what's-her-name are burning up with fever." He squatted down and poured a cup of coffee. "And both women have spots on their upper body."

"Oh, damn!" Blackjack said.

"I don't think it's typhoid," the Delaware said. "The spots are larger and look different." He shrugged. "I don't know what it is. The whites have many diseases that are unknown to the Indian."

The men looked at one another and then without a word, quickly stripped down to the waist. Rupert could not help but notice that Preacher was a ruggedly built man, lean and with tremendous power in his arms and shoulders. They inspected each other. No spots.

"Whatever it is," Snake opined. "I'll bet you a gold eagle we'll be right here for a week or better."

"I won't argue that bet," Preacher said.

The next morning, most of the women were so sick, they had trouble raising their heads.

Eudora, Faith, April, Lisette, and a few others were not affected by the malady, and they gathered with the men in the coolness of dawn.

"Any of you women got any notion what this is?" Preacher asked.

They shook their heads. Eudora said, "It looks like typhoid. And has many of the same symptoms, but I'm sure it isn't that."

"How, Miss Hempstead?" Rupert asked.

"There are no signs of diarrhea, coughing, nosebleeds, or constipation. Some women have fever, some don't. This is not typhoid."

"But we have some awfully sick women on our hands," Faith said.

"We have one that isn't sick anymore," Claire Goodfellow said, walking up.

They all looked up at her.

"Tessie Malone just died."

Preacher took charge immediately. "Strip her and burn her clothing and blankets. Wrap her in canvas and bury her away from this camp. Get movin', damnit! We got a plague on our hands."

Four more women died within the hour. Preacher ordered every kettle hung over a fire and to get a lot of water boiling. Every stitch of clothing in the wagons was boiled. Every blanket, every cloth was sanitized in the boiling water. Preacher ordered the canvas taken down from every wagon and boiled. Every wagon was emptied of its cargo and the beds scrubbed down. The mules and oxen were bathed with strong soap. They all seemed to enjoy the new attention.

The men didn't like doing it, but there were so few women still able to stand, that they had to strip many a woman that day, bathe her, and wash her hair. Most of them soon found that they could detach themselves from their task and just get it done without undue embarrassment.

"If you get tired, stop and rest," Preacher told everybody. "Don't let your body get run-down."

Preacher sent the Delaware out for herbs to crush, combine, and make into a syrup that could be drunk. He didn't know if that would do any good, but it damn sure couldn't hurt nothing.

"This has to be the cleanest bunch of trailsme . . . ah, trails-peoples I ever seen," Blackjack observed much later on that day when the men were stretched out wearily on the ground, eating supper and drinking coffee. "I know I'm damn shore cleaner than the day I was birthed."

All the men were cleaner than they'd been since the trip began. They had scrubbed with strong soap, cut their hair and beards, and washed good, and then had boiled their clothing. They had discarded their buckskins and were now dressed in homespun. At least somebody spun it, Preacher reckoned.

Faith came up and joined them, sitting down on the ground beside Preacher with a tired sigh.

"You get anything to eat?" he asked.

"I'm too tired."

"No, you ain't. You got to eat. Go without vittles at a time like this and your body gets weak and then you'll get sick like them others over yonder." He dished up a tin plate of stew, tore off a hunk of frying pan bread and handed it to her. "Now, eat. Steals Pony made up an Injun puddin' that's tasty. But eat this stew first."

She took the plate and soon found that to her surprise, she

was famished. She ate another plateful and a goodly portion of Steals Pony's puddin'. "This is delicious. What's in it?"

"Don't ask," Steals Pony urged her.

She took the warning to heart and didn't. But she ate all the puddin'.

Twelve women died over the next several days. Then those who had made it through the worst began to slowly recover. They asked what had made them sick. What disease had befallen them?

No one could tell them anything because no one knew. They were glad they made it and could get well.

"Be a lot more graves 'fore the West gets settled," Preacher said, resting on his shovel for a moment in the graveyard beside the trail.

"Amen, brother," Blackjack said. "Amen."

Preacher was right in his dire prediction. Years later, when the great movement west had abated, experts began theorizing that there had been one grave dug every eighty to one hundred yards between Missouri and the Willamette Valley. And many times whole families, six or seven people, were buried in the same shallow pit. So there is really no way to judge how many people died on the Oregon, Mormon, and California trails. Hundreds, certainly. Thousands, probably.

At the wagons, Preacher and the others could only guess as to why none of the men and some of the women were not at all affected by the strange disease, while others were incapacitated for days, and still others succumbed to it. And it was just as baffling as to why once the malady had run its course, the women, who hours ago, were so sick they could not raise their heads, were now getting to their feet so quickly.

"It's a miracle," one woman exclaimed. "God's work surely."

Preacher didn't know about that. He was just glad it was all over. He lifted his eyes heavenward. "Thank you," he muttered. "Stay with us, won't You?"

"Who you talkin' to, Preach?" Snake asked.

"God."

"He reply?"

"We're alive, ain't we?"

"You do have a point."

Steals Pony then said, "I think the women will be fully recovered and ready to travel in another two days."

Preacher nodded his head in agreement. "We haven't lost much time. Even when the women was kidnapped, the wagons still kept on west. But we damn well better be over them mountains 'fore the snow flies."

"Where do we take them across the Platte?" Blackjack asked.

"I give that some thought. It's been fairly dry this year. River ought to be low enough to make crossin' pretty easy. We'll stay south 'til we get up to the Buttes. Then we got to cut south and cross the Sweetwater. We'll stay north of the basin and head for the Green. We'll see how the cutoff looks when we get there." He smiled. "I figure ten days to two weeks and we'll hit the Laramies. Then these ladies will really see what they got themselves into."

"And so will we," Steals Pony said solemnly.

"Chimney Rock, ladies," Preacher said, swinging down from the saddle and using his hat to slap the dust from his clothing.

Dry. Awful dry. But to Preacher's way of thinking, that was better than mud and slow going.

The women had been stoical when they rolled away from the cross-marked graves, now days and miles behind them on the trail. A few had had tears in their eyes, but by and large, they had controlled their emotions.

"I can see why it got its name," Eudora said, standing up from the wagon seat to stretch and to rest her rear from the pounding it had taken that day.

Since this party had ample mounts, few were forced to walk, but many still chose to, just to stretch out some. And in the case of many of the women on this train, for other reasons.

"Arapaho coming," Snake said, riding up. "Pretty good-sized bunch, too. But I talked to 'em, and they ain't on the hunt for trouble. Just curious."

"How much time do we have?"

" 'Bout a minute and a half."

"Rupert," Preacher said. "Tell the women we got Injuns comin'. And tell them to stand easy but ready to grab guns. Here we go."

The Arapaho were not hunting for trouble, but neither were they out to win any prizes for sociability. One big buck made that clear right away.

"Get off the land," he told Preacher.

"What would you have us do, fly like eagles?" Preacher asked. "We're not stayin' here. We're just passin' through and we're peaceful."

A warrior rode up to Eudora's wagon and stared at her. She met his eyes with a look that was as cold and fierce as his. Faith was writing in her journal and the Arapaho jerked the journal out of her hands. Faith jerked it right back and the Indian lifted his hand to strike her. But before he could, Faith conked him on the head with a heavy club she'd found and the brave hit the ground with a thud. He did not move.

Only Preacher and the sub-chief had conversed, and the Arapaho were not sure whether the majority of these people were men or women. They could tell that some were women. But they knew the mountain men, and knew that Preacher and his kind would spill a lot of Indian blood before they could be brought down.

The sub-chief said he wanted a tribute before he would allow the wagons to cross.

"We'll cross," Preacher told him. "And we don't have nothin' to give you."

"Preacher plays a dangerous game," the Arapaho said, his eyes turning mean.

"This ain't no game," Preacher assured him. "If you think it is, just start some trouble."

"This is our land!"

"This ain't nobody's land. You use it, the Pawnee use it, the Cheyenne use it. Lots of tribes use it. Now we're usin' it. You can have it back when we're done passin' over it. That's the deal."

"Bad deal."

"It's the only deal you're gonna get."

The sub-chief had been sizing up the situation. He knew that everybody on this train was armed with guns, and plenty of them. He wanted those guns. But he could see no way to get them without losing a lot of his people. To his mind, it was a bad deal in more ways than one.

The Arapaho cut his eyes to Steals Pony. He knew the Delaware. He was both afraid of him, and jealous of him. The Delaware moved with ease among the whites. And that infuriated not only him, but many other Indians. He hated the way Steals Pony sat his horse and smiled arrogantly at him.

"I will kill you someday," he told Steals Pony.

"It is a good day to die," Steals Pony told him. "You want to see which of us die this day?"

The Arapaho glared at the Delaware for a moment. Slowly, reason began to overtake emotion in his mind. His body lost its tenseness. "It is not the time and this is not the place, Steals Pony. But someday."

"Surely," Steals Pony replied.

The brave that Faith had conked on the head moaned and stirred on the ground. He had a knot on his head about the size of an egg. He sat up and put both hands to his head, his fingers feeling gingerly at the goose egg. When he spoke, it was in his own language and evident to all that he was cussing.

One of his friends laughed at him and pointed at Faith.

The buck with the sore head rose to his feet with as much dignity as possible and hopped on his pony. He sat there for a moment, staring hatefully at Faith. When he spoke, his words were hard and tinged with hate.

The Arapaho sub-chief rode down his side of the wagon train for a couple of minutes, looking at the drivers and those mounted on horseback. When he returned, there was a different light in his eyes. "You will not go much further," he told Preacher. "What you will be is a lesson to any who might want to follow you."

"Is that right?" Preacher replied, in the sub-chief's own language. "I'd give it some thought, was I you."

"Why? I know your secret now. You shall see us again." He wheeled his pony and left, the others galloping behind him.

When they were gone, Eudora said, "He knows we're women. Right, Captain?"

"That he do. They's a right nice crick just a few miles up ahead. It's got some graze for the animals. The attack won't come today. He's got to get back to the main camp and talk it over. When he returns, it's doubtful he'll have many more than's with him now. Most of the Arapaho ain't much when it comes to war. They'd rather be friends with ever'body. They pretty easy to get along with. Some of the other tribes call them the Blue Cloud People 'cause they so peaceful. We'll make the crick and get ready for a visit."

When the wagons were rolling, Blackjack rode up to Preacher. "You neglected to tell the ladies that that bunch just might have some Kiowa or Southern Cheyenne friends that'd just love to come along on the raid."

"That did slip my mind, Blackjack. I just plumb forgot it, I did."

"You think you just might tell them after we make camp?"

"I probably will. But it's doubtful the Southern Cheyenne and the Kiowa is this far north. But you never know, do you?"

Blackjack smiled. "No, Preacher. You never do."

* * *

Preacher walked the tight half circle. The open end faced the creek, which had high bluffs behind it. The attack could only come from the front and sides. So the stock was safe and had water and some graze.

"Load up every gun," Preacher told the ladies as he passed by the wagons. "Keep hatchets close by; a few of them are sure to get into the circle."

Preacher sat down to eat only after he was satisfied that no more could be done. Steals Pony was absent. He had gone outside the circle to prowl.

"Once this journey is concluded, I will be able to correct certain theories about Indians never attacking at night," Rupert said. "That's what we were taught."

"Injuns will attack whenever they feel their medicine is good," Snake told the young officer. "I don't know who started that crap about Injuns being afraid to fight at night. What many of them is afeared of is gettin' kilt at night and not bein' buried proper. If that happens, they believe they'll wander forever, never findin' peace, never seeing family or friends. The Injuns is a tad more superstitious than most whites. Although I have seen some mighty goosy white folks."

The young officer leaned back on one elbow and smiled in the waning light. "Here we are, expecting an attack from the savages, and I am not afraid, not apprehensive—just enjoying the company of friends and savoring the taste of coffee after a good meal of camp stew. It's . . . well, *amazing!*"

Blackjack smiled slowly at him. "Ain't no point in worryin' 'bout what *might* happen. You can't change it no matter how much you roll it around in your head. You see, an Injun don't worry about much. Or so they claim. Personally, I think an Injun worries pretty much about the same things me, Preacher, Steals Pony, and Snake do. Something to eat, a warm place to rest, a good horse, a good gun, a good woman." He smiled. "Forget about the woman on Snake's part. He's too damn old to do much except remember." Snake grunted, but he didn't dispute it.

"On the other hand," Blackjack continued, "You folks east of the Mississippi, hell, you worry 'bout all sorts of things. You worry about the rain and the wind and the heat and the cold—you worry 'bout all sorts of things that can't none of you do a damn thing about. I don't know why you fret your heads so much 'bout things you can't change."

Steals Pony had returned and was standing, listening to the men talk. He looked at Rupert. "You recall Blackjack saying, in his quaint way, about there being a *time* to worry?"

"Did I say that?" Blackjack asked.

"In a manner of speaking," the Delaware replied.

"Yes," Rupert said. "I do."

"Now is the time," Steals Pony said. "The Arapaho are about a half mile from the wagons. And they are painted for war."

6

Steals Pony had not seen any Cheyenne or Kiowa with the bunch, and Preacher would have been surprised if he had seen any. This was mostly a band of young men led by a sub-chief called Broken Nose. Steals Pony said that Broken Nose was always leading young men off to fight.

"How many in this bunch?" Preacher asked.

"Forty perhaps. No more than fifty."

"We'll drive them off with the first volley," Rupert said.

"Don't count on it, son," Snake told him. "When the Arapaho decides to fight, he's a fighter. They might spend all night just creepin' up on us, and be five feet away from us come the dawnin'. Then they'll hit us. Don't never underestimate an Injun. They'll fool you ever' time."

"I should take you men back east with me so you could teach classes on frontier fighting."

"They wouldn't believe us, son," Preacher said. "You didn't, so why should they?"

"We ain't got no fancy de-grees from universities," Blackjack said.

"Let me inject this viewpoint here," Steals Pony said. "I

started to say that what we all lack in book knowledge and formal education, we probably more than make up for by possessing a deep well of basic common sense. But then I quite suddenly realized that any man who would voluntarily choose to spend his entire life, more often than not, alone, with no one to converse with except his horse, in the deep wilderness and towering, snowcapped mountains, with violent, sudden death all around him every day, sleeping on the ground instead of a bed, and wandering as aimlessly as the wind and as free as an eagle, really might not be as smart as he thinks he is."

"Ain't that purty?" Snake said. "That damn Delaware is a regular poet, by God."

"Yeah," Blackjack agreed. "Go on, Steals Pony. Say something else."

"You really want me to?"

"Shore! That was plumb purty."

"All right. How about this: here come the Arapaho."

The first attack was only a feeler on the part of the Indians. A few arrows were hurled at the wagons and a few shots were fired at the attackers. Neither the arrows nor the lead balls hit anything of importance.

"Hold your fire until you're sure of your targets!" Preacher shouted. "They're just feelin' us out, lookin' for weak spots."

Steals Pony retrieved several of the arrows and carefully inspected them. They appeared to be newly put together and were finely made, the arrowhead made of carefully worked bone. He knew the glue that helped hold the feathers to the shaft was made of a mixture of buffalo hooves and hide, the strings from a bull buffalo's sinew.

"What's wrong?" Preacher asked in a hoarse whisper, after watching Steals Pony for a few seconds.

"The arrows are new," the Delaware said.

"All of them?" Blackjack entered the conversation.

"All of them."

"We're in trouble." Snake added his voice. "Them arrows more than likely mean they've planned and prepared for this. I got me a hunch Bedell and what's left of his bunch came through here and stirred 'em up. Maybe by ambushin' a small band of 'em. Kilt women and kids, probably. Damn trash."

"Broken Nose!" Preacher shouted from his position. "Why are you attackin' us? We ain't done you or your people no wrong."

But only the silence of early night greeted Preacher's question. And that told Preacher and the other mountain men a great deal.

"Why won't he reply?" Eudora asked.

"Because they're close and that would give away their positions. Them firin' the arrows is back a good ways. We got Injuns layin' out yonder not more than twenty feet from the wagons. They'll lay still as a rock for hours. I don't think they're gonna give up this fight as easy as I first thought. They're mad about something."

Those Arapaho who were laying back some distance from the wagons began shouting taunts at the pioneers. But since only the mountain men spoke in their tongue, the shouted insults and taunts were incomprehensible to the women. But they still got the message.

Steals Pony grunted as one particularly offensive insult was hurled directly at him.

"Wagh!" Blackjack said. "That there was right personal, Steals Pony."

Blackjack raised his voice and told Broken Nose that before this was over, the Arapaho was going to find his tongue cut off and shoved up into a place that was located very near where Broken Nose surely kept his brains.

Broken Nose screamed his outrage at that.

"What did Steals Pony say to make that savage so angry?" Eudora asked.

Preacher told the women close to him.

"My word!" Faith exclaimed.

The Arapaho laying back then really started shouting the insults, filling the air with obscenities.

"They're gettin' ready to charge," Preacher said. "That hollerin' will cover any slight sound the attackers will make. Get ready. Pass the word."

The faint sound of weapons being cocked was heard all around the wagons. Preacher had his rifles propped up against a wagon wheel; his hands were filled with his multi-shot pistols; half of the barrels were double-shot. He knew that the first wave would come in fast and close, and probably several, or more, would get inside the protective circle of wagons. And he wanted all the firepower he had for this first, close-up charge. Since there was practically no chance of an attack from the rear, due to the bluffs, Preacher had assigned only a few of the women to guard the rear. "Hold your fire until you're sure you can put one down," Preacher told the women. "They're gonna be real close—close enough to smell the wood smoke on 'em—so don't panic. They're countin' on you ladies to panic. Let's give 'em hell, gals."

With a silent urge the first wave of attackers came out of the night like deadly wraiths.

The attacking Arapahos were met by an almost solid wall of heavy-caliber lead balls. One buck leaped between two wagons directly at Preacher. Preacher lifted his right-hand gun and stopped the Arapaho in midair, the twin-balls slamming into his belly and chest. He fell back—his bare chest and belly torn open and bloody—dead before he hit the ground.

One suddenly screaming Arapaho leaped at Faith, his lips peeled back in a snarl. She lifted her rifle and shot him in the face, the ball entering his open mouth and exiting out near the top of his head. He fell soundlessly to the earth and did not even twitch.

Yet another enraged buck got inside the circled wagons and managed to get his hands on Eudora's shirt. She bodily threw him against the side of a wagon and proceeded to club his head in with the butt of her rifle.

"Come on in, you bastard!" Blackjack roared over the sounds of screams and gunfire, closing his hands around the neck of a very surprised buck and dragging him over a wagon tongue. With one quick and powerful move, the huge mountain man snapped the warrior's neck. Blackjack then picked the man up effortlessly and tossed him back outside the wagons.

Snake looked down to see a dusty hand closing around one of his spare rifles. The aged mountain man slashed down with his razor sharp knife and the Arapaho was suddenly one-handed. The Indian screamed in pain and rolled back out into the night, blood streaming from his mangled arm.

The attack ended abruptly, the brown shapes rushing back into the darkness, carrying or dragging their wounded, dead, and dying.

"Get a head count, Rupert," Preacher said. "Let's see what damage they done. Every other woman reload and face forward and keep your eyes sharp; the others tend to the wounded. And we got some. I heard 'em scream."

One woman was dead, four were wounded. But the wounded were not hurt too bad. They were in some pain, but would live.

Preacher knelt down beside one woman with an arrow stuck in her shoulder. "Get some whiskey," he told Eudora. "And pour some down her throat." When the lady had taken several good slugs, Preacher took a taste himself, wiped his mouth, and grasped the shaft of the arrow. "This ain't gonna be no fun, but I got to do it."

"Do it," the woman said through gritted teeth.

Eudora and Wallis held the woman's arms while Preacher pushed the point of the arrow all the way through. The woman shrieked once and then passed out.

"Good," Preacher said, breaking off the arrowhead and then pulling the shaft out. He poured whiskey into both entry and exit wounds and then left her for the women to bandage and tend.

"Who's dead?" Preacher asked Rupert.

"Miss Shivley. She took an arrow right through the throat."

"Let's wrap her up and stash her under a wagon 'til mornin'. We'll plant her then. Any livestock get hurt?"

"None. Will the savages return this night?"

"They'll be back."

The attackers were back long before Preacher anticipated their return. Something was really eating at them and he could not figure out what it was. But nevertheless, he had his people ready for the angered Arapaho. But this time they not only came slipping out of the night on foot, they were charging their ponies into the battle, with many of them leaping over the tongues and into the circle.

"It's all up to you, ladies!" Preacher yelled. "We're gonna have our hands full out here." He was yelling as he ran to face a buck charging him in the semigloom, the only light coming from the moon. The warrior had a long lance and there was murder in his eyes. Preacher lifted his right hand pistol and fired, the ball striking the Arapaho in the throat, lifting him off his horse and sending him tumbling and rolling on the ground.

Ol' Snake had two bucks backing up. Neither one of them liked that long bladed Bowie knife that glistened and gleamed in the faint light. And they didn't like the sight of the blood that dripped from the blade. Arapaho blood. Snake faked to one side while a buck went with the fend, and Snake brought up a pistol with his left hand and shot the Arapaho through the heart just as Steals Pony picked up a dropped lance and threw it. The lance went all the way through the other brave and pinned him to the side of a wagon. He died soundlessly.

Blackjack picked a buck up bodily and brought him down back-first over his knee. The sound of the Indian's back breaking was audible even over the screaming and gunfire.

Preacher jerked a buck off his horse and both of them fell
to the ground. They came to their feet fighting and the Arapaho swung a war-axe, but Preacher caught the Indian's wrist
and stopped his swing cold in an iron grip. The brave tried to
kick Preacher and Preacher flipped him over one hip, bouncing him off the side of a wagon. The Arapaho lost his axe and
jerked out a knife. Preacher jerked out a pistol and ended
that brief argument with one ball through the heart.

He looked around. The clearing held no more live hostiles. Preacher raced to the wagons and faced the attack from
the night. But the attack was over. The Arapaho had taken
quite a beating in the two charges and they had had enough.

Preacher had him a sudden thought. "Broken Nose!" he
shouted. "Wait."

"Have you lost your mind?" Faith demanded angrily.

"Hush up, woman. Broken Nose! You hear me?"

"I hear you, Preacher. What trick do you have now?"

"No tricks, Broken Nose. You and your people fought
bravely and well. I would not have such brave men to wander
forever in the darkness. That would be wrong. We will carry
them to the edge of the wagons. You and your people can
pick them up there for proper burial. Is that fair?"

"Good thinkin', Preacher," Snake whispered, walking up.
"He'll owe you for that and won't attack no more."

"It is a trick!" Broken Nose called.

"No trick, Broken Nose. I give you my word. And you
know I don't break my word."

"That is truth," the voice came out of the night.

"Think of the wives and mothers of your fallen men. If
you bring them back home, the women won't have to slash
themselves in grief."

"That is also truth," Broken Nose said, his voice calmer
now.

Preacher stepped into the space between two wagons,
holding his rifle high. "I'm puttin' down my rifle, Broken
Nose. And my pistols." He laid his Hawken down and his

pistols beside it. "I'm goin' back to fetch one of your brave men, Broken Nose."

"And the rest of us, too," Blackjack said, laying down his weapons.

"We'll tote them to the clearin'," Snake said.

"I shall meet you at the wagons," Broken Nose said. "And I, too, will be without weapons."

"Bring some of your people with you," Preacher said. "With horses so's you can take your dead back home," Preacher told Eudora, "Put on some coffee and fix something to eat," I'm gonna get to the bottom of why peace-lovin' Arapaho attacked us."

Preacher and the mountain men handled the bodies with the respect due to the dead and the Arapaho noticed this. When the dead had been carried off, Preacher invited Broken Nose and some of his people inside the circle.

"No tricks, Broken Nose. We fought us a fight, now it's over. I want to know why you wanted to fight us. Let's have coffee and food and talk some."

Broken Nose stared at Preacher for a long moment. Then a very faint smile creased his mouth. "Yes. That would be a good thing. There is no need for more blood to be spilled. Your women are warriors, Preacher."

"Ain't they, though?"

Broken Nose waved a few of his men forward and stepped over the tongue and into the clearing. "Leave your weapons outside the wagons," he told them. When they hesitated, he again said, *"Leave your weapons!"*

They dropped their weapons and followed him.

The women had heated up a stew and made strong coffee. The men ate without speaking. When all had finished, Broken Nose rubbed his belly and belched loudly. The others too laid their bowls aside and belched. When the chief quit eating, everybody was finished. They all wiped the grease from their fingers on their skin and leggin's. "Good," Broken Nose said, in perfect English. "Very good. Your women not only can fight like men, they can cook too. How are they in the robes?"

"Tolerable," Preacher said, keeping his face straight despite the hard looks shot his way by Faith, Eudora, and others within earshot. "Only tolerable."

"That is too bad," Broken Nose said sorrowfully, looking at Bertha Macklin. "Nice round ass on that one." He shrugged his shoulders philosophically. "Well, one cannot have everything. At least they are good for something." He did not see Faith pick up a frying pan and start toward him, nor did he see Eudora grab the skillet from her and lead her off. "It is time for the truth. We were lied to, Preacher. A man by the name of Be-bell passed by and told us of a wagon train with women dressed like men. He said that from the seas of grasses to the east, all the way across, the women had lured Indian children to the wagons and then slaughtered them. I should have known when I saw you with the wagons that it was a lie. For that I am truly sorry."

"If we didn't make mistakes, Broken Nose, we wouldn't be human, would we?"

"Preacher, as always, speaks the truth."

"I wonder if he's spreadin' that lie all the way across?"

"Probably. But the closer he gets to the great mountains, the Ute, the Shoshoni, the Cheyenne, and the Crow, they will know he speaks nothing but lies. They might cut his tongue out."

"No, I want do to that," Rexana said, walking up to collect the bowls. She added another part of Bedell's anatomy she wanted to cut off.

When she had gone, Broken Nose shuddered. "Sleep lightly, Preacher. You are in the midst of savages, surely."

7

Louis, the boy the group had taken from Bedell's outlaws, had suffered a slight wound during the Arapaho attacks, but the wound was not a serious one. The boy had done well and proved himself a person who would stand his ground and fight.

The only casualty, Miss Shivley, was buried the next morning, just as dawn was lighting the sky. The ladies gathered around and sang "Where Is Death's Sting," Eudora read from the Bible, and the wagon train pushed on.

Broken Nose had taken his band of warriors and his dead, and left, after swearing that his people would not bother the wagons again.

"Do you believe him?" Rupert asked.

"Oh, yeah," Preacher said. He smiled. "At least for this trip."

Preacher was keeping a good eye out on the building storm clouds in the west. Only a few drops of rain had fallen thus far, but the lightning was fierce and the clouds promised one hell of a storm.

After only a couple of miles had passed, Preacher ordered

the train stopped and the canvas double-lashed. "We're in for it," he told the ladies. "You ain't seen hail 'til you've gone through what this country can give you. Pray that them clouds hold only rain and not ice."

"If it's rained much to the west," Snake said to Preacher, "we might have to cross the Platte more times than we want to."

"If she's spillin' over, we'll cross at the rocks," Preacher said, looking around and receiving nods of approval from his friends. "If not, we'll press on and plan on crossin' at the Buttes."

This storm held no hail—which the mountain men were thankful for—but it dumped torrents of water on the west-ward travelers and slowed them down to a mere crawl across the land. Once, Preacher had to halt the wagons because it grew so dark, and the storm was so intense, that the only way the drivers could see the wagon in front of them was by lamplight. By midafternoon he halted the wagons and told the ladies to circle. There wasn't no point in goin' on through this.

Squatting under canvas, Preacher told Eudora, "It ain't worth the strain it puts on the animals and the risk of broken axles and wheels to go on. We'll just sit it out."

Covering three times on horseback what the wagons could do in a day, Bedell had linked up with his cohorts far to the west and was laying out his plans.

One man shook his head in doubt. "I know Preacher," Villiers said. "I been in this country for years. Tanglin' with Preacher ain't smart, Vic. And Blackjack, Steals Pony, and Snake is just about as mean. I wish to hell your boys hadn't a-killed his horse. Preacher set store by Hammer. He ain't never gonna let you rest for doin' that."

"It was just a damn horse!" Bedell said to the Frenchman. Another Frenchman, Trudeau, added, "Most men grow fond of their animals, Bedell. Out in this country a good horse is the most valuable thing a man can have. I'm in agreement with Villiers. Preacher ain't never gonna forgive you for killin' Hammer. But I'm in agreement with you 'bout the wagons. We can't let them reach no post and make a report. If that was to happen, we could never show our faces in no civilized place again. All them folks got to die. That's all there is to it."

"Perhaps the Arapaho finished them off," Bedell said, a hopeful note to his words.

"Don't count on that," a man called Tater said. "And don't be tellin' that big whoppin' lie to no more Injuns we come up on out here. They know Preacher. This is Preacher's stompin' grounds. And whilst some of them might not like him much, they respect him a whole bunch, and they know Preacher wouldn't have no part in harmin' no woman nor child . . . no matter what color the skin. They'll cut your tongue out for lyin'. And they'll do it, too. I've seen them do it. It's right unpleasant."

Right unpleasant, Vic Bedell thought with a hidden shudder. Interesting way of stating it. "All right," he said. "Let's get to work on planning this out. I want this done right the first time."

Steals Pony had been gone for several days. When he returned, his horse was tired and so was he. He was covered with dust—they had left the rain far behind them—and he swung wearily down from the saddle.

Preacher handed him a cup of coffee and the Delaware took it with thanks.

"Bedell waits for us about a hundred miles ahead," Steals Pony told them. "I spoke with several Indians of different tribes. They all told me the same thing. Bedell's force was just too large for them to attack. The outlaws are well-mounted, well-supplied, and well-armed. Several trappers gone bad are among them, so they will know this country."

"Who?" Snake asked.

"Trudeau, Villiers, Logan, and Tater. There are many more in the gang, but those are the only ones I could identify from their descriptions."

"I owe that damn Tater a lead ball or two," Blackjack said. "He shot me some years ago. From ambush. He's a no-count from way back."

"I know him," Preacher said, "and Trudeau too. They teamed up some years back and killed a friend of mine. Shot him in the back one evenin' for his furs. Left him to die alone and hard. But they're experienced men, and you're right 'bout them knowin' the country. And they ain't cowards neither. If Trudeau and Villiers is there, you can bet their partner, Pierre, ain't far away. Well, we shore can't go back. All we can do is push on and stay alert."

It was a strange sense of relief for the men, but relief nonetheless, to know that Bedell was waiting for them, and to know approximately where he was waiting. It ended speculation. The mountain men knew now they had a fight waiting on them.

The next morning, Preacher gathered the women around him.

"Steals Pony brought news yesterday evenin'," he told the group. "And it ain't good, but it's what we all been expectin'. Bedell's linked up with his gang and they're waitin' on us 'bout a hundred miles ahead. You signed on to go west, and that's where we're goin'. Y'all done told me you wasn't goin' back so we ain't even gonna talk about that.

"Bedell wants the wagons and the supplies, and he wants us all dead. He has to kill us, all of us. If he don't, if just one of us gets through to tell our story, he'll be a wanted and hunted man the rest of his unnatural life. Y'all let that sink in your heads for a minute or so."

Preacher then eyeballed each woman for a moment. Their faces were set in grim and unyielding determination. They stood, all dressed in men's britches and shirts, with pistols shoved down behind their belts, and many of them leaning on their rifles. They bore little resemblance to the women who had left Missouri weeks back. The group seemed small and very insignificant against the vast backdrop of lonely land that stretched for hundreds of miles all around them.

Preacher nodded his head. "All right, ladies. Let's head west."

Twice during the next five very long, hot, dusty, and monotonous days Indians were sighted. But the Indians kept their distance and did not show any signs of hostility. That was due in no small part to the size of the wagon train. Word had spread quickly—thanks to Broken Nose and his people—that the train was made up almost entirely of women, and also that the women were savage fighters. Mostly, the Indians were curious. They wanted to see what manner of females these were, who rode, dressed, and fought like men.

Both times Indians were sighted, Steals Pony rode over to talk with them. And both times he returned with the same news: A large band of men waited just up the trail. They had some women with them, too. When the wagons were a day's distance from where Bedell and the men were supposed to be, Steals Pony left the train to scout ahead.

"They sure picked a piss-poor place to ambush us," Preacher said to Blackjack. The two men were ranging about a mile ahead of the wagons. "Must be a thousand better places on up ahead."

"I got me a hunch that the Delaware is gonna come back and tell us the gang pulled out," Blackjack said. "Them trappers with the bunch got more sense than to try something out here in the open."

"A body would think that," Preacher agreed. "Yonder's

Steals Pony comin'. He's takin' his time so's I 'spect you're right, Blackjack."

"Gone," the Delaware informed them. "Ashes are cold. They headed west."

"You called it right, Blackjack. Now we got to worry for another week or so." Preacher thought about that for a moment while his friends looked at him and waited. "They want us deeper in," he finally said. "Somebody finally got through to Bedell that this country is lousy for an ambush. Too bad. I was lookin' forward to endin' it right now."

"Yeah, me too. But it sounds right to me," Blackjack said, removing his battered hat and scratching his head. When the sickness hit them, all the men had let the ladies cut their hair much shorter than they normally wore it. But oddly enough, no fleas had been found on anyone, and not in any of their clothing or blankets. The sickness still baffled them all.

"Bedell has given up on the supplies," Steals Pony ventured his opinion. "He is going to content himself with our deaths. So when the ambush comes, it will be the most advantageous place he or his men can plan."

"You're right," Preacher said. "Steals Pony? You been talkin' more on this trip than I ever heard you 'fore. You've said more words in a month and a half or so than I've heard you say in twenty years."

The Delaware smiled. "Maybe I just haven't had anything to say until now." He rode off, leaving the men looking puzzled at each other.

"Sometimes you can get more sense out of a Chinaman than you can out of that damn Steals Pony," Blackjack said.

Preacher just smiled and rode on ahead.

The seemingly endless land stretched out before them, hot and dusty. The mules and the oxen plodded on. They were making good time, and Preacher did not push them. They rested when necessary, and made camp early enough so that everybody had good light to do their chores and get supper fixed. The weather held fair, albeit hot and extremely dusty, and so far only a few iron rims had wobbled off and no axles had broken. The shoes on the animals had held, and no hooves had split, but that would come later on. And the Indians continued to leave them alone.

Preacher sent Steals Pony on ahead again, to scout for signs of Bedell and his gang. But the Delaware came up empty. It was as if Bedell and his band of cutthroats had dropped off the face of the earth.

"Our luck ain't that good," Snake groused.

The wagons rolled on and the men and women did not encounter another human. They seemed to be lost on a barren, lifeless planet, void of others like them. Many of the women began to wonder if they'd ever see a stand of trees again.

The wagons crossed the Laramie range and made the Buttes. From there they headed slightly south and west toward what would someday be called Independence Rock. In the years to come, thousands of pioneers would chisel their names or initials into the rocks overlooking yet another barren stretch of this westward route. They had left the murky, lumbering Platte behind them now, and few of the women missed it, although it did provide water for the livestock.

And there was still no sign of Bedell or his gang. Preacher knew there was no point in his going out or sending Snake or Blackjack to look for Bedell. If Steals Pony couldn't pick up a trail, no one could.

A few days later, the snowcapped mountains began looming up in front of them. Soon the women were shivering, although it was the summertime. Preacher smiled and said, "This here's called Ice Slough. Get your axes and shovels out and dig down about a foot. They's solid ice under the sod. Makes your water taste a whole heap better. Go ahead. I know you don't believe me, but it's true. We're seven to eight thousand feet up, ladies. We're on the crest of the Divide. This here's the Wind River Range."

The ladies started digging and chopping and squealing with delight at the ice under the sod.

Preacher waited until supper and then told them, "We'll go through what's known as the South Pass. A trapper named Stuart found it back 'bout thirty years ago. After that, we'll take the cutoff," Preacher added, conscious of Snake, Blackjack, and Steals Pony looking at him. "Day or two past South Pass, we'll stop and fill every barrel and bucket we got, and I mean brim full."

"Are you sure about this, Preacher?" Steals Pony asked.

"Yeah. I'm sure. I don't see no point in pullin' an extra hundred miles."

"What's the problem with this cutoff?" Eudora asked.

"No water," Preacher bluntly told her and the other ladies. "And I mean, no water at all. It's a good eighty or ninety miles from the cutoff to the Green. It's a hard pull, but we can do it. I warn you all now, it sure ain't no pretty route. Not much grass, lots of ravines, gravel, and dried-up lakes. Alkali lakes. A lot of it is flat as a tabletop, and probably comes close to resemblin' hell. But we'll make up for a lot of the time we lost." He looked into the tanned and windburned faces of the women. They were all leaned down and toughened up. "Are you ladies all game for it?"

"We're game," they said in unison.

Snake smiled, then chuckled for a moment. "Wait 'til we get to Soda Springs. The water there tastes like beer and if you add a little sugar to it and maybe some syrup if you got any, it tastes like lemonade."

The ladies all laughed.

"It's true." Blackjack backed up his friend. "They's all sorts of wonders out here."

"Outlaws and highwaymen, wild savages, ice under the boiling hot ground, water that tastes like beer or lemonade,"

Faith said, her lips curved into a faint smile. "I should have brought more writing tablets. What other wondrous surprises do we have in store for us?"

"Plenty," Steals Pony said, no humor in his words. "Believe when I say that the worst is still ahead of us."

Faith cut her eyes to Preacher. He nodded his head. "He ain't lyin' about that. These past weeks has toughened up you ladies quite a bit. I know you think I been rough on you, and I have, but I done it for a reason. You're gonna need all the strength you got 'fore we get to the coast. We got mountains, ragin' rivers to cross, and there's still Indians to fight. It'll turn cold 'fore we get there, so we'll have to fight our way through winter storms. When we get to the Snake . . ." He paused. "Well, there ain't no way to describe that. You got to see it to believe it. Then we got the Blue Mountains to cross. And beyond that it's two hundred and fifty miles either raftin' down the river or goin' over and through the Cascades to get to the valley. I ain't gonna sadden you no more. But the country behind us was a church eatin' on the grounds compared to what's ahead. Get some sleep, ladies. It gets worser and worser from here on in."

8

The way was every bit as tough as Preacher and the other mountain men had promised . . . and more.

South and slightly west of South Pass, Preacher halted the wagons early and told the women to make camp. They were going to rest up and fill every barrel and container they had with water. Preacher had had them gathering up twigs and sticks and buffalo chips for a week. " 'Cause if you think it's been slim pickin's so far, just wait 'til you see this trail."

"Hell," Faith summed it up the middle of the next day, fanning herself with her hat.

It was a fairly apt description, for the sun was beating down mercilessly and the powderlike dust whirled under the hooves of the animals and the wheels of the wagons.

"It gets worser," Preacher said, riding up to end the short break. "Let's go."

When they made camp for that night, after having traveled about fifteen miles, the women were furious with Preacher because he would not let them use one drop of water for anything other than cooking and the taking care of their animals. He even rationed the drinking water.

"We are *filthy!*" Faith told him. "I positively *reek!*"

"You'll get reeker," Preacher informed the indignant lady. "Whatever that means. Beat the dust offen you with your hat and quit gripin' about it."

"Ohh! You insufferable ass!" Faith said, then wheeled around and stalked off.

"You lost a little ground there that time, Preacher," Blackjack said. "You keep on like that, you'll never get that woman 'tween the blankets."

"She'll get over it," Preacher replied. "Eudora'll settle her down."

Whether the tall and handsome New England woman settled her down or not, Faith did stop her complaining and rode stoically on westward, grimy hands, dusty face, disheveled hair, and all. But she didn't speak to Preacher for the next four days.

Which was sort of a relief for Preacher. Faith Crump could be a real pain in the butt when she took a mind to be.

"Green about five miles ahead," Steals Pony informed Preacher, reining up in a cloud of fine dust.

Preacher rode back to Eudora. "Keep a firm hand on them reins, ladies. The mules and oxen will be smellin' that cold, clear water in a minute, and they'll try to run."

"I certainly wouldn't blame them," Faith said, more ice in her voice than it took to cool off a barrel of beer.

The other men were riding up and down the wagons, warning the drivers to keep a tight rein on the mules and the drovers and prodders to grab ahold of the oxen and try to hold them back when they smelled the water.

"The Green's fed from the snow up yonder in the mountains," Preacher said, Faith's words not fazing him one bit. "She's cold and sweet and once you've drunk your fill, y'all can move upstream a bit and take shifts a-bathin'. But wait a time so's you can wash down the livestock. They deserve a good bath, too. They sure earned it."

"I certainly concur," Eudora said. "They have performed magnificently."

"We bathe the animals before we bathe ourselves?" Faith questioned.

"You take care of what's the most important on the trail first," Preacher said with a straight face, then rode on back to the head of the long train, leaving Faith sputtering and Eudora smiling.

The drivers and drovers tried their best, but they could not contain the animals' excitement when they smelled the cold fresh water of the Green. Mules and oxen broke into a lumbering trot when the river was near. After days of savage heat and choking, blinding dust, the animals headed for the river despite everything that could be humanly done to hold them in check, which included a lot of fancy cussing by the ladies. And Preacher discovered that Eudora really knew how to sling the four, six, and eight letter words around. One wagon overturned, but suffered only minor damage, the driver sustaining nothing more than a few cuts and bruises and loss of temper.

The overturned wagon was righted and checked for damage and declared trailworthy. The driver had her scratches tended to and her temper calmed. Although it was only midday, Preacher told the ladies to make camp. They all needed to rest and they sure needed a good bath.

"How far is it to this Soda Springs?" Rupert asked.

" 'Bout a week, I'd say," Preacher told him. " 'Bout fifty miles past that, they's a tradin' post. Belongs to the Hudson's Bay Company. We can stock up on provisions there."

"A few folks have taken to callin' that the split-up post," Snake offered. "Just past the post is the trail—if that's what you want to call it—that leads to Californy. But it's a killer, I tell you. I wouldn't lead no wagons crost it."

"What's that like?" Faith asked, walking up to join the group with a few other ladies. Faith had her writing tablet in her hand.

"Hot and dry," Preacher told her. "Rocks, sagebrush, dust, and alkali water. That place ain't fit for man nor beast. Hell on earth is what I call it."

"And the route we'll take from the post?" Eudora asked.

"As we have tried to tell you all," Steals Pony said. "It's very dangerous. It's, well, difficult to describe. At the Columbia, I suggest rafting the final leg. But Preacher is the only man to ever take a train through the mountains. Is that the way this train is going, Preacher?"

"That's my plan now. We'll just have to wait and see the condition of the women, the wagons, and the livestock when we get there. And let's don't forget Bedell. We still got him and his scum to deal with. Despite all the misfortune the ladies has gone through, we been lucky so far. Real lucky."

"Lucky!" Faith blurted.

"Yes," Blackjack spoke up. "You see, Missy, what them people from back east didn't tell y'all, is that they's been several wagon trains 'fore this one that just vanished on the trail. I mean, no trace of them has ever been found and no trace of them ever will be found. All we had was a few minor run-ins with the Injuns. We got that to face on the next leg of this journey. Plus Bedell and his trash. You'll see. All of you. You'll see just how lucky you've been so far."

Faith scribbled in her journal for a moment and then lifted her eyes to Preacher. "The animals have been watered and bathed, your dictatorship. May we now take *our* baths?"

"Have at it, Missy. Just do it in shifts with ample guards all around. When y'all are done we'll take our spruce-ups. Take your time a-splashin' and a-soapin' and a-rubbin' this and that."

"Oohhh!" Faith said, tossing her head. She stalked away.

The ladies marched off, Eudora lingering with the men

for a moment. Eudora smiled and asked, "When do you intend to temper that fire in her, Captain?"

"Why, Miss Hempstead," Preacher said with a grin, "whatever in the world do you mean?"

Eudora laughed and walked off.

"That New England woman, now," Blackjack said, with
admiring eyes on Eudora, "she's the first woman I've met in
many a year who could make me settle down to hearth and
home."

"If I was fifty years younger," Snake said. "I'd bundle her
up and tote her off. That there is one hell of a woman, I tell
you. Mighty fine. Mighty fine."

"Be right interestin' to see what kind of man she's got all
staked out on the coast," Preacher opined. "If she's got one
a-tall."

"What do you mean?" Steals Pony asked.

"I just got me a hunch that maybe that government man
lied," Preacher replied. "I think they's some men in the valley who knows these ladies is comin'. But not many. Maybe
they's another government plan in mind. Hell, there ain't a
hundred an' fifty spare men in the whole damn Willamette
Valley."

"I think you be right, Preacher," Snake agreed. "This
setup didn't seem right from the git-go. Not to me."

"But what do the government hope to gain by doin' this
foolishness?" Blackjack asked.

Preacher shook his head. "To in-tice more men from the
east, maybe. Government wants this area settled. And fast. I
mean, ever'thing from the Mississippi to the Pacific."

"That's foolish thinkin'," Snake said.

"Yes, it is," Steals Pony said. "But I agree with Preacher.
The government wants this nation settled. What better way
to get men out here than with the knowledge that women are
waiting for them. I think you are correct, Preacher."

"Why, them lyin' no-counts!" Blackjack said. "The government ain't supposed to lie. They supposed to be honorable men, doin' the biddin' of them that voted for them."

"You livin' in a dream world," Preacher countered. "I allow as to how I seen more politicians than near'bouts any one of you. And I ain't got no use for none of them."

Rupert had been listening, saying nothing. But now he nodded his head. "I am forced to agree with you, Preacher. A mere few weeks ago I would have taken exception to your words. But no more. I now believe the government wants the entire Willamette Valley firmly established in American hands. And this wagon train is just one of their plans for doing that. But we'll never know for sure, will we?"

"If the men in Washington ain't honorable men now," Snake said. "Reckon what it'll be like there a hundred or so years from now?"

"Awful," Preacher replied.

The wagons reached the trading post without event and the trappers and fur buyers gathered there stood and looked on in astonishment as the women stepped down and returned their stares.

"Women!" one man said, awe in his voice. "I ain't never seen so many women in one place in all my life."

"That there's Preacher!" another said. "Preacher! What the hellfire's goin' on, you old warhoss?"

"I'm a-leadin' these ladies to the promised land," Preacher said. "You git whiskey around here?"

"What's wrong with right here?" another man asked, eye-balling Faith. She was mighty fetchin' in her men's britches. Especially walking away.

"There ain't nothin' wrong with right here," Preacher said, taking the jug offered him and knocking back a huge swallow of whiskey. He lowered the jug and wiped his mouth with the back of his hand. "But these ladies is bound for the Willamette."

Much to the surprise of the men who ran the huge trading post, after the women had seen to their teams, they all crowded into the dark and dank-smelling building and were pawing through blankets and cloth, holding up this and that, and generally having a good time. This was the first small touch of civilization they'd experienced in several months, and they were determined to make the most of it.

"Why Willamette?" a trapper asked.

Preacher started to tell him because it was another of the government's damn fool ideas, but he'd given his word not to talk about that, so he said, "They got men waitin' on 'em out yonder. Gonna get all hitched up." He took another swig. "You boys seen a big bunch of men anywheres around here lately?"

"A bunch come through here about ten days ago," a man behind the counter said. "And they bought too many supplies for their number. I figure they was buyin' for a lot of people. I didn't like the looks of them at all."

"How many in the bunch that stopped by here?" Blackjack asked, after buying a huge handful of twist chewing tobacco.

"Ten. But they bought enough for fifty or so. Had them a string of packhorses that was loaded down when they left. Headed in the same direction you folks are going."

"Know any of them?" Snake asked.

"Yes. That no-good Villiers was with them. But what made me suspicious was that Pierre and Trudeau were nowhere to be seen. You boys know something that we need to know?"

Preacher poured himself a brimming cup of whiskey and sat down at a table. He first drank half the cup, then he told the sordid tale of Bedell from the beginning, telling everything that had occurred on the trail since leaving Missouri. The trappers, traders, scouts, and Hudson's Bay men, all seasoned veterans of the wilderness, were shocked and their faces showed it.

One man broke the silence. "They're dead men if they return here," he said, his voice thick with anger. "I can guarantee you they will be shot on sight."

"You were right, Godfrey," a trapper said to the counterman. "We should have put lead in the scummy whole bunch of them."

"We were just about to set out for Canada, Preacher," a buckskin-clad man said. "But we can change our plans and ride with you."

Preacher drained his cup and shook his head. "No. No point in any of you riskin' your skins for this government foul-up. And you people keep your mouths shut about what I told you. Bedell and his crew find out you know about the evil deeds, they'll come back here and do some butcherin' in the night. If any of 'em get away from me, that is," he added.

The men gathered in the trading post exchanged knowing glances. They all knew Preacher, and his reputation. Preacher had been wronged, and his good horse had been killed. Those who had done it would be called to account. And with Preacher that usually meant guns or knives.

"Preacher," a man called. "Them's the most terriblest lookin' pistols you got strapped around you I ever seen. Where can I get me a set?"

"I don't know. Feller back east made 'em. I took 'em off a dead outlaw I kilt last year. I . . ."

"He was a friend of ours," a voice spoke from the open doorway.

Preacher turned around and faced the three men. They were dirty, stinking, and the fleas and lice were fairly hopping on them. Probably jumping from one to the other, Preacher thought. Maybe for a change in menu. Preacher grinned at the thought.

"Whut are you grinnin' about, you ugly bastard?" one of the trio asked.

Several of the men who knew Preacher well and could guess what was about to happen, hustled the women out a side door. Eudora and Faith were standing off to one side in the shadows, and did not move.

Preacher smiled slow and easy. "Why . . . I'm laughin' 'cause in my mind, I just told myself a joke that I never had heard before. It was right funny."

The trio of brigands looked at one another, all of them attempting to figure out what Preacher had just said. "He's makin' fun of us," the original loudmouth said. "What he just said just ain't possible."

"Whut did he say?" another asked.

Preacher laughed at him.

"It ain't possible, I say," the spokesman insisted. "It just ain't."

"Are you callin' me a liar, you bear-butt ugly son of a bitch?" Preacher asked, his voice suddenly hard and all traces of the smile gone from his lips.

"Take your troubles outside," Godfrey said from behind the counter.

"Shut up!" one of the men told him. He cut his eyes back to Preacher. "Yeah, I reckon I am callin' you a liar. Now let's see what you intend to do about it."

"Well, I reckon I'll just have to kill you," Preacher replied.

And the huge room became as quiet as a tomb.

9

Faith and Eudora stood mesmerized. The counterman stood with both hands palms down on a blanket Claire Goodfellow had started to purchase. Snake and Blackjack were over near the bar, holding cups of whiskey. Steals Pony was outside, talking with several Indians. Rupert stepped to one side, quickly getting out of the line of fire.

"You got it to do," the lout told Preacher.

"I reckon I can do it," Preacher replied. "Make your play."

The brigand grabbed for his pistol, which was tucked behind his belt.

Preacher's right-hand gun flashed into action and boomed before the brigand could cock his pistol. The heavy ball struck the man in the center of his chest and knocked him back outside. He hit the ground on his back and twitched once as his brain told his body he was dead.

"Never seen a man git a pistol into action so fast." A trapper broke the silence. "I believe Preacher's got something goin' for him, I do."

"That was certainly a fast-draw," Godfrey said, craning

his neck to see if any blood had gotten spilled on his freshly mopped floor.

"Yeah," another said. "He's a regular gunfighter, he is."

And the term was born.

Preacher cut his eyes to the dead man's friends. They stood poised, their hands hovering near their pistols. But they were smart enough not to try a grab.

"You kilt Hill," one finally said.

"I sure did," Preacher replied. As soon as he had fired the first ball, he had cocked the hammer on another barrel of the awkward-looking pistol. "You boys want to join him?"

"Cain't say as I do," the other one of the pair said. "That was his friend you kilt last year, not ours."

"The hell you say!" his buddy shouted. "You just stand aside." He glared at Preacher. "I ain't no fast hand at pistols, but I'll fight you fair with a blade, Preacher."

Godfrey lifted a double-barreled shotgun out from under the counter and pointed it at the mouthy brigand. "Outside," he ordered. "I'll not have blood all over my merchandise."

"Suits me," Preacher said.

"You best think about this, Jackson," the other friend of the dead Hill said.

"Shet your mouth, Cecil," Jackson told him. "I ain't a-feared of this ignorant bastard."

"Your funeral," Cecil replied. He looked at Preacher. "I'm out of this."

"Good enough," Preacher said, easing the hammer down on his pistol and holstering the weapon. "Outside, Jackson."

"Oh, sure. You want me to go furst so's you can shoot me in the back?" Jackson said with a sneer. "No, thanks."

Preacher smiled and shoved past the man, stepping outside. A large crowd had gathered, most coming running at the sound of the shot. They backed away when Preacher pulled out his long-bladed knife.

"Come on, you misbegotten sot!" Preacher shouted. "Time's a-wastin' and I got better things to do."

"Somebody drag that stinkin' body out of the doorway," Godfrey called. "You!" He pointed at Cecil. "There's a shovel around back. Get it and bury him in the woods."

Jackson was showing signs of having regretted his challenge. He was slow in walking toward Preacher. Preacher saw it and offered the man a way out.

"This don't have to be, Jackson. Just get on your pony and ride on out of here."

"Yeah, it has to be," Jackson said, baring his blade. "It has to be."

"I don't know why," Preacher said. "But if that's the way you want it, come on."

Jackson cursed and sprang at Preacher, his knife held low for a gut-cut. Preacher sidestepped, whirled, brought his razor-sharp blade down, and cut Jackson on the buttock. Jackson yelped in pain and the blood flowed from the deep cut.

Cecil, dragging the body of the dead man toward the woods, heard the cry of pain and shook his head. He was sorry he'd ever gotten mixed up with this bunch. Ever since he'd come west he'd been hearing tales about a mountain man called Preacher. He hadn't believed them. But he sure did now. Them was the most awfulest lookin' pistols on Preacher he'd ever seen in his life.

"You cut my ass a-purpose!" Jackson squalled.

"Sure did," Preacher said, grinning.

Jackson cussed him and took a swipe. Their knives clashed and locked at the cross guards. Preacher smiled at Jackson and hit him in the belly with a hard right fist. The wind whooshed out of the man and his eyes glazed. Using his knife, Preacher tore Jackson's knife loose from his weakened grip and shoved the man back.

"I don't really want to kill you, Jackson," he told the startled man, as he was sheathing his blade. "I just want to beat the snot out of you." Then, before Jackson could get set,

Preacher flattened him with a right to the jaw. Jackson landed on the ground flat on his back, the wind knocked clear from him.

Preacher stepped back and let the man get slowly to his boots. Jackson looked at his brace of pistols on the ground where he'd dropped them. But what really got his attention was the sound of Steals Pony cocking his Hawken.

"Touch those pistols," the Delaware warned him, "and I will certainly drop you where you stand."

"Goddamn wild savage!" Jackson cussed him.

Steals Pony laughed openly at the absurdity of the remark.

Jackson turned to face Preacher. He lifted his fists. Preacher raised his fists; there was a strange smile on his tanned face.

"You really think all this is funny, don't you, Preacher?" Jackson asked, a trickle of blood leaking from one corner of his mouth.

"Well, not really. It's more sad than funny. You so damn clumsy. But I know who you are, now. You're Jackson Biggers, ain't you?"

"That's right. And you kilt a runnin' buddy of mine last year."

"I disremember the time and place 'xactly, but I 'spect he was tryin' to kill me."

"So what? You been needin' killin' for a long time. I'm sick of hearin' your pukey name."

"So come on, Biggers," Preacher laid down the challenge. "I've seen men killed with fists. You think you're hoss enough to do that?"

Biggers stepped forward and smashed a right to Preacher's jaw. But Preacher had been expecting something like that. He turned and the blow only landed with about half-power. Still, it was enough to hurt, and Preacher knew the man was no pushover.

Preacher countered with a left and then a right to Jackson

Biggers' belly and face. With blood streaming from his newly busted beak, Biggers backed up, shaking his head to clear away the blood and the birdies and cobwebs.

Preacher pressed him hard, punching fast, landing body blows that he knew were hurting the man. Biggers was slightly taller than Preacher, and outweighed him by twenty or thirty pounds. But Preacher was all bone and hard-packed muscle. His legs were spring-steel strong and Preacher was a runner, nearly always winning the footraces at the rendezvous.

Biggers dropped his guard and Preacher landed a hard right to the jaw that staggered the man. Biggers backed up and Preacher bored in. He landed a left to the belly and a right to the mouth. Biggers spat out teeth and blood and cussed Preacher.

Preacher didn't waste his breath with words, obscene or otherwise. He just proceeded to beat the crap out of the bigger man. In a few moments, Biggers' face was a mask of blood and torn skin. His nose was flattened and both his eyes were closing.

Preacher took one look at the man and measured his next blow. It sounded like the flat side of an axe hitting a side of raw beef. Biggers went down and didn't move. One side of his jaw was all cattywhompous; busted all to hell and gone. Cecil came and dragged the broken-nosed, busted-jawed, unconscious, and ass-cut Biggers off behind the trading post.

"He never did have no sense," was Cecil's summation of the entire affair. "I can't speak for Jackson, but you'll not see me no more."

"Good," Preacher said, taking the water bucket that Snake handed him and pouring it all over his head right good. He slicked his hair back with his fingers and looked around him. The women were all standing around, staring at him.

"All right. Let's get this circus on the move, people," Preacher said, plopping his hat on his head. "We got mountains to cross."

* * *

And cross them they did.

Rejuvenated by the stop at the first lone light of civilization after hundreds of miles of plains and wilderness, the women picked up the reins, took their prod sticks, swung into their saddles, and pressed on westward. Preacher had warned them that the hardest part was still ahead, and they believed him. But they were trail-wise now, and felt that nothing could stop them—and nothing was going to. The mountain men knew that, too. They saw the change in the women, in the set of the jaw, the way they sat their saddles or handled the reins, and in the way they walked.

These women who now pushed westward bore little resemblance to the band of powdered, perfumed, and soft-handed ladies who had gathered back in Missouri for a grand adventure. Most had cut their hair short so they wouldn't have to fuss with it. The women had become more proficient with weapons than most men of that time, handling them with an expert's ease and sureness.

And Preacher, Steals Pony, Blackjack, and Snake were proud as punch of these women. They had taken more than their share of hard knocks and had bounced right back. These women would make fine partners for men, but the men who chose them had damn well better know right off the mark that these ladies would be their equals. The first men to raise a hand to these gals had best understand that when they did, odds were good they'd spend the rest of their life one-handed.

The hot and dusty days creaked and rattled past and the wagons pushed on without seeing any sign of Bedell and his gang. Two days after crossing the river, Steals Pony rejoined the train.

Before he said anything, he squatted down by the fire and poured a cup of coffee. "Tomorrow we fight," he told Preacher and the other men. "Bedell and his men have laid out what appears to be a very elaborate ambush." The Delaware smiled. "Perhaps too elaborate."

"How many men?" Blackjack asked.

"I counted forty. They have pulled in their scouts and now wait in hiding."

"You got a plan?" Snake asked.

"I do," Steals Pony said. "But it is a very risky one for us. It could misfire."

"Lay it out," Preacher said.

The Delaware took a twig and started drawing in the dirt. He had worked his way in close to the encampment and memorized the positions of Bedell's men. He now highlighted each ambush point. As before, it appeared to Preacher that Bedell was supremely confident. And now that overconfidence was going to blow right up in his face.

"He's a fool," Preacher said flatly. "He ain't lookin' to his back. Seems like Trudeau or some of them others would point that out to him."

"I think that Bedell is a man who does not take kindly to the suggestions of others," Steals Pony said.

"Ten women up here," Preacher said, pointing to the top of the cliffs surrounding Bedell's position. "We go in from the rear. The wagons stop here on the flats." He jabbed at the ground. "And don't move no further. They'll be gone out of rifle range and safe. There ain't no way Bedell's men can approach them from any direction without gettin' the crap shot out of them. The women on the ridges open fire and we move in. That it, Steals Pony?"

"That's the way I see it."

"Let's do it."

10

Preacher chose the women carefully and moved them into position that night. Ten women would be firing, and ten others would be reloading. Each woman carried two rifles. The hard practice Preacher had put them through at the beginning of the trip would now prove to be invaluable. There would be a nearly constant barrage from the ridges. The first wave of fire would cut Bedell's band down by a full ten men. The rifle fire after that would keep them pinned down and cut off, allowing Preacher and the other men time to work their way in among those trapped near the rear. It would be a very bloody dawn.

"The man is no soldier," Rupert pointed out, after reviewing the plan. "He positioned his forces all wrong. For which," he added, "I am everlastingly grateful."

"You real shore in your mind that you want to go in with us?" Preacher asked the young officer. "We ain't plannin' on takin' no prisoners, son."

Rupert cut his eyes over to Snake. The old man was patiently and skillfully sharpening his scalping knife to a razor's edge. He was planning on taking some hair. All the mountain men had unpacked their bows and quivers of arrows for that first silent kill at dawning's light. Steals Pony had gathered up some plants, pounded them into a thick and smelly pulp, and soaked his arrow points in the solution overnight.

"Poison," the Delaware had told him. "Kills slow. Very painfully. These men deserve no better. I would not use it on an animal. I have too much respect for them."

"Oh, yes," Rupert said, a steely edge to his voice. "I'm going in."

Preacher looked hard at the young man. He saw a very different person from just a few months ago. Rupert Worthington would never again fit entirely into genteel Virginia society. The west and the wilderness had left its mark on the career army man, and like a deep tattoo, it could never be removed. There was finely tempered steel in the man now. Many of his past illusions about right and wrong and the treatment of career criminals had been blown away like smoke in a high wind.

"You'll never leave the west again, will you, boy?" Snake asked softly.

"I don't plan to, sir. I will ask that I be posted to the wilderness. You see, I happen to know a new fort is to be built in the Dakota territory. I shall ask to be sent there. I have some experience in construction and engineering."

"I wish you luck," Snake said, sheathing his blade and getting up and walking away.

"Is he ill?" Rupert asked.

"No," Steals Pony said. "He goes off to quietly sing his death song."

"His *death song?*"

"He does not believe he will live to see another nooning. He told me."

"But . . ."

"Leave it alone," Preacher told him. "We know what to do. I done promised him I'd bury him high. Get some rest. Tomorrow's gonna be right busy."

After Rupert had gone to wrap up in his blankets, Preacher looked at Steals Pony. "You know something I don't?"

"Snake has a sickness inside him. A growth that keeps getting bigger and more painful. I have seen them in others. The pain just gets unbearable at the end. He chooses to go out as a warrior. It is a good thing, I think. He told me about your promise to him."

Preacher nodded. "He see a doctor?"

"Snake? You surely jest. No. Of course not. But he's tired, Preacher. He wants to rest. Forever."

"Ought to be right interestin' come the dawnin'."

Steals Pony smiled. "Quite."

The women were in position an hour before dawn. Preacher, Snake, Steals Pony, Blackjack, and Rupert had Injuned up to the sleeping camp and were silently waiting for dawn and the wagons to start rumbling westward. Bedell had chosen a good ambush spot; Preacher himself couldn't have done better. Only thing was, Bedell had not counted on having to protect his back and his north side. He was as exposed there as a newborn baby's butt.

Slowly the east began to lighten, and the camp began to stir. No fires were built, and the mountain men could tell that the outlaws were not happy about a no-coffee morning. They were going to be a hell of a lot unhappier in about an hour.

The mountain men were spread out well, effectively covering the canyon floor from side to side. At the sound of the first fusillade, the leading wagons were to wheel and present their broadside to the outlaws. The teams would be quickly unhooked and led to safety. The wagons had been reinforced on the sides and now held half a dozen women each, all heavily armed and all good shots.

Preacher knew that some of the outlaws would get away. There were several shallow canyons running off to the south for a few hundred yards before they leveled out and met ground level amid a jumble of rocks. Preacher just didn't have enough people to cover all of it. But with any kind of luck, they would break the back of Bedell's gang and be done with the bastard once and for all.

The mountain men watched as the gang members got into place for their planned murderous ambush. Invisible from the front, their backs were in full view of Preacher and the others. There were a half dozen or so women with the gang, dressed in men's clothing and armed, taking up positions along with the men in Bedell's gang. Preacher held no sympathy for them. They'd chosen their lot willingly and had held their fate in their own hands. And according to the ladies rescued, the outlaw women had been just as bad, or in many cases, worse, than the men who had kidnapped, raped, and abused them. So to hell with the outlaw women. Preacher had a hunch that Eudora and her crew up on the ridges would make short work of them.

Preacher and the others felt, rather than heard, the wagons approaching. The mountain men saw the outlaws tense as they, too, felt the ground rumbling. Only a few of the outlaws had chosen positions that covered their backs; Bedell, naturally, was one of them.

Slowly, ever so slowly, the wagons came into view and the outlaws made ready their weapons. It was evident by their actions that they planned on taking no prisoners. When the wagons were about five hundred yards from the ambush site, Preacher lifted his Hawken as the others followed suit and sighted in. On the ridges above them, Eudora and her ladies did the same.

Fifteen rifles roared from the rear and from above the ambushers and the life was ripped from that many outlaws. The lead wagons quickly turned and the teams were unhitched and led out of the field of fire. Canvas was flipped back and the besieged outlaws found themselves facing the long rifles of twenty-five women.

Eudora and her ladies on the ridges kept up a savage fire,

so savage that Preacher and the others chose not to close in and mix it up with Bedell and his scum. All but one: Snake. The old mountain man left his position to tangle hand to hand with several of Bedell's men. Preacher lost sight of the old man as Snake jumped into a jumble of rocks, his knife blade flashing in the early morning sunlight.

Through the confusion of smoke and dust, Preacher watched helplessly as half a dozen or so made it to their horses and raced down the canyons to the south.

"That's it!" Preacher shouted, standing up and waving his arms. "Stop shootin'!"

Eudora and her sharpshooters ceased firing—the women in the wagons had not had to fire a shot—and Preacher and the men worked their way into the rocks. It was carnage.

Many of the dead had taken the heavy rifle balls through the head or neck; several had been shot half a dozen times or more. A few were still alive, but their wounds were grievous and none of the mountain men—Rupert included—felt any great compulsion to offer any comfort or aid.

Snake had gone in cutting and slashing and he lay among the dead, shot several times. The old man had sliced the life out of three outlaws before his soul had left his body to meet the Man Above. Snake lay on his back with a smile on his lips, his right hand still gripping his knife.

One of the wounded outlaws that the rescued women had said had been particularly cruel, savage, and twisted, both to the kidnapped women and the boys, let out a fearful shriek as Steals Pony took his scalp. The Delaware left the pervert flopping around on the rocky ground. Rupert's eyes took in the scene with no emotion showing on his face.

A dying outlaw, his chest and belly covered with blood, gasped to the young officer, "You a white man, but you as bad as that damn Injun!"

"Thank you," Rupert said. "I consider that quite a nice compliment." He walked on.

"How many dead?" Preacher called.

"Thirty-four," Rupert said, completing his body count. "Well, when the six still alive do expire there will be thirty-four dead."

"Help me!" one gut-shot outlaw called out weakly.

One of the women from the train helped him. She remembered him as one of those who had raped her repeatedly. She shot him between the eyes.

After that, the five outlaws still alive did not call out for help.

Preacher gently wrapped up Snake's body in his blankets and tied the old mountain man across his saddle. He sighed and then turned to face the others. "Y'all go on. I'll catch up with you in a week—maybe less than that, maybe more than that. All depends. You won't have no more problems. Injuns witnessed this here fight . . . such as it was. They pulled out when the shootin' stopped. They'll pass the word. The train won't have no more trouble from Injuns. They ain't never seen so much firepower as we showed today. They won't want to come up against that."

"You wish us to bury the dead, Captain?" Eudora asked.

"Hell, no! Leave 'em for the buzzards and the varmints. Take their horses, guns, and supplies and head on west." He looked at Steals Pony. "How many you figure got clear?"

"Twelve or so, I think. Not many more than that. Bedell, of course, was one of them."

"We get these women to the Willamette, then I'll take care of Bedell and what's left of his gang. I'll do it if I have to track that bastard clear to New York City." Preacher swung into the saddle and took up the lead rope to Snake's pony. "I'll catch up with you. Move 'em out, Blackjack."

Preacher headed for a place that he knew the Indians called the Silent Rocks. On a hill there, he buried Snake and covered the grave with rocks. He buried Snake facing west, for the old man had requested that, said he always liked to sit and smoke his pipe and watch the sun goin' down. Gave him a right peaceful feelin'.

Preacher took off his hat and held it by his side while he pondered on what he might say. "You done good, Snake," he said softly in the waning light of day. "You was a man to ride the rivers with, and we sure nuff rode a many of 'em, didn't we? We seen some country and had some fights. But it's your time to rest now. You sure earned that right. If any man did, you did. There ain't a whole hell of a lot of us left, Snake. And ever' time I plant another, I feel like I'm losin' a part of myself." He sighed heavily.

"I'm gonna turn your pony loose. You caught him wild, and he's a good'un. He'll hang around here for a day or two, doin' his grievin' for you in his own way, and then he'll find him some mares and sire some fine offspring. I ain't gonna chisel your name in no rocks, 'cause you asked me not to. I don't know what else to say, Snake."

Preacher sat for a time by the mound of rocks, smoking his pipe as the sun went down. His thoughts were all jumbled up. Talkin' with that man from Washington had got him to thinkin' hard 'bout his mother and father. After all this was over, he thought he might just take him a ride back east. See his ma and pa . . . 'fore it was too late to see anything except a grave. But first he had to get back to his valley and get his Appaloosa. Then he was going after Bedell and what was left of his gang. The ones that had got away were the bad ones. Villiers, Trudeau, Pierre, Gar, Slug and Pug—two brothers—and Tater had all run, one of the dying outlaws had told him. He had also begged for forgiveness, but Preacher had told him he was sorta short on that at the time.

There was also Able, Eli, Monroe, Logan, Wade, Jack Hayes, Rat-Face, Tom Cushing, and of course, Victor Bedell still alive. Preacher knew some of them, but some of them were completely unknown to him. 'Ceptin', of course, the knowledge that there wasn't a single one in the bunch worth a bucket of scummed-over, stinkin' buzzard puke.

Preacher sat by the grave of his old friend for a long time, lost in his many thoughts. The sun was long gone over the mountains and darkness had settled in hard around him before he made a move, and then it wasn't very far. He'd already unsaddled and picketed his horse, so he just ate a couple of biscuits, drank some water, and rolled up in his blankets.

Preacher was up before the sun and fixed coffee and bacon, sopping out the grease with chunks of pan bread he'd taken from the wagons. In the saddle, he paused and turned once to look at Snake's grave. "Goodbye, ol' hoss. You rest easy and be sure to ride ol' Hammer ever' now and then for me. Tell Hammer I'll be along sometime. We still got trails to ride."

Then he rode toward the west.

BOOK THREE

The sword of justice has no scabbard.
—Joseph De Maistre

1

It was several weeks before Preacher caught up with the wagons, and all could sense the change in him. And not just because he was riding a beautiful gray rump-spotted Appaloosa. The spotted horse was bigger than most of his breed, and had a mean look to his eyes, although he was gentle with Preacher and seemed devoted to him, which he was.

"What's his name, Preacher?" Rupert asked.

"Thunder."

"You've changed," the young officer said.

"I reckon I have."

"Why?"

"I got to get these ladies to the coast, and then I got Bedell and his bunch to deal with."

"Vengeance is mine, sayest the Lord."

"Not this time, Rupert. Not this time." Preacher rode on ahead.

He kept mostly to himself, ranging miles ahead of the wagons.

"I can't believe a man would love an animal so much that he would be obsessed with revenge over it," Faith remarked to Steals Pony one evening.

"There have been more men killed over horses and dogs than over women, lady," the Delaware replied. "Long years ago, Preacher found a little wolf pup whose mother had been killed. Preacher raised that wolf. Some whites say a wolf cannot be tamed. Whites say many foolish things. A wolf cannot be tamed like a dog, but if you gain that wolf's trust, in that respect the wildness within can be tempered. Preacher and that wolf were inseparable for several years. Then, a man named Ben Parsons killed the wolf. Killed it because he didn't like Preacher. This was back in, oh, I just don't remember. Preacher finally caught up with Parsons at the rendezvous of '28, on the south end of Bear Lake. Walked up to him, called him out, leveled a pistol, and shot the man dead. Preacher is not a man you want to cross."

"Preacher killed a man over his *wolf?*"

Steals Pony shook his head. "No. Preacher didn't own the wolf. You can't own another living thing. You can take care of it, love it, be a friend, but you can't *own* it. Preacher and the wolf were friends. Like that young man who lives down in the Colorado Rockies with a cougar and a wolf. Jamie Ian MacCallister."

"What do you mean, he lives with them?" Eudora asked. "You mean, they stay in the *house* with him?"

"If they want to, yes. His wife doesn't seem to mind. His young son sleeps with the puma. Rest assured, no one is going to bother the child when that puma is near," Steals Pony added very dryly. "That cat weighs about a hundred and fifty pounds. Very impressive animal."

Faith shook her head, sensing a story here for her father's paper and for her own fledgling publication. "Where have I heard the name MacCallister?"

"The lone survivor of the Alamo," Blackjack said. "Jamie came out here right after the Alamo fell. He married up with the gal who helped nurse his wounds and they come west soon as they could. I understand it took her a few months to get used to the way certain dangerous animals flocked to

Jamie, but she soon settled right in. She don't allow bears in the cabin though. She do draw the line there."

"Imagine that," Faith said, the sarcasm thick in her voice.

"What happened after Preacher shot that man?" April asked.

"Nothing," Steals Pony said. "Nobody liked Ben much anyway."

"It's finally getting through to me," Rupert said, refilling his coffee cup. "And I don't mean any ugliness or criticism in what I'm about to say. You people have brought it all back to the basics. Your laws are so simple that they are difficult to understand. You have taken your laws from the ways of the animals, in a manner of speaking."

"You're right to a degree," the Delaware agreed. "Back when we were actively trapping, a man would see another person's traps, but you never bothered them. Stealing from a man's traps could get you killed, and rightly so. Same with a man's cabin. If you were in need, you could use it, but if at all possible, replace what you used. Steal a man's horse, kill his horse or dog, and you get killed. Respect is the key. I respect your way of life, you respect mine. I respect what is yours, you respect what is mine. If a person chooses to disrespect the rights and property of others, well, we don't see the point of keeping that person alive. Because he isn't worth much. He takes more than he gives."

"But among civilized people, that way of thinking went out centuries ago," Faith pointed out.

The Delaware smiled. "Civilized people, you say?" He chuckled. "On this journey, dear lady, you have seen many Indian tepees. But you have yet to see one with a lock on the entrance."

Five and a half months after leaving Missouri, the wagons were at last within sight of their destination. Since the aborted ambush by Bedell, there had not been a single shot fired in anger, and very few other mishaps for the ladies on the train.

Madeline Hornbuckle said, "Perhaps God, in His Wisdom, decided we had been punished enough."

The women had forded rivers, struggled over mountain ranges, fought Indians, outlaws, and the elements, seen their numbers cut by a third, and now they were within an easy day's ride to the valley.

Eudora abruptly halted the wagons.

"What the hell's goin' on?" Preacher demanded, riding up to the lead wagon. "Yonder's the damn valley!"

"We camp here," Eudora told him.

"What!"

"We camp here," she repeated.

"Why?"

"So the ladies can bathe and fix their hair and change into proper attire," Rupert said. "It will do you no good to protest, Preacher. Believe me."

Preacher opened his mouth, then closed it shut after taking a good look at the set features of Eudora and Faith. He slowly nodded his head and swung down off of Thunder. "I reckon we'll camp here for the night."

The men were quickly ordered to stay the hell out of the circle of wagons. Eudora pointed to a grove of trees about a hundred yards or so from the wagons and the mountain men needed no other instructions. They dutifully trudged over to the trees and made their own camp. Young Louis thought he might be exempt. Eudora gave him a swift kick in the butt with her boot and Louis quickly joined the men.

Some of the men from the Willamette Valley decided they'd ride over to check out the ladies. It took them about fifteen seconds to realize they had made a ghastly mistake. Looking at the muzzles of fifty rifles will do that to a man. They joined the other men under the trees.

And it was then that Preacher realized he had been wrong about the man from Washington. The ladies were expected, and they were spoken for. It made him feel some better about politicians . . . but not much.

"This is becoming a regular yearly visit for you, Preacher," the chief banker of the post said to him, accepting a cup of coffee.

"Not no more," Preacher told him. "This is my last run. Somebody else can look out after them poor pilgrims from here on in. You got my money?"

The banker handed Preacher a thick envelope. Preacher thanked him and took his friends aside to divvy up.

"More money than I've seen in many a year," Blackjack said. "I think I'll leave the mountains and head on down to Californey and buy me a little business of some sort."

"You lie," Steals Pony told him.

"Shore, I do," Blackjack replied indignantly. "You didn't expect me to tell the truth, did you?"

"That would be a novel experience, to say the least," Steals Pony replied.

"What you gonna do, Delaware?" Blackjack asked.

Steals Pony cut his eyes to him. "Ride with Preacher if he wishes."

"Yeah," Blackjack said brightly. "I think that there's a right good idea."

But Preacher shook his head. "No, I 'ppreciate it. I truly do. But it's my fight, boys. And mine alone. It's a personal thing with me. I lost good friends on this run. They'd still be alive if it wasn't for me. Now they lay moulderin' in the ground. Them that we could find, that is," he added bitterly. "Y'all lay around the post and enjoy yourselves. After I say my goodbyes, I'll be pullin' out 'fore the dawnin'."

Preacher walked away.

"I don't feel a bit sorry for Bedell and them scum that ride with him," Blackjack said. "But I'd shore hate to have Preacher on my trail."

Faith had walked up while Preacher was stating his intentions of going it alone. She had just washed her hair and was toweling it dry. "Don't tell me," she said. "Let me guess.

He's going after those men, but the reason for his doing so, other than they killed some of his friends, is mainly because they killed his horse."

"You're learning, lady," Steals Pony told her. "You're learning."

"I never will understand that man!" she said, stamping her little foot.

That night, long after the wagons and most of the tents had gone dark and nearly everyone was sleeping, Preacher pushed back the flap on Faith's tent and stood for a moment.

She lay in her blankets, the lone lit candle highlighting the sheen of her strawberry blonde hair. Her shoulders were bare, and it wasn't hard for Preacher to see that under the blankets, everything else about her was bare, too.

"I thought you'd come by to say farewell," she said.

"I'm here."

"And?"

Preacher smiled and laid his rifle aside. She watched him kneel down by her bed and take off his shirt. She noted the bullet scars and knife scars and the place where he'd once had an arrow cut out. He was powerfully muscled. He reached out and gently touched her face with a hard and calloused hand.

"Is that the best you can do?" Faith asked.

Preacher chuckled softly and pinched out the candle.

When she awakened the next morning, Preacher had been gone from the camp for several hours. He had left her a note on his pillow.

"I know yore goin to writ about me. I dont mind. Just tell the truth."

"I shall, Preacher," Faith whispered. "Oh, I shall!"

2

The Appaloosa was a strong horse and loved to roam. Preacher had known when he'd first laid eyes on him he was the first horse he'd seen in a long time that would be a match for Hammer. By the time Faith had awakened, Preacher was miles from the Willamette Valley, heading east.

Preacher knew he had a long way to go and not a whole lot of time in which to do it. He guessed that it was the first week in September, and in the high-up country, light snow would already be dusting the land. What he had to do was talk to some Indians and they'd spread the word about Bedell. Then it wouldn't be long before somebody would have seen something and reported it. He did feel for certain that Bedell and his men would not chance heading back east. To do that would risk a hangman's noose.

Preacher headed straight east, taking the trails that he knew would get him there the fastest. After traveling for days, and speaking with dozens of Indians from many tribes, he got a fix on Bedell's location. A band of friendly Nez Perce did their best to trade him out from under Thunder, giving up when they only realized Preacher was not about to trade away his horse. It was then they told him about the band of white men—not mountain men—who, so they had heard, had been spotted repeatedly in the area of the land that smokes and thunders.

Preacher smiled at the news. He knew exactly where the land was that they were talking about. He'd wintered south of there a time or two, in a place called Jackson's Hole, and knew the area the Indians stayed out of 'cause they considered it to be spirit-haunted. A Frenchy had named the place Roche Jaune. Yellow Stone.

If Bedell and his people wasn't real careful, they'd get lost as a goose in that area, for the place had canyons that were so deep, they would boggle the mind, and dotting the landscape were holes, from which there were sudden fountain bursts of scalding hot water.

Preacher headed out, a grim smile on his lips. He figured he knew that area 'bout as well as any man and better than most. It was high-up country, in the Absaroka Range, and it was country to Preacher's liking. Bedell figured that the country was so isolated he'd be safe there. He was wrong. Dead wrong. With emphasis on *dead*.

Preacher stayed north of Hell's Canyon and rode through the Clearwater Mountains, heading for the Bitterroot Range. The nights grew colder and Thunder's coat began turning shaggy, in preparation for the bitterness of the harsh winter that was only weeks away. Preacher knew he had him a horse that was a stayer and a friend, but there would always be a soft spot in Preacher's heart for Hammer. He hoped that Man Above had allowed Ol' Snake to get together with Hammer, so's they could ride the clouds and the valleys of the Beyond. Ol' Snake would take good care of Hammer until the day come that Preacher would finally meet up with the Man Above.

Preacher was not a religious man, not in the sense of a Bible-shouter or them that followed the fiery spoutin' of gospel-thumpers. Preacher had been raised in the Church, but for years now he'd subscribed to the Indian way of thinking. Man Above had created all living things, and all living things that was useful to mankind had them a place up in Heaven. To the Pawnee it was Tirawa that was their principal god. The Cheyenne danced the Massaum, the animal dance, to ensure that the earth would remain bountiful—their main god was Wise One Above. To the Cheyenne, the soul was Tasoom. The Sioux, and many other plains tribes, had a dance they called Gazing At The Sun, which they did to help keep troubles from them. The Mandans danced and tortured themselves while doing the O-kee-pa, dressed as animals. To the Indians, and to Preacher, it was stupid to think that animals did not have a place beside Man Above up yonder in the Beyond.

The beaver was an engineer. The horse and the dog was man's friend, protector, and worker. Dogs came from wolves so the wolf certainly had a place Up Yonder. Buffalo kept the plains Indians from starving, kept them dressed, and provided material for their tepees, cooking utensils, and weapons. They, too, had them a place, as did the coyote, the bear, the eagle, and lots of other animals. Preacher did have some doubts about whether the rattlesnake would make it to Up Yonder, but he figured that since Man Above had created it, the damn thing had to be good for something. He just hadn't as yet figured out what that might be. He'd eaten rattlesnake more than once, when pickin's was slim. They were right tasty, but he wouldn't want to maintain a steady diet of it. Damn things was hell to catch.

Preacher stayed just south of the Salmon River and crossed over into the Beaverhead Mountains. He was camping in the Tendoys when the first big snow of the season came. Preacher knew it wouldn't last, and there would be many more pleasant days before winter locked up the high country, but when he pulled out, he quickened his pace, as much as the terrain would bear.

He crossed the Divide and headed down for the Tetons, after talking with a hunting party who told him that fifteen or so white men were in the Hole. Unfriendly white men. Quarrelsome and not prone to washing very often.

With few exceptions, the Plains Indians felt the white man was dirty most of the time . . . and they were right more often than not. An Indian would break the ice in a river or pond to bathe, and do it several times a day.

Preacher was camped along Bitch Creek when he caught the smell of wood smoke, and knew it wasn't coming from his fire. He took his Hawken and went looking. He grinned when he slipped up on the camp and eyeballed the three men around the fire. He started coughing like a puma and watched as the mountain men jumped up, grabbed their rifles, and started looking all around them. Preacher then howled like a wolf.

A man known only as Clapper narrowed his eyes as Preacher attempted, unsuccessfully, to contain his laughter. Clapper lowered his rifle in disgust. "Preacher!" he shouted. "Damn your eyes. Come on in here and sit and eat."

Clapper's companions were Joe Morris and Dave Nolan. After swapping some highly profane insults about each other's character, the men sat down to drink coffee and eat.

"I heared tell you was surrounded by petticoats earlier this year," Clapper said.

"I was. Got most of 'em over to the Valley. Now I'm lookin' for the men who ambushed the train and killed my good horse."

"Hammer's dead?" Joe asked.

"Buried him on the plains. You boys seen any signs of life over to the Hole?"

"Not personal, we ain't," Dave said. "But some wanderin' Flatheads told us they's a group of damn fools thinkin' 'bout winterin' in the Hole." He chuckled. "I allow as to how I near'bouts froze my butt off that winter me and Russell spent there. Back in '33, I think it was. We reckoned—without tellin' no lies 'bout it—it got down to close to seventy-five below at times. Joe Meek wintered in there last year, even after me tellin' him it was a frozen hell."

Preacher nodded his head and was silent. Clapper stared hard at him. "You huntin' these men, Preacher?"

"Yeah. I damn sure am." Then he told the mountain men about Bedell and what was left of his band, ending with, "On top of everything else, they killed Hammer."

The trio of mountain men all shook their heads in disgust, Clapper saying, "Me and the boys here would sure be proud to ride along with you, Preacher. Men like that don't need to be out here."

Preacher shook his head. "No. But I thank you boys. This is my show."

No one bothered to point out that one against fifteen was really lousy odds. Mountain men had been fighting against odds like that from the first moment a white trapper set foot in the wilderness, sometimes winning, sometimes losing.

Preacher stood up. "I'll go get my gear and bring it over here."

"Then you can tell us all about what it's like to be surrounded by a hundred and fifty fillies for two thousand miles," Dave Nolan said.

Preacher's eyes twinkled for a second or two. "Not the good parts, boys. Them's private."

Preacher stared out over what was then called Jackson's Hole. The mountains around the valley—approximately eighty miles long and fifteen miles wide—have been referred to as Teewinot by the Shoshoni. Others called them Shark's Teeth and Pilot Knobs. But the name a French trapper gave them has topped the list and remained constant over the years: The Grand Tetons. Big Breasts.

Preacher dismounted and squatted down for a time, studying the land below him. He was high-up, just below the timber line to give him some cover. He couldn't spot any smoke from cookfires, but he hadn't expected to see any. Bedell wasn't stupid, just arrogant. And he wasn't at all certain Bedell and his gang were even in the hole. They might have moved north to the land that thunders and smokes.

Preacher figured that's where he'd find most of them. A couple of Shoshoni had told him that the white men had split up, the larger band moving north out of the hole and into the place of haunted spirits.

If Preacher had his way, and he figured he damn sure would, he'd leave some more spirits up yonder to haunt the place.

He took his time heading down, staying with the timber whenever possible and utilizing every bit of cover he could find. The temperature, he figured, was in the fifties, with nighttime temperatures in the low thirties, and snow staying in the high country, melting during the day in the valley.

Reaching the valley, Preacher stayed away from the scrubby floor and stayed near the base of the slopes, weaving in and out of the timber. He paused often to swing down from the saddle and view his surroundings through his spyglass. Nothing. Then he left the slopes and headed onto the valley, staying to the west side of the Snake River.

Then he smelled the smoke. He stopped and looked all around him. But he could see no signs of fire. That meant the fire was a small one and built under low branches to dispel the smoke. The men weren't entirely stupid, he thought.

He swung down and picketed Thunder. Then he stood for a moment, sniffing the air. Taking his rifle, he headed out on foot, following the smoke odor as it became stronger.

He almost blundered straight into the small camp, catching himself just in time. The camp was a good one, well concealed, with a little lean-to built up against the side of a bluff. The lean-to told him it was a one-man camp. But he could see no man.

Preacher didn't want to harm some innocent, so he waited for the better part of an hour. He heard one shot, coming from the north, and figured the man had killed him a deer or elk. He made himself more comfortable and waited.

Sure enough, the man soon came trudging back in, toting the whole carcass. Preacher figured he planned on using the hide and didn't want to leave none of it behind for the wolves, coyotes, and bears. Although had it been Preacher who made the kill, he at least would have gutted the animal and spared himself some weight.

The man laid the deer down with a sigh and propped his rifle against the carcass. Then he straightened up, with both hands to the small of his back, and arched backward, sighing with relief, for the deer was not a small one. Preacher stepped out, his Hawken leveled, and the man's eyes widened in shock.

"Just stand easy and raise your hands," Preacher told him. "And I might decide not to kill you. Start makin' funny moves and I'll blow your kneecap off and leave you here to die."

"I told Bedell you was a devil," the man said. "I told him you'd not give up. And I was right," he added bitterly.

"Where's Bedell?"

"Gone north, up into the Absarokas. Him and most of the gang."

"How many?"

"Hard to say and I ain't lyin' 'bout that. Half a dozen more finally linked up with us some weeks after the failed ambush in the rocks. They got six of the women with 'em. Lara and Kim died on the trail."

"Give me a guess."

"I'd say twelve men and the women. They's five or six others like me who decided to go it alone. Providin' you let me live, what's my chances of makin' the winter here?"

"Poor to none," Preacher told him. "If Injuns don't get you, a grizzly might. If the bears don't eat you, the weather will more than likely kill you. This ain't no place for a damn pilgrim. Whereabouts in the Absarokas?"

"I don't know, and that's the God's truth. Somewheres along the river is all I know. Them Frenchies with Bedell said they knowed a place."

Preacher stared at the man for a moment. "When did you join up with Bedell?"

"I didn't leave out from Missouri with him, if that's what you mean. And I didn't have nothin' to do with the ambushin' of the train and the usin' of the women. I ride the dark trails, I'll admit that. But I ain't no rapist."

"But I only got your word for that."

"That's true. But I got me a tintype of my mother in my purse. How many outlaws you know would do that?"

Preacher grunted. "You got you two pistols outside your coat. How many you got *inside* your coat?"

"None."

Preacher leveled the Hawken, the muzzle straight at the man's belly. "If you're lyin', you're dead. Drop them pistols on the ground and open your coat."

The man did exactly as he was told. He was carrying no other weapon save a knife on his belt.

"Dress out that deer and fix us something to eat," Preacher told him, sitting down on a large rock. "You cook me a nice meal and I might just go on and leave you be. I'm a man who 'ppreciates good food."

"I'll fix you a feast!"

"You better."

He did. After Preacher had eaten enough for two men, he belched and wiped his hands on his buckskins. "You missed your callin', man. You ought to open you a eatin' place."

"You let me go, and I will. I'll swear on the Bible and my mother's picture."

Preacher thought about that for a moment. "You pack your gear and get gone from here. Take the south trail out of the Hole. They's a tradin' post south and some east of here. On the Green. If the Injuns ain't burned it down, that is. Follow the Green on down and you'll find the trail back east.

West is the cutoff, east is back home. Go back home. Don't never let me see you west of the Mississippi again."

"You're lettin' me go?"

"Git!"

Fifteen minutes later the man was gone. Preacher had let him take his rifle, his pistols, and a bait of grub.

Preacher followed the man for a-ways, and then brought his horses in close and cleaned out the lean-to, laying down fresh boughs for his bed. Then he set about jerking some of the venison. He fixed another steak for his supper, hung the meat up high, away from his camp, so's the bears couldn't get at it, and lay down to rest, his rifle and pistols at hand just in case the man he'd cut loose had a change of heart. He rested well that night and awakened fresh and ready to go.

A light snow had dusted the Hole during the night, but Preacher knew it would be gone by midmorning. The sky was blue and nearly cloudless and the sun was bright. He had him another venison steak for his breakfast and stowed his smoked meat, leaving the deer carcass for the animals. They had to eat too. He pulled out, taking the west trail, following Cottonwood Creek up to Jenny Lake. There, he camped for the night, after eating enough fresh-caught fish to grow gills. Five miles out of camp the next morning, he smelled smoke, and it wasn't no little one-man fire, neither. He felt he'd finally come up on the breakaway band of Bedell's men that the outlaw he'd cut loose had told him about. Checking his rifle and pistols, Preacher set out on foot.

"Now, by God," he muttered. "I start riddin' the land of two-legged vermin."

3

Preacher approached the outlaw camp cautiously. He was already sure that's what it was, for Indians had told him several times that no trappers were in the Hole or in the land that thunders up north of the Hole.

Three men and a woman were sitting around the fire. But there were five saddle horses at the picket line. Preacher sank down in the brush and waited. He was not close enough to make out what they were saying, only able to catch a word or so every now and then. They would all laugh from time to time. It was a dirty sort of laughter, followed by a lot of profanity, exactly what he'd expect from the low-life types in the rough camp. Preacher winced at some of the language being spoken. Preacher and his friends were no angels, and they could cuss with the best of them, but the language being used around the fire was of the sewer variety, and the words from the woman's mouth were just as bad, or worse, as the filth coming from the men.

When the fifth man finally made his appearance, coming in from the north, Preacher used the noise the man made settling in, as a cover to move in close enough to catch all the words being spoken. The newcomer poured a cup of coffee and sat wearily down with the group. "I went up high," he said; now Preacher could hear the words clearly. "No signs of anybody else in here with us. No smoke, no movement. Nothing. I think we're clear."

"Curtis's camp ain't that far to the south," a man said. "He'd have smoke from a fire."

"I 'spect he pulled out shortly after he left us," another man offered. "He never did have no stomach for this kind of work. He was a cook back east."

"But he killed three people!" the woman protested.

"He poisoned them," yet another man spoke.

Oh, wonderful! Preacher thought. And I et up his cookin' like a starvin' hog.

"Curtis never did like it out here," the first man said. "He wanted to go back to civilization. Hell with him. I don't trust no poisoner no way."

"You reckon Preacher give up the hunt?" the woman asked.

"I 'spect he did, Nelly. There ain't no one man gonna take out after no twenty men alone. I just wish we'd have brung along some of them women we had. I liked to hear 'um holler when all of us started humpin' 'um."

Then the men and the woman started mouthing and laughing about some of the most perverse and vulgar re-membrances of the kidnapping, and the days and nights that followed. It made Preacher's stomach churn. He lifted his rifle and ended the foul discussion by putting a ball right be-tween the eyes of one of the men. The outlaw's head snapped back and for a moment, he had a very odd expression on his face, before his heart told his brain he was dead. Then the man fell forward, face-first into the fire.

Preacher jerked out his pistols and let them roar just as the outlaw's hair caught on fire with a flaming, whooshing sound. Preacher was now standing up, a pistol in each hand, and he was cocking and firing the complicated weapons as fast as he could. When the pistols had emptied, Preacher stood completely enveloped in a thick cloud of gunsmoke and the campsite was littered with the dead, the screaming, and the dying.

Preacher shifted positions and reloaded, paying no attention to the howling of the badly wounded. The woman was screaming vile curses at him—the worst language he had ever heard come out of a woman's mouth. He reloaded his rifle last and then stepped into the clearing. Two were left alive, a man and the woman, and they would not be long for this earth.

The first dead man's head had cooked to steaming and it was a dreadful smell. Preacher pulled him out of the fire and rolled the carcass off to one side.

Nelly, screaming the vilest of curses at Preacher, reached for a gun and cocked it. Preacher quickly leveled a pistol and put an end to the profane shrieking.

The camp was suddenly very silent. The one mortally wounded survivor lay on the ground, shot twice through the stomach, and stared in silence at Preacher.

"You got anything to say," Preacher told him, "I 'spect you better get it said quick-like. 'Cause you sure ain't long for this world."

The last words out of the man's mouth were horrible curses, all directed at Preacher. Then he gasped, closed his eyes, and died.

"I sure wouldn't want to go meet my Maker with them words bein' my last," Preacher remarked. "But trash is trash right to the end."

Preacher put out the fire and packed up what supplies he felt he could use. He took powder, shot, caps, and lead and secured his new supplies on a second packhorse. He'd be damned if he was going to waste his time and energy on burying such trash as these. He left them where they lay and pulled out, heading for the land that smokes and thunders.

As he rode away, he did not look back at the dead. Overhead, the buzzards were already circling.

Miles to the north, Villiers stared morosely into the fire. The grease from the meat on the spit cracked and popped as it hit the flames. To the east and north, Granite Peak, almost thirteen thousand feet high, was clearly visible, the summit poking out from the clouds.

"You reckon Preacher's a-comin'?" Logan asked him in a low voice.

"Yeah," Villiers replied in a whisper. "You can damn well bet he's comin'. And he'll keep on comin' 'til we're all dead or gone to China or some goddamn place. I wish I'd never got mixed up in this mess."

"Let's you, me, Trudeau, and Pierre slip out and get gone." Logan's voice was very low. "We'll head to Canada, change our names, and start over."

"Man, can't you understand what I been tellin' you people over and over?" Villiers replied. "We done a harm to Preacher. He don't forgive and he don't forget. Not ever. He'll hunt us all to the grave. And then probably come back and haunt us. We got to stay together and stop him. Splittin' up is the worst thing we could do."

"Are you skirred, Villiers?"

Villiers slowly nodded his head. "Yeah. I'm scared, Logan. Preacher tracked a man from down near the Sangre de Cristos to clear up into Canada years back. He found him camped along the Battle. Left him dead on the riverbank. Wouldn't even bury him. You know what that man done? Stole his pelts. That's all. Just stole his pelts. You understand what we've done? We've kilt his friends and his horse, kidnapped women and girls and boys and tortured 'em and raped 'em and worser. And you ask me if I'm scared? Man, I'm so scared, I'm bound up so's I can't even take a decent crap. Now go away and leave me alone."

Sitting away from Villiers, Bedell's own thoughts were very much like those of the Frenchman. For the very first time in his long life of crime and mayhem, Victor Bedell was frightened. He had not been frightened of Preacher before. Yes, the man had thoroughly whipped him in a fight in St. Louis, but it had not been a fair fight. Preacher had fought like a savage, kicking, gouging, and biting, and otherwise engaging in pugilistic conduct unbecoming of a gentleman.

But now Bedell knew that Preacher was never going to give up. He was going to track them all down and kill them. Over a goddamned *horse!* Bedell had never heard of anything so ridiculous. A horse was just a damn dumb animal. Like a stupid dog. You beat it until it minded you, or if it didn't, then you killed it.

"But no one tracks down and kills another human being over a goddamned horse!" Bedell blurted out loud.

Villiers turned his head to stare at the man. "That's what you think," he said sourly. "I have. You kill a man's horse out here, you damn near condemn him to death. Logan's killed a man over a horse." Logan looked up and grinned when Villiers added, "Of course, Logan was stealing it from the man at the time."

"Ridiculous!" Bedell said, but all the men could detect the slight note of fear in his voice.

Preacher tracked the band of outlaws north over the Divide and up the east side of the lake and into the Absaroka Range. Whoever was doin' the guidin', Preacher deduced was keepin' way to the east of the scalding waters. Preacher had high hopes of sitting Bedell down on one of them big holes just about a minute before she blew. That blowhole would give his arrogant butt a cleanin' the bastard would never forget.

But Preacher concluded the chances of his bein' able to do that were slim to none.

Preacher figured he'd just have to settle for shootin' the no-count.

Maybe he could find him some wanderin' Blackfeet and hand Bedell over to them. The Blackfeet could get real inventive when it came to ways of dealin' with the likes of Bedell. They could make it last a long time.

Preacher went to sleep thinking of how Bedell would look after the Blackfeet got done with him. He knew one thing for a fact: that way of gettin' rid of Bedell would damn sure please the ladies who survived the wagons' trip west.

Preacher spent the next two weeks scouring the land for some sign of Bedell and his bunch. He roamed from Avalanche Peak clear up to Slough Crick looking for a sign of them. But Bedell and his pack of hyenas seemed to have just dropped off the face of the world. That would have been just fine with Preacher, but he knew that men like Bedell and them who rode with him seemed only to survive when the good and the decent died young.

Preacher was determined to change that, at least for this go-around.

When Preacher awakened the next morning, he stretched in his blankets and took him a lung full of high mountain air. With the cold air, he sucked in the strong smell of wood smoke and the faint odor of frying bacon.

He smiled and came out of his blankets like a puma on the hunt. He dressed quickly, knowing that it was no bunch of Indians fryin' bacon. "Got you!" he said.

4

Making certain that Thunder was safe in a brush corral—which he could easily break out of, should Preacher not return—with plenty of graze and water available, Preacher took his rifles, his bow and quiver of arrows, his pistols and ample shot and powder, and struck out on foot, literally following his nose.

Bedell and his gang had either been so close to him, it was like that old saying about not seeing the trees for the woods, or the outlaws had shifted their camp and moved in close while Preacher was asleep. Either way it went, Preacher was about to end this show. The fact that he was going up against fifteen-to-one odds never slowed his step. He figured the more people in the camp the more confusion he could cause. Hell, some of them just might end up shootin' each other 'fore he got through.

The smell got stronger and Preacher slowed his step, weaving through the thickening timber as he worked his way down near to the flat valley floor.

He stopped, not believing his eyes. Bedell had picked the worst campsite Preacher had ever seen. The man was either a total fool or so arrogant that he believed he and his gang were all alone in the wilderness.

They were camped smack in the middle of a clearing, with timber all around them. They had them a fire going that you could roast an ox over, and they were all huddled around it, cookin' breakfast and boilin' water for coffee. And there was Bedell, just as big as brass, with Jack Cushing and Rat Face right beside him. That damn Villiers was standin' beside Trudeau and two others that Preacher didn't know right off.

Preacher carefully worked his way closer to the clearing. If he made the spot he'd chosen, he would be less than seventy-five yards from the group when he opened fire. My, but the smell of bacon and coffee was making his mouth water. After he did the deed, he just might sample some of that breakfast. Preacher lifted both rifles, holding them like pistols, and blew Eli and Able straight to hell, the heavy balls doubling them over and sending them lurching to the ground. Preacher jerked out both pistols and charged up to the edge of the timber, screaming like an angry panther.

Two men jumped up from the ground and ran into the timber on the far side of the clearing just as Preacher opened up with his pistols. Trudeau and Logan went down next, both of them belly-shot. A woman that Preacher recalled was named Ruby something or another grabbed up a pistol and fired it at Preacher. The ball came so close Preacher could hear the whiz and feel the heat. Preacher grabbed up a rifle and fired just as Ruby turned to charge up her pistol. Preacher's ball struck her at nearly pointblank range and took part of her head off.

Preacher ducked back into the timber and frantically reloaded, looking up every few seconds to scan the scene in front of him. His guns just half-loaded up, Preacher started shooting arrows into the clearing. He could not understand why the men and women did not run for the timber. After a man and woman went down from the arrows, the others seemed to realize that they were terribly exposed and as one, they hit the air for the timber, on foot, leaving everything behind them in their frantic retreat.

Preacher shifted positions, bellied down in some brush, and quickly reloaded everything up full. Some of the horses had broken free from their ropes and had run off, out of the clearing, away from the noise of guns and the screaming and yelling of people. Preacher lay still as death in the brush and waited. Near as he could figure, there was twelve or thirteen men still out yonder, and five women. The woman who'd stepped into the path of an arrow meant for Bedell had taken it in the throat and was making all sorts of horrible noises as she thrashed around. The man had taken Preacher's arrow in the center of his chest and he was not moving. The woman suddenly rolled onto the fire and her dirty, greasy clothing burst into flames. She hollered and jerked and squalled awhile longer and then fell silent as the cold hand of death shut her evil mouth and stilled her vile oaths.

Preacher had not moved anything except his eyes since he'd crawled under the brush. His eyes caught movement across the clearing. Rat Face was slippin' around, nearly as furtive as the rodent he was named after. Preacher let him slip. He was after bigger game. He could not use his bow; the brush prevented that. He did not want to fire and give away his position . . . unless, that is, he could get a shot at Bedell. And Bedell was not about to expose his arrogant butt for that. He'd probably crawled up inside a hollow log. Preacher hoped the bastard came nose to snout with a bear.

"He's gone!" someone yelled.

"Don't you believe it," another voice said. "He ain't gone. He's waitin' for some of us to show."

"Somebody kill that son of a bitch!" Bedell screamed from deep in the brush.

"You can't kill something you can't see," Villiers said. "Just stay put. He's got to move sometime."

"What's that horrible smell?" a woman called.

"Nina," Villiers said. "She rolled into the fire."

And shore ruined my breakfast, Preacher thought. Damned inconsiderate of her.

"That's disgusting," another whore said.

"I'm sure she would have preferred not to do it," Villiers called.

"She still stinks."

"I think he really is gone," a man called, and Preacher almost jumped out of his skin. The man was not more than five feet from where he was hiding in the thick brush. "I've worked all around the clearing and didn't see a thing."

"You won't see anything of Preacher," Villiers said. "The Injuns don't call him Ghost Walker for nothin'."

"He's gone," another voice said from Preacher's left. "I can see Gar from where I'm at and no sign of Preacher."

"Then if you're so sure, Wade," Villiers called, "you and Gar step out into the clearin'."

But neither man was that sure Preacher was gone.

Preacher waited, as silent as the ghosts that were his namesake.

"How many's down?" Bedell shouted from deep in the timber across the way.

"Eli, Able, Trudeau, Logan, Nina, Ruby, Pete, Dixon."

Bedell cursed.

"Everybody stay right where they are," Villiers called from his hiding place. "Nobody move. We got all the time in the world."

No, you haven't, Preacher thought. The sands of time is runnin' out fast for all of you.

The minutes ticked past and the outlaw men and women got restless, just as Preacher figured they would. Villiers and Pierre didn't, however, and Preacher had figured that, too. Those were mountain men turned bad, and they had just about as much patience as Preacher.

The man to Preacher's close right suddenly sprang out of the timber and into the clearing. He ran for a pile of supplies and disappeared behind it. Then the man on Preacher's left did the same. Preacher did not move anything except his lips, which curved into a knowing smile.

Another man cautiously stepped out of the timber across the clearing. Another followed him; then another man and a woman stepped from the timber sanctuary.

"He's gone," Jack Hayes finally said. "The ambushin' sorry son is really gone."

Preacher then shot Jack through the head, and, grabbing up his second rifle, he gave Rat Face the same, but just a mite lower. Rat Face doubled over as the big ball tore into his innards and blew out the back of his shirt. Rat Face sat down on the ground and yelped once, very weakly. Then he toppled over dead.

Preacher grabbed up his pistols and gave those in the clearing every barrel, and he had double-shot several. Wade and Gar had ridden their last dark trail.

The sounds of galloping horses reached Preacher as he was reloading as quickly as he could. The bloody ground grew silent and the gunsmoke wafted away on the fall breezes. Preacher worked his way out of his cover. Staying in the timber, Preacher made his way all around the clearing, then through to a patch of clearing. Far away, he could see the riders still galloping on their horses. He counted nine, maybe ten. At this distance, he couldn't be sure. One thing he could be sure of was that he had played hell with Bedell's gang and that he now had most of their supplies. And winter was only a few weeks off.

Preacher returned to the clearing and packed up what he felt he could use and secured the riggin' on a big packhorse that had broken loose. He took all the powder . . . and there were several small kegs, in addition to the horns each man and woman had carried. He smashed the rifles and pistols so the Injuns wouldn't get them and turned the horses loose to run wild. He rolled the bodies away from the fire and opened the lid and took him a sniff of the nearly full coffeepot.

Smelled all right to him. But Nina had fallen across the bacon and ruined the hell out of that.

Preacher drank a cup of coffee and felt better. He chewed on some bread he'd found and poured another cup.

"You . . . cold, black-hearted bastard!" A man gasped the words at him.

Surprised the hell out of Preacher. He was sure he'd inspected all the bodies and found them dead. He turned to look at the man who'd spoken.

"Who be you, Pilgrim?"

"John Lucas. From Arkansas." The man's coat was soaked with blood. Preacher wondered how the man was still alive.

"You shoulda stayed to hearth and home, John Lucas. You look sort of peaked to me. And you damn shore shoulda picked better company to ride with."

"Don't you . . . preach no sermons to me . . . you godless heathen! Sittin' there . . . stuffin' your mouth full . . . amid the dead . . . damn your eyes."

"I hate to see vittles go to waste." Preacher looked around the body-littered clearing. " 'Sides, they don't appear to be a bit hungry."

"You're a . . . savage, man! A savage, I . . . say." He moaned out the last word.

"I'm a savage, hey?" Preacher said with a smile. "Me and you, John Lucas, we have shore got different interpertutions of that word."

"You can't even . . . speak proper English," John gasped.

"Can too. If I want to." Preacher finished his coffee and bread and poured another cup. "You want a cup, John Lucas?"

"No."

"It's gonna be the last one you ever taste on this earth. You reckon they got coffee in hell?"

"I wouldn't know. I'm a baptized Christian."

Preacher had him a good laugh at that. "Christian, hey? Church shore ain't what it used to be."

"If I had the strength, I'd kill you!" John Lucas said, blood leaking out of his mouth and nose.

"Oh, and I wouldn't blame you, neither. I 'magine I did mess up your day quite a bit."

"I feel sorry for my . . . poor mother."

"I do too," Preacher said solemnly, nodding his head in agreement. "I 'magine it grieved her old heart something terrible to see her boy turn out to be such a rotten no-count scallywag like you. You want me to post a letter to her?"

"I don't want you to . . . do anything 'cept . . . die, you bastard!"

"You closer to doin' that than me, John Lucas. But I will be nice and plant you. I ain't plantin' none of these others though. You was kind enough to engage me in civil conversation over vittles, and that was fairly polite, so I'll bury you."

"Oh, Lord!" John shouted. "I'm comin' home!"

"I hate to break this news to you, but you shoutin' in the wrong direction, John Lucas."

"I see the light, Lord!" John gasped.

"Them's probably the flames of the pits," Preacher muttered.

John Lucas belched, broke wind, and died.

"Hell of a way to check out," Preacher said, pouring the remainder of the coffee over the fire.

He then buried the man like he said he would and, using a knife taken from the scabbard of one of the others, Preacher carved into a tree: JOHN LUCAS, 1839. HE WAS A FOOL.

5

Preacher took his time tracking the remnants of Bedell and his gang as they headed deeper into the Absaroka wilderness. Wilderness to most of them, home ground for Preacher. He suspected that sooner or later, probably sooner, they would have an ambush set up for him.

They had to be hurting, for Preacher knew they had precious few supplies left, and if they had doubled back—which they had not done, as yet—they would have found that Preacher had burned all the supplies he hadn't taken with him. So far he had heard no shots at all, so they weren't eating any fresh meat. He didn't know what they were doing for food, for they were no more than a few miles ahead of him and in this country he would have heard any shots.

"Goin' hungry, probably," he muttered.

Just then his ever-roaming eyes caught a bit of color that didn't fit in with the surroundings. He left his saddle about one second before the rifle boomed. Rolling to his knees, Preacher brought his Hawken to his shoulder and sighted in. His shot was true and the man stumbled out of cover, both hands holding his punctured belly, his face pale with pain and shock. Tom Cushing fell to his knees and cried out.

"You've killed me, Preacher!" he screamed.

"I damn sure tried my best," Preacher called over the distance.

Tom Cushing fell forward on his face and began sobbing like a baby.

Preacher squatted where he was and reloaded. Then he slowly looked all around him. His packhorses were grazing and Thunder, after looking around, joined them. Preacher walked up to the crying man and stood over him. Tom rolled over onto his back and stared up at the mountain man.

With tears cutting paths through the grime on his face, Tom said, "You played hell with us, Preacher."

"You should have took my advice back in Missouri, Tom. I told you to go on home and leave me alone."

"You gonna bury me proper and read words from the Good Book over my grave?"

"I ain't plannin' on it."

"But you cain't just leave me for the varmits!" the gut-shot man wailed.

"Why not? That's what you'd a-done for me. And don't say you wouldn't have. You don't wanna die with a lie on your lips."

"Oh, Lord!" Tom squalled. "My poor body's gonna be et by a bear."

Preacher kicked the man's rifle away from his reach and threw his pistols into the brush. Then he sat down on a rock and chewed on a piece of jerky. "You best hurry up and expire," he told Tom. "I ain't gonna sit around here no two or three days and listen to you complain."

"Sweet Baby Jesus!" Tom said. "You the hardest man I ever seen in all my borned days!"

"You come after me, Tom. I didn't start this affair. I told you to leave me alone."

"Do something for me!"

"Cain't. Ain't nothin' I can do. Can you move your legs?"

"No. I can't feel nothin' from my waist down."

"You're done for."

That really set Tom to hollerin'. He squalled and blubbered, prayed and cussed.

"If you'll shut up and stop all that blasphemin', I'll bury you proper," Preacher finally told him. "Way you're actin' now, you're givin' me a headache."

"You promise you'll see me in the ground proper?"

"Yeah, yeah. I promise."

"Bless you, Preacher."

"Just get on with it, Tom."

It got kind of rough for Tom toward the end, as Preacher knew it would. But he could work up no sympathy for the man. Folks who choose to ride a dark and twisted trail do so willingly and with full knowledge that at trail's end lies a violent passage to the other side. But Preacher had to admit that Tom's end was sort of pitiful. He didn't go out like a man. One minute he was cryin' and prayin', hollerin' and turnin' the bloody ground into a revival, the next instant he was gone.

Preacher had dug the hole while Tom was implorin' Heavenly choirs to sing him home gently. Preacher had found Tom's horse and stripped saddle and bridle from the animal and turned him loose. He rolled Tom up in his blanket and laid him to rest, then covered the shallow grave with rocks.

Preacher took off his hat and looked up at the amazing blue of the skies. "Lord, You do what You've a mind to with this sorry piece of crap. That's all I got to say."

He then swung into his saddle and headed out. "One less," he muttered. "Eight or nine to go."

That afternoon, he rounded a curve in the animal trail and whoaed up at the sight before him. Four women were sitting on a fallen log. They had propped their rifles against a tree and their pistols were lying on the ground a dozen feet from them. Their horses were picketed nearby. The women looked up at Preacher and one said, "I'm Camille. This is Lydia, Nadine, and Melba. We left Bedell. We're tired, hungry, cold, and lost. We give up. We surrender to you."

"Hell, I don't want you," Preacher told them. "I wouldn't even take the lot of you on a bet."

"You can't just leave us here!" Nadine screamed loud enough to shake leaves from the trees.

Preacher winced and Thunder laid his ears back. Damn whore had a voice that would put a puma to shame. "I'll give you enough food to see you through and blankets to keep you warm. And I'll point you in the right direction. Other than that, you ladi . . . women is on your own." And God help any Indian who blunders up on you, he added silently.

To a person, the ladies cussed him loud and long. Preacher swung down from Thunder and faced them. When they had paused for breath, he said, "You cuss me one more time and I'll leave you out here with just what you got, and you damn well better believe I'll do it, too."

The four whores sat in sullen silence and stared at him. "That's better," Preacher told them. He unloaded supplies and laid them out on the ground. "That way," he said, pointing.

"But what if we're taken captives by the red savages?" Camille hollered.

"Just squall once or twice," Preacher replied. "I guaran-damn-tee you they'll turn you loose faster than you can blink. Injuns ain't stupid. Goodbye."

Preacher got gone from there as fast as he could. The women could not tell him where Bedell and his shrinking band of crud and crap had gone, and Preacher believed them. He didn't know if the women would make it out of the wilderness, and he didn't much care. But they had a pretty good chance of making it. They stunk to high heaven and no self-respecting Injun would get within ten feet of them. They were as vicious a lot as Preacher had ever run across and he wouldn't trust none of them any further than he could throw a grizzly. But he was glad he wouldn't have to harm no more of them. Shootin' a woman sort of cut across the grain . . . even women like them that had thrown in with Bedell.

Bedell looked at what was left of his gang. The brothers, Slug and Pug, and the two French trappers turned outlaws, Villiers and Pierre. So this was the end of it, Bedell thought. All my fine plans, hopes, and dreams, smashed to naught by a damn ignorant, savage mountain man. He watched as Villiers straightened up from warming his hands over the little fire.

"This is it for me," the man announced. "I ain't runnin' no more. I been in these mountains for most of my life. And if I'm to die, it'll be right here."

Pierre nodded his head. "I'm with you. I'm tired of bein' chased."

Slug looked at Pug and the brothers slowly nodded their heads. "We'll stand with you," Pug spoke for both of them.

"I'm leaving," Bedell said, standing up and walking toward his horse. "I'll not just give up and let that wretched bastard kill me." He swung into the saddle and rode off, taking one packhorse with him.

"Good riddance," Villiers said, watching the man ride away to the east.

"I never did like that man," Slug said. "I ain't got no use for nobody who thinks he's better than me."

"Look at him now," Pierre said. "Dirty, ragged, and scared." He laughed aloud as Bedell vanished from view. "Think about it, boys. We had, all told, about a hundred men. And this is what's left. Squattin' over a fire in the Absarokas, waitin' to shoot it out with a human wolf. I . . ." He stopped as the howl of a timber wolf cut the cold air. Pierre shivered. "There he is, boys."

And he was very close.

Pug looked up, his eyes wide with fear. "Can we make a deal with him?"

Villiers laughed bitterly. "Deal? With Preacher? Forget it. Load up full, boys. Now we really get to see the elephant."

Slug stood up in time to catch an arrow directly in the center of his chest. His hands clutched at the arrow for a few seconds, then he fell over backward.

"No!" his brother screamed, snatching up his rifle and firing it blindly at the timber.

"Damn fool!" Pierre shouted. "Get down."

But the admonition was too late. Preacher's second arrow took Pug in the neck and dropped him, the bloody point sticking out the other side.

The two renegade trappers exchanged glances. "Can we talk, Preacher?" Villiers shouted.

Silence greeted his question.

"Damnit, man, I didn't kill your horse!" Pierre yelled.

A funny-looking arrow came whizzing out of the timber.

"What the hell is that thing?" Villiers asked. "What's that tied to the end of it?"

"It's a fire arrow," Pierre said. "Oh, shit!" he hollered. "It ain't either. It's a . . ."

The bag of black powder exploded. The explosion didn't do a lot of damage, but it did scare the crap out of the men as it showered them with dirt and burning bits of cloth that Preacher had stuffed in with the powder. Both men instinctively jumped up, slapping at themselves and hollering. It was to be their last jump before slipping into hell. They both realized their mistake too late.

Preacher shot them both.

Villiers opened his eyes. He wasn't in a lot of pain, but he knew he was hard hit. He cut his eyes over to Pierre. He was dead, sitting with his back to a boulder, a bullet hole in the center of his forehead. He slowly moved his head. Preacher was sitting by the fire, drinking the last of their coffee and staring at him.

"How bad am I, Preacher?"

"Lung-shot. I dusted you from side to side. You want some coffee?"

"Yeah. Thanks."

Preacher put the cup in his hand.

"It don't hurt none, *mon ami.*"

"Mayhaps it won't. You ain't got long."

"We played out our string with the wrong man, didn't we?" He took a sip of coffee and slipped his left hand behind his sash.

Preacher smiled. "I tossed away that little pistol of yours, Villiers. Yeah, you shoulda stayed with trappin'. Bedell was a bad choice."

"That's a good little derringer pistol, Preacher. That's an Ethan Allen."

Preacher nodded.

"Gettin' dark, Preacher."

"I'll tell the boys you died well."

"Merci. Did the others die well?"

"Not many of them."

"That does not come as any surprise to me. They were riffraf."

"Got any kin, Villiers?"

"Non. But thank you for asking." Villiers began coughing hard. He spit out blood.

Preacher waited and then asked, "Vic Bedell cut and run, did he?"

Villiers caught his breath and nodded his head. *"Oui.* He was a coward. But you watch him, Preacher. Cowards are dangerous when cornered."

"I know."

The coffee cup had overturned, the hot coffee scalding Villiers' hand. The man seemed not to notice. Preacher reached over and took the cup. Villiers didn't notice that, either.

"I'm glad it was you who did the deed, Preacher. I'm really glad it . . ."

Villiers fell back and died.

Preacher did not bury any of the men. They would not have expected that courtesy and he damn sure didn't offer it.

He'd seen Bedell's tracks and had guessed accurately that Bedell would try for the east. "Run all you want to, Bedell," Preacher said. "I'm right behind you."

6

Preacher lost the trail.

He tracked him to Rock Creek, and then the trail went cold. He just couldn't believe it. Preacher hadn't lost a trail in years. He sat on Thunder and did some fancy cussin', turnin' the air fairly blue. But he still knew Bedell was headin' straight east, so that's the direction Preacher took. It was getting cold. Preacher headed south and west, making about twenty-five to thirty miles a day. By the time winter struck its first hard blow, he was out of the high country and onto the plains, heading east. Not that it wasn't cold on the plains, for it damn sure was. But nothin' like bein' caught ten thousand feet up and the temperature seventy below zero and the winds screamin' at better than fifty miles an hour.

Preacher stopped at an Indian village and swapped his spare packhorses for a new set of buckskins, and they was fancy ones, too. He'd save them to wear when he hit the civilized middle of the nation. A couple of days out of the village, some young bucks come along lookin' for a fight. There was four of them, and they wanted to impress the girls. Preacher spoke to them in sign language and they relaxed when they learned who he was and what he was doing. Preacher continued on without incident.

He rode across Missouri in the middle of winter, and he marveled at the nice roads. Why, they was even graded ever' now and then to smooth them out. Folks back here sure lived an easy life.

And St. Louis liked to have plumb startled him out of his 'skins. The place was boomin'. People ever'where and both the gentlemen and their ladies walked around all gussied up and fancy lookin'.

Didn't take Preacher long to get his fill of that place. Some folks was beginnin' to look down their snooty noses at him. By talking with tavern owners that knew him from the past, and trappers who were now in other businesses, Preacher learned that Bedell had come through. He had conned money out of some people and headed on east. One of Preacher's old friends told him on the quiet that he'd heard that Bedell was heading for the southern part of Ohio.

"Totin' guns is rapidly becomin' a thing of the past once you cross the Mississippi, Preacher," a friend told him. "Law and order is the thing now."

"They leave me alone and I'll damm shore leave them alone," was Preacher's reply.

He pressed on, determined to find Bedell.

He rode the ferry 'crost the Mississippi and stepped onto Illinois soil. It was like a whole new world to the man who had spent nearly his entire life in the wilderness. He hadn't ever seen so many people. They were everywhere he looked. And they was all lookin' at him! He didn't understand how anybody could ever get any rest with all the commotion. Why, you couldn't ride an hour on the roads without seein' somebody a-foot, or in a wagon, or on a horse. Damned if he'd want to live like this.

In a small town just across the Wabash, Preacher had his first run-in with civilization. He had stopped at a tavern on the edge of town, a coach stop, for a glass of ale and a plate of food. He had become accustomed to the stares and whispers from people and didn't pay much attention to it anymore. He had cut his hair and shaved, leaving only a mustache, and he had bought himself a new hat in St. Louis. Other than that, he still wore his buckskins and high-topped Apache moccasins. If people didn't like the way he dressed, they could all just go right straight to hell.

He heard the door open and felt the blast of cold air. But he did not turn around to see who it might be. He just wasn't that interested.

"Who owns that funny-looking, rump-spotted horse in the livery?" a loudmouth asked.

Preacher took him a swig of ale and turned his head. A big-bellied man wearing a star on his chest stood in the center of the room. Preacher took a dislike to him right off. He knew the type and had no use for them. "I do, lard-ass," he told the man. Then he resumed his eating.

The room became very quiet, very quickly.

"What'd you call me?" the badge-toter said in a shocked tone.

"I said you was a lard-ass." Preacher raised his voice. "And don't you be callin' my horse funny-lookin'. You'll hurt his feelin's. I got to live with him, you don't. You ever tried to ride a humiliated horse?"

Heavy footsteps shook the floor. The badge-toter stopped at Preacher's table and stared down at him. "I'm the law around here."

"Congratulations. Now go away."

A heavy hand fell on Preacher's shoulders. It was a very bad mistake. "I think you better come with me to the jail. I don't like you very much."

Preacher drove his fist into the big man's groin. The marshal hit the floor, both hands to his groin. He rolled around and moaned and groaned.

Preacher ignored him and finished his meal, laying a coin on the table when he was done. Then he stood up and plopped his hat on his head just as the marshal was slowly getting to his boots. The marshal made his second mistake when he reached for the pistol in his belt. Preacher flattened him, stretching him out stone-cold unconscious on the floor. Feller seemed to like the floor a lot, Preacher thought.

Preacher turned as several men crowded in through the front door. One of them was an older feller, an intelligent-looking, nicely dressed man who bore an air of importance about him. Preacher got the impression that the man had been across the river a few times. He had that look about him.

The older man sized up the mountain man quickly. He'd seen the type and knew them for men who could be extremely dangerous at the blink of an eye. "Why did you knock Marshal Bobbins to the floor, young man?"

" 'Cause he insulted my horse and then put his goddamn hands on me and tried to tote me off to jail. No man puts his hands on me. Not you, not nobody."

The older man could not contain his smile. "And your name, sir?"

"Preacher."

All heads turned. Preacher was one of the most famous mountain men in all the nation. Right up there with Carson, Bridger, Beckwourth, Smith, and Hugh Glass.

"I . . . see," the man replied. "Well, I am Judge Madison. I'm pleased to make your acquaintance, Mister, ah, Preacher."

"Same here," Preacher said, and stepped over the unconscious marshal, who had not moved since his latest encounter with the tavern floor.

"Might I have a few words with you, sir?" the judge asked.

"All right."

"We'll use your back room, Sidney," the judge told the barman. Sidney nodded.

Preacher picked up his rifle and followed the judge and the other men into the vacant room. "Ale, Sidney," the judge said. "And some of you men carry the marshal back to his office." Then he closed the door.

Seated at the table, the pitcher of ale and glasses before them, the judge asked, "Your first time back to, ah, civilization, Preacher?"

"It's been a while."

"Things have changed, sir."

"I noticed. You folks give badges to loudmouthed bullies, do you?"

"It can be a very rough job, Preacher. Takes a rough man."

"He wouldn't last fifteen minutes in the wilderness," Preacher countered. "He'd be totin' that badge in a mighty uncomfortable place."

The judge could not contain his chuckle while one of the other men looked embarrassed. "Preacher," the judge said, "I must give you some advice. You may take it, or ignore it. But I assure you, I mean well."

"Speak your piece."

"You have come from a land filled with hostiles and fraught with danger. But it isn't that way here. We have laws and codes of conduct that most obey and follow. The marshal was out of line. Frankly, I feel he deserved what he got. Others will not see it that way. They would feel he was only doing his job the best he saw fit. You are traveling east, sir?"

"I am."

"The laws will become more firmly enforced the further east you travel. You will be seeing more towns and villages with more marshals, more constables, and more sheriffs. The wearing of skins has almost passed. So you will be attracting more and more attention as you travel. Most lawmen will be cordial and civil with you. There will be some who might take a more aggressive stance."

"If they bother me whilst I ain't done nothin', they won't be aggressive for long." Preacher spoke the words hard and flat and no man there doubted the famed mountain man's intent.

"Some cities have passed laws forbidding the carrying of firearms."

"I hope they don't try to forbid me."

"Do you understand what I am trying to tell you, Preacher?" the judge pressed him.

"Sure I do. And I thank you kindly." He stood up. "I'm not a trouble-huntin' man, Judge. I come east to do two things. One of them is to see my ma and pa. I ain't seen them in over twenty years. Now compared to you-all and your hand-sewn pretty duds, I know I just look like a savage, but fancy clothes don't no gentleman make. As long as people leave me alone, there ain't nobody got nothin' to fear from Preacher. Oh, tell your marshal he best find a job farmin'. Constablin' seems to be a mite wearin' on the man."

Four days later, Preacher swung down from the saddle and gave the reins to a livery boy. "Rub him down and feed him good, boy," he told the young man, who was staring openmouthed at Preacher's manner of dress. "Dave Mott still own this place?"

"Yes, sir."

"Fine." He gave the boy a coin and walked into the combination general store, tavern, hotel, eatin' place, and livery.

An old man looked up from behind the counter and grinned hugely. "Wagh!" he hollered. "Ain't you a sight to behold, Preacher."

The two men hugged each other and done a little dance, much to the delight of several of the patrons, who were shopping in the store.

"You old mountain lion!" Preacher said. "How can you stand it out here amongst all these pilgrims?"

Dave Mott had left the mountains about ten years back, bought this place, and settled in. Had said his rheumatism was gettin' too bad for him to stay up in the high country any longer. Dave had kept in touch right good though. Why, he'd posted three letters west in ten years. Even though it sometimes took them two years or so to reach the addressee.

"I heard you got married, Dave."

"I did. My wife's visitin' her sister up country. You let me wait on these customers and we'll crack us a jug and talk some, Preacher."

When the customers were gone, Dave closed the store, and then he and Preacher went into the tavern part and opened a bottle of whiskey, taking a corner table. They had the place to themselves.

"I come east for two reasons, Dave," Preacher said. "I want to see my ma and pa one more time, and I'm huntin' a man."

Dave slugged back a snort and said, "I got a man stayin' here who acts like he's bein' hunted. Funniest-actin' feller I ever did see. Name is Bedell."

Preacher set his cup down with a bang. "Vic Bedell?"

But Dave shook his head. "No. But they might be brothers. This man's name is Chris Bedell."

"Age?"

"Oh, 'bout fifty, I'd guess. Slender man but well put together. Gray hair."

Preacher shook his head. "That ain't the one I'm huntin'."

"Be that as it may, I don't trust this gent. He's got a shifty eye and a sharp tongue. But . . . he pays hard coin and don't cause no trouble. Maybe he's waitin' on this feller you're huntin'."

"Could be."

"Let me get the girl to fix you up in the best room I got, Preacher."

Preacher waved that off and Dave laughed, knowing why he was refusing a bed. Took Dave five years before he could be comfortable in a bed.

Preacher said, "You know me, Dave. I don't care for no

feather ticks. I git all smothered up in them things. Too soft. I got to sleep where I can breathe and move around. I'll pile up in the barn and wait around for a few days. Bedell ain't no common name." He told Dave why he was after Bedell and Dave's face hardened.

"I won't suggest you callin' the law, Preacher."

"Good. 'Cause I ain't. But I won't kill him here and bring no trouble down on you. That's my word on it."

"Good! Now let's have us some drinks and then we'll table up. I got meat and potatoes and gravy, and fresh baked bread and sweet butter and jams."

"I got a better idea, Dave."

"What?"

"Let's eat *now!*"

7

Preacher stayed close to Dave's businesses for several days. He kept to himself and away from Chris Bedell. But after seeing the man only one time, he knew it was Vic's brother. The family resemblance was strong and undeniable.

Chris Bedell kept to his room most of the time, leaving only to check for mail in town every day, and to take his meals, which he did sitting alone in the tavern part of the business. No doubt about it, according to Preacher's mind: the man was waiting for his brother.

Thunder was getting plenty of rest, food, and care, and Preacher was getting downright lazy, with no Indians to have to watch out for, or grizzlies or pumas. Damn place was just downright borin'.

On the fifth day of Preacher's stay at the roadhouse, slimy Vic Bedell showed up. Preacher watched from the loft of the livery stable and smiled as the stagecoach stopped and Vic stepped out. His valise was tossed down to him and the stage rattled off. Chris Bedell hurried out and shook his brother's hand and then the two of them disappeared into the large building.

Preacher was sort of at a loss as to what to do next. He didn't want to bring no grief down on ol' Dave's head, so whatever he did would have to be done away from the tavern. So that meant he had some more waiting to do. He'd already told Dave that he might leave real abruptlike, so Dave wouldn't get alarmed if Preacher just didn't show up for mealtime one day.

Preacher waited.

About an hour after the Bedell brothers had disappeared into the hotel, Dave came strolling out to the barn carrying a bundle and set about fiddlin' with some bridles.

When he knew they were alone, he said, "The brothers has arranged to buy two horses from a local man. They'll be leavin' first thing in the morning. They're headin' east. They's some dark woods about half a day's ride from here. Runs for miles. Used to be highwaymen's favorite place to force a stage driver to stand and deliver. Here's food for you. It was good seein' you again, Preacher. Give my best to all the boys back in the high country."

Dave walked away and entered his business by the back door. He did not look back. Fifteen minutes later, Preacher had saddled up, packed up, and was gone.

The woods Dave had told him about were dark and dank, eastern woods, not like the timber in the high country. But they'd be perfect for what Preacher had in mind. He wasn't sure what he was going to do with Vic's brother. But he was equally certain the man knew all about Vic's dirty dealings. So to Preacher's mind, that made him just as black-hearted as Vic.

It was bitter cold, but despite that, Preacher's fire was a small one, just enough to heat food and boil coffee. Preacher was used to the cold and did not wish to draw any attention to his presence by a lot of smoke.

He had picked his ambush point with care and was waiting there at dawn. He still didn't know exactly how he was goin' to pull this off. But he knew that it would come to him.

He figured it would be about noon 'fore the Bedells reached the woods. Preacher settled in. One thing he had was patience.

Wagons rumbled by, and one stagecoach heading west passed Preacher. Several horsemen rode past, but they rode swiftly, for the woods were not a very inviting place. They seemed somehow evil to Preacher.

"A right fittin' place for Bedell to meet his end," Preacher muttered.

When the sun was directly overhead, Preacher heard the sounds of horses. He peeked out of the brush and pulled his pistols. Vic and Chris Bedell were walking their horses through the timber. When they reached the ambush point, Preacher stepped out and leveled his pistols.

"End of the trail, Vic," he said. "Dismount. The both of you."

"What?" Chris Bedell blurted, clearly frightened at the sight of Preacher.

Vic just sat his saddle and cussed Preacher.

Preacher cocked his pistols and Vic and his brother fell silent. "Dismount or I kill you both right here."

"The mountain man you spoke of?" Chris asked.

Vic was so angry he could not speak. He merely nodded his head.

"I am a man of some means, sir," Chris Bedell said. "A thousand dollars to you if you'll go and leave us. I think that is a fair offer."

"You know what your brother done?" Preacher asked.

"Yes. But killing him won't bring those women back. Take the money, man, and leave us be. I must warn you, sir, I am a man of importance in this state. Harming me would ensure a noose around your neck."

The woods seemed to grow colder and Preacher felt a dark anger seize him in a hard grip. He thought of Snake, of Charlie and Ned and Ring. Of the bodies of the women, raped and abused and tortured, lyin' cold in the ground. The boys and girls buried in the lonesome. The brave soldiers all dead. Hammer galloped through his mind, wild and free. He just could not believe what the older Bedell was saying. How could anyone cloak over what Vic had done?

"You know all that your brother done and you want to defend him?" Preacher's words were hard-spoken, choked with emotion. "You're as sorry as your no-count brother."

"We're brothers!" Chris Bedell said. "Blood is thick, mountain man."

"Not none of yours," Preacher said. "Bedell blood is tainted. You're both evil."

Chris Bedell cursed, then grabbed for a pistol and Preacher drilled him clean, the ball dead-centering the man in the chest. Chris's horse panicked and the horse charged into the trees. Chris's foot was hung up in the stirrup and horse and man disappeared into the woods. Vic spurred his horse and Preacher dropped his pistols and leaped forward, dragging the man from the saddle.

Preacher did not know how long he took or how many times he struck Vic Bedell, but when he finally let the man fall, Vic Bedell was dead. Preacher had beaten the man to death with his fists. The mountain man stood for a moment by the side of the dark road, his chest heaving. He caught his breath and gathered up his pistols, then dragged Vic's body into the cold timber and dumped him several hundred yards from the road. He stripped saddle and bridle from Vic's horse and turned him loose. Preacher found Chris Bedell—what was left of him after having been dragged for hundreds of yards—and left him where he lay, a bloody heap of rags and torn flesh in a shallow depression. He found Chris's horse and freed the animal of saddle and bridle and whacked him on the rump, sending him galloping off. He took all papers and wallets from the men, not checking the contents.

Preacher erased all signs of his tiny camp and got gone from there. In this weather, the bodies of the Bedell brothers would not begin to stink for days or weeks, or they might never be found. Whatever the case, the deed was done and Preacher put miles behind him before he swung off into timber along a tiny crick and made his lonely camp for the night.

One thing he knew for certain, Victor Bedell's reign of terror was over and done with.

Sitting by his tiny fire that night, Preacher inspected the contents of the wallets he'd taken. He burned all papers that identified the men—Vic had changed his name to Walter Burdette—and counted the money. A lot of money. More paper and gold than Preacher had ever seen. It boggled his mind. But it was dirty money; had blood on it.

On his way east, Preacher stopped at a store and bought clothes to fit the time and locale, carefully stashing his buckskins among his belongings on the packhorse. He stored his pistols with his clothing and carried only his knife on his belt and his Hawken in the saddle boot. And he began dropping off the dirty money along the way, giving it to poor houses and orphanages and churches and down-on-their-luck families who was havin' a tough time of it in this hard winter. Never no huge amount in any one place—not enough to draw any particular attention to him—but stretching it and doling it out a bit here and a bit there.

He neither heard nor read any news about the bodies of the Bedell brothers ever being found. After this long a time, if the bodies had not been found and planted, they would have been gnawed on by varmints and the like, and positive identification would be near impossible.

And Preacher was amazed, awed, and, he had to admit, a bit frightened as he rode deeper and deeper into civilization. He saw a huge train roarin' through the countryside on steel tracks, the damn thing a belchin' smoke and spewin' out sparks and racin' along at a terrible rate of speed. Made a horrible noise, too. Couldn't even think until the thing had passed. Scared his horses something awful. Preacher couldn't imagine how anybody would be comfortable riding that fast.

Wasn't a natural thing to his mind. Damned if he'd ever get on one of them things.

He saw some amazing things as he traveled, things that he'd only read about and never dreamt of actually seeing. He saw new inventions and learned that the U.S. Government now had over ten thousand post offices and two hundred thousand miles of postal routes. Preacher couldn't figure out just who in the hell would have that much to say to a body that they'd have to write it down and post it clear across the country. He learned that there were over half a million people now living in Indiana. He couldn't even imagine that many people. And he read in a newspaper that Chicago now had over six thousand people living there, and New Orleans had over seventy thousand people all jammed up there. Preacher sure didn't have any desires to visit them places. All crowded up like that, a body would be sure to catch some horrible disease.

Even with his store-bought clothes he drew stares. For he did not belong in this part of the country and clothing would not hide that fact. The women cut their eyes to him and the men were a tad on the hostile side. But not too hostile. For the men pegged the hard-eyed and wind-burned and sun-darkened man as being a man one had best not push. And they were damn sure right about that.

He crossed over into Ohio and stopped at a roadhouse to ask directions. The man was friendly enough and told Preacher that he was only about a two hours ride away from the village where his family lived. The innkeeper knowed them all and said they was right nice people. But he didn't care much for their kids. They was all a tad on the uppity side to suit him.

Preacher didn't tell the innkeeper that he was kin to the old man and woman. Just a friend of the family. He thanked the man and rode on.

Then Preacher got him an idea. He reined up in a copse of woods and damn near froze his privates off changin' back into his buckskins; the new ones that he'd swapped from back on the Plains. My but they was fancy and fit him to a fare-thee-well, they did. He unwrapped his new bright red sash he'd bought back in the city and wound it around his flat and hard-muscled belly, sticking one of his big pistols behind the sash.

By God, he was a mountain man, not a damn pilgrim. These were his clothes, and if anybody didn't like the way he dressed, they could go kiss a duck.

Now, he'd go see his ma and pa.

8

Preacher got all choked up and sort of misty eyed when he swung down from the saddle in front of the neat little home on the edge of town. There was an old man choppin' kindlin' wood by the side of the house, and some good smells comin' from the house. His ma was bakin' bread. But why was pa havin' to chop wood? Seemed like some of his brothers could come over every day and tend to that. Preacher would have to talk to his brothers about that, and make arrangements of some sort. One way or the other.

Preacher pushed open the gate and stepped inside the small yard, walking around to the side of the house. He stood for a moment, looking at his father. The man grew conscious of eyes on him and straightened up with an effort, to stand staring at the rugged-looking stranger in buckskins.

"Can I help you, stranger?" the old man asked.

Preacher had to clear his throat a time or two before replying to that. *Stranger?* Then Preacher realized that he'd been gone for twenty-odd years. And he had changed.

"You want me to finish up the choppin' and tote that wood in for you, Pa?" he managed to say.

The old man moved closer. "Arthur? Art, boy? Is that really you, son?"

"It's me, Pa."

The back door opened and a gray-haired lady stepped out. "Who's there, Homer?"

The old man smiled. "The wanderer's come back, Mother. It's our son, Art."

The lady caught her breath and then quickly dabbed at her eyes with a tiny hanky. Then she was off the porch and into Preacher's arms.

The mountain man had come home.

COURAGE OF THE
MOUNTAIN MAN

Necessity brings him here, not pleasure.
—Dante

Those who'll play with cats must expect to be scratched.
—Cervantes

SMOKE JENSEN

He drifted West with his pa, just a boy, right after the War Between the States ended. Hard work was all he'd ever known. After his ma died and his sister took off with a gambling fellow, Young Jensen had worked the hardscrabble farm in the hills and hollows of Missouri and just did manage to keep body and soul together. Pick up one rock and two more would take its place the next morning, seemed like. Then his pa came home.

They pulled out a week after the elder Jensen's return home. Heading west. Young Jensen had him a .36-caliber Navy Colt that Jesse James had given him after the boy had let some of the guerrilla troops of Bloody Bill Anderson rest and water their horses at the farm. Jesse had seemed a right nice person to Young Jensen.

Jesse had give him an extra cylinder for the pistol, too. Neighborly, that's what it was.

On the way West, an old mountain man fell in with the pair on the plains. Said his name was Preacher. Not thirty minutes after the introductions, a band of Indians looking for scalps hit the trio, and it was there that Young Jensen got the name hung on him that would stay with him forever. Although only a boy, Young Jensen fought a man's fight and killed his share of those who were trying to kill them.

A thin finger of smoke lifted from the barrel of the Navy .36 Young Jensen held in his hand. The old mountain man smiled and said, "Can't call you no boy now. You be a man. I think I'll call you Smoke."

1

Smoke Jensen stepped out of the café on the main street of Big Rock, Colorado. He leaned against an awning post and rolled a cigarette, lighting it just as Sheriff Monte Carson strolled up.

"Need to talk with you, Smoke," the sheriff said. "You like a beer?"

"No," the ruggedly handsome man with the cold eyes said with a smile. "But I'll watch you drink one."

The sheriff and the most feared gunhandler in all the West walked to the saloon, pushed open the batwings, and stepped inside. Monte ordered a beer and Smoke ordered coffee.

"I hear you're selling your stock, Smoke."

"Most of it. I'm going to raise horses, Monte. Oh, I'll keep a small herd. But nothing like we've had out on the Sugarloaf."

"You using the rails?"

"I wish, Monte. No. This will be a hard drive. All the way up to Montana. Into a big valley. Town's called Blackstown. Fellow up there name of T. J. Duggan wants the whole damn herd."

"The whole herd? Why?"

Smoke shrugged heavy muscular shoulders. "Beats me. He's an Eastern fellow. Said he was in a hurry to get into ranching. He's paying me good money, Monte. I couldn't turn down the offer."

"How about your hands once the drive is over?"

Smoke chuckled. "A few want to drift; you know cowboys. But I couldn't run most of them off with a shotgun. I'm going to be running a lot of horses, Monte. You know how I love the appaloosas. I'll be needing hands."

"When will you pull out?"

"Oh, about ten days, I think. Why? You want to come along and do some honest work for a change?"

"Hell, man! I'd love to. But no. We have trials set for all of next month. Smoke, you know you're going up into Clint Black's country."

"Clint Black doesn't bother me. I don't even know the man. All I know is he's a rancher who thinks he owns the whole damn Montana Territory."

"He's got some rough ol' boys ridin' for him, Smoke."

"I've run up against some rough ol' boys a time or two in my life, Monte." Smoke spoke the words softly. But there was lead and fire and gunsmoke behind them.

Clint Black better rein in his hands and his mouth when he meets up with Smoke Jensen, the sheriff thought. *If you aggravate him too much, Smoke will come after you lookin' like a demon out of Hell.*

Both men watched as three young riders came walking their horses slowly up the street. Both men noted that the riders sat on Texas saddles—without the wide skirt, the saddle horn was thicker and stronger for roping, and the stirrups were of the heavy-duty type. The brands were unfamiliar. All three cowboys wore their holsters tied down. One of the trio wore two guns.

"You know them," Smoke asked.

"Never saw them before this day. What do you think?"

"Wild and woolly and full of fleas, probably. Might even be on the prod, looking for trouble. They're young. Oldest one's not out of his early twenties, I'd say."

"This place does have a back door," Monte said with a wide smile. But there was a hopeful note in his voice. If the three young punchers wanted trouble, Smoke Jensen was the last man in the world they should brace. He didn't want trouble in Big Rock, and if it started, Smoke would not have initiated it. But there would be three dead rowdies on the barroom floor when the silence prevailed.

Smoke chuckled. "Then use it."

Sheriff Monte Carson laughed softly. "I was rather hoping you would."

Boots sounded heavily on the boardwalks and spurs jingled.

"Too late now."

The riders took off their hats and beat the trail dust from their clothing before stepping into the saloon. The one leading the pack slammed open the batwings, and that irritated Monte. He looked at Smoke. There was no change in his expression.

The trio ordered whiskey with a beer chaser. Their voices were too loud and too demanding.

"Huntin' trouble," Monte said softly.

"They came to the right place," Smoke replied in a soft voice.

"Hey!" one of the riders yelled. "What you two whisperin' about over yonder? You talkin' about us, maybe?"

Monte was sitting in a way that only presented one side of his torso to the bar. He shoved back his chair and stood up. His badge was now visible. He walked to the three young would-be gunhands and faced them.

"The name is Carson. Sheriff Monte Carson."

The trio stiffened. Monte Carson had been one of the West's premier gunfighters until he married and settled down in Big Rock. Everybody had heard of Monte Carson.

"If you boys are lookin' for a drink, some food, and a place to spend the night, you found it, right here in Big Rock. If you boys are lookin' for trouble, you found that. Right here and right now!"

One of Monte's deputies had seen the rowdies ride in. The back door of the saloon creaked. One of the young Texas toughs cut his eyes. The deputy stood behind them, a sawed-off double-barreled shotgun in his hands. He cocked both hammers. The slight sound was enormous in the now-quiet room.

"I'll take this punk here," Monte said, his temper rising. "Jimmy, you blow the guts out of two-gun over there by the bar . . ."

"And I'll take Tall Boy," Smoke said, pushing back his chair and standing up. It seemed like he never would get through standing up. Smoke Jensen was several inches over six feet, with the weight to go with it. Huge hands and wrists. Thickly muscled with massive shoulders and a barrel chest, he was lean at the hips, and his jeans bunched with powerful leg muscles. His hair was ash blond, worn short; his eyes were brown and cold. Smoke wore two guns, .44s, the left-hand gun worn high and butt forward, the right-hand gun low and tied down. He was snake-quick with either pistol. He carried a long-bladed Bowie knife behind his left-hand six-shooter. He could and did shave with it. Or fight with it, didn't make any difference to Smoke. "The name is Jensen. Smoke Jensen."

A sigh came from Tall Boy. Slowly he let his hands drift to the bar, where he placed them palms down. "Fightin' Monte Carson would be bad enough," he said. "A deputy with a Greener makes it worser. Add Smoke Jensen and a body'd be a damn pure idiot."

"Drink your drinks, get something to eat, and behave," Monte told them, his anger fading. He turned his back to them and started to the table and his unfinished beer.

"No, Jack!" Tall Boy yelled. "Don't do it."

Jack was grabbing for his gun. The sawed-off roared. The heavy charges nearly cut the Texas boy in two, flinging him against the wall and leaving a bloody smear as he slid down to stop butt-first on the floor. He died with his eyes wide open, staring into a terribly bleak eternity.

"I'm out of this!" the third rider screamed. "Jesus Christ, I'm clear out."

Folks came running, for gunfights were not a common thing in Big Rock, not with Monte Carson, Smoke Jensen, Pearlie, Johnny North, and half a dozen other heavy-duty gunslicks, who had turned into respectable citizens, only a breath away.

Dr. Colton Spalding stepped into the saloon. He needed only one look at the puncher. "Get the undertaker," he told the barkeep.

"Was that boy born a damn fool?" Monte asked, pointing to the dead would-be tough, "or did he have to work at it?"

"He . . . fancied hisself good with a gun," one of his shaken-up buddies said.

Monte shook his head in disgust and walked to the table. Smoke had sat down and was drinking his coffee.

"What do you think about it?" Monte asked.

"I think my coffee got cold," Smoke replied.

Sally, Smoke's wife, read the letters from her parents and their children, who were all in France attending school. One of their children was there for health reasons, being tended to by specialists. Smoke had picked up the letters in town and had not opened them, leaving that small pleasure for Sally.

"Any word on when they'll come back home?" Smoke asked.

"No. When do you leave?"

"Probably next week. I'd like to take you with me, honey. But a cattle drive is rough work."

"I'll be fine here," she assured him. "Just who is this Clint Black person?"

Smoke sipped his coffee for a moment. "A hard, unyielding tyrant of a man. I suspect that somebody sold this T. J. Duggan a bill of goods with this ranch he bought. Somebody wanted out of that country and found themselves a sucker. I don't even know the man and I feel sorry for him."

"Oh, my!" Sally said, but with a smile.

Her husband looked at her. "What's that all about?"

"I feel a quest coming on, oh man of La Mancha."

"Sally . . . !"

"I gave you the book to read."

He looked puzzled for a moment, then a wide grin cut his face and softened his eyes. "Oh, yeah. Don Quixote."

She gently corrected his pronunciation.

"Am I the Knight of the Woeful Figure?"

"Hardly," she said with a laugh. "But you do have this tendency to stand up for lost causes and the little person."

"You knew that when you married me, honey."

She stood up and walked to him, kissing him on the cheek. "And I love you all the more for it. Now stand up and put on an apron," she told the most feared gunfighter in all the West. "I'll wash, you dry."

"Yes, dear."

Smoke Jensen had not sought out the reputation of gunfighter. Most of the known ones hadn't. For several years after he and Sally were married, he had changed his name and lived quietly. Then outlaws come to town and he was forced to once more strap on his guns to protect hearth and home and kith and kin. He never went back to his false name. He was Smoke Jensen, a man of peace if allowed, a warrior when he had to be. Back in '72, when he was just out of his teens, Smoke Jensen tracked down the men who had raped and killed his wife, Nicole, and had brutally murdered their baby son, Arthur. He cornered them in a raw silver-mining town in the Uncompahgre. Writers of dime novels wrote that there were fifty gunhands in the town, and balladeers sang that Smoke Jensen killed a hundred or more desperados. In a play later written about him, with Smoke portrayed in New York City by a dandy who had never been west of Philadelphia, Smoke was portrayed to have killed five hundred men on that fateful day. In reality, Smoke faced fourteen men that day. Smoke rode away, wounded a half a dozen times. The miners buried fourteen gunhands.

A month later, his wounds nearly healed, Smoke went after the men who had killed his brother and his father years back. He found them in Idaho. When he rode away, he left a burning town and the streets littered with dead.

It was there that Smoke met Sally.

No one really knew how many murderers, outlaws, rapists, and other assorted human slime had fallen under the guns of Smoke Jensen. Smoke himself didn't know. And he didn't worry about it. But the figure was staggeringly high.

Around Big Rock, Smoke was known as a man who loved kids and dogs and horses, who sang solos in church every now and then, and would pitch in with a barn or house-raising. He would climb a tree to rescue a cat, take in stray dogs and make sure they had good homes or keep them himself. There were at least twenty running around the fenced-in acres where the house stood on the Sugarloaf. He would help a stranger in need and had completely outfitted, at his own expense, numerous settlers who had lost everything in their march West.

But crowd him, insult his wife, make a hostile move against an innocent—as Sally had pointed out in the kitchen, even an innocent he didn't know—hurt one of his dogs or horses, and Smoke Jensen would hunt that man down, call him out, and either beat him half to death with those huge fists, or kill him.

There is an old Western expression that men would use to test another man's courage. It reads, "I ain't never seen none of your graveyards."

Nobody ever said that to Smoke Jensen.

On this drive north to Montana Territory, Smoke had hired eight boys who were out of school for the summer. One sixteen-year-old, four fifteen-year-olds, and three fourteen-year-olds. They were young, but they were good hands. Willie, Jake, Bobby, Rabbit, Louie, Dan, Sonny, and Guy. In addition to his regular hands, Smoke had hired on four more men who had drifted through. He wired their former employers— the telegraph was making life a lot easier in the West—and received replies that the men were good hands who would give a day's work for a day's pay. That would give him seventeen men for the drive. It wasn't enough, for the herd was very large, but he could pick up other hands along the way.

The drive would be hard work for the boys, and it would also be an adventure for them.

Smoke was kind of looking forward to it himself.

2

On the morning of the pullout, the boys from the neighboring farms and ranches were so excited, they could hardly contain themselves. Not only were they going on a real cattle drive, clear up into Montana Territory, but they were in the company of Smoke Jensen. How much better could it get?

The boys knew they would be close to the drag most of the time, herding the remuda on either the right or left flank of the cattle, but that was all right. It was a very responsible job, and they knew it.

Smoke had figured it close as far as manpower was concerned. Some trail bosses figure one cowboy for every 400 cows. Smoke figured one cowboy for every 250 cows. They would be pushing slightly over 3,500 head, not all belonging to Smoke. A half a dozen other ranchers had put a number of their cattle up for sale as well. The price Duggan was paying was more than fair, so why not throw in with Smoke?

The remuda was made up of more than a hundred horses, so the boys would have their young hands full.

Just before pullout, Smoke found two more punchers drifting through and hired them. They were down at the heels and looked like they needed a good meal just to stay alive one more day. But their horses were in good shape and they had honest eyes and easy grins. Their hands were so calloused from handling cattle and ropes, Smoke knew they couldn't be outlaws.

The cook was a sour-faced old coot with never a kind word for anybody. But he was the best trail cook in five counties and could be counted on to have coffee ready anytime the men wanted it. While they were in camp, that is.

"Damn bunch of snot-nosed boys gonna eat us out of grub 'fore we get fifty miles," he had groused. "This many men, we're gonna need another wagon and I got to have me a helper, too. That's that, or I ain't goin'."

"Will I do, Denver?" Sally asked, stepping up.

"A *female?*" Denver shouted. "Hell, no!"

"She's a durn sight better cook than you, you old goat," one of Smoke's regular hands told him.

Denver threw his hat on the ground. "That's a tooken bet, boy!"

"Now wait just a minute," Smoke said. "I run this outfit. I say who goes along, and Sally is *not* coming along on this cattle drive."

The hands all gathered around, grinning like a bunch of fools. None of them would have missed this for a month's wages and a little speckled pup.

She marched up to him. She wore men's britches and the men all admired that sight too. But there wasn't a man among them—including the new hands—who wouldn't stomp any man who said anything about Sally's shape. Outside of their own bunch, that is, and that would be said very respectfully.

"I see, Mr. Jensen," Sally said, her head just about reaching the center of Smoke's chest. "It wasn't too dangerous for me to ride all over Hell's creation a few months back with a rifle in my hand, getting you out of a bad situation . . ."

"Now, Sally," Smoke said.

"Oh, no. That was quite all right for me to do that . . ."

Smoke sighed.

"Why, there ain't no way this little bit of thing could keep up with me," Denver stuck his mouth into the situation. "And what if we run into quarrelsome Injuns? I never seen a woman who could shoot worth a damn."

"I really wish you hadn't said that," Smoke muttered.

Sally jerked one of Smoke's .44s from leather and put all five rounds into the knot on a log some fifty feet away. She handed the pistol back to Smoke.

Denver chewed his tobacco for a moment. "What do you know about a chuck wagon, little lady?"

"I wish you hadn't asked that, either," Smoke muttered, reloading his .44.

"I know how to doctor cuts, drive a wagon, prepare three hot," she smiled, "and *tasty* meals a day. And I know to point the tongue of the wagon toward the north star every night."

Denver chewed, spat, and then grinned. "You and me, little lady, are gonna get along just fine."

"I didn't say she was coming along," Smoke protested.

"I reckon you didn't, boss. But I can see that you ain't the only one who wears pants around here neither."

The drive was delayed for one day while Sally got ready to go and made arrangements for this, that, and the other thing, as females are wont to do before a journey. Just as dawn was cracking the sky, the drovers hi-hoed the herd and started them moving north. One of the boys would take turns driving Miss Sally's wagon, which was not a chore for any of them. Miss Sally was beautiful and she smelled good, too.

Only bad thing was that all the hands, men and boys, knew that Miss Sally had laid in a goodly number of bars of soap—like about five *cases*. And that meant that every time they stopped, if there was water handy, everybody was going to take a bath. Whether they needed it or not. And the boys were looking forward to doing a whole lot of cussing on this trip. That was out too. Well, they all could gather in a bunch and cuss quiet, they reckoned.

After the second day out, the lead cows were established and the herd moved along. "Keep them out of the dew in the morning," Smoke reminded the men. Dew tended to soften the cattle hooves.

They would average ten to twelve miles a day. The chuck wagons were new, both bought from the Studebaker Brothers Manufacturing Company. Sally had seen to it that the coffee beans were Arbuckle's, which always had a stick of peppermint packed in each one-pound bag. Cowboys had been known to come to blows—and sometimes guns—over who got the peppermint. Sally straightened out that problem easily by buying a huge box of peppermint candy before leaving. Everybody got a peppermint occasionally. Even Smoke, if he behaved.

Sally and Denver worked well together, and the meals, although simple, were tasty and, with Sally along, varied. Smoke picked up the Western Trail just outside of Cheyenne and headed due north. They would stay on that trail until they got into Montana Territory. Once they crossed the Powder in Montana, Smoke would cut north and west, heading for the mountains and the town of Blackton. That final leg would be the real test, for the drovers would be pushing the huge herd over no established trail.

"Are we going to see wild Indians, Mr. Smoke?" young Rabbit asked.

Smoke looked at the boy across the flames of the fire. He'd been just about his age when he killed his first man, back on the plains of Kansas. He smiled at Rabbit. "I'm sure we will, Rabbit. But it's unlikely they'll be hostile ones. More than likely they'll be begging for food. The route I've mapped out will keep us off of any reservation land. But not by many miles."

Later, when the crew had bedded down, Smoke was having a cup of coffee with Denver. "You know Clint Black, Smoke?" the cook asked.

"Not personally. Only by reputation."

"He's a bad one. Tried to hire me one time, right after the war, when he first come out here. I wouldn't work for him."

Smoke sipped his coffee and waited, knowing there was more.

"He runs the biggest cattle operation in the territory. Hundreds of thousands of acres. He started the town of Blacktown. It's grown so much now that he don't control it no more. But he does swing a mighty big loop when it comes to town matters. In my opinion, this Duggan feller's a damn fool for goin' up agin someone as powerful as Black."

"Surely Black is not the only rancher in the county."

"Oh, no. 'Course he ain't. But the others is just hangin' on. Black controls the best water, the best graze, the best everything. This is a story that's been played out a thousand times in the West, Smoke. But . . . this Duggan feller just might hold the joker in the deck."

"How do you mean?"

"Several rivers and some fair-sized cricks run through that part of the country. Black is big, but he ain't so big that all the water, or all the best graze is on his holdin's. You say Duggan's brand is the Double D?"

"That's right."

"More than one Duggan, then."

"Unless his name is Don Duggan."

Denver smiled. "Dumb Duggan is more like it."

"What's Black's brand?"

"The Circle 45. And brother, his hands don't hesitate to back up that brand with lead."

"If he leaves me alone, I'll certainly leave him alone."

"This many cattle comin' into a part of the country Black thinks he's the lord and master of? No, he'll stick his nose in to see what's goin' on. And if he thinks he can get away with it, he'll take this herd."

"No law in that part of the territory?"

Denver snorted. "The sheriff is Clint's brother."

Smoke delayed the start of the drive the next morning. He sat alone, drinking coffee and giving some serious thought to sending the boys back home. Sally came over and sat down beside him, on the ground.

"What's the matter, honey?"

Smoke laid it out for her. He never kept anything from her and was going to ask her opinion anyway.

"Well, the boys would be awfully disappointed. Do you really think this Black person would harm a boy?"

"From what I've heard about him, I think he's probably capable of doing just about anything. But it's hard for me to believe that a man who would do that could make it as big as he has here in the West. You know how Western people feel about kids. But all that means is he's either never done something like that before, or didn't get caught. Maybe Denver is stretching the truth a bit. I don't know. I do know that I've got a contract to deliver this herd and I'm going to push it through. Come on, let's go meet with the crew."

Smoke laid it out for them all. He knew what the reaction of the men would be and Shorty put it into words.

Shorty spat on the ground and hitched up his gunbelt. "Sounds like this ol' boy is meaner than a snake, Boss. But I've killed a lot of snakes in my time. As far as him hurtin' these youngsters, I can't see him doin' that. Western folks just wouldn't stand for it. No matter how big and powerful he is, if he ever done something like that, a lynch mob would string him up real quick."

The other men nodded their heads in agreement. Even Denver agreed with the majority. " 'Specially if the boys wasn't totin' no iron," the old cook said.

Smoke looked at the boys. "Any of you packing guns?"

They shuffled their booted feet and exchanged sheepish glances that silently spoke volumes.

"Get your saddlebags and bedrolls and spread them out right here in front of me," Smoke told them.

Every boy had a pistol tucked away. Smoke took the guns and gave them to Denver. "Tuck them away." Smoke looked hard at the youngsters. "Boys, you know that out here, if you strap on a gun, that makes you a man on the spot. Now if we're attacked, you certainly have the right to defend yourself. Your guns won't be locked away. They're handy if you need them. I'm going to squat down by the fire and have another cup of coffee. All of you talk this out and come up with some sort of decision. You let me know what it is."

Smoke chewed on a biscuit and drank a cup of hot, strong coffee while he waited. Sally stayed with the hands.

Smoke's drive foreman, Nate, broke off from the group and came over, squatting down and pouring a cup of coffee. "Boss, me and Miss Sally voted against these boys goin' on. I think this drive is shapin' up like trouble. But the others, they voted to go on. I reckon it's up to you."

Smoke shook his head. "No. If the majority voted to go on, that's it. Finish your coffee and let's put some miles behind us."

There are those who paint a cattle drive as romantic and exciting. A cattle drive is just plain work. Hot, hard, dirty, dusty, muddy, often dangerous work. If it wasn't too dry, it was too wet. If it wasn't too hot, it was too cold. Mosquitoes could drive both man and beast half crazy. Rivers and creeks could be no more than a trickle or flooding over their banks. Water holes might be no more than caked mud. There wasn't a damn thing romantic about it.

People have been led to believe that the man who rode at the head of the drive was the point man. Not true. That was the trail boss. The chuck wagon was to the left of the trail boss. The point men—always two—rode behind the trail boss, on the left and right of the cattle. Behind the point men rode the drovers in the swing position. Behind them were the cowboys on the flank. The remuda was just behind and outside of the left flank, with the wranglers. In the rear were the drovers who made up the drag. It was the job of the trail boss to scout ahead for water and pasture. The other cowboys rotated positions. How often that occurred sometimes depended on the disposition of the trail boss, but usually it was left up to the cowboys to equally share the good and bad positions found on any drive.

No sooner had the herd entered Wyoming than one of the point men shouted, pointing to the west. A dozen riders were coming up, trotting their horses. The riders didn't look a bit friendly.

3

Smoke rode out to meet them, putting some distance between himself and the herd. If there was to be shooting, he didn't want the herd stampeded. The riders pulled up and sat looking at Smoke. They were all pretty well set up, so they probably weren't rustlers. But they all appeared sullen and Smoke didn't take to them at all.

"We're from the cattlemen's association," one finally said, after Smoke refused to be stared down. His tone indicated that was a big deal to him. Didn't impress Smoke at all.

"Congratulations. Do you want applause?"

"Oh, we got us a real smart-mouth here, Walt," another said.

Walt pointed a finger at Smoke. "You best button your lip, mister."

"I wasn't born with a button on it," Smoke told him. "Now state your business and get out of my way. I've got cattle to drive."

Nate and Shorty had left the herd, to ride up alongside the boss. While neither one was a gunslinger, they could both shuck a Colt or Remington out of leather mighty quick and they were crack shots.

"By God!" another member of the association said. "I'll not stand for talk like that. We're here to inspect your herd and you best just stand aside."

"Inspect my herd for what?" Smoke asked, his right hand resting on his thigh, close to the butt of his .44.

"Been a lot of rustlin' goin' on," Walt said. "You're a stranger here, so we take a look at your cattle, whether you like it or not."

"I don't care if you inspect my herd. But you'll do it while they're moving. Now get out of the way."

"Just who in the hell do you think you are, buddy?" another asked, belligerence in his tone.

"Smoke Jensen."

Those among them with any sense at all made certain their hands were in plain sight and they made no quick moves. But there is always one. . . .

"That don't spell jack-crap to me," a burly, unshaven man said. "I never believed nine-tenths of them stories 'bout you no way."

"That is your option," Smoke told him. He glanced at Shorty. "Get the herd moving. If these gentlemen want to inspect it, that's fine with me. But they'll do it on the move."

"Right, boss." Shorty wheeled his horse, took off his hat, and waved it in the air. "Head them out!" he shouted.

"You gonna sit there and let this two-bit fancy-dan gun-hawk get away with this, Walt?" the loudmouth asked.

"Shut up, Baylis," a man whispered hoarsely.

Smoke lifted the reins and walked his horse into the group, stopping by the side of Baylis. He smiled at the man. Baylis not only didn't believe in shaving every day, he didn't bathe much either. "What's your problem?" Smoke asked him. "Other than having to smell your own stink, that is."

"Baylis," Walt said. "Close your mouth and keep it closed. I recognize the gentlemen now."

"Jensen," Baylis said, "I think I'll just get off this horse and whup your butt."

"Oh, I don't think so." Smoke pulled his hat brim lower and then sucker-punched the man. He busted Baylis smack in the mouth; the blow knocked the man out of the saddle. Baylis sprawled on the hoof-churned ground, his mouth a bloody mess.

Smoke backed his horse out of the group, stopping between Nate and Shorty. "If you gentlemen wish to ride along and inspect the herd, feel free to do so. We'll be stopping for lunch in about an hour. You're welcome to eat with us. And that includes the fool on the ground."

Several of the men tried to hide their smiles.

"That's very kind of you, Mr. Jensen," Walt said. "We'll just ride along for a time and then take you up on your most generous offer of a meal."

Smoke nodded and he and Shorty and Nate rejoined the herd. Walt looked down at Baylis, who was hanging on to a stirrup, trying to get up. "Baylis, I always suspicioned that your mamma raised at least one fool. Now I know I was right."

Over lunch, which was the thick rich stew sometimes called Sonofabitch Stew, with sourdough bread to sop in it, dried apple pie for dessert, and all the coffee anybody could drink, Smoke asked Walt about Clint Black.

"I never met the man, Smoke. But I know about him. Runs the biggest spread in all of Montana Territory. The Circle 45. Has maybe . . . depending on the time of year . . . anywhere from fifty to a hundred men on the payroll. You're not taking these cattle to him, are you?"

"No. To a man named Duggan. Runs the Double D spread."

"I never heard of him."

"I think he's new out here. He bought my whole herd and about a thousand from neighboring ranches. Said he wanted to get into the cattle business fast. I've never met him. Everything was handled through lawyers."

"Gettin' to be a man can't break wind without checking first with a lawyer," Walt grumbled.

Smoke grinned at him. He shared the same opinion of most lawyers. "Speaking of sons of bitches, have some more stew, Walt."

Walt laughed and a new friendship was bonded.

Baylis glared at Smoke and hatred was fanned.

Walt gave Smoke a handwritten note and with it said, "You'll have no trouble in Wyoming. Just show anyone who stops you that note and they'll wave you right on through and help you with the drive for a time."

The men shook hands all the way around. All but Baylis. He rode out alone right after lunch. Nobody missed him until he couldn't be found and a drover told them he saw him ridin' out toward the northwest.

"I hope he keeps on riding," Walt said. "Baylis is a troublemaker. Runs a little rawhide spread not far from here. There is a mean streak in the man that I never could cotton to. Shame too, 'cause he came from good stock. I knew both his parents 'fore they died."

"How's he live?" Smoke asked. "That was a good horse and a fancy rig."

"Lot of us have wondered that," another association member told Smoke. "I ain't sayin' he's crooked, but it wouldn't surprise me to find out he was."

"Maybe he's headin' back to Montana," yet another suggested. "He worked up there for years. Say! I think he worked for the Circle 45, come to think of it."

The herd pushed on and for a time they had nothing but beautiful weather. The boys were turning into good hands, and it surprised everybody to see how closely they watched the remuda and how well they took to accepting responsibility.

The days began to blend together as they pushed north. The herd was stopped several times by cattlemen association members, and by curious ranchers, but the letter Walt had given Smoke quickly brought smiles and offers of meals and a chance to take a real bath in a tub, something Sally jumped at.

"I've heard about you for years, Smoke," a rancher said, over a fine meal of fried chicken and potatoes and gravy. "I figured you'd be a much older man."

"I got started young," Smoke said with a smile.

"Oh?"

"After my pa was killed, an old mountain man name of Preacher took me in . . ."

"Why, say! Preacher's famous. He took the first wagon train over the Oregon Trail, didn't he?"

"Something like that. Preacher was the first to do a lot of things out here. My teenage years were spent in the company of old mountain men. I got a pretty good education."

The rancher's kids, ranging in age from about twelve to twenty, sat at the long table, eyes bright with excitement. Smoke Jensen, the gunfighter who'd killed about a zillion bad hombres was really here and eating fried chicken just like everybody else.

"And you and Sally have been married . . . how long?" a teenage girl asked.

"Well," Smoke said. "Ah . . ."

"You'd better get it right," Sally warned and everybody laughed.

"We've been married, ah . . . ten years," Smoke said.

"That's close," Sally said.

"Your first wife was . . ." The boy closed his mouth at a hard glance from his father.

"It's all right," Smoke said. "Her name was Nicole. We

were married, sort of. Had a bent nail for a wedding ring. We had a son. Named him Arthur, that was Preacher's name. Outlaws came one day while I was gone. They killed the baby and then raped and killed Nicole. I tracked them down and called them out in a mining town."

"How many of them were there, Mr. Smoke?" a girl asked.

"Fourteen."

"Jesus," the rancher whispered.

"Did you get them all, Smoke?" the oldest boy asked.

"I got them all."

"How old were you, Smoke?" the rancher's wife asked in a soft voice.

"I think I was twenty-one. I'm not real sure how old I am," ma'am.

The father put a stop to it. "No more questions."

The young kids were off to bed; the women went to the parlor—much to Sally's disgust—while the rancher, his oldest son, and Smoke, went into the den for whiskey and cigars. Smoke waved off the cigar and rolled a cigarette.

"What do you know about a man named Clint Black?" Smoke asked.

The rancher's eyebrows lifted as he was lighting his cigar. When he had the tip glowing just right, he said, "He's a bad one, Smoke. I'd say he's probably in his mid-to-late forties. Ruthless and dangerous and powerful. He took country that was untamed and built an empire out of it. He's big and strong as a bull. And there is no backup in him. It's his way, or no way at all."

"Nobody is right but him."

"That's it. Anybody gets in his way, he just rides right over them."

"Would he hurt a boy? Those boys I have with me, for instance?"

"Oh . . . I wouldn't think so. But with a man like that, hell, you never know. I know he's run off nesters, but I never heard of him or his men ever harming a child. Hell, I ran off nesters, 'til I got tired of it and learned to live with them."

"You know anything at all about T. J. Duggan and the Double D ranch?"

The rancher shook his head. "Can't say as I've ever heard of him or his brand. T. J. Duggan. Don't ring a bell with me."

The herd slowly put the miles behind them. They crossed rivers, pulled cattle out of quicksand and fought the heat and ate the dust and endured the loneliness of the trail, with the older men remembering how it was years back, when there were no towns along the way. When there was nothing except an empty, seemingly never-ending vastness and then screaming Indians that came out of nowhere.

It was bad now, but it was worse back then.

About fifty miles after crossing the North Platte, they hit a vast grassland, and the cattle slowly ate their way across, regaining the few pounds lost on the way north.

Holding the herd outside of a small town in northern Wyoming, Smoke and several other riders accompanied the wagon in for supplies.

It wasn't much of a town, even by Western standards. A large general store, a blacksmith, a saloon. The stage stopped twice a week. The town had sprung up out of nowhere, had lasted a few years, now was dying. Another couple of years and it would join the many other towns that failed in the West.

Not too many miles to the west, there was another settlement called Donkey Town, although some were trying to get its name changed to Rocky Pile.

While the supplies were being loaded, Smoke walked the short distance to the saloon. If there was any news worth hearing, he would learn of it at the saloon. There were half a dozen horses at the hitchrail and two wagons in the street. Smoke pushed open the batwings and the buzz of conversation slowed, then stopped as he ordered a beer and leaned against the bar.

He was used to that. Nearly everyone in the rural west carried a gun; few carried two guns; almost no one wore his guns the way Smoke wore his. It branded him. Smoke moved to the shadows at the far end of the bar. He hadn't had time to lift the mug to his lips when the batwings flew open and two young men stomped in.

"Hell of a herd outside of town," one said. "And, boy you ought to see the cook. She's a looker, let me tell you.'

"Wears men's britches," the second one said. "Rob here like to have fell off his horse starin'.'"

"Got a bunch of snot-nosed kids wranglin'," Rob said. "Might be fun to go out there and hoo-rah 'em some. What'd you say, Carl?"

"Kids?" a man questioned. He sat at a table with three other men. "What kind of a damn fool outfit hires kids as drovers?"

The pair obviously had not seen any hands except the boys at the remuda. Smoke sipped his beer and waited and listened. Talk was one thing, but hoo-rahing the herd was quite another.

The batwings were shoved open and a young man rushed in, his face flushed. "You heard the news?" The words rushed out of his mouth. "That herd outside of town belongs to Smoke Jensen!"

"You're crazy!" Carl told him. "Who told you that?"

"One of them kids at the remuda."

"Aw, he's just sayin' that so's no one will bother 'em. Smoke Jensen ain't got no herd. I don't even think there is such a person noways. I think all that's made-up stuff."

Rob hitched at his gun belt. "Oh, he's a real person, all right. My brother seen him a couple of years ago. Backed him down, too, my brother did. Jensen ain't much. I'd like to see Jensen in action. I think I'm faster."

"Your brother's got a fat mouth," a cowboy spoke from a table. "Smoke Jensen ain't never backed down from no one.

And leave them boys out yonder alone. Nobody but a tinhorn would hoo-rah a herd."

"If my brother was here, you'd not be sayin' them words," Rob yelled.

"Go get him," the cowboy said. "I'll say it to his face. As far as you bein' better than Smoke Jensen . . . you're a fool. You best take them pearl-handled six shooters off before somebody snatches 'em offen you and shoves 'em down your throat. Or shoves 'em up another part of your a-natomy."

"You think you're big enough to do it!" Rob screamed.

"Yeah," the cowboy said. "I sure do."

"How have you been, Al?" Smoke broke into the conversation.

The cowboy smiled. "Pretty good. I wondered if you recognized me."

"Stay out of this!" Rob yelled at Smoke.

Smoke ignored him. "I heard you were working up this way. Heard you had your own spread."

"Sure do. Got married and all that. How's things down on the Sugarloaf?"

"Couldn't be better."

"Keep your mouth shut!" Rob yelled at the tall man in the shadows. "When I want you to butt into my affairs, I'll let you know. You hear me?"

"Al Jacobs will eat your lunch, boy," Smoke told him. "He's a bad man to tangle with. Me and Al go way back. He used to work for me down in Colorado."

"I don't give a damn where he used to work and I don't give a damn about you. Now why don't you just shut up and mind your own business. That two-bit rawhider insulted my brother and insulted me. Stay out of things that don't concern you 'fore I call you out too."

Al laughed at that. "The kid's sure got his dander up, don't he?"

"Hey, don't you call me no kid, you son of a bitch!" Rob yelled.

The saloon became very quiet. Call a cowboy a flea-bitten, no-count, worthless saddle bum, and he'll probably laugh at you. Besmirch a cowboy's mother's name, and in all probability he'll kill you.

Al slowly rose from his chair, his hand hovering over the butt of his .45.

"Back off, Rob," Smoke said quietly. "Back off and apologize to Al. That remark was uncalled for."

Carl decided it was time for him to stick his mouth into the tense situation. "Hey, mister! Who the hell asked you to butt in? You a friend of Al?"

"That's right," Smoke said, still standing in the shadows.

"Then you get your butt out here and face me."

"Now boys," the barkeep said. "I just mopped this floor."

"Shut up!" Carl told him. He stared into the gloom where Smoke stood. "You! Get your butt out here."

Sonny, one of the boys who had come into town for some licorice, stood at the batwings. "We're all loaded and ready to go, Mr. Smoke," he called.

The saloon became as quiet as a grave.

4

"Go on back to the herd, Sonny," Smoke told him. "I'll be along presently."

The boy had sized up the situation instantly. "Yes, sir!" Sonny hit the air.

"Jesus God Almighty," one of the seated men breathed.

Smoke stepped out of the shadows. He didn't have to wonder if he'd slipped the hammer thongs from his .44s. That was done by reflex as soon as his boots touched ground out of the stirrups. "This does not have to be," he told Rob and Carl. "Rob, you insulted a man and you owe him an apology. Carl, from now on, you'd best think before you challenge a man."

"You can go right straight to Hell," Carl said, his words thick, almost slurred.

"Don't do this, Carl." The barkeep said his words softly. "Don't do it, son."

"Shut up!" Carl told him. "I'll be famous. I'll be the man who killed Smoke Jensen."

"No, you won't," one of the card-playing men called. "You'll just be dead."

"We'll pull together, Smoke," Al said. "If it comes to that."

"All right," Smoke replied, his eyes riveted on Carl. "It won't be any disgrace for you to just walk out of here, boys."

"I ain't no boy!" Rob screamed. "I'm a man grown."

"Then act like one!" Smoke snapped at him. "Men admit their mistakes and grow more mature each time they do. Boys let their mouths get them into trouble and then let pride get them killed. A man is dead a long time. Think about that."

"I think he's yeller," Carl said, a mean smile moving his lips. "The big shot Smoke Jensen is takin' water."

"Yeah," Rob said, his eyes lighting up. "Both of 'em are pure-dee yeller-bellies."

"It's no use, Smoke," Al said. "You and me, we've seen this played out ten dozen times."

"I'm afraid you're right," Smoke admitted.

"Damn, they're gonna do it," a man said, as chairs were pushed back and the tables emptied with men moving about, hoping to get out of the way of any stray bullets.

Smoke felt a sadness take him. The young man was obviously scared, but his stupid pride was crawling all over him, refusing to allow him to back down.

The young man jerked his iron. He was pitifully slow.

Smoke put two rounds into Carl's gun hand. The first hit his gun and tore it from his hand, the second round smashed into the hand, breaking it. Al's draw had been smooth and his aim true. Rob stood holding a bloody shoulder.

"I just don't want to kill no more, Smoke," the gunfighter turned rancher said. "Not unless I just have to do it. You know what I mean?"

"Oh, yes. I sure do."

"You ruined my hand!" Carl sobbed. "It's all busted up."

"My shoulder's broken," Rob moaned.

"But you're both alive," the barkeep said, after picking himself up off the floor. "Now get the hell over to the barber shop so's Ed can patch you both up. Go on, now, move. You're leakin' blood all over the floor."

Sobbing and stumbling, the two young men whose gunfighting days had just begun and ended staggered to the batwings and into the street.

Smoke and Al holstered their guns. Al smiled. "Good to see you again, Smoke."

"Same here, Al. You take care."

"Will do." The man walked out of the saloon and mounted up, riding away without even so much as a glance over his shoulder.

Smoke held up his empty mug. "Want to fill this up?"

"Oh, yes, sir!" the barkeep said. "It's on the house, Mr. Jensen. Yessiree, bob. On the house."

Smoke took his drink to a table by the window and sat down. "What about this brother of Rob's?" Smoke tossed the question out.

"Oh, I reckon he'll catch up with the herd and call you out, all right," a man said. "He ain't got no more sense than Rob. But he is a mite faster, I'll warn you of that. But I don't think you're in any mortal danger," he added drily.

"I already know that."

"They call him Rocky," another said.

Smoke was thoughtful for a moment. "He live far from here?"

" 'Bout three miles out of town."

"I don't want my herd stampeded or any of my hands hit by stray bullets. Go get him and let's straighten this mess out right now."

A man stood up. "I'll do that, Mr. Jensen. Yes, sir, I sure will."

The barkeep opened his mouth.

"I don't wish any further conversation." Smoke spoke the words softly.

"Right," the barkeep said. "Mouth is hereby closed."

It didn't take long for Rocky to ride in and swing down

from the saddle in front of the barber shop. Two guns and all. Smoke knew, by the way he walked, the man wasn't in any mood to talk. The man who had fetched him got him a beer and returned to his table.

"He says he's gonna kill you, Smoke."

"No, I don't think so."

"Well, here he comes," another stated.

Smoke waited about four feet inside the batwings. He had slipped on leather gloves.

Boots thudded on the old boards. "Jensen! You better make your peace with the Lord. 'Cause I'm shore gonna kill you for what you done to my brother."

Rocky slammed open the batwings and charged inside. Smoke hit him flush in the mouth. Rocky's boots went out from under him and he sailed right back out into the street, landing on his butt. The dust flew.

Smoke stepped out and kicked the gun from Rocky's hand. He reached down and slapped the man hard, twice across the face, addling him, and then jerked out his other Colt and tossed it into a horse trough. Then he hauled Rocky up and proceeded to beat the snot out of him.

Rocky didn't get a chance to land a single punch. All he did was receive them, and he received a goodly number of them, divided about equally between ribs and face.

When Smoke finally let the would-be gunslinger fall, he was pretty sure that Rocky's jaw was broken in at least two places and he had numerous broken ribs. Rocky would not be riding for a long time.

Smoke swung up into the saddle and faced the crowd of men and women. "Give him a message from me. Tell him I gave him his life. This time only. Explain to him that Carl and Rob crowded Al and me. Not the other way around. Try to get it through Rocky's head that if I ever see him again, and he's wearing a gun, I fully intend to kill him. On the spot." He turned his horse and rode out of town.

"I do like a feller who knows his mind and speaks it," a

man said. "And Jensen can sure enough speak it plain. Well, come on. Let's drag Rocky over to Ed's. Most excitement we've had in this town in ten years."

At the herd, Sally walked to her husband's side. "Any trouble in town?"

"Not to speak of. Saw Al Jacobs and we had a beer together. He's ranching and married now. I forgot to ask if he had any kids. He looked real good."

Sally looked at the blood splattered on Smoke's shirt. "It must have been a lively conversation. Get out of that shirt so I can soak it before the blood sets. What in the world did you two talk about?"

Smoke stripped off his shirt and handed it to her, then rummaged around in his bedroll for a fresh shirt. "We saved some lives there in the town. Al and me, we put two young fellows back on the right road. You might say we read to them from the scriptures."

She patted his arm. "I'm sure it was quite a sermon. Do we stay here for the night?"

"I think it would be best if we moved on for a few more miles. No point in wasting good weather."

Sally put hazel eyes on her husband. "Someday you must tell me about your impromptu Bible reading."

"Oh, I will. When we get a few more miles up the road."

They experienced no more trouble as the herd moved slowly north. The drovers pushed them into Montana, and after three days drive they turned the herd west. Now the real test began, for they were on no known trail. That meant that Smoke stayed busy all day, seeking a right of way for the herd and being careful not to damage the property of other ranchers and farmers. And the drovers had to work twice as hard in order to keep the herd together and not pick up anyone else's cows.

Hands from other ranches willingly pitched in to help. They did it for many reasons, including the chance to pick up news and to taste some of Sally's cooking, for the word had spread before them.

Many of them also wanted the chance to size up Smoke Jensen. The majority of the hands and ranchers who met him quickly found themselves liking the man, for they found in him a man who worked just as hard as his hands and who told it the way he saw it, pulling no punches. That was the Western way.

And the story of the shoot-out back in that little Wyoming town, and the fistfight that followed, had already spread, to be told and retold around the campfires of the West.

The boys in the drive got their wish, and they met some Indians. They were not hostile and appeared to be starving. But there was no way they were going to beg. They had been defeated on the battlefields, and now were not much of a threat to anyone. But beg they would not. Smoke could see that. He could also see hungry children and he couldn't stand that. Smoke gave them ten of his own cattle and wished them well.

"What kind of Injuns were those, Mr. Smoke?" Young Guy asked.

"Cheyenne. Proud people."

"They didn't look like very much to me."

"Some of the fiercest warriors that ever lived," Smoke told the boy. "Back when I was not much older than you, I lived with them part of one winter. Me and old Preacher. Indians are good people . . . in their own way. Their ways are just not like ours, that's all."

Smoke cut north for several days, to avoid the Indian reservations, then again pointed the herd west. They had one hell of a time crossing the Yellowstone, almost losing a hand when his horse panicked and floundered. They saved the hand, but the horse was swept downstream and the cowboy lost his horse, saddle, saddlebags, and Winchester.

Then they hit days of hot, dry weather before they reached

the Sweet Grass River. The cattle almost stampeded when they smelled the water. One old mossyhorn bull who had joined the herd a few days back charged a horse and gored it so badly, the horse had to be shot. When the horse fell, Harris was pinned under the saddle. The bull took out his anger on Harris before Smoke could kill it. Harris was buried beside the trail. He wasn't the first to have been killed on a cattle drive, and certainly would not be the last.

Smoke made a short talk after the body was lowered and covered, saying a few good things about Harris, and Denver read words from the Bible. Some of the boys had a hard time keeping back the tears.

When Sally sang "What A Friend We Have In Jesus," several of the boys and more than one of the men could no longer contain themselves and even old Denver had to horn his nose a couple of times. The whole affair just about did Smoke in, too, and he was glad to be back in the saddle and moving. It wasn't the first lonely grave he'd helped dig.

Smoke led them south of the Crazy Mountains and then led them north and west across the Sixteenmile River, keeping the Big Belt Mountains to the north. Smoke told his people they could visit Helena after the herd was delivered and have a rip-roarin' good time. Right now, the herd needed to be delivered.

Mountains towered all around them as Smoke wound the herd through valleys lush with summer vegetation. These were not yet the towering peaks that lay farther north, but they were respectable mountains just the same.

Smoke halted the herd in a long, wide, beautiful valley and told his people to let them graze. "This is where Duggan said he'd meet us," he told his crew. "So make camp and relax. We're a couple of days early." He smiled. "Give or take a week or so."

"This is puzzling," Sally told her husband, snuggled next to him that night. "Why didn't this Duggan want the herd taken straight to his range?"

"I don't know. Unless he doesn't want Clint Black to know about it, just yet."

"That must be it."

The next morning, Nate came fogging his horse into camp. "Two women comin', boss. Ridin' sidesaddle an' all. They some duded up, too. Funniest lookin' hats I ever did see."

"Two *women?*" Smoke asked. "Here?"

"There they come, boss. See for yourself."

The women were twins, and identical twins at that. They were elegantly dressed, in the very latest Eastern riding habits. Their hats were huge things, with what looked to Smoke like mosquito netting tied under their chins. They walked their horses over to a natural rise and stepped daintily from the saddle, handing the reins to a dumbstruck young Rabbit, who was bug-eyed staring at the pair.

"Which one of you is Mr. Jensen?" one twin asked.

"Right here, ma'am." Smoke walked toward them and took off his hat. "And you two would be . . . ?"

"I am Toni and this is my sister, Jeanne. Duggan."

Smoke got it then. T. J. Duggan. "You have got to be kidding!"

"Quite the contrary, Mr. Jensen. We own the Double D ranch."

Everybody gathered around, staring.

"Ah . . . this is my wife, Sally," Smoke finally managed to say.

"Pleased, I'm sure," the other twin said, and then dismissed Sally silently.

"Of the New Hampshire Reynolds," Smoke said, before Sally could step forward and bust one of these ladies right in the chops.

"Oh, my!" the other twin said. "I didn't realize. Of course! We've read about you, Sally. How wonderful to find some degree of breeding out here in this . . ." She looked around. ". . . bastion of coarseness and vulgarity."

"What the hell did she say?" Denver whispered to Shorty.

"Don't git me to lyin'," Shorty told him. "But I don't think it was no compliment."

"That's what I think, too."

"Where are your hands, Miss Duggan?" Smoke asked.

"I beg your pardon?"

"Your hands? No. I don't mean them. Not your hands. Your crew? Your cowboys?"

"Oh, we don't have any yet."

"You . . . don't have any? Well, how in the he . . . heck are you going to handle these cattle without a crew?"

"Oh, we'll leave that up to you," Toni said brightly. "I mean, that's what you do, isn't it?"

"On my own ranch, yes. I don't hire out to other people."

"Well, I'm certain we can work something out," Jeanne said. "Come now, time's wasting. Let's don't dawdle. We have quite a distance to go."

"Wait a minute!" Smoke said, exasperation in his voice. "Where is your ranch?"

"Twelve miles, that way," Toni said, pointing. "We camped in the timber last night. We'll pick up our equipment on the way back. We're quite expert in the woods, you know."

"No, I didn't know," Smoke said. "Camped in the woods," he muttered. "Experts, no less. All right," he said. "Get the cattle ready for the trail."

Sally was laughing at his expression. "Don't dawdle now, honey."

Smoke was muttering low curses as he mounted up.

"Did we do something wrong?" Jeanne asked Sally. "We've been out here from Boston for several months and we seem to, well, anger all the people we've come in contact with."

Sally climbed up on the wagon seat and took the reins. "I wonder why?" she said drily.

5

The ladies' camp was equipped like an African safari. Smoke and the other hands had never seen so much junk in their lives.

"What's that thing?" Rabbit asked, pointing to a canvas tent at the edge of the camp area. "It ain't even got no top to it."

"Don't ask me," Smoke said.

"One side is for bathing and the other side is a toilet," Sally informed them.

"Do tell?" Rabbit muttered.

"We're not going to make the ranch by nightfall," Smoke told the twins. "We'll be lucky to make two miles in this country. Best thing we can do is camp here for the night and leave early in the morning. You really have no one at the ranch?"

"Well, we have a cook and a nice young Spanish boy who takes care of the horses and does the lawn work," Jeanne replied. "We just can't get anyone else to work for us. We're obviously doing something wrong but no one will tell us what it is."

"You're just new out here," Smoke told them, putting on his diplomat's hat and lying through his teeth. "Takes Western folks a while to size a person up." He wanted to tell the twins that if they'd stop looking down their blue-blood noses at everybody, things might ease up a mite.

"Oh!" Toni said. "Well. I have an idea. We'll give a party and that will break the ice. What is it called out here? A whigdig?"

"A shindig, ma'am," Smoke corrected.

"Yes! That's it. I don't suppose there are any violinists close by?"

"I rather doubt it," Smoke said.

"Oh, well. My sister and I will entertain. We're very accomplished musicians."

"Wonderful," Smoke said.

"Yes. Jeanne is a flutist and I was trained as a classical pianist."

"Ought to be a real entertaining evening," Smoke said.

"Oh, quite! Are you familiar with Chopin?"

Smoke shook his head. He was getting a bad case of indigestion.

"Do you know the closest place where we might order caviar, Mr. Jensen?"

"No, ma'am," Smoke said wearily. "I sure don't."

"You see," Toni said during supper. "After our parents were killed, my sister and I came into quite a sizable inheritance. We have funds in other businesses, of course, but we felt it would be exciting to own a ranch."

"Right," Smoke said. "Have you met your neighbor yet, a Clint Black?"

"He came to call. He found something hysterically amusing. He laughed the entire time he visited. I found him quite boorish, to be truthful."

"What's boorish?" Ben whispered to Duke.

"Hell, I don't know. But I bet it ain't real nice."

"Yes," Jeanne said. "Mr. Black is a rather nice-looking man, in a rugged sort of way. But he's terribly coarse. His table manners were an abomination. We fixed cucumber sandwiches for him and he said he wouldn't feed those to his horse."

"You have to understand," Sally said, "that Western fare is simple, but filling and wholesome. Most out here grew up on beef and beans."

From the expression on her face, that cuisine didn't meet her approval. At all.

"Just where is the town of Blackstown?" Smoke asked.

"About twenty-five miles west of our location," Toni said. "A rather quaint little town."

The way she said it gave Smoke the idea that Blackstown appealed to her about as much as sticking her big toe into a fresh pile of cow droppings.

"Did Clint Black say anything, well, threatening to either of you?" Smoke asked the twins.

They exchanged glances. Toni replied. "Not . . . directly, Mr. Jensen. But we both feel there were some thinly veiled threats."

"Tell me about them."

"Well, he is an unmarried man and women are scarce out here. He made some rather crude advances at Jeanne, and then when she rebuffed him, he directed his attentions toward me. I told him that I was not interested. He said I'd come begging before all this was over. I asked what in the world he meant by that. He just laughed and walked away."

Jeanne said, "Then I noticed that we were being watched and followed constantly. When we tried to hire people to work on our ranch, they would just shake their heads, mumble something and walk off. It's obvious that Mister Black had ordered us boycotted, for some reason. We are able to shop in the town, for many of the merchants there don't care for the man or his high-handed tactics. Mister Black's brother,

Harris, a thug if I ever saw one, is the Sheriff, and his deputies are just as bad as he is, if not worse. All in all, it is not a pleasant situation."

"Who sold you this ranch?"

"It wasn't sold directly to us," Jeanne said. "Our attorneys are always looking for places to make our monies work, and when this property came on the market, they bought the ranch. However, they had no idea that we would personally come out here to run it." She looked directly at Smoke. "You think that we are ill-suited to do so and that we were wrong to come out here, don't you, Mr. Jensen?"

"Smoke. My name is Smoke. And in answer to your question, yes, I do think you're out of place here. Clint Black is a dangerous, ruthless, and power-hungry man. From what I was able to learn about him, he's about as easy to get along with as a rattlesnake."

The twins smiled, Toni saying, "Our attorneys said much the same about you, Mr. Jensen."

Smoke chuckled. "Have your attorneys ever been west of the Mississippi?"

"Heavens no!" Jeanne said. "But everyone they communicated with said you were a bad man."

Sally laughed. "Out here, Jeanne, the phrase 'a bad man' doesn't hold the same connotation as back East. It doesn't mean that person is evil, or not to be trusted, or anything like that. It means that person is a bad man to crowd or try to harm. It might mean he's a dangerous man in a fight. My husband is known as a bad man because he has the name of 'gunfighter.'"

"We saw the play," Toni said.

"That's too bad," Smoke told her. "I'm told it's terrible."

"And we've read the books," Jeanne said.

"They're even worse," Smoke replied.

"I must admit," Toni said, "that you are a rather, ah, imposing figure of a man. Have you really gunned down five thousand men?"

Smoke laughed aloud. "If I had done that, when would I have had the time to get married, build a home, father children, and run a ranch? I'm afraid the stories about me are highly exaggerated." He stood up and tossed out the dregs of his coffee cup. "I'm going to make a turn around the herd. It's getting late. We'd all best get ready to hit the sack."

"He's only gunned down about a thousand men," Sally said, with a mischievous glint in her eyes.

Smoke sighed.

"Oh, my!" the twins gasped.

A shot brought Smoke lunging to his feet, grabbing for his guns. He could hear the bawling of cattle and the thunderous roar of a stampede building. He jammed his feet into his boots and slung his gun belt around his waist just as the camp filled with horses. He could just make out hooded men, all wearing long dusters, and all with guns in their hands. A horse hit him and knocked him sprawling.

"Sally!" he called. "Run for the timber. Run, honey."

He struggled to get to his feet. A bullet tore into his shoulder and staggered him. He could hear the cries of wounded men as his crew was being shot to pieces. He was again knocked spinning by a running horse. He grabbed ahold of a rider's leg and jerked him out of the saddle, smashing him in the face with a big fist. A bullet nicked his head and he fell to the ground calling out Sally's name. Through the painful fog in his brain, he could hear the screaming of men and women and boys and the roar of a full-blown stampede. Clint Black! he thought. I should have placed more men on guard. I should have guessed he'd have the twins followed.

Then there was no more time left for thinking. Smoke had to stay alive. He had to find Sally. He had to fight.

He jumped up behind a rider and hammered blows at the man, knocking him out of the saddle. In the saddle, Smoke fumbled for the reins and found them. The night was so black, he could not see five feet in any direction. Something struck him on the head and the last thing he remembered was grabbing hold of the saddle horn as the badly frightened animal took off in a panicked run.

Warmth awakened him. He lay on the ground for several moments, not moving or opening his eyes. He listened. He could hear squirrels chattering and birds singing. A bee hummed past him. Without lifting his head, he opened his eyes. He was in the high country, he could tell that. But he didn't have the vaguest idea where in the high country. To make matters worse, he didn't know who he was.

He rolled over and pain tore through his left shoulder. Groaning, he sat up. His left shirtsleeve was bloody. Part of a large splinter was sticking out of his flesh. He remembered being shot, or thinking he'd been shot. He must have been hit with the stock of a rifle. The stock might have been broken and it ripped apart when whoever it was had hit him, driving the splinter into his shoulder. Gritting his teeth, he pulled the long piece of wood out of his shoulder. He looked at it and threw it away. He gingerly felt his head. It hurt. There were two lumps on his noggin and dried blood.

"Sally!" he said aloud, his voice a croak. He cleared his throat as the events of the night before came crashing back to him.

He looked up at the sun. About ten o'clock. He felt sudden panic try to overtake his emotions. He pushed panic aside and regained control. He pushed himself to his boots and almost fell, reaching out to grab a small tree for support. He leaned against the tree for a moment. Damn, but he was weak.

The camp had been attacked—he tried to sort out the jumble in his aching head. He remembered yelling for Sally to get away. He recalled the shooting and the hooded riders. He suddenly and vividly remembered the screaming of the women, the yelling and moaning of his hands, and the stampeding herd.

And he was thirsty; God, what he wouldn't give for a long drink of cold water. Taking several deep breaths, he looked around him. He had absolutely no idea where he was. But at least now he knew who he was.

He inspected himself for further wounds and could find nothing except bruises from being knocked down several times by running horses. Maybe he'd been kicked too. He just couldn't remember. Smoke started carefully down the slope, for he was strangely weak. And that was a condition he was unaccustomed to.

He dropped his hands to his guns. They were in place. He felt for his knife. It was there. Obviously, the attack had come so quickly, he had not had the time to pull his guns from leather.

He had to find Sally.

He fell twice on the way down the steep slope. He sat down and removed his spurs, sticking them in his back pocket. He found some berries and ate them and felt better. A few hundred yards later, he found a spring and bellied down on the ground and drank his fill. Smoke took off his bloody shirt and bathed his wounds. He found moss and placed that over the jagged rip in his shoulder, tying the moss secure with his kerchief. He drank again and could feel the strength returning to his powerful muscles and his head clearing.

A cold anger was filling his head. Smoke knew the sensation well. If Sally had been hurt, or killed—he knew he had to face that possibility—this countryside was going to run red with blood. Any man who would order the killing of women and boys did not deserve to live, and Clint Black had made one very large mistake. He had let Smoke Jensen live.

In a clearing, Smoke got his bearings. He picked out landmarks he had seen coming in and now knew his approximate location. He started toward the last camp they had made, figuring it was about five miles away.

He found a body but the rampaging cattle had trampled it beyond recognition. Then he found a boot and recognized it as belonging to one of the new hands. Eton. Smoke stuck a stick in the ground to mark the spot and walked on. He would be back to bury the remains.

He found Willie next. He knew it was the fifteen-year-old because of his overalls. He preferred them over jeans. Using another stick, he marked the spot and walked on, sadness mixed with the coldest anger he had ever experienced washing over him with every step.

Duke lay on the ground facedown. He had been shot a dozen times. In the back. Rabbit was next. Someone had roped and dragged him.

"Fourteen years old," Smoke muttered. "Fourteen years old."

He walked on. He could smell the wood smoke now. The raiders had probably torched the wagons. And probably piled on as many bodies as they could find.

Shorty had made a stand of it behind some rocks. But it didn't do him much good. He was riddled with bullet holes. Smoke took his rifle and all his cartridges. Davy had taken a round right through the head. Smoke took his leather waistcoat and slipped it on. He found Johnson and took his hat and gloves. A horse nickered close by and Smoke turned. The foreman's horse walked slowly toward him. Nate had managed to get saddled up. Smoke had no way of knowing the foreman's fate—but he could guess.

He pulled the saddle off the horse and rubbed him down with dry grass, talking to the animal, calming it. He smoothed out the saddle blanket, saddled up, and swung into the leather. Nate's Winchester was in the boot, so Smoke rode with Shorty's rifle across the saddle horn. He only rode a few hundred yards before he found his foreman. Nate and Little Ben had stood and fought it out to the end. Smoke took their weapons and ammunition and the canteen that one of them had grabbed.

"Goddamnit!" he cursed. "I'll see you in Hell, Black. I'll personally send you there."

He looked around him. "Where are you, Sally?"

The wind sighed and gave no answers.

"But, Jeanne . . . ?" Toni said.

"If she's alive, we'll find her," Sally assured the woman. "Right now we've got to stay low and quiet. The raiders are still beating the bushes for us. Now stay calm. We'll get out of this."

"Your husband . . . ?" Toni whispered.

"My husband is a hard man to kill. Now listen to me, Toni. These words are going to sound unfeeling to you. But I know how Smoke thinks. Smoke can take care of himself. If he's alive. And I've got to face that. Right now, he would want me to concentrate on survival. That's what we've got to do. We're no good to anybody dead. Come the night, I've got to strip some pants off of a dead hand and get you in them and out of that stupid-looking riding habit."

"Men's pants!"

"Yes, damnit, men's pants. That thing you're wearing would hang up on every twig and branch. We've got to be able to move quickly and silently. Have you ever fired a gun?"

"Heavens no!"

"This valley we're in. How long is it?"

"I . . . don't know. But it's very long and winding. Miles. And Sally? There aren't that many ways in and out."

"I was afraid of that. They chose the ambush site well. We're boxed in and you can bet they've got the passes covered. So we're better off staying right here for the time being. Well, I've got a rifle and my pistol, and my cartridge belt is full. Right now, we need blankets and food and water. Horses would be nice, but I think we're probably better off on foot. Now, Toni, you stay right here. Don't you move one inch from this spot. Do you understand me?"

"Don't leave me, Sally!"

"I've got to. I've got to get supplies. If I don't, we'll die. Don't move from here, Toni. For God's sake, *don't move."*

"I promise I won't. I swear it, Sally."

"I won't be gone long. Perhaps an hour. If I'm lucky, less than that. You stay low and quiet." She smiled at the woman. "You're tougher than you think, Toni. We all are when the going gets rough." She patted her arm and slipped into the brush. Away from Toni, she paused to compose herself. She was scared, but she couldn't let Toni see that.

"Smoke, honey," she muttered. "Where are you?"

6

Sally found Jake's body. The boy had been gut-shot and had dragged himself off in the bushes to die.

"Dear merciful God," Sally murmured. "Fifteen years old." She tugged the boy's jeans off and started to cover him up, then thought better of it. That would be a sign that she sure wouldn't want the raiders to find. "Sorry, Jake. You were a good hand."

Unlike Smoke, she had caught a glimpse of the brand on the horses of the raiders. The Circle 45. And one had seen her looking at the brand just a second before she leaped into the darkness of the bushes, dragging Toni with her. So they had to kill her. They couldn't afford to let her live and be a witness against them.

Circling, Sally found the body of one of the new men. Forrest. She took his gun and gun belt and hat and left him as she had found him. She made her way cautiously to the campsite and studied it for several moments before slipping up to the smoldering ruins of the wagons. All the bodies had been dragged away. She could see that sign. She grabbed up two blankets, a full canteen, a tarp, a knife still in its sheath, and a sack of canned foods. She was disappearing into the brush just as Smoke made his way up to the ruins.

Smoke had found no more bodies, and, like Sally, he read the sign where the bodies had been dragged off. He squatted, only his eyes moving, picking out the scattered articles he wanted. He moved very quickly, scooping up a blanket— there was a ground sheet and a blanket tied behind the saddle of his horse—a side of bacon that was half buried in the dust, a battered coffee pot and a sack of Arbuckles, another canteen and a loaf of bread that had been only slightly scorched by the fire. Then he was gone.

"You made a big mistake, Mr. Black," he muttered, swinging into the saddle. "You left me alive."

"Now listen up," Bobby told the young cowboys. "We're afoot, we ain't got no weapons, and we're in big trouble." He looked at Louie, Dan, Sonny, and Guy. "And yeah, I'm just as scared as you are. But Mr. Smoke made me ramrod of the remuda crew, so I'm givin' the orders. You take them. Understood?"

The quartet of very scared boys nodded their heads.

"We're in a pretty good place here. This blowdown ain't gonna let no horses through, and there ain't no cowboy gonna do nothin' much that he can't do from the saddle. So we stay right here. There's water to drink from that crick over yonder, and we all got a little poke of food. It ain't much. But it's got to do. We can't talk above a whisper. We can't move around. Just remember this, we seen them brands. Circle 45. So that means them thugs got to kill us all. If we keep our heads, maybe they'll give up after a time, thinkin' they got us all. It's the best I can do, boys."

Denver eased his old bones into a more comfortable position in the rocks where he lay about a mile from the ambush site. He wasn't hurt bad, just bruised all to hell and gone. He'd managed to grab some gear just as that damn horse hit him and knocked the crap out of him. He had a canteen of water, some biscuits, and a rifle. And he was alive.

Harvey and Jeff, Smoke's regular hands, lay in a thicket and tried to blend in with the earth. Jeff had a bullet in his leg and Harvey's left arm was busted. But they were alive.

Tim was the only one of the new hands to make it out alive. But he was weaponless, except for the sheath knife he carried in his boot. He'd seen those dirty bastards shoot down and ride down his friends with no mercy. One thing Tim knew for a dead-bang fact was that he was going to find those responsible and make them pay a terrible price. He'd prayed to God to give him the wherewithal to do just that.

Jeanne lay behind a log and listened to the men search for her. She cringed when she heard the things they said they were going to do with her and to her when they found her. She clutched a butcher knife in her right hand. Maybe they would do those terrible things. But she'd make one of them pay a fearful price before the others got to her. Then she listened to them ride off and the silence that followed was just about as terrifying. Jeanne did not think she had ever been this frightened. She rose from her hiding place and had not walked a hundred yards before discovering the body of one of Smoke's men. She stifled a scream and knelt down by the body, making up her mind to do what she felt she must.

She tugged off his boots and forced herself to pull off his jeans and shirt. Always keeping a wary and watchful eye, Jeanne undressed and then dressed in jeans and a men's shirt.

The cowboy's holster was empty. She looked around frantically for his gun. No gun; she couldn't find it.

Now she felt she had a chance of staying alive. If she could just get her fear under control.

Smoke picketed his horse near water and sat down to think matters through. Several times he'd come very close to being spotted on horseback, so he decided to stay on foot until he had scouted the valley through and arrived at a plan of action.

Clint Black had no choice but to kill them all. He could leave not one of them alive. Keeping that in mind, Smoke had ridden back to the bodies he'd found and pulled out the marking stake. That was a sign of a survivor that he just couldn't leave behind. Then, only a short time afterwards, from where he sat on the ridges, he had watched Circle 45 riders return to the bodies and drag them off. There was to be a mass grave somewhere to the south of the ambush site.

He and Nate had scouted out the long valley and found only a few passes. Clint had planned his ambush well. But how did he know a herd was coming? How could he have known? Toni and Jeanne's attorneys were Boston-based, and the twins had assured Smoke they had told no one locally about the herd. A puzzle.

Smoke tensed at the sound of a steel-shod hoof striking stone. He quickly shifted locations, moving into brush at the edge of the small clearing. His big hand closed around a rock about the size of an apple. His smile was hard, for Smoke had always been pretty good at chunking stones.

A Circle 45 rider, his dark duster tied behind the saddle, walked his horse slowly into the clearing. He gave the area a close once-over and then turned his horse, putting his back to Smoke. Smoke rose up, took aim, and flung the stone. The rock smacked into the rider's head and knocked him slap out of the saddle. He hit the ground and did not move. His horse trotted off a few yards and stopped.

Smoke moved from his hiding place and walked slowly toward the seemingly lifeless form. He walked slowly so he would not alarm the horse. He wanted that canteen, rifle, and rope. And he might have a bait of food in the saddlebags.

The rider's skull was busted open. He was alive, but just barely. Smoke looked down at the man and felt no pity, no remorse. Nothing. The man had chosen his way of life. To hell with him.

Smoke took the man's gun belt and then dragged the raider into some bushes and dumped him. He pulled the saddle off the horse and picketed it with his own. The saddlebags contained a sack of cartridges, some dirty socks, and two biscuits and bacon wrapped in paper. Smoke ate those, drank some water, and felt better. He then wrapped the dead man's weapons in a ground sheet and carefully hid them under a rotting log. If he found any of his own people alive, the chances were, they would need weapons.

With a grim expression on his face, Smoke picked up his rifle and started walking. He was going hunting.

Toni had not moved. But she was so relieved to see Sally that she could not contain her tears. Wiping her eyes, she whispered, "They came so close, I thought sure they would see me. I could hear them talking. They were saying vulgar, filthy things about what they would do to the women once they found us. I have never heard such disgusting things."

"They're not going to do anything to us," Sally assured her. "Put these jeans on while I go through the supplies I brought back. Go on, Toni, do it."

So they searched this area, Sally thought. *Good. Maybe they won't be back.*

But deep inside, she knew they would. And the search

would be much more thorough this time, probably with men on foot. But she didn't share that with Toni.

Clint Black stood in the big family room of his house and glared at his foreman, Jud Howes. He got his temper back under control and took several deep breaths. "You're certain that none of the bodies found were those of women?"

"Positive, boss. We checked real close. All men and boys."

"And the bodies have been disposed of?"

"They'll never be found."

"What'd you do with them?"

"Put 'em in Jackson's Cave. Way back in there. I'll take dynamite up there later and seal the entrance."

"That's good. But be sure that you do that, Jud. The cattle?"

Jud shook his head. "They're scattered from one end of that valley to the other, boss. It'll take every hand we got a good two-three weeks to round them all up."

"We'll deal with that problem later. Just be sure that no one enters that area until we're done."

"Right, boss. I've got them covered."

"Get every hand we can spare in there. Search that area, find those damn people, and kill them."

"Right, boss. One thing puzzles me, though. Some of the guys we found didn't have no pants on."

"Probably didn't have time to pull them on, don't you imagine?"

"Yeah . . . we hit 'em hard and fast, for a fact."

"Get busy, Jud. Let's wrap this thing up and put it behind us."

Smoke rested the rest of that day and tended to his wounds and bruises. There was a bottle of horse liniment in the dead raider's saddlebags—the one with a busted head—

and Smoke treated his bruises with that. He bathed his splinter wound and bound it with a strip of the dead man's shirt, once it had dried after Smoke washed it in the stream. One of the night herder's horses had found him, seeking human company, and Smoke found a pair of fresh socks and some .44 rounds in the saddlebags. As soon as the sun went down, Smoke went on the prod.

He had caught the smell of food cooking and decided he'd drop in for a bite . . . uninvited. He wanted a cup of coffee in the worst way.

And he wanted to spill some Circle 45 blood.

He put Sally as far out of his mind as he could. It wasn't a heartless act on his part, it was just practical.

He could hear the lowing of cattle from various parts of the valley, some faint, some no more than two hundred yards off. The cattle were probably scattered all to hell and gone. Smoke left the timber and fell in with a small bunch of cattle, slapping a few on the rump to get them moving in the direction he wanted to go. He got in the center of the bunch and crouched low.

When he drew close to the dot of flames from the campfire, he left the cattle and moved into the timber. He began huffing and coughing like a puma. The sound was so real it scared the cattle and they ran off a few hundred yards. Smoke used their noise to work close to the camp.

"Damn painter out yonder," a man said. "And close too."

"He won't come near the flames," another said. "Turn that bacon, Wilson. I'll give these beans a stir."

"You hope he don't come close," another said.

Smoke had pinpointed the raider's fires. The nearest one to his location was a good two miles away. Smoke moved in closer. Four men sat around the fire. A real stupid thing to do, for it destroyed their night vision. But that didn't make any difference, for in about thirty seconds, the only thing they'd be seeing was Hell.

He lifted his rifle and let it roar, working the action as fast as he could. When the roaring was only an echo, Smoke was running toward the fire and the food and the dead and dying bodies. He stripped the bodies of weapons and ammo.

One was still alive. "Damn your eyes!" he groaned.

Smoke, normally not a profane man, told the dying raider what he thought of men who would kill boys and women. The venom in his words shocked the man. Then, as the raider lay bleeding and dying by the fire, Smoke took two thick slices of bread, made a sandwich of the bacon and dug into the beans, then calmly poured himself a cup of coffee.

"You ain't human!" the raider managed to gasp the words.

Smoke threw back his head and howled like a great gray wolf, the howling echoing around the valley. Another wolf across the valley joined in the night's chorus as the raider lay on the ground, his eyes wide in astonishment.

Smoke huffed and coughed like a puma and then smiled at the man. But he was smiling at a dead man. Smoke dumped the weapons on a ground sheet, bundled it up, and, taking the pot of beans and the bread, vanished into the night.

A mile away, Sally smiled. "That first call was no wolf," she told Toni. "That was Smoke. He's *alive!*"

Jud was the first to reach the death scene. He looked at the four men sprawled in their own blood and cussed.

"Jud," a Circle 45 hand said. "They was cookin' beans when I was over here."

"So what?"

"The pot's gone. Whoever done this took their guns and the bean pot."

"I think we're in trouble, Cleon. Big trouble. I don't think that body Fatso thought was Jensen was really him. I think Jensen's out yonder. I think that was Jensen howlin' like a lobo."

"He ain't but one man, Jud. And we got fifty men."

"Forty-six," Jud quietly corrected.

7

Harvey and Jeff had heard the gunshots and then the howling of a lobo wolf. They had looked at each other and smiled. They'd been with Smoke a long time, and they'd both heard him talk to the wolves and the pumas many times. They snuggled back into their hiding place. The raiders didn't know it, but they were in trouble.

Sally lay back on the ground sheet and smiled as she snuggled into her blanket. Her man was alive and on the prowl. The Circle 45 men had grabbed onto something they couldn't turn loose of. And they were about to find that out . . . in blood. Their own.

Smoke returned to his hidden camp and ate the beans, sopping out the juice with the bread. He wished he had another cup of coffee, but a man can't ask for everything.

Jud Howes was riding hard for the ranch. Clint had to be informed of this new development. With Jensen alive, that really put a fly in the ointment. Jud had heard about that crazy German fellow who'd chased Smoke all over the country—with a passel of hired gunslingers helping him—hunting Jensen like you would an animal. Smoke had turned the whole thing around and the hunters became the hunted in the deadliest game they'd ever found themselves in. Jensen won.

"Damn!" Jud said. "I wish that fool Baylis had stayed down in Wyoming and kept his mouth shut."

Denver eased his bruised body and smiled when he heard the wolf howling and the gunshots. He had him a hunch that Smoke Jensen was alive and well and on the prod. He just hoped that Miss Sally and those other two women were all right.

Smoke rolled up in his blankets and went to sleep. Tomorrow was going to be a busy day.

Just as gray was tinting the skies, Smoke took his rifle and eased down toward the valley floor. He'd picked out a good location the past afternoon and planned on really getting this war under way.

His anger and grief and sadness were buried deep within the man, the coals banked, kept hot and smoldering. Today was the day he was going to show Clint Black and his renegade hands that wars are not that easily won.

He just wished he knew whether Sally was alive or dead.

Harvey held the limb back with his good arm, but if that rider didn't come on, he was going to have to turn loose; his arm was trembling from the strain.

The Circle 45 hand looked around, was satisfied that this area was clean, and rode on. Harvey released the thick limb and the green, springy wood impacted with the raider's face. Harvey cringed as the sound of bones and teeth breaking came to him. The thick limb had caught the Circle 45 hand smack in the mouth, knocking him out of the saddle, knocking him unconscious, and smashing his face.

Harvey grabbed the reins and calmed the spooked horse. He limped over to the unconscious raider and ripped off his gunbelt, slinging it around his waist. He took the Winchester from the boot and removed the saddlebags and canteen. He turned around and almost messed his longhandles when he saw a man standing a few yards away. The Colt leaped into his hand and he almost killed a friend.

"Whoa, Harvey!" Tim said in a hoarse whisper. "For God's sake, man, don't shoot."

"Jesus, Tim. I'm sorry, boy." He holstered the Colt.

The men grinned and shook hands. "You alone?" Tim asked.

"Got Jeff with me. He's got a slug in his leg. But I don't think it's broke. Come on, help me tie this no-count in the saddle."

They took the raider's blanket and ground sheet, tied him, belly across the saddle, and slapped the horse on the rump. The animal went bumping out of the timber and loping across the meadow.

"As many tracks as there is out yonder," Tim said, "they'll have a time tryin' to track that horse back to us. You got a good hole to hide in?"

"You bet. Come on."

Jeanne pulled back into a thicket as the search intensified. Once the searchers came so close, she could have reached out and touched the leg of a horse. She was still badly frightened, but that fright had been tempered by anger and a strong resolve to survive. She knew nothing of guns, but if she could get her hands on a weapon, she would by God learn. What had happened, and what was happening to her and the others, was an outrage that she was not going to tolerate. She knew from listening to the raiders talk that her sister and Sally were alive. She knew that Smoke Jensen was alive and fighting back. She knew that some other cowboys had not been found. So that meant they had a chance of surviving this terrible act of . . . of what? She didn't know why Clint Black had done this. Could think of no logical reason.

She fought back tears.

Smoke sighted the rider in and the Winchester roared. It was a righteous hit, the slug knocking the Circle 45 hand from the saddle. The man did not move. Smoke bellied down and waited. It was not a long wait.

Three Circle 45 riders came pounding to the scene, which told Smoke they didn't have a whole lot of sense. Smoke emptied two of those saddles before the third one could lay on his horse's neck and get the hell gone from that place.

Smoke ran down the slope, ripped gunbelts from the three and gathered up the reins and ran back up the slope into the timber. He quickly roped the horses together, mounted up, and changed locations, moving about a mile before he once more left the saddle and got into position behind some rock, an earthen embankment behind him.

"Mr. Smoke?" The boy's voice came from behind him.

Smoke turned his head and looked up into the pale face of Bobby, peering over the lip of the embankment.

Smoke grinned at the boy. "You're pretty good, Bobby. Not many men could have Injuned up on me."

"I didn't, sir," the lad admitted. "I was layin' up here watchin'. I got Louie, Dan, Sonny, and Guy hid out in a blowdown about five hundred yards from here."

"Good! Good! Take those guns I've got looped on the saddle horns and those canteens and food and bedrolls. Get back in there and stay put. Don't use those guns unless the night riders are right up on you and there is no way out. I know where you are, now, and I'll be back. We'll get out of this, Bobby. I promise you."

"Yes, sir, Mister Smoke. I'm gone."

"Get the men out of there," Clint told his foremen. "We're losing too many hands to that damn Jensen. He's turned into a savage. Get them all out and plug up the passes. Hell, we can keep them in there forever."

Jud wasn't too sure about that, but he wasn't running this show. He pulled out his pistol and fired the prearranged signal. From his hidden position, Smoke watched the hands stop, listen to the shots, then turn and ride toward the north end of the long valley.

"Your boss doesn't have much taste for the battle," he said aloud, then stood up. "Dirty, low-down, cowardly, ambushing son of a bitch!" he added.

Jeanne rose up to her knees just as the unshaven lout spotted her and opened his mouth to yell. She threw the butcher knife with all her strength, with no hope of doing any damage to the rider.

The knife turned slowly in the air and an astonished Jeanne watched as the blade buried itself in the rider's shoulder. He dropped his six-gun and yelled, the scream startling the horse. The animal took off like a lightning bolt, the rider holding on. Jeanne ran to the gun, picked it up, and cocked it. Holding it with both hands, she pointed it and pulled the trigger.

The slug just nicked the horse on the butt and he pitched his rider; the Circle 45 hand landed on his head, breaking his neck. Jeanne ran to the man; fighting back waves of nausea at the sight of the corpse, she jerked off the man's gun belt and ran back into the timber.

"Missy!" The call turned her around, bringing up the pistol.

Jeanne started weeping tears of joy at the sight of Denver, hobbling painfully toward her. "Oh, my God!" she cried.

"Hush, now, Missy," Denver soothed her. "We're all right. We made it. Them hands done been called back to the barn, so to speak. Smoke's been raisin' hob and hell with 'em. I think I know where he is. Come on."

"Let's go, boys," Smoke called from the saddle. "Let's see

who is left alive. Ride single file, behind me and keep your eyes open."

Jeff, Harvey, and Tim hailed them from the timber and Smoke swung down and got Jeff into the saddle. They moved on toward the ambush site.

Sally had heard the signaling shots and watched as the riders gathered on the floor of the valley and pulled out. She walked back to Toni. "They're all leaving, Toni. Come on. Let's get back to the ambush site."

"Why?"

"Because that's where Smoke will expect to find me. Come on, Toni. We made it."

Smoke and Sally held on to each other for a long moment. Then they pulled back and smiled for a second. Sally sobered her smile.

"This is all that survived?" she asked, cutting her eyes.

"Yeah. We lost thirteen, all told."

"The boys?"

"Willie, Jake, and Rabbit. They dragged Rabbit."

Denver cussed, low and long. For all his grousing, he liked the boys, and had let Rabbit swipe a cookie every now and then when Rabbit thought he wasn't looking.

Smoke said, "The cattle trampled Eton. I recognized him by a boot. The herd got Willie. He was wearing overalls. Duke had been shot a dozen times, in the back."

Jeff and Harvey loaded their pistols up full and closed the loading gate. Tim continued pushing cartridges into his Winchester.

"Shorty made a stand of it, and he probably got lead in a few of them. Davy took a slug through the head. Johnson made a fight of it. Nate and Little Ben fought them to the end."

"I found Jake's body," Sally said somberly. "They shot him in the belly. He died hard."

"I found one of the men," Jeanne said. "I changed into his clothing. I'm sorry. I didn't know his name. Only his face."

"He'd be honored to have you wearin' his duds, ma'am," Tim said.

"We found several cases of food, boss," Denver said. "I reckon them raiders didn't do a good job of searchin'. And I dragged the big coffee pot out and we'll have some coffee directly."

"Good. You boys scrounge around and see what pots and pans you can come up with. Tim, ride over to that little bunch of cattle over there"—he pointed—"and cut one out and butcher it. We'll have steaks, if nothing else. Sally, take a look at my shoulder and then we'll cut the slug out of Jeff's leg."

"Why?" Jeanne asked him, while Sally was cleaning out and redressing the splinter wound, and washing out the bullet groove in his scalp. She had never seen so many muscles on a man. The man's upper torso was huge. "Why did they attack us. Why?"

"To kill you, get the cattle, and then take possession of your ranch. By the time your Eastern attorneys got wind of your deaths, and that might take months, and found their way out here, everything would be settled. False bill of sale, the whole bit."

"The man is *mad!*" Toni said.

"No. He's not crazy. He's just ruthless and greedy. Clint probably thinks he's got us trapped in here. But there are ways out he doesn't know of." Smoke smiled. "A cowboy will explore as long as he can do it sitting in leather," he said to the twins. "But walking for long distances is not something he's real fond of doing. They'll have the north and south ends guarded. They'll be guarding the trail that you ladies used coming in. And they'll have that notch over there on the other side guarded." He pointed across the valley. "But there are other ways in and out. We just have to find them."

"And you are confident that you will be able to do that?" Jeanne asked.

Smoke's smile was brief and savage. "I'm confident that I will find a way out this valley. I'm confident that I will get us out. And I am confident that I will kill the dirty son who ambushed us."

"Coffee's ready," Denver called.

"I found our saddles!" Guy called from the edge of the timber. "Them raiders wasn't gonna burn no good leather. They was gonna keep them for personal use. Includin' all our saddlebags."

"One more mistake Clint made," Smoke muttered.

"You damn fool!" Clint's brother raged at the man. "Don't you realize what you've done?"

Clint lazily lifted a hand and waved it off.

"No, Clint," the sheriff corrected. "You can't wave this off. The times and the ways may have changed somewhat in the West, but the treatment of women has not. You even had four of your rowdies ride out when you told them of this ambush. Oh, I don't think they'll talk about it. They were loyal to the brand. But you've put something into motion that's like an avalanche. It can't be stopped; it's got to come crashing down and run its course."

"You worry too much," Clint said, pouring a fresh cup of coffee. Harris waved off the offer of coffee.

"Smoke Jensen! My God, man! Of all the herds to strike at, you picked one belonging to Smoke Jensen."

Clint looked at his brother. "You know him, Harris?"

"Not personal. But I saw him in action one time down in Colorado. The man is awesome. He's fearless. There ain't a nerve in his body. You can't beat him with guns. You can't beat him with fists . . ."

"I have never seen the man I couldn't stomp into the ground," Clint replied coldly.

"Don't try Smoke Jensen," his brother warned. Harris shook his head. "I thought we agreed the lawlessness was to end?"

"You goin' soft on me, brother?" Clint asked the question quietly.

"You know better. But times are changing and you're not changing with them. I say that in ten years we'll be a state. And with that comes a state police force and better law enforcement." He rose from his chair and paced the room. "I don't know how we can cover this up, Clint."

"We kill the rest of them in the valley," the rancher said. "It's simple."

Harris turned from the window to stare at his brother. "Women and boys, Clint? No. This ends now. You . . ."

Clint flew into a rage. He jumped from his chair and stalked across the large room to face his brother. "Goddamn you! Don't you be givin' no orders to *me*. I put you in office, I . . ."

"The *people* elected me, Clint," Harris corrected. "Yeah, yeah, you hung this badge on me years back. But then we held elections, and the *people* voted on who they wanted to be their sheriff. And they chose me. It's taken me ten years to weed the deputies loyal to you out of my department. But I did it. And now, you, by God, are going to listen to me. I'll cover for you just this one time. Then it's over. I'll not cover for you again."

Brothers stood toe to toe and eyeball to eyeball for a very long moment. Finally Clint grunted and winked. He walked back to his desk and sat down. "All right, Harris. Lay it out."

"I'm taking a posse out to the valley. This afternoon. All your rowdy hands had better be gone from the passes. Where were the bodies dumped?"

"I don't know what they done with them," Clint lied.

"I'll listen to the survivors' stories. I'll probably hear that the brand on the night riders' horses was Circle 45, since you gave me a report stating that a number of horses were stolen from you the other night. I'll apologize to the survivors. Smoke Jensen won't buy it. And he might come lookin' for you. I don't know. But if he calls you out, I won't interfere. The war is over, Clint. The lawlessness is over. I won't stand for it. I never liked your high-handed and roughriding ways. You're not the Almighty, no matter what you think. I've got a tarnish on my name just from being your brother. I'm going to clear my name, as best I can. Seeing you behind bars won't bring back the dead out there in that valley. Those . . . boys that came along for a summer's adventure. I don't see how you sleep at night. I can't undo what you and your men have done. But I can, by God, see that it never happens again. And I mean it, Clint. I mean it. I don't want to have to lock you up. But I will. After this day, I've told the last lie for you. You and me, we're flesh and blood, Clint. But you took a wrong road. You and me, Clint, we took separate trails. And Clint? Don't ever think you're better with a gun than I am. I'll shoot your ears off if you ever drag iron against me."

Harris Black plopped his hat on his head and stalked out of the office. He slammed the door behind him.

Clint Black sat behind his desk, his mouth hanging open. He was very nearly in shock.

8

"Riders comin'!" Tim yelled from his lookout post. "Boss, I think it's the law."

"Is this Harris Black as bad as his brother?" Sally asked the twins.

"Some say yes, others say no," Jeanne said.

"He was elected by a clear majority of the people," Toni added.

The sheriff and four tough-looking deputies rode up to the ambush site and dismounted. They all took off their hats in deference to the ladies. They all stared briefly at the ladies dressed in men's clothing.

Sally accurately pegged the sheriff as a man torn between loyalties. A man in a mental quandary. His face was a study.

"Somebody tell me what happened," Harris said.

"That murderous brother of yours sent hooded night riders against us," Toni said. "They stampeded the herd and killed more than a dozen men and boys."

Harris sighed as his deputies exchanged glances, looks that were not lost on Smoke.

"If they were hooded, ma'am," Harris said. "How do you know they were from the Circle 45?"

"By the brands on the horses," Jeanne said.

Smoke and Sally were staying quiet.

"Clint Black reports horses stolen from him the other night," Harris said. "That might account for it. And I said 'might.' "

Jeanne and Toni snorted quite unladylike.

Harris cut his eyes to Smoke. Lord, but the man looked awesome. He just stood there, big and tough and no backup in him. Harris knew there was no way he could stop the war that was about to start. He wasn't sure he wanted to. "I saw you once or twice. You'd be Smoke Jensen."

"That's right. And the hands that were murdered worked for me. Three of them young boys. It takes brave men to attack women and children. The boys, I'd like to add, were unarmed. I saw to that on the trail."

The sheriff rubbed a big hard hand across his face. That he was in mental pain was obvious to all.

"How did you hear about this, Sheriff?" Sally asked.

"My brother told me," the sheriff replied truthfully.

Smoke sensed that the man had carefully rehearsed this in his mind on the ride out.

"And you intend to do what about it?" Toni asked.

"See that it never happens again. And if it does, it'll be only over my dead body. Now, these deputies will stay out here with you to see to your safety." He tried a smile. "You feed 'em right and they'll probably help you round up your stock and get it over to the Double D. Your place is all right, Miss Toni, Miss Jeanne. I checked on that comin' out."

"Thank you, Sheriff," Jeanne said. "I just may have to revise my opinion of you."

Harris nodded his head. He chose not to reply to that.

Smoke said, "Start rounding up the cattle, boys. Dan and Guy, you'll come with me into town at first light. We'll rent a wagon to haul back supplies."

"The supplies will be paid for, Mr. Jensen," Harris said. "I've seen to that. Whatever you need, you just pick up and lay on the counter at Hanlon's Emporium. Leather goods and clothing and guns and so forth is waiting for you at shops all over town. There are rooms at no cost for you at the hotel." He didn't tell them his brother was picking up the tab for everything. His brother didn't know it yet.

Smoke and Sheriff Harris Black were left together for a few moments. "You real fond of your brother, Sheriff?" Smoke asked.

"I wonder now if I ever even liked him." He cut his eyes to the man some called the last mountain man. "Why do you ask?"

"Because it's real easy to prove that your brother sent his hands to ambush us."

"He lost some," Harris spoke the words very softly.

"Yeah. And I got them laid real neat, all in a row, about a half a mile from where we're standing."

"Why are you telling me this?"

"So you can take a probably much-needed vacation."

Harris stood silent for a few seconds. "I don't think I like that idea."

"Sheriff." Smoke spoke low. "I can have twenty-five or so of the randiest old gunfighters the West has ever known in here in a week. I can travel about fifty miles from where we're standing and round up just about that many old mountain men—they raised me, Sheriff. Or helped to. You don't think those men would like to go out of this life in a blaze of glory? Think again. My neighbor down in Colorado is Johnny North. The sheriff is Monte Carson. One of my best friends in this world is Louis Longmont. I'm friends with the Mexican gunfighters, Carbone and Martine. Cotton Pickens is a friend of mine. Do you want me to continue with this list, Sheriff?"

"It won't be necessary," Sheriff Black said, some stiffness to his words. He got Smoke's message, very loud and clear.

"What I'm going to do, Sheriff, is this: I'm going into the horse-breeding business. So I think I'll just stick around this part of the country, looking at horses. And while I'm here, I'll just act as the foreman of the Double D. I'll do the hiring. After I send a few telegrams for hands. Hands, Sheriff. Hands. Not gunfighters. Just good steady cowboys who ride for the brand. You know the type, don't you?"

Oh, yes, Harris Black knew the type. Men born with the bark on. Men who were not gunfighters, but who could and would damn sure use a rifle or pistol. Men who rode for the brand and God help anyone who tried to rustle cattle from that brand or who bad-mouthed the owner of that brand. Peaceful men for the most part, men who would give you two days' work for a day's pay. Men who would eat dust, ride through torrential rain or blizzards, work from can to can't, all for thirty or forty a month and grub. The American cowboy. And his brother didn't have a man on his place who could shine a cowboy's boots.

"I figure there are probably two hundred head of cattle, maybe more than that, that were injured so badly in the stampede, they'll die or have to be destroyed. I expect your brother to replace every one of them. And make sure that a half a dozen of them are bulls."

The sheriff looked at Smoke for a moment, then shrugged his shoulders philosophically.

"Your brother have many gunslicks on his payroll?"

"Most of them are gunhands. Or fancy themselves as such. I got out of that business before the name stuck to me."

Smoke smiled. "Yeah, I know, Sandy."

Harris cut his eyes and smiled. "I wondered if you'd recognize me. I was hoping you wouldn't."

"It's safe with me. Gunslicks and cattle aren't a good mix. What's your brother doing about branding and roping and night-herding and such?"

"He sold off most of his herd."

"And had plans to seize this one."

Harris's eyes tightened just a bit before he spoke. "Your words, not mine."

"Your eyes gave you away."

"I'm hoping my brother will pull in his horns and get straightened out."

"Too late."

"Why?"

"Because I'm going to kill him, that's why."

The blunt statement from Smoke had shocked Harris. He was still thinking about it as he rode back to town. Blood was thick, yes, but on the practical side of it, he could not be angry with Jensen for going after his brother. His brother had plotted the coldblooded murders of over a dozen men and boys, and had planned on killing three women.

That was inexcusable and unforgivable in a country where even a careless remark to a lady or a slight jostling of a woman on the street could culminate in a killing.

It had been the matter-of-fact and careless way Smoke had stated his intentions that had shocked Harris. He had spoken the words with no more emotion than if he had said he was going to kill a rattlesnake.

Well, the thought came to him, his brother could be compared to a rattlesnake, he supposed.

He was still ruminating on the subject when he swung down in front of his office. His one remaining deputy in town was sitting on the bench on the boardwalk.

"Jensen gonna come hell for leather, Sheriff?" the deputy asked.

"No," Harris said, sitting down. "But he is going to kill my brother. He told me so."

The deputy took his time rolling a cigarette. He lit it and said, "That's something that's past due."

Harris looked at the man. He could not even work up a

slight anger at the words. Not anymore. He knew how true they were. But it did hurt just a little. His baby brother.

He had been in another part of the west when Clint came into this area, and Harris still had never found out where and how his brother had started his empire. Probably with stolen cattle . . . and killings.

Harris had accepted the badge he now wore because he felt his brother was an honorable man. It didn't take him long to see how wrong he was. But still he stuck it out while the town and the country grew, turning his back on his brother's schemes and cheating and the night-riding of his men. Finally Harris had told him, "No more. No more burning out of farmers and small ranchers. It's over."

And surprisingly, it had stopped. But by then, Clint had grown so wealthy and powerful and land-rich that he could afford to stop it.

Now this . . . disgrace.

He stood up from the bench. "Pitiful sight out there, Harry. Make a man's blood run cold. And Jensen killed about a dozen of Clint's men. Had them all stretched out neat and in a row for me to see. No question that Clint was behind it. Then he looked at me with those cold rattlesnake eyes and told me flat out he was going to kill my brother."

"And you said . . . ?"

"Nothing. I just walked off. I never met a man like Jensen before. And you can believe I've known some damn salty ol' boys in my time. I've covered up a lot for Clint over the years, but nothing like this. I've never covered up murder. That I know of. He's got all his hands ready to testify that no one left the ranch the night of the raid. And Clint's gonna say that he fired them dead hands a week before the raid. It would be Jensen and them's word against forty or more hands. No court would convict any of them. I don't know what to do, Harry."

"You want a suggestion?"

"I'm open."

"Back off. Don't get in Jensen's way. It's a hard thing to have to swallow, but your brother is no good. Now he's tangled with a man who don't have no backup in him and who's got the wherewithal to stand tough. Don't get caught up in the middle of this."

Harris shook his head. "I'm a poor excuse for a lawman, Harry."

"That's not true," the deputy said sharply. "We've got a good department. Judges have complimented you on your performance. There is a legal word for what you ought to do in this, but I can't think of it right off. It means stay the hell out of it, or get someone else in here to handle it, or something like that."

"I do that, it just proves that I'm not capable of sheriffin' this county. But I think, Harry, there comes a time when the law's got to back off and let men settle their own affairs. There ain't no law against men callin' each other out. Not yet anyways. If that happens, it happens. Tomorrow is gonna be an interestin' day, I'm thinking."

The townspeople gathered on the boardwalks as the line of horses came walking slowly up the street. The bodies of the Circle 45 night riders were tied belly down across the saddles. It was not a pleasant sight and the smell was more than slightly worse. Smoke stopped the grisly parade in the center of town and dumped the bodies in the dust of the street.

The foreman of the Circle 45, Jud Howes, was standing under the awning in front of a saloon. Several of his men stood with him.

"Oh, hell," Harry whispered.

"Yeah," Harris replied. "Me, too."

Smoke stood by the pile of bodies and said to the crowds that lined the streets, "I'm Smoke Jensen. These dead men are, or were, Circle 45 riders. They attacked our camp a couple of nights ago. They killed ten of my men and murdered three young boys. They tried to kill the Duggan twins and my wife. Dispose of the bodies in any manner you see fit."

Smoke turned, spotted the horses wearing the Circle 45 brand, and lifted his eyes to the men in front of the saloon. They were fine animals and the saddles were top quality.

"Who rides these horses?" Smoke called.

"Me and these boys here," Jud said. He was thinking that this just might be his last day on earth.

"Write me out a bill of sale for them. All of them. Including the saddles and the rifles and the ropes."

"Do . . . what?" Jud asked.

"A lot of our stock was killed, run off, or maimed in that ambush the other night. I'm claiming these horses as part of the replacement. Now either write out a bill of sale, or drag iron. Either way. It doesn't make a damn to me."

"We can take him, Jud," a hand called Ron said. "Let's do it."

"Shut up," Jud whispered. "You know what Clint said. All right, Jensen," he raised his voice. "We didn't have nothin' to do with that raid. But if you think these horses will help make up for your loss, you're welcome to them."

"I'll be damned!" Ron said. "I paid Clint a hundred and fifty dollars for that roan. That ain't no rough string horse. That's mine! And you can go to hell, Jensen."

Smoke shot him. His draw was so smooth and quick, it was not possible for the human eye to follow. The slug took Ron in the center of the chest and he was dead before he hit the boardwalk. His hand had not even closed around the butt of his .45.

"Good God!" Harry whispered.

"And I thought I was fast," Harris said.

"Your play," Smoke said to Jud. He had slipped his .44 back into leather.

"I said you could have them horses, Jensen," Jud replied, his voice husky from shock. He had never seen anyone draw a gun that fast. "Soon as I can find pen and paper, I'll write out a bill of sale."

"That's good. And you boys are gonna walk back to the Circle 45."

"We gonna do what?" a hand named Cleon asked.

"I said you're going to walk back. Because no one in this town is going to sell or loan you a horse. Now write out that bill of sale and start hoofin' it. Now!"

A shopkeeper came up with a tablet and a pen and ink. With a smile, he handed them to Jud. The smile infuriated Jud, but he wisely said nothing about it. Smoke couldn't hang around forever. Their day would come. He wrote out the bill of sale, waved the paper dry, and held it out to Smoke.

Smoke stepped forward, took it, inspected it, and then said, "Start walking."

"What about Ron?" Jud asked, pointing to the dead night-rider.

"He'll be taken care of," Smoke told him. "And your boss will receive the bill for the burying. Now unbuckle your gun belts and let them fall. We lost guns in the raid, too. Do it and then move out."

The astonished and mostly amused townspeople watched as the Circle 45 men dropped their gun belts and slowly stepped off the boardwalk and began the long trek back to their range. There would be several gunslicks soaking their blistered feet that night.

The undertaker strolled up and began measuring Ron for a box.

Smoke turned to face the sheriff. "You said something about wagons to haul the supplies back?"

"Down at the livery," Harris replied. "You do have a way of getting your point across, Smoke."

"Yeah, I do, don't I?"

9

Smoke walked into Hanlon's Emporium where the boys, Dan and Guy, were waiting for him. A nervous Hanlon was behind the counter.

"That was some shooting there, Mr. Jensen," Hanlon said.

"Yes, sir. That's something I can tell my grandchildren about, for sure. Anything in the store you want, sir, you and your hands just lay it out here on the counter and it's all taken care of. Yes, siree."

Smoke had taken all the raiders' guns, so they were high on guns and ammo and low and out of everything else. It didn't take long to fill the bed of the wagon.

"Charge it all to my brother's account, Hanlon." Sheriff Black spoke from the door.

"Yes, sir, Sheriff. I'll certainly do that."

Harris walked in and got him several crackers from the barrel and cut off a wedge. He looked at Smoke and held out the crackers and cheese.

"Yeah," Smoke said. "And the boys too." He smiled. "Since your brother is buying."

Harris laughed and cut two enormous slices for the boys

and a smaller slice for Smoke. "Pickles in that barrel, boys," he said. "Help yourselves."

Smoke had noticed two hands lounging out front. "You know those fellows, Sheriff?"

"Oh, yeah. That's Ted and Stony. Good punchers and they ride for the brand. They're out of work."

"They can be trusted?"

"They hate my brother," Harris said simply.

"That's good enough for me." Smoke walked to the door, digging in his pocket for folding money. "You boys looking for work?" he asked the pair.

"You bet we are, Mr. Jensen. I'm Stony and this terrible-lookin' feller with the mop of red hair is Ted."

Smoke handed them each fifty dollars. Their eyes widened. "That's a bonus just for going to work for me and after I'm gone, sticking with the Duggan twins at the Double D. Can you use those guns you're wearing?"

"We can hit what we're shootin' at, Mr. Jensen," Ted said. "But we ain't gunhands."

"That's fine. You got horses?"

They both looked embarrassed and Smoke knew they were down on their luck. They were young, probably in their mid-twenties, but fate had dealt them a hard hand. "We had to hock our saddles just to eat, Mr. Jensen. And we ain't done that in two days."

"Get yourselves some cheese and crackers and a pickle. Cut off a wedge for the trail while you're at it. Clint Black is paying for this treat."

A wicked glint sprang into the eyes of both young punchers at that news.

"Then go down to the livery and rope out what you think you can ride. After that, ride escort for these boys and drive those horses with the 45 brand back to the valley." He handed them the bill of sale. "Pull the rig of that puncher I just shot off his horse and one of you use that. There are plenty of other rigs over across the street."

"Why don't we just ride the 45 horses?" Ted suggested.

Smoke had anticipated that. He shrugged massive shoulders. "You can if you want. But there might be trouble in the days ahead."

They both smiled. "I 'spect there will be," Stony said. "But we'll face that when the time comes."

"Fine. Get yourselves something to munch on."

Sally, Toni, and Jeanne had handed him a shopping list . . . for new jeans and men's work shirts. If they ever rode into town decked out like that, they'd scandalize the territory— and they probably would ride in just like that. Do it for pure spite.

The wagon was going to be groaning and squeaking when it pulled out.

"You're not riding back with the wagon?" Harris asked.

"No."

"You're crowding, Smoke. You know that?"

"I sure do."

"What if my brother comes riding hell for leather into town with about forty hands while you're here?"

"Be a hell of a fight."

"You'd fight forty men!"

"If they pushed me to it."

Exasperated, the sheriff stalked away, muttering to himself. Smoke watched him go, smiled, and then stepped across the street to the saloon. As soon as he entered, men, women, and small boys and girls crowded the boardwalk, peeping through the windows of the saloon. Actually, he planned on leaving shortly after the wagon. He just liked to needle Harris Black. Basically, Smoke felt the man was a decent sort. He just had a bastard for a brother, that's all. And blood was thicker than water. Smoke thought it best to bear that in mind.

He drank a beer and left, walking up to the doctor's office. He'd dug the slug out of Jeff's leg, and there was no sign of any infection, and he'd set Harvey's arm—the man refused to come in and see the doctor. Said he didn't trust them.

Smoke wanted some medical supplies just in case. While he was there, he had the doctor look at his shoulder. It was healing nicely and nearly all of the soreness was gone.

The doctor insisted upon checking Smoke's head where the bullet had grazed him. He looked disgusted when he found the slight wound was nearly healed.

"You have amazing recuperative powers, Mr. Jensen."

Smoke gathered up his medical supplies and was walking back to his horse when he heard the thunder of hooves. He stowed the supplies in the wagon and stepped up onto the boardwalk in front of the emporium.

"His Majesty, himself," Stony said, rolling a cigarette. "Lord of the county and all you can see. Clint Black and some of his gunslicks."

"I can't stand to see a man abuse a horse that way," Smoke said. "No need in it. Any man who'd deliberately abuse an animal is a no-good."

"Clint likes to shoot dogs," Ted said. "Just for the hell of it. I had me a little mutt when I worked for him. He killed it. I hate that son of a bitch."

Harris Black and his deputy suddenly appeared, walking up the boardwalk, both of them carrying sawed-off shotguns. Takes a mighty foolish man to go up against a sawed-off, and the sheriff knew it.

Clint Black jerked and fought the reins and came to a dusty halt facing the men on the boardwalk. His own riders left and right of him.

Smoke fanned the dust. "You always this inconsiderate of other people, Black?" he asked.

Clint ignored that. "I found my men hoofing it back to the ranch. You're Jensen, aren't you?"

"Yeah, Black, I'm Jensen. And yeah, I took your hands' horses. Got a clear title to them. And yeah, I put lead in some loudmouth named Ron."

"That's it!" Harris said, cocking both hammers to the shotgun. "There will be no trouble in this town. Damn you,

Clint. I sent a note for you to stay clear of Blackstown. I know you can read, 'cause mother taught us."

"Me? You order *me* to stay clear. I built this town, damn you. I brought the people in. I brought the stage in. I *own* the bank."

"Oh, that's something else that slipped my mind, Sheriff. You met my wife, Sally? Well, she is a woman of considerable wealth. Comes from a long line of bankers. And the Duggan twins, you know, I'm sure, are quite wealthy. So we decided, last evening, that this town needs another bank. That empty building right over there will do nicely, I'm thinking. I've got to send a wire off and start making arrangements." Actually, nothing of the kind had been discussed. But it would be discussed at length that night. And Smoke knew Sally would jump at it and in all likelihood, so would the Duggan twins.

Clint looked like he was working himself up into a good case of apoplexy. His eyes were bugging out and his face was turning red.

"Why are your ears red?" Smoke asked him.

"My ears are not red!" Clint yelled.

"Oh, yes, they are," Smoke said. "Don't you think the man's ears are red, boys?"

"Sure are," Stony said. "Look like two little jugs of beets." He stared. "Well, maybe not so little."

"Red as can be," Ted said. "Looks plumb funny to me."

"Both of you saddle bums shut up. Another bank!" Clint yelled. He sputtered for a moment. "You can't do that."

"Who is going to stop me?" Smoke asked in a calm tone of voice. "You?"

"Back off, Clint," Harris said in a warning tone. "If another bank wants to come in, there is nothing you can do about it. Is that understood?"

The citizens of the town had gathered left and right of the confrontation. Those in front and back of the volatile situation had cleared out, getting away from the line of fire. Stony and Ted stood left and right of Smoke, the three of them facing Clint and his dozen or so rowdies.

"How's the feet of your de-horsed boys?" Smoke asked the rancher, smiling as he spoke.

"Don't worry about it," Clint replied, regaining what composure he had left him, which was very little when he didn't get his way in any given situation. "I hear you're accusin' me of raidin' your camp. I didn't have a thing to do with that, Jensen. And if you say I did, you're a damn liar."

"I say you did, Black," Smoke told the man and everybody else who was close enough to hear. "I say you gave the orders to kill men, women, and kids. And that makes you snake-low and dirty. You don't have the nerve to do your own fighting. You're a coward, Black. Step out of that saddle and fight me. Right here and now."

The sheriff walked between the men. He put his back to Smoke and faced his brother. "Take your men and get out of town, Clint. Right now. Leave now or I'll put you in jail."

"On what charge?" Clint asked. He wanted to leave, wanted desperately to leave. But how to do that without losing face in front of the townspeople and his men? Clint was many things, but a fool was not one of them. After getting a good look at Jensen, Clint, for the first time since he was a boy, had experienced fear. And he hated himself for it.

"Refusing to obey the orders of a peace officer," his brother told him. "Now take your men and leave. Jensen, you do the same. And do it right now."

"All right," Smoke said. He looked at Clint. "Some other time, Black. Let's go, boys."

With his brother and his men heading in one direction, Smoke and his hands going in another, Harris eased the hammers down on his sawed-off and his deputy relaxed.

"All you did was put it off for another time," the deputy said. "It's bound to come."

"Yeah, I know," Harris said. "But I got it out of town." He stepped back, leaned the shotgun against the building, and rolled a cigarette. "My brother was scared this day," he remarked, lighting up. "I saw fear on his face."

"Hell, who wouldn't be scared?" The deputy bit off a chew from a plug. "Jensen would have been killed, for sure, but he would have emptied eight or ten saddles before he went down. A man that size can take a lot of lead."

"What bothers me is that a scared man will do desperate things, Harry. My brother took water this day. I gave him a way out, but he still took water. He was shamed this day, and he'll not forget it. He was always a vain and a vengeful person."

"Well . . . like you say, we got it out of town."

Riding back to the valley of death, Smoke asked the new hands, "You boys know of other men who might like a job?"

"I know of a few," Stony said. "And I 'magine Ted knows of several." Ted nodded his head.

"OK. You two veer off now and find them. I'm offering top wages and the best food you ever put in your mouth." He dug in his pocket and handed Stony a wad of bills.

Stony looked at the money and whistled. "How do you know we won't just take that money and clear out, Smoke? That's two years' pay for most hands."

Smoke grinned. "I'm a good judge of character, Stony. See you boys later on."

The new hands headed off, leaving Smoke and the boys and the heavily laden wagon. "Ol' Waymore hates Clint Black," Stony said. "He'd jump at this chance."

"You bet," Ted agreed. "And I was thinkin' 'bout Rich and Malvern."

"They'll do to ride the river with. How about Paul and Cletus?"

"Suits me. Say, I just remembered something. Jud accused Joe Owens of stealin' that time. Pistol-whipped him."

"Yeah. And Joe never stole nothin' in his life. His shack ain't a mile from here."

"I think we got the makin's of a pretty good crew and don't none of 'em live more'un a half hour away. We could be back in time for supper."

"Let's go round 'em up, then. I'm hungry!"

10

Stony and Ted showed up at the camp in the valley just at sundown. They brought with them the most disreputable-looking bunch of men Toni and Jeanne had ever seen. Sally had lived nearly all her adult life in the West, and she knew that appearances could be very deceiving out here. She suspected these new men were top hands who, for whatever reason, had been blackballed for employment in this area by Clint Black. Turned out she was right.

"We just didn't cotton to takin' orders from the likes of Clint Black and Jud Howes and that pack of gunslingers they got workin' out on the Circle 45," Waymore said, accepting a plate of food.

"They's other smaller ranches scattered all over this country," Cletus added. "But Clint's got them buffaloed. Didn't none of them dare hire us. We don't hold no grudges against them for it. Man has his entire life put into a small spread, well, he can't stand up to a rich and mean person that has forty or fifty gunslicks on the payroll. Or men who fancy themselves slick with a short gun."

"Mighty good grub," Malvern said. "Best I think I ever eat."

"When was the last time you did eat, Mr. Malvern?" Toni asked.

"Just Malvern, ma'am. Mal for short. Oh, I been eatin' regular. Seems as how one of Mr. High and Mighty Clint Black's cows wandered over to my place and fell down. Broke its leg and I had to put the poor thing out of its misery. It was the Christian thing to do. I can't stand to see no animal suffer. And it seemed right foolish of me to just let all that meat go to waste. So I butchered it and ate some and smoked and jerked the rest. Then, lo and behold, about a week later, durned if *another* one of Mr. Black's cows didn't come over to my place and fall down. Right in the same spot. Poor thing broke its leg. Well, I had to end its sufferin', so I shot it, too. This has been going on for about six months. Now, since Mr. Big Shot Black has forbid me from ever settin' foot on his land, there just wasn't no way I could get word to him about his cows. It's really put me in a state of confusion." He shook his head. "And I do try to do right by my fellow man, ma'am."

Toni looked at him for a moment, then slowly smiled. "You, Mr. Malvern, tell big whackers."

"Occasional, I do, Miss Toni," Mal said with a grin. "Occasional, 'deed I do."

The next week went by in a blur of work, with everybody who was able pitching in and rounding up cattle and stampeded horses. Smoke would work until noon and then go off exploring. The bodies of his men had to have been dumped somewhere, and he was determined to find that location.

On the afternoon of the seventh day, he found a boot. Smoke swung down from the saddle and knelt down by the ripped boot. he ran his hand over the dead leaves that were all around it.

Dead leaves? In the middle of summer? He swept them away and looked at the clear impressions of hooves. Leading his horse, he began following the trail of dead leaves that led upward. Someone had gathered up great handfuls of leaves and scattered them over the tracks. He climbed on. Now he could clearly see the tracks of horses and something else, too: a clear path where bodies had been dragged up this way.

It had gotten back to Smoke that Clint had been saying Smoke had made the attack up. That there were no bodies, so how could an attack have ever taken place?

Smoke began carefully looking around him as he moved along the ridge. Here the trail was harder to follow because of the rocks. Then the smell of death reached him.

He picketed his horse on a small stand of grass and walked on, the smell growing stronger. He could see the mouth of the cave now, and he walked to it. The smell was very nearly overpowering. He picked up a dry branch and tied twigs to the end of it, using some dead vines and then lighting the brand. It would only burn for two or three minutes, but that would be time aplenty.

He stepped into the mouth of the cave and almost lost his lunch. He struggled to keep it down. Smoke walked into the foul semigloom. He did not have to walk far. The first body he found was that of fourteen-year-old Rabbit. Then he saw the others, all piled like garbage. He walked back out into the sweet air. He was sweating and mad clear through. He stood for a moment, composing himself, and then rode back down to the valley, stopping the first hand he found.

"Cletus, ride for town and fetch the sheriff. Tell him I've found the bodies of my men . . . and boys."

It was late afternoon when the sheriff arrived, and growing dark when Smoke pointed out the cave. "I hope you have a strong stomach," Smoke told him. "You're going to need it."

The sheriff and two of his deputies lit torches and stepped

inside. Harry came out much quicker than he entered, kneeling by the side of the mouth of the cave and puking.

Harris Black came out. He was badly shaken by what he'd just seen. He leaned against a tree and struggled to regain his composure. Smoke walked over to stand by the man. All work had stopped and everyone was gathered around the cave, as close as they could get without being overpowered by the terrible smell.

"I'll bring Doc Garrett out with me in the morning," Sheriff Black finally said. He refused to meet Smoke's steady gaze. "I want him to see this and write up a report. This is the worst thing I have ever seen. Horrible."

"Maybe this will shut your brother's mouth." Smoke spoke the words harshly.

Harris said nothing.

"You know he's responsible for this, don't you, Sheriff?"

Harris remained silent.

"How long are you going to keep covering for him, Sheriff. How long?"

Harris wiped his sweaty face with a handkerchief, wiped the sweat band of his hat, and plopped it back on his head. "I won't stand for vigilante action, Smoke."

"Oh, I wouldn't dream of that, Sheriff. Your brother has already cornered the market."

When Dr. Garrett emerged from the cave, he was pale and badly shaken. He had to sit down on the ground for a moment before he could speak. He finally took a shuddering breath and looked up at Smoke and the sheriff.

"I've ordered canvas to be sent out from town. I'll ask for volunteers to help place the bodies on a tarp and wrap them. Once they are out in the light, I will inspect each body more carefully. Then I would suggest they be buried close by. Perhaps on that flat right over there." He pointed. "Their names could be chiseled on the face of that huge rock, or perhaps on the face of the mountain itself. That's up to you." He shook his head. "The bodies are in a terrible state of decomposition. Thirteen men and boys, trampled and shot. My God, it's hideous. It's . . . unthinkable. The man behind this must be mad. Mad, I tell you!"

Sheriff Black opened his mouth to speak, then thought better of it. He turned and walked away.

Dr. Garrett looked up at Smoke. "You're going to start a war over this, aren't you, Mr. Jensen."

Smoke shook his head. "The war has already begun, Doctor. And I didn't start it."

"The families of the men and boys?"

"I've wired them. Services have already been held down home."

"I don't know what else to say or do, Mr. Jensen."

"Time for talk is over. As for what you can do. you can stock up on medical supplies. I think you're going to be treating a lot of gunshot wounds."

Smoke left the rounding up of the cattle in the hands of his men. He kissed Sally and saddled up the next morning. No one spoke to him. No one had to. Nearly everyone in the camp knew what he was going to do. His face was hard and uncompromising as he swung up into the saddle. He pointed his horse toward town and rode off without a look back.

"What is he going to do, Sally?" Jeanne asked.

"He's going to make war," she replied, busying herself washing dishes.

"By *himself?*" Toni asked.

"Smoke Jensen is a one-man army, missy," Denver said, drying a plate. "He's tooken on meaner odds than this. 'Sides, this is real personal for him. He feels responsible for what happened to them men; 'specially the boys."

"But if it's anyone's fault, it's ours," Jeanne said.

"No, it ain't neither," Denver said. "And don't you be thinkin' that."

"Denver is right," Sally said. "You had no way of knowing something like this would happen. Neither did we. Only Clint Black and his men had knowledge of it. The responsibility for it lies squarely on their shoulders. I think Sheriff Black is covering for his brother, but I don't believe he knew about the ambush—until after it happened."

"You don't appear worried about your husband," Toni said, looking at Sally.

"Oh, I'm plenty worried about him. But he has to do what he has to do, that's all. I would have been shocked had he not. He's waited a week for the law to do something. The law has done nothing. Now Smoke will see to the administering of justice. The Western way."

There was something about the way he sat his horse, something about his bearing, that cleared the streets of Blackstown the instant he rode in. Smoke stabled his horse and checked his guns. He had seen horses at the hitchrail in front of the saloon; horses that wore the Circle 45 brand. He walked slowly up the boardwalk. Sheriff Black stepped out of his office, blocking Smoke's way.

"Goin' somewhere, Smoke?"

"To the saloon for a drink. You have some objections to my doing that, Sheriff?"

"Damnit, Jensen. You know there are Circle 45 hands over there."

"It's a free country."

"You know what I mean."

"The services for the dead will be at sundown this evening, Sheriff. You plan to attend?"

"Which dead?" the sheriff asked sourly. "The dead found in the cave or the men you're about to kill?"

Smoke stood and stared at the man. Finally he said, "I waited for the law to act. The law did nothing. You know your brother ordered that ambush. And you know that all the Circle 45 hands either took part in it or had direct knowledge of it. Now you either stand aside, or you help me kill dangerous rabid animals. You really don't want to get in my way, Sandy," he called him by the name the sheriff used back when he was a gunfighter. "The choice is yours to make."

Sheriff Black knew he was not as fast as Jensen. And he also knew that Smoke was right. He was sworn to uphold the law and protect decent, law-abiding citizens, but the words "decent and law-abiding," he knew, did not include his brother or the men working for his brother. The sheriff sighed. "Go stomp on your snakes, Jensen." He turned and walked back into his office, closing the door behind him.

Smoke walked on up the street, then cut across to the other side, approaching the saloon from the one side that butted up against another building. He pushed open the batwings and stepped inside. Four men sat at a table, drinking beer and playing cards. Everybody else had vacated the saloon at the news of Smoke Jensen riding into town.

Only the barkeep was left, and he was so scared he looked like he was going to pass out any moment.

Smoke put his hand on a chair back and said, "You boys dumb enough to ride a Circle 45 horse?"

The card players sat quietly, their hands on the table. They knew better than to have them by their sides when Jensen walked in, for he was on the prod. "We're ridin' 'em, yeah," one hand said.

"Did you steal them or are you on Clint Black's payroll?"

"We ride for the Circle 45," another said. "And we been ridin' for Clint for a long time."

"Is that a fact?"

"That's a fact, Jensen."

Smoke cut his eyes to the barkeep. "Is there a dentist in this town, friend?"

"Why . . . ah, yeah. There is. Right over the undertaker's place. You got a toothache, Mr. Jensen?"

"No. But this dirty, back-shooting, murderous ambusher here does."

The hand just had time to turn around and say, "Who are you callin' a . . . ?"

Smoke hit him in the face with the hickory chair. Blood and teeth and snot flew. The chair splintered. Holding the back rail of the busted chair, Smoke hit another hand smack in the mouth, then bounced the hickory off the noggin of a third. The fourth jumped up clawing for his six-gun. Smoke hit him right between the eyes with the hickory club and the Circle 45 rider went down like a sack of potatoes.

Smoke grabbed the first one he'd hit and tossed him through the big window. The hand smashed through the hitchrail and landed in the dirt, out cold with several broken ribs. Smoke backhanded another and sent him sprawling, then the third 45 hand staggered to his feet and Smoke sent him sailing out the batwings. Smoke hit another five times in the side, the blows sounding like swinging a sledge hammer against a side of raw beef. Ribs cracked under the blows and the man fell to the floor, moaning in pain.

The one Smoke backhanded came to his feet, his face bloody and ugly and one hand closing around the butt of his Colt. Smoke stepped forward and clubbed the man with one huge fist. Then he grabbed the man's gun arm and broke it by slamming it against the bar. The would-be gunhandler screamed and passed out.

Smoke dragged them outside and threw them in the dirt. Sheriff Black and his deputies stood on the other side of the wide main street and did not interfere. Smoke dunked one in the horse trough several times and got him on his feet. His nose was spread all over his face and his lips were pulped.

"I'll say this one time, mister," Smoke told the man. "You and the rest of this trash here ride out of this part of Montana. Go back to the ranch, pack your kit, and ride out—

today. If I see you again, I'll kill you where you stand and I won't give you one second's warning. Do you understand all that?"

"Yes, sir," the man mumbled through ruined lips.

"Ride!"

Smoke released the man and the cowboy almost fell down. He managed to get his friends on their feet and on their horses. They left town without looking back.

Smoke went back into the saloon and tossed money on the bar. "That will pay for the busted window and the chair. Give me a beer."

Smoke was sitting down sipping his brew when the sheriff walked in and over to the table. He sat down and stared at Smoke for a moment.

"You do understand that you just whipped four pretty tough ol' boys?"

"So?"

Harris shook his head. "You think they'll really haul their ashes?"

"They'll either pull out or be buried here. I meant what I said."

"I could wire the territorial governor and have him send the state militia in."

"Go ahead."

"That wouldn't stop you, would it?"

"No."

"You're really going to kill my brother, aren't you?"

"First I'm going to bring him to his knees."

"That will never happen."

Smoke's smile was close to a death's-head. His words were very softly spoken. "You want to bet?"

11

Clint Black sat in the study of his fine home and pondered his future. At the moment, it did not appear to be very bright. He had seen the four punchers come riding in, all beat up to hell and back, and watched as Jud paid them off and they left, that day, taking their broken ribs and busted arms and tore up faces and hauling their ashes out of the country. It had not set well with his other hands.

That Jensen had whipped four pretty rough ol' boys in a fight shocked the rancher. He'd whipped two men at a time more than once. But *four* men! Nobody whips four men at a time. But Smoke Jensen had done it, and then, according to what Clint had heard from spies in town, Jensen just calmly sat down and had him a beer with the sheriff.

He had made a mistake by attacking the camp site. He admitted that. He was sorry he'd done it. He was genuinely sorry about it. But he wasn't sorry enough about it to admit to it in any court of law. Clint certainly was sorry, but not for the right reasons.

So some forty-dollar-a-month cowhands and some snot-nosed kids had been killed. Well, big deal. Clint could buy people like that all day long. They were nothing. Nobodies.

He didn't know what to do. He couldn't admit his part in the attack. At worst he'd be hanged; at best he'd be run out of the country. And now Jensen had bragged that he was going to put Clint Black on his knees. Well, that had been tried before. Clint was still standing tall while the men who'd tried to bring him down were rotting in the graves.

And Jensen moved fast. Already carpenters were banging away inside and outside the new First United Bank of Blackstown. And Clint had heard rumblings that most of his depositors were going to pull out, once the new bank opened. He sighed heavily. That wouldn't hurt him; the bank was solvent. It was losing face that bothered Clint. Worse than that, it was a slap in the face.

All in all, Clint concluded, Smoke Jensen was becoming a royal pain in the butt.

"What happened to the man who owned this spread?" Smoke asked.

The herd had been rounded up and moved to Double D land. Clint had yet to replace those cattle that had been lost; indeed, nothing had been heard from the man or any of his hands and it was a week past the fight in the saloon.

"Rustlers," Stony told him. "Ever' time he'd get his herd built up, night riders would come in and wipe him out. He finally gave up and sold out. But not to Clint, and that really galled Black. Boss? Have you given any thought to grabbin' one of the Circle 45 bunch and makin' him talk?"

"Torture, Stony? No. For a lot of reasons. It boils down to it'd be his word against forty others. It wouldn't even come to court. I've got all summer. We'll just keep whittling away at Clint. Nipping at his heels and being a splinter in his butt that he can't get to. It'll get to him. He'll eventually lose his temper and make that one big mistake."

"And then, boss?"

"And then he'll face me."

Stony looked at Smoke and felt a chill crawl around in his belly. He knew then for an ironclad fact that his boss had placed a death sentence on Clint Black and meant to carry it out. And Smoke Jensen didn't give a tinker's damn what the law might have to say about it. Jensen was going to angle Clint into a position where he had no back-out room, and then Smoke was going to force-feed him lead.

But first he was going to break Clint Black, slowly and steadily.

Stony shifted his eyes for another look at Smoke Jensen. He had ridden back to the camp after the saloon fight and had not said one word about it. Only after a hand had ridden into town for some tobacco had the word come back. Jensen had walked into the saloon, tossed down the gloves and proceeded to stomp the snot out of four men. Stony hid a smile. Things were sure going to be interesting this summer. Real interesting. And he sure was glad he had stuck around.

Lucas, one of Sheriff Black's deputies, noticed the men ride slowly into town. Six of them. They wore long dusters and rode fine horses. Horses way too costly for the average cowhand to ever afford. Then his half-rolled cigarette was forgotten as he recognized the man on the big, high-steppin' bay. Yukon Golden. He stepped to the office door.

"Harris," he said softly. "I think your brother's done gone and hired himself some real gunslingers. That's Yukon Golden in that bunch reinin' in by the hotel."

With a curse, Harris shoved back from the paperwork at his desk and grabbed his hat. He stepped out onto the boardwalk for a look.

"Bronco Ford," Harris said, eyeballing the six men as

they dismounted and stood on the boardwalk in front of the hotel. "He's a bad one."

"You know them yahoos, Harris?"

"I know them all, Lucas. That short stumpy one is Austin Charles. He's hell on wheels with a gun. That's Red Hyde next to him. That long tall drink of water is Slim King. The big one in the bunch is Carson. They call him Grub 'cause he eats all the time. When he's not hiring out his gun to kill people."

"We got trouble."

"Oh, they won't mess with any of us. But they'll sure try Smoke Jensen. The man who kills Smoke Jensen can name his price after that."

"That sorry-lookin' bunch is that fast?"

"They're professional gunhandlers, Lucas. It's how they make their living. Damn my brother. Damn his eyes. He's declared war and he doesn't know what he's begun."

"Harris?"

"Huh?"

"Smoke Jensen's ridin' in."

Harris cut his eyes. "Oh, hell!" he said.

Smoke walked his horse over to the hitchrail and swung down. He had seen the six men lounging in front of the hotel, and his eyes had picked up on the strange brands. He knew the men for what they were. They had the mark on them just as plainly as the brands on their horses.

Smoke stepped up on the boardwalk and nodded at the sheriff and his deputy.

"Trouble over yonder, Smoke," Harris said.

"I see them. Did your brother hire them?"

"I don't know, Smoke. He no longer speaks to me. But I'd say it would be a safe bet that he sent for those men."

"Then they'll be more coming in," Smoke said. "Men like those over there smell blood money. They've got the damndest pipeline I have ever known. Word gets around like lightning. Your brother's made up his mind."

"To do what?" Harris asked. "Defend his own land? God-damnit, it's his, Jensen. He settled it and proved it up years ago. You came in here and laid down your challenge. What the hell do you expect him to do?"

"You defending him now, Harris?"

"No. No, I'm not. He did wrong and I know it. But even if I went to a judge and signed a deposition that my brother told me he planned the raid, it's doubtful that the judge would let it be entered as evidence. Yes, Jensen, damn you, yes. My brother admitted to me that he ordered the raid. But it comes down to my word against his. I can't show any solid proof that Clint engineered the ambush. That's the way it stands now."

"I see. Well, you ask what I expected of your brother, now let me ask what you expect of me?"

"Take your wife and what hands you have left and go back to Colorado."

"And let murderers go unpunished?"

"It's not up to you, Jensen!" Harris flared at him. "That's my job, and the judges and the lawyers and the juries. You don't want justice, Jensen. You want revenge. Just like when the Slater gang attacked Big Rock and shot up the place. How many of them did you kill, Jensen?"

"All of them."

"Just tracked them down, one by one, and killed them?"

"We faced each other, Black. You know me that well."

"Suppose . . . suppose I could guarantee you that my brother would never harm another person? That I would personally see to that. That he would fire his gunhands—his whole crew—hire nothing but cowboys, and stick with ranching his property. If I could convince him to do that, would you leave?"

Smoke took that time to roll a cigarette and light it. He took a draw and said, "Yes. Yes, I would. When he comes to me and faces me and tells me that personally. When he swears to me that the Double D, and all the other ranches in this area will be left alone and I see his hands leave and new men come in, cowboys, I'll leave. You have my word."

"Fine. I think I can get him to agree to that. You meet me here at my office, first thing in the morning."

"I'll be here."

"You've got to be out of your mind," Clint told him. "You want me to apologize to Jensen and crawl around on my belly like a whipped dog? You go to hell, Harris. You just go straight back to town and take your stupid suggestions with you. Just go to hell, Big Brother. And stay out of my affairs."

"You break the law, Clint, you're going to jail. That's a promise."

"You'll never put me behind bars, Harris," his brother warned. "Don't ever try to do that."

"If the time comes, I won't try to do it, Clint. I'll just do it. Clint, think about this offer. Think on it, man. It means peace. Clint, my God, you're a wealthy man. You have all the money you could ever spend. You've got a fine home, great holdings of land. You've got it made! Jensen is willing to ride out and put this . . . tragedy behind him."

Clint shook his head and laughed at his brother. "Sure, Harris. But only after I grovel in the dirt like a bum begging for a handout. No way."

Harris opened his mouth to plead with his brother. Clint's hard words closed it.

"I don't want to hear any more of your sniveling. No more of it, Sheriff Black." He slurred the word "sheriff." "Not another word. Leave me alone about it and stay out of my affairs. Now get out of my house, Harris. And don't come back. You hear me? Don't come back!"

"You're a fool, Clint. You're a fool. I don't care how many gunslicks you hire, you're not going to win this fight with Jensen. He'll kill you. He'll break you, humiliate you, and then he'll kill you."

"Get out!" Clint screamed, half rising from his chair. "Get out of my house, goddamn you. Get out, I say!"

Harris picked up his hat and started for the door. He turned around and looked at his brother. "Goodbye, Clint. I used to think that mother and father would be proud of you. They wouldn't be. Ma would have prayed nightly for you, and Dad would have slapped you down to the ground for what you've become. You're a common thief, a treacherous schemer, a cheat, and now a murderer. You're a disgrace to our parents' good names. I'm glad they're dead so they don't have to see this."

"Why . . . you hypocrite!" Clint sputtered the words. "You were nothin' but a goddamn paid gunfighter for years. I dragged you out of the gutter and made you what you are."

"I was never in the gutter, Clint. And yes, I hired my gun. But I never shot a man who wasn't facing me with a Colt in his hand or in his holster. And I never bushwhacked or drew first. Like Jensen, I never had to. And I never harmed a child, or a woman, or killed anyone's pet dog or cat or horse for meanness. Like you've done more than once."

"I don't need a damn sermon from you!"

"I was proud to come be the law in Blackstown, Clint. Chest-swellin' proud. My little brother had made it big. I was so proud of you. I just didn't know at the time how you made it. Then I finally pieced it all together and found out it was by lying and cheating and stealing and . . ." He swallowed hard. "I reckon by murder too. But you kept me out of that. 'Cause you knew I wouldn't stand for it. You dragged my name down in the filth with you, Clint. But I stood by and let you do it. 'Cause we're brothers, I reckon. But this tears it, brother. This is the end of it."

"Who the hell needs some broken-down old gunhawk?" Clint sneered the words at his brother. "You're nothin'. *Nothin'!* You got nothin'. I got it all. Money, the finest wines and whiskeys, all the women I want any time I want them. Hell, you don't even own a decent pair of boots! I got a dozen pair in my bedroom. The finest made. You got nothin', Harris. Holes in your socks, probably."

Harris put his hat on his head and smiled. "You know, Clint, you were almost right about one thing. Only it wasn't the gutter I was in, it was the sewer. A stinking, slimy sewer. And I climbed in it when I went to work for you. But I climbed out, Clint. You're still wallowing around in the filth. You stink of it."

He jerked open the door and left the great room, slamming the door behind him.

12

Smoke took one look at Sheriff Black's face and knew he had failed in his mission to convince his brother to pull in his horns. He said as much as he poured a cup of coffee.

"So I guess the next move is up to you, Smoke," Harris said.

Smoke sugared his coffee and sat down in front of the desk. "I am sorry that you failed, Harris."

"I believe that, Smoke. You could have killed those hands in the saloon. But you were content to hang a pretty fair country butt-whippin' on them and let them go. That tells me a lot about you." He stood up and warmed his own cup of coffee. "One of my men spotted a couple more gunslicks this morning. They avoided town and headed for the Circle 45. It looks like trouble is coming and there is nothing I can do about it."

"I'm going to call your brother out, Harris," Smoke said.

"Yeah. I figured you were. But you're going to wait until he comes to town and make him take water. I told him last night that he couldn't win this fight. That you would humiliate him. He didn't believe me."

"Will he fight?"

"No," Harris said without hesitation. "He's a vain, strutting rooster, but he's not a fool. He's not going to pull on you. It would surprise me if he even came to town wearing his gun. I know my brother, Smoke. I don't think he brought— is bringing—those hired guns in here to kill you. I think he's bringing them in to protect himself. From you. He's going to try to wait you out."

"He's got a long wait."

A deputy stuck his head into the office. "Here comes your brother, Harris. And he's got a lot of men with him. Includin' them new-hired gunhandlers."

Harris cut his eyes to Smoke. He knew the man had ridden in alone. The expression on Smoke's face had not changed. Harris didn't think Jensen had one ounce of fear in him.

"They're goin' into the saloon," the deputy reported.

Smoke sipped his coffee.

Harris stared at him for a moment. "Well, damnit, man! What are you going to do?"

Smoke set his coffee cup on the desk and rose from the chair. He smiled at the sheriff. "Why . . . go pay my respects to your brother, of course." He turned and walked out of the office.

"Damn!" The word exploded out of the sheriff's mouth. He rose quickly and took a sawed-off shotgun from the rack, calling for his deputies. "Everybody get a Greener and load it up. I'm not going to have trouble in this town."

Smoke pushed open the batwings and stepped inside the beery-smelling saloon. As Harris had predicted, Clint was not wearing a gun. But those men surrounding him had plenty of six-guns belted around their waists. Smoke unbuckled and untied and hung his guns on a peg of the hatrack. Clint watched him, puzzlement in his eyes. The gunhands exchanged glances, not understanding what was going on.

"Is that a fresh pot of coffee I smell?" Smoke asked the barkeep.

"Yes, sir, Mr. Jensen. Just boiled it."

"I'll have a cup with a little sugar in it, please. Down there at the end of the bar."

"Yes, sir."

Smoke paused at Clint's side. "Morning, Clint. Fine day, isn't it?"

Clint grunted and turned his back to Smoke.

"What's the matter, Clint?" Smoke asked. "Didn't you sleep well last night?"

The owner of the Circle 45 turned to face Smoke. "What the hell's that supposed to mean?"

Harris and his deputies had entered the bar, spreading out, all of them with sawed-off shotguns in their hands.

"Why . . . I'm just concerned about your health, that's all," Smoke told the man. "You seem a little out of sorts this morning. Maybe you need a good dose of salts."

"Why don't you just mind your own damn business?" Clint replied. "And don't you worry about my health. It's none of your business."

"My, my. How touchy we are." Smoke walked to the end of the bar and picked up his coffee cup and took a sip.

Clint and his hands all ordered either beer or whiskey.

"Alcohol this early in the morning is not good for a body," Smoke chided them all. "I read that in a medical article."

"Who the hell cares what you read?" Clint told him, anger in his words. "If I want a drink in the morning, I'll have a drink in the morning." He knocked back his shotglass of whiskey and shuddered as the booze hit his stomach.

"Oh, by all means, go ahead." Smoke sat his coffee cup on the bar. "A man never knows when it might be his last one."

Clint cut his eyes. "What the hell does that mean?"

Smoke shrugged. "Oh, you know how it is out here, Clint. A man's horse might throw him, a snake might bite him, some Indian might leave the reservation looking for a scalp. Lots of things could happen. Have another drink."

"I don't want another drink!"

"Your option." Smoke sipped his coffee. "Mighty good coffee, barkeep. Mighty good. Coffee, now, that's good for a man. Sharpens the senses. Whiskey, now, it fills a man with false confidence. Makes him do foolish things. You're wise not to have but one drink, Clint."

"Gimme another damn drink!" Clint snarled at the nervous barkeep.

"Two whiskeys, now, that probably won't hurt a thing," Smoke said. "Man takes more than two, though, 'specially this early in the day, he's asking for trouble."

"Will you shut up?" Clint yelled.

"I'm not talking to you, Clint," Smoke told him. "I was speaking to the barkeep."

"Well, I'm tired of hearin' your mouth rattle."

"Free country. Of course, if you feel like you're a big enough man to shut me up, come on."

"That's it!" Harris said, moving toward the men. "I'll have no trouble in this town."

"Damnit, Harris, I come in town for a drink and some conversation," Clint said. "I don't have to listen to someone pop off at the mouth."

"Neither one of us is armed, Sheriff," Smoke said. "What trouble could we cause?"

Dr. Garrett had quietly entered the saloon, taking a seat at a far table.

"Of course now," Smoke took it further, "I see all these gunslingers are totin' two guns, at least. Yukon there, I know he carries a .41 derringer in his boot. Slim King's got a knife hung down his back. And a man doesn't ever want to turn his back to Red Hyde, he's a back-shooter . . ."

"By God," Red stepped away from the bar. "You can't call me no back-shooter, Jensen. Git a gun."

"I said no trouble!" Harris said. "You, Red, get out of town."

"Me!" Red hollered. "I ain't done nothin'."

A deputy lifted his sawed off, those cavernous muzzles pointed right at Red's stomach.

"All right, all right!" Red said, sweat suddenly beading up on his face. "I'm goin'. But you, Jensen . . . you and me will meet up sometime, and we'll settle this."

"We can settle it now," Smoke said. "With fists. But you won't do that, will you, Red? No. You won't. You're yellow without those guns of yours."

"Smoke . . ." Harris warned.

"That's you, Red. A damn coward."

"You dirty . . ." Red cussed him.

Smoke laughed at him. "Come on, Red. Show everybody how bad you are without those guns. You're afraid to take them off, aren't you, Red. Because you know when you do, the whole roomful of people will see you for what you are: a dirty back-shooting coward!"

Red grabbed for his guns. Deputy Harry Simpson's Greener roared, the buckshot taking Red in the side and almost cutting the man in two. The force of the impacting buckshot lifted Red off his boots and slung him against the bar, splattering bits of Red all over the front of the long bar.

Sheriff Black looked at Smoke while some of the gunhands coughed and struggled to keep down their breakfast at the sight of what was left of Red. "Very neatly done, Smoke," the sheriff complimented him. "Very neat, indeed."

Smoke lifted his cup in a mock salute and finished the coffee.

"What are you talking about?" Clint said.

"How about you, Clint?" Smoke asked from the end of the bar. "Do you have the guts to fight me?"

"That's all for this day, Smoke," Harris warned. "No more of this. I'm ordering you from this town, and you'd better heed that order."

"Fine," Smoke said. "I'm a law-abiding man, Sheriff." He paused by Clint and whispered, "You're about six feet, three inches tall, aren't you?"

"Yeah. What of it?"

"I just didn't know that crap would stack that high, that's all."

Jud grabbed his boss and spun him around before he could take a swing. "Don't do it, Clint. That's what he wants. Can't you see that?"

Smoke stood smiling at Clint. Then he arrogantly tipped his hat at the man and walked out of the saloon, lifting his gunbelt from the peg on his way out.

"Somebody pick up Red and tote him to the undertakers," Jud ordered.

"What are we gonna use?" Fatso Ross asked. "A shovel?"

Clint Black sat in his study, in a leather chair by the fireplace, drinking shot after shot of whiskey. Drinking it neat and chasing it with water. He had thanked Jud for stopping him that morning back in the saloon. Clint was under no illusions about who would have been the victor in that fight. Smoke Jensen would have killed him with his fists, or at least crippled him. He could see it in Smoke's eyes. A cold, killing fury.

He poured another glass of whiskey. It was one of those times when the alcohol had no effect on him. He reached for a cigar then pulled his hand back. He didn't want another cigar and really didn't want the whiskey he'd just poured. He threw glass and contents into the fireplace. The small fire to chase away the evening's chill exploded harmlessly when the whiskey hit the flames.

He thought about Red and the supper he'd eaten turned sour in his stomach. Once he had gotten over his anger, he realized what his brother had meant that morning when he spoke to Smoke and said it was neatly done. Jensen had set that killing up as coldly as a striking rattler.

Clint sighed and rose to his feet. He walked to the window and looked out at the lamplit windows of the twin bunkhouses, set off to the side and slightly in front of the big house, a respectable distance away. He had more than fifty men at his command, hard men, good men with a gun, ruthless men who would kill man, woman, or child . . . and most had killed all three, at one time or another. He had more money than he could ever spend and vast holdings of land. And yet Clint felt a helpless sensation sweep over him. He didn't know what to do about Jensen. The man made him feel . . . well, *inadequate*.

Clint had expected Jensen to come charging in days ago, waging war. Instead, he was laying back and biding his time . . . but for what reason? What was his plan? The man had to have one. Clint just couldn't figure out what it might be.

Smoke and Sally were staying in one of the bedrooms of the ranch house on the Double D spread. It was a sturdy home, with half a dozen big, comfortable rooms. The man who built it, or had it built, had looked to the future in his planning . . . but for him, it hadn't panned out well here.

Smoke was going to see to it that it did work out for the Duggan twins.

Lying in bed, with Smoke snuggled close to her, she asked, "What is your plan, honey?"

"My plan? I don't really have one. I almost made Clint mad enough to fight me this morning, but the foreman apparently has more sense than his boss and grabbed him. I don't think Clint's not wearing a gun will last long, though. But I can't see him pulling on me. No matter what I might say. But I will see him dead, Sally. Either by my hand or at the end of a rope. One way or the other."

"Do you trust Sheriff Black?"

"Up to a point. But that point is broadening. I think after he failed to convince his brother to back off and live in peace with his neighbors, Harris began to see him in a much different light. I get the impression that Harris is very disappointed in his brother."

"Disappointed enough to shoot him if it came to that?" Sally asked.

"I don't know, honey. I just don't know about that. I've known brother to shoot brother, and father to shoot son and the other way around. But I think for all his past, Harris Black is a good, decent man at the core. Could he kill his brother? I don't know. One thing I wish I did know: I wish I knew what Clint's next move was going to be."

13

Clint called his foreman over for breakfast at the main house. All the hands knew something was up, for anytime Jud was asked to eat with Clint, something big was in the works.

"When I came in here, Jud," Clint said, after shoveling food into his mouth, "I wasn't no more than a kid. Not yet twenty years old. There wasn't nothing in this part of the country exceptin' Indians and outlaws. Few nesters. I run the nesters off, fought the Indians, and killed the outlaws. This part of the territory is mine. Has been for years, and I intend to see that it remains that way."

The foreman ate slowly and said nothing. He listened.

"Tell the men they're going to start earning their money today," Clint told him. "I want Smoke Jensen dead."

Jud nodded his head and continued eating. The cook came in with a fresh pot of coffee, set it on the table, and quickly left the room. For a fact, Jud thought, things had sure changed in only a few weeks. Used to be that when a Circle 45 rider came to town, folks stepped lively in serving them. A person could smell the fear in them. All that had changed since

Jensen arrived. The townspeople and even the damned farmers around the area were not properly respectful like they should be.

"Jensen's gone out of the cattle business for the most part," Clint said. "He's gonna raise horses. So he's got time on his hands to hang around up here and meddle in everybody's business. Well, I'm tired of him meddlin' in mine. Can't count on Harris anymore. But that don't make any difference. He never really was included in any major plannin'. Next thing we know, he'll have got religion and be goin' to church. The new hands arrive?"

Jud nodded his head. "Eight of them. We still got empty bunks we could fill. Problem is, Clint, there ain't nothin' for them to do. They're just hangin' around the bunkhouse loafin' and drawin' their pay."

"Weldon and Tex come in?"

"Late yesterday."

"We start crowdin' the Double D hands. Push 'em into a fight. But make sure our boys got lots of witnesses. Leave the women alone."

"How about them snot-nosed kids Jensen brung up with him?"

"They're drawin' a man's pay and sittin' a saddle. If they get in the way, too bad. After breakfast, send the boys out in groups of five and six." Clint raised his head and smiled at his foreman. "Tell them to get into trouble."

Raul, the young Mexican who took care of the house and the lawn at the Double D, had taken the wagon into town for supplies early that morning. When he wasn't back by mid-afternoon, the twins got worried.

"Raul does not drink," Toni told Smoke. "And he is very dependable. He's stood by us through the worst. I'm afraid something has happened to him."

"I'll ride in and check on him."

Smoke found the wagon a few miles from the ranch. It was overturned and the supplies scattered. The harnesses had been cut and the horses were gone. A few minutes later he found Raul. The young man had been badly beaten and then dragged. He was alive, but just barely. Smoke emptied a pistol into the air, knowing that would bring the Double D hands at a gallop.

Waymore and Cletus were the first to arrive. "Get to the ranch and get a buckboard, Cletus. Waymore, you get Stony and Ted and start tracking the raiders. Ride with your rifles in hand."

Smoke got his canteen and bathed the young man's badly battered face. Raul opened his eyes. "Lie still, you're bad hurt, Raul."

"Fatso was in the bunch, Mr. Smoke," Raul whispered. "So was Art Long. They beat me and dragged me."

"Don't talk anymore. We'll get you into town to the doctor. You'll be all right. Just lie still for now."

Everybody came fogging down the road with the buckboard. The bed had been filled with hay and Raul was lifted as gently as possible and placed on the softness.

"Get him to town," Smoke told Jeff, who was driving the wagon. He looked at the boys who'd come on the drive north. "You boys are now in charge of the house and the grounds, including the barn and corral. You are not to leave the grounds unless I say so. Is that clear?"

They nodded their heads.

"Get back up to the ranch and see to things. And stay in sight of the house. I'll tan your butts if you disobey me. Get moving."

The boys gone, Smoke looked at Denver. "Look after them, Denver."

"Will do, boss." The old cook swung into the saddle and headed back to the ranch.

"No riding, Sally," Smoke told her. "You keep on teaching the twins how to shoot a rifle and stay close to the house and go armed at all times. Load up all the guns, especially the shotguns, and place them in every room and on the front and back porches. The war has started."

Smoke waited on the boardwalk in front of Dr. Garrett's office and small clinic. He turned as Sheriff Black quietly closed the door and stepped out.

"Doc says he'll probably make it. But he's busted up pretty good. I got his statement, for all the good it'll do." The Circle 45 hands will alibi for each other." It was not put as a question.

"You know it. Raul is well-liked in town. He was polite and would do anything in the world for people. He came in with some sheepmen. My brother ran the sheep off, killed a lot of them, and probably had a hand in killing the sheepmen. Raul stayed around doing odd jobs. When the Duggan twins came in, he went to work for them . . . in direct defiance of Clint's orders. I warned Raul to go armed. But he didn't like guns. Goddamnit!" Harris summed up his feelings in one word.

Smoke said nothing.

Harris hitched at his gun belt. "I'm going out to my brother's place. But don't expect any arrests."

"I know you'll do all that you can, Harris. And I'm not being sarcastic. I mean that."

The sheriff nodded his head and walked toward the stable. "Try to keep your guns in leather," he said over his shoulder.

Smoke didn't reply to that. He stood on the boardwalk until after the sheriff had ridden out, then crossed the street and took a chair in front of the hotel. He figured some of the Circle 45 rowdies would be riding into town shortly for a drink. He would be waiting.

It was not a long wait, and Smoke smiled when he saw the Wyoming man, Baylis, riding in with several of Clint's men. One of the deputies, Benny, stood across the street, watching Smoke and the Circle 45 men. The rest of the deputies were out tracking the men who'd attacked Raul. The Circle 45 men went into the saloon. Smoke stood up and headed for the saloon.

As he passed by the deputy, he paused and said, "I just heard there was some trouble out at that farm about three miles west of here. Maybe you'd best go check on that."

"Huh? I haven't heard about any trouble."

"I just told you."

The deputy got the message and nodded his head. "That would be the Jeffersons' place."

"Probably."

"It'll take the rest of the afternoon for me to do that."

"Pleasant ride, though. See you."

"Ah . . . right, Mr. Jensen. See you."

Smoke walked over to the saloon and pushed open the batwings. A dozen locals were sitting at tables. The Circle 45 hands were lined up at the bar, Baylis among them. Smoke stepped to one side, away from the batwings, and put his back to a wall.

"Any of you trash seen Fatso and Art Long today?" Smoke called.

Baylis froze in the lifting of his glass to his mouth. He cut his eyes to Smoke. "You callin' me trash?"

"That's right, Baylis. And worse. You're the one who beat it up here from Wyoming to tell Clint about the herd. I can't say that you were in on the night attack, but you're just as guilty. You wanted to brace me back on the trail, Baylis. Still want to pull against me?"

Baylis lifted the shot glass and downed his drink. He thought for a moment, nodded his head, and turned, his hand by the butt of his gun. "Why not, Jensen? I think all that talk about you is bull anyway." Then he grabbed for his Colt.

Smoke's .44 roared and Baylis was leaning against the bar, his belly and chest leaking blood. The three Circle 45 hands jerked their guns and both of Smoke's hands were filled with .44s as he went to one knee and began thumbing and firing in one long continuous roll of deadly thunder.

A round blew Smoke's hat off his head and another slug came so close to his leg, he could feel the heat. But Clint Black was four hands short.

Baylis was sitting on the barroom floor, his hands by his side and his dead eyes staring at eternity. Two other Circle 45 riders were dead and the fourth was not long for this world. He had taken two .44 slugs in the chest. Smoke walked to him, reloading as he went, and kicked his gun away. The man stared up at him.

"You played hell, Jensen," he gasped.

"I usually do, partner."

"I guess I took a wrong turn in life and just never got back on the right road."

"I reckon you did. But you can clean the slate some this day."

"How's that?"

"Did Clint Black order the attack on my herd?"

"Yeah. I won't lie for him no more. He ordered us to hit your camp and kill everyone there. Told us to bring them good-looking twins back to him. He wanted to have some fun with the gals before he got rid of them."

Dr. Garrett and Bigelow from the hotel had entered and were listening.

"Did you know about Raul being dragged and beaten today?"

"No. But Jud said Clint told him to have us start earnin' the fightin' wages we was gettin'. He put a bounty on your head, Jensen. Whichever one of us kills you gets five thousand dollars."

"Anything else you want to tell me?"

"Gettin' dark, Jensen. I think I'm goin'. Funny . . . but there ain't no pain. Yeah. Clint's done sent word all along the owlhoot trail for gunhands. I don't know how many's comin' in, but they'll be some, you can bet on that."

"What's your name?" Smoke asked, kneeling down beside the dying puncher turned gunslick.

"Doug. Doug Randel."

"I'll have that put on your marker."

" 'Preciate it. Maybe we'll get to ride down a better trail someday. I'd like that."

"Me, too, Doug."

Doug smiled, coughed up blood, and died.

Smoke looked around for his hat. He found it, stuck his finger through the bullet hole and shook his head. "Hat's not ten days old." He put it on and settled it. He looked at Dr. Garrett, who was inspecting the downed men for signs of life. He didn't find any and stood up with a sigh.

"A dead man's confession might hold up in court," the doctor said. "But I doubt it."

"We'll all testify that we heard it," one of the local men said. "If that'll help."

"Here comes Lucas," another local said, looking out the window. "Looks like his horse come up lame. Little Billy Thompson is tellin' him about the shootin', I reckon. Here he comes."

The deputy walked in, looked at the bodies by the bar, and cussed for a few seconds.

"Jensen didn't pull first," a local said. "But he shore laid him out neat, didn't he?"

"The sheriff ain't gonna like this," Lucas said. "All right, somebody tell me what happened."

Clint's joy at hearing about Raul was short-lived when one of his hands told him about the shooting in town. The hand took one look at Clint's face and immediately found an urge to be somewhere else . . . quickly.

"I put one of theirs out of action and Jensen kills four of

mine," Clint muttered darkly. "I won't have any hands left at this rate."

His brother had been to see him and Clint told him he didn't know anything about Raul. Fatso and the others were working the range clear on the other side of his place and he'd swear to that in a court of law. And to get the hell off his property and stay off.

Clint had slammed the front door in his brother's face.

Furious, Harris Black wired a judge for advice. When the judge in the territorial capital of Helena ruled that the death-bed confession of Doug Randel could not be used in a court of law, the people in the sparsely populated area around Blackstown braced themselves for war.

It was not long in coming. Less than twenty-four hours after the attack on Raul and the shooting in the saloon, a group of Circle 45 riders—after getting juiced up on whiskey—decided to have some fun and hoo-rah a local farmer. They rode their horses through the family's vegetable garden, shot the milk cows and the pigs, and trampled the chickens. The farmer grabbed a rifle and blew one rider out of the saddle. The Circle 45 riders shot him to bloody rags and as they were riding away, accidentally ran down one of the man's children, a six-year-old girl. She died in the back of the wagon long before the nearly hysterical mother could get her into town and to Doc Garrett's office.

So angry he was nearly trembling with rage, Harris Black rode out to confront his brother.

"It was a damn accident," Clint told him. "The punchers was just having some fun, that's all. The nester opened fire on them. What the hell was they supposed to do?"

"Fun!" Harris yelled at him. "Fun? A man and a little girl are dead. All because you think you're some sort of king around here and the law doesn't apply to you. I want the men responsible for this and I by God want them now, Clint."

"I paid them off and fired them."

"You're a damned liar, Clint."

Clint sucker-punched his brother, knocking him off the porch. The two brothers fought for a moment before Jud and half a dozen other men could pull them apart.

With hands holding both men, Clint yelled, "Get off my land, Harris. Get off and stay off. If you ever call me a liar again, I'll kill you!"

"I'll see you hang, Clint," Harris told him. "You're my brother, but you're no good. You're trash. You better toe the line from now on, Clint. Fire these no-count gunhands and walk light."

"Get him on his horse and out of my sight!" Clint screamed. "Right now."

In the saddle, Harris Black looked down at his younger brother. "You don't even realize what you've done, Clint. You're filled with such hate, you don't know that I could arrest you for attacking me."

"You want to try it now?" Clint challenged, as more of his hands gathered around.

"I'm not a fool, brother. I might get lead in you and a couple of your men before I was shot out of the saddle, but it's just not worth it. You're not worth it."

"Get out while you still can, Harris," Clint warned him. "Before your big flappin' mouth gets you in trouble. And there isn't a damn thing you can do to me; I run this country. Not you. Don't get in my way, you might get hurt."

Harris lifted the reins. "Mother would want you buried proper, Clint. I'll see to that." Then he added, "You poor damn pitiful fool." He turned his horse and headed back to town.

14

Almost everyone who lived in the vicinity turned out for the funeral of the farmer and his daughter. Feelings were running very high and there was some talk of a hanging. Harris knew it was just talk and let it ride. But he knew that if more of this continued, the talk just might change to action. Just about an hour after the funeral, he watched it do just that.

An even dozen of Circle 45 riders came galloping into town, raising a cloud of dust and scattering people. A little dog was caught in the thundering hooves and was trampled. A small boy ran out and picked up the lifeless body of the pup.

"You dirty scum!" he screamed at the Circle 45 men. "Murderers. All of you. Patches didn't do none of you no harm. Why'd you run him down, you . . . crap?"

One of the rowdies walked to the boy and slapped him down into the dirt. The blow brought blood to the boy's lips. He lay in the dirt, sobbing, his arms wrapped around his dead pet.

"I'll kick your guts out, you little turd," the Circle 45 hand said menacingly.

The boy's father ran out of his store, a shotgun in his hands. He was just lifting the weapon to his shoulder when six-guns roared. The father fell back into the store, dead.

Suddenly, the street was filled with armed men and women. The Circle 45 riders looked into the muzzles of six-guns, rifles, and shotguns.

Harris walked through the crowd of armed and angry citizens. "Put those pistols back in leather and get off those horses," he told the bunch. "If you want to stay alive."

The riders slowly complied.

"Doc," Harris called. "How many bullet holes in Mr. Wisdom?"

"Eight," the doctor called.

Harris pointed to the man who'd slapped the boy. "You're under arrest for assault and battery against a child." He turned and smiled at the 45 hands. "The rest of you are under arrest for murder."

"He was fixin' to kill Ned!" a hand yelled.

"After Ned threatened to do more harm to his son," Harris reminded the tough. "Not a court in the land would have convicted him. But they'll damn sure convict you boys."

The deputies had collected the guns from the Circle 45 riders.

"You boys know the way to the jail," Harris told them. "Now, move!"

Harris knelt down by the boy, who was still somewhat addled by the brutal blow from the tough. He helped the boy to his feet and handed the trampled little dog to a man standing near. "We'll see that your puppy gets a proper burial, lad. Now you go on over to your ma. She needs you right now."

Harris walked over to the tough who'd slapped the man and flattened him with one hard fist to the mouth. The Circle 45 hand lay in the dirt and kept his mouth shut. He could see cold, killing fury in the sheriff's eyes.

"Goddamn filth!" Harris's words were spoken low and

hard. "If I wasn't wearin' this badge I'd kick your face clear off your brainless head and let the hogs eat it."

The tough lay still in the dirt, blood leaking from his mouth. He knew that he'd get no more than a few days in jail and a fine for slapping the boy. He had not fired at the boy's father, and he could not be charged with murder. When he got out of jail, then he'd settle with Sheriff Harris Black.

Harris jerked the tough to his boots and threw him toward the jail. When he was slow getting to his feet, he felt the sheriff's big boot impact against his butt. He hollered and went sprawling face first into the dust. He crawled to his hands and knees and then came up cussing. He took a swing at Harris. Bad mistake.

Harris hit him five times. Blows so fast they seemed to come out of nowhere. The rowdy was slammed back against a hitchrail and Harris plowed in. Since the man's face was already ruined, Harris concentrated his big hard fists against the man's belly and sides. Ribs popped and the Circle 45 hand screamed in pain as the blows kept coming. When Harris was through, the rowdy fell to the dirt, his jaw broken, his nose flattened, his lips pulped and half a dozen ribs broken.

"Why?" he managed to gasp through his pain, looking up at the still enraged Harris Black.

"I like kids and dogs," Harris told him.

Clint Black and his hands rode into town the next morning. He had sense enough to come in unarmed. He left his horse at the livery and he and half a dozen of his men walked to the sheriff's office. They walked in a sweat, all of them knowing at least fifty or more guns were trained on them from doorways and windows all along the main street.

At the sheriff's office, they were met with sawed-off-shotgun-carrying deputies. More sweat.

"Keep your gunslicks out on the boardwalk," Harris told

his brother. "And you don't sit down. You're not going to be here that long. State your business and then get the hell gone."

"Bail for my hands," Clint said.

"No bail for murderers." He held up a telegram. "Judge's orders. That all you got to say?"

"You won't get a conviction from the people around here," Clint boasted. "And you know it. I'll hire the best lawyer in the state and beat it."

"Trial is not going to be here," Harris told him. "It'll be held in Helena. Hire your lawyer and go to hell with him. Anything else?"

"You want a war, Harris?"

"Is that a threat? You want to join your no-count hands behind bars for threatening a peace officer?"

Smoke sat on a bench outside the jail. He smiled at the Circle 45 riders.

They did not see any humor in their situation.

"You mind if me and my boys have a drink in town?" Clint asked.

"Don't cause any trouble. The townspeople will shoot you to ribbons. They've had it with you, Clint. They won't stand for any more crap from you or your hired guns. You can try to buy a drink. But I doubt if the barkeep will serve you."

"Can I see my men?"

"After I search you."

That infuriated the rancher. He drew back from the desk and straightened up, his face flushed with rage. "You tin-star piece of crap. Who in the hell do you think you're talking to?"

"A thug," Harris replied. "One that needs to be back there behind bars. And I'm going to put you there, Clint. Believe that."

Clint balled his hands into big fists. He struggled to keep control. He took several deep breaths and calmed himself. "Are my men being fed?"

"You know they are. Three meals a day. Now if there is nothing else, I'm busy with paperwork."

"You're . . . *dismissing* me?"

"That's right, Clint. Good choice of words. I am indeed dismissing you. Oh, it might be a nice gesture on your part to go see the widow Wisdom. Since it was your men who killed her husband."

"Go to hell!" Clint spun around and stalked out of the office. He pulled up short at the sight of Smoke, sitting on a bench smiling at him. "You!"

"Just me," Smoke said. "You were expecting maybe the President of the United States? I mean, with you being such an important person and all, it wouldn't surprise me."

Clint stared at Smoke for a moment. He knew he'd been insulted and cut down, but he couldn't think of a proper response.

Smoke lifted a big hand and waggled his fingers at the rancher. "Run along, now, Clint. Bye-bye."

"Run along? I don't take orders from you, you sorry . . ." He started cussing Smoke, screaming the obscenities. Several women across the street covered their ears and ran into the nearest store.

Harris jerked open the door and stepped out. "Shut up, Clint! I said shut up!" he hollered.

Wild-eyed with fury, Clint turned on his brother, his fists balled.

"Don't even think about doing that," Harris warned him. "Calm down and ride out of here. That's right, Clint. I'm ordering you from town. Right now."

Clint cut his eyes to Smoke. Smoke smiled, lifted his hand, and waggled his fingers at the rancher. "Like I said, bye-bye."

Clint reached down and grabbed Smoke by the front of his shirt and hauled him to his boots. Bad mistake.

Smoke popped him on the side of the jaw with two short punches, left and right, that jarred Clint down to his toenails.

He released the grip on the shirt and Smoke popped him again, this time right in the mouth. Clint's head jerked back and blood sprayed from his lips.

He screamed in fury and waded in, swinging with both fists. Smoke sidestepped and ducked and swung one foot, catching Clint on the ankle and sending the man tumbling to the boardwalk. Smoke backed up. "You better stop it now, Harris," he warned. "Because if he gets up, it'll be the last time he does it in this life."

"Grab him, boys!" Harris yelled to the men gathered around.

They all piled on, deputies and Circle 45 riders. Deputies and punchers were flung around like rag dolls as the enraged Clint Black struggled to get to his feet. Smoke had backed up farther, his fists up and ready to go.

"I'll kill you, Jensen!" Clint screamed, as the big man was once more ridden down to the boards by a pile of men. "You're a dead man."

"All I did was say bye-bye," Smoke told a gathering of women across the narrow alleyway.

"Disgusting," one woman said.

"He's an animal," another said.

"Is there anything wrong with saying bye-bye?" Smoke asked the ladies.

Clint was cussing to the high heavens and throwing men off as fast as they could pile on the fist-throwing rancher.

"Oh, hell," Harris said, as he reached behind him and pulled a leather-bound cosh from his back pocket. He shifted a couple of times, for a better angle, then rapped his brother on the noggin.

Clint's eyes rolled back in his head and he stopped thrashing and cussing.

"Jesus," one of the Circle 45 men said, holding a bandanna to a busted lip. "He's strong as a bull."

"Tie him across a saddle and get him out of town and by God, I mean right now!" Harris ordered. "Move!" he hollered.

Clint was tossed belly-down across a saddle, tied securely, and the horse led out of town.

Harris looked at Smoke for a few seconds, then walked back into his office. Smoke went across the street to buy a new shirt. Clint had torn the whole front out of the one he was wearing. But it was worth ten shirts just to get a couple of good licks in on the man.

That night, several holes were blown out of the back of the jail and all the Circle 45 hands except the one charged with assault and battery escaped. He was lying on his bunk, hands behind his head, and smiling when Harris and his deputies arrived.

"What can I say, Sheriff?" he asked. "I ain't no criminal. No point in me runnin'."

Harris opened the cell door. "Get out. Your horse is at the livery. Be kind of stupid leaving you in here with that hole in the wall behind you."

"Now what?" a deputy asked.

"They're out on the Circle 45 range. You can bet my brother had fresh horses stashed every few miles along the way. He got this idea from me," Harris said ruefully. "Twenty years ago I busted some friends of mine out of jail down in Kansas. They weren't in there for murder, just for barroom fighting. Clint took a page from out of my past in doing this. He'll think it funny. We'll ride out come first light. I'll get flyers made up at the print shop and get them posted out across the territory. Come on, let's get this mess cleaned up."

That morning, Smoke did something he felt he should have done as soon as they cleared the ambush valley. He brought the teenage boys into town and sent them home on the stage. Three went one day and the remaining two the next day. He wanted them out of harm's way.

He walked down to Garrett's office and checked on Raul. The young man was looking and feeling better and the doctor said he could be taken back to the ranch in a couple of days. After talking with Raul for a moment, Smoke walked over to the jail and looked at the holes blown into the rear of the jail building. Benny was the only deputy left in town. Harris and the others had ridden out to Circle 45 range.

"How mad was Harris?" he asked the deputy.

"Not too bad. Not as upset as I thought he'd be."

"The sheriff knows this situation is coming to a head and he's feeling his way slow," Smoke said. "I don't blame him. He's taking his life in his hands just by riding out to his brother's place."

"Oh, they might tie up in a fistfight," the deputy said. "But when it comes to killing, I think Clint will walk up to the line and then back off on that. Look at all he's got to lose if he pulls a gun on Harris. If he just keeps that temper of his in check, maybe this thing can be smoothed down."

"If I'd leave the country, you mean?"

"Something like that." The deputy wasn't going to push the issue too hard.

"And if you were me?"

Benny met the cold steady gaze from Smoke. Without giving much away, he said, "A man's got to do what he's got to do, I reckon."

15

"They're up in the high country, staying out of sight," Harris said to Smoke the next afternoon. "Clint was actually civil to me yesterday. But he couldn't keep from smiling. He feels pretty good about what he did." He stared at Smoke for a moment. "You look like a man who just ate a sour apple. What's your problem?"

"I feel responsible for that merchant getting killed the other day."

"That's nonsense. You didn't start this war, my brother did. No one in this town blames you. Hell, if you did anything, you stuck some steel into a lot of backbones around here. No, Smoke. No. In one way, my life would be a lot simpler if you'd leave, but that would just make my brother even more cockier. I am glad you got those boys out of this mess."

"I should have done it days ago. I don't know why I waited so long."

Boots sounded on the boardwalk and the door was flung open. "Sheriff!" a man shouted. "Come quick."

Smoke and Harris stood on the boards and looked to the west. Plumes of dark smoke were spiraling into the sky.

"The Crawford farm," Harris said. "Clint's been trying to buy it for years. Good water and good graze. Crawford's told me that Clint's threatened him a time or two. Feel like taking a ride?"

"Let's go."

The farmer lay face down in his wife's flower bed. He'd been shot twice in the head. The woman and three girls stood under a huge old tree, sobbing. The house and barn were gone, burned to the ground. The cows, pigs, and horses were dead, all of them shot.

"In broad open daylight," Harris muttered.

"They were wearing hoods," the woman said, tears still streaming down her face, reddening her eyes. "And their horses were wearing brands that I'd never seen before."

Smoke dismounted and began inspecting the tracks left by the churning hooves. He found one horse with a nearly perfect Z somehow cut into the shoe. He waved Harris over and pointed it out.

"Let's look at the dead horses over there, just to be sure," Harris suggested.

The dead animals bore no such cut on any horseshoe.

Harris turned to his deputies. "Take off after them. But I've got a pretty good hunch where they're going. They'll probably get into the river and try to lose you that way. Then they'll come out on the gravel and probably go back in the river where it curves. Stay with them. Provision at the Bell spread."

"I'll ride back to town for a wagon," Smoke said. "Ma'am," he turned to the woman, "do you want to stay on this farm and work it?"

"No," she shook her head. "No. I want to leave this awful place."

"All right. When you get to town, go to the new bank and tell them who you are. I'll have everything set up. I'm buying your place. You just name your price."

Harris stared open-mouthed at Smoke. This would really

anger his brother. Jensen was pushing and pushing hard. He closed his mouth before a fly could find it.

Smoke swung into the saddle. "See you, Harris." He headed into town.

"Was that Smoke Jensen, Sheriff?" the woman asked.

"Yes."

"He doesn't look at all like the stories depict him. What a nice young man."

Harris cut his eyes to the woman. "Believe me when I say there are those who do not share that opinion, Mrs. Crawford."

"Including your brother, Sheriff?"

"Especially my brother, Mrs. Crawford."

Smoke tossed the deed to the Crawford farm to Denver. "It's big enough to run a few head of cattle, some horses, and it has a whale of a garden there now. You said this run was going to be your last one. So happy retirement, Denver."

Sally smiled. Nothing that Smoke did surprised her any longer. If he liked a person, that person had a loyal friend for life. If he disliked a person, that person had better leave town on the first available horse, stage, or train.

Denver turned his head so those gathered around would not see the quick tears. He brushed them away and said, "You're a puzzlement, Smoke. I thank you."

"Well, you can't leave until we get this Clint Black situation put aside. You certainly don't want to stay over there by yourself. You'd end up like Crawford. Besides, there is no house or barn. When the time is right, the First United Bank will loan you the money to get started."

"Count on that," Sally said with a smile

"They killed the man right in front of his family," Toni said. "Horrible. Clint Black has certainly lost his mind! "

"Oh, he's mad, all right," Smoke said, after thanking the cook for the cup of coffee she handed him. "But not in the way you think. He's crazy-killing angry because for years he was the top fish in a small pond around here. He yelled frog and everybody jumped. Now the pond is a big lake and nobody is paying any attention to him. He's striking out at anybody he sees. He thinks everybody is his enemy, and he's just about right on that."

"And the sheriff seems powerless to act," Jeanne said.

"Harris is straight arrow, Jeanne," Smoke told her. "He wants everything done legal-like. All the T's crossed and the I's dotted. He'd put him in jail in a heartbeat if he had some proof that would stand up in a court of law. But he doesn't have it."

"And not much chance of getting it," Denver said. He was still in mild shock upon learning he was now a landowner.

"Sadly true," Smoke agreed.

"So we're right back where we started," Toni said.

"Oh, no," Smoke told her. "You and your sister have the herd on Double D range, the people in the community have risen up against Clint Black and his men, the sheriff now sees his brother for what he really is, and I doubt that Clint's bank will last out the summer. A lot has been accomplished, I'd say."

"I just feel responsible for what's happened," Jeanne said. "All the tragedy."

"Don't," Smoke said. "Harris told me that before we came in, he'd heard rumblings of a citizens' group forming to fight Clint and the Circle 45 hands. The good people of the community had decided to make their stand. The fuse was already lit when Clint ordered the raid against us. Harris said, very reluctantly, that our coming in might just have prevented a lot more spilled blood of innocent people than has occurred since we arrived. I like to think so."

"What's next?" Denver asked.

Smoke shrugged his shoulders. "That's up to Clint, I reckon."

* * *

Jud walked slowly toward the big ranch house. He had to speak his piece to Clint, and he was not looking forward to it. What he had to say would not be said out of any compassion for his fellow man, for Jud was just as sorry and miserable and low-down a person as Clint and all the other Circle 45 hands. But the situation had reached the point where a man had to step back and do some thinking. It was down to survival now. The whole country was lined up solidly against the Circle 45. Once they left Circle 45 range, none of them had a friend within a hundred-mile radius. It wouldn't be long before the whole kit and caboodle of them would be barred from town. Jud had seen that happen before. Back when he was a young hellion riding the owlhoot trail.

His head down, deep in thought, he was surprised to see Clint sitting on the front porch.

"We got to talk, boss," the foreman said, stepping up on the porch.

Clint waved the man to a chair. "You going to tell me to pull in my horns, Jud?"

"I'm sure gonna suggest it."

Jud hollered for the cook to bring them a pot of coffee and be damn quick about it. The cook might not like being hollered at, but there was precious little he could do about it, since Jud knew he was wanted for murder back in Missouri. All in all, the Circle 45 riders, including Jud and Clint, made up just about the sorriest gathering of humanity anywhere west of the Mississippi.

Coffee poured, Clint sipped in silence for several minutes. He sat the mug down and said, "What else were you going to tell me?"

"George Miller just come in from town. He said he was walkin' real light in there. It was some kind of scary. Everybody was carryin' guns. And he also said that Smoke Jensen bought the Crawford farm."

Clint hurled his coffee mug out into the yard and cussed. Then he yelled for the cook to bring him another cup. In a calmer voice, he said, "That five thousand dollar bounty on Jensen's head still stands, Jud."

"What good would it do, Clint? When an old elk turns to make his final stand against the wolves or a cougar or a fight for who's boss, he's made up his mind to stand or die. Same way with the people around here, now. The killin' would never stop. Two more hands rode out this mornin'. Clint, there ain't a real cowboy left on this place, 'ceptin' maybe you and me. You got thousands and thousands of acres with no cattle to speak of."

"You going to start attending church, Jud?" Clint asked sarcastically.

"Probably wouldn't hurt neither of us, although it's more 'un likely too late to do us any good. Clint, Smoke Jensen ain't even broke a sweat yet in this fight. You and me, now, we know all about the man. He's hell when he gets goin'. He'll do anything. Guns, dynamite, fire . . . you name it and Jensen will use it. He's a wild man when he gets riled up."

"He's just one man, Jud. Just one man. And I don't agree with you about the people around here. They kowtowed for years. They're yellow clear through. With Jensen out of the way, they'd slink back into their holes."

"There is one more thing: what about your brother?" Jud asked softly.

"I have no brother," Clint said. "He's turned his back to me and shown me his true colors. As far as I'm concerned, he's an enemy."

"You're going all the way with this, Clint?"

"Yes, I am. I don't have any choice in the matter. Do you see a choice for me?"

Jud looked at his boss for a moment, wondering if the man was kidding? But Clint's face was granite. Then he got it: Clint was talking honor. *Honor!* There wasn't a shred of honor between the two men. Both of them had cold-bloodedly murdered and stolen land and cattle and horses and God alone knew what else, and Clint was talking about *honor?*

Jud stood up. "All right, Clint. You know I'll stand with you all the way."

"I appreciate that, old friend. We'll whip Jensen. You just wait and see. We'll whip him."

When pigs fly, the foreman thought. But he kept that to himself.

On Stony's word, Smoke hired two more hands for the Double D. Two young, easy-to-grin men who had been working over in the Dakota Territory and had drifted back home when they learned that someone was fighting Clint Black.

"This here's Davy and Eli, Smoke," Stony said. "They ain't gunslingers, but they are good punchers. And they both hate Clint Black."

Smoke shook hands with the men and could feel the calluses on their hands. "What did Clint ever do to you boys?"

"Put my daddy out of the ranchin' business," Davy said. "I was just a kid. Clint and his no-count hands stole our cattle just after we rounded 'em up. Killed my brother and when ma heard that, she just collapsed. Died a couple of days later. Doc said it was a heart attack. Pa, he went after Clint, but Jud Howes found him first and stomped him half to death. Pa died a few years after that. Lost the ranch and that stompin' broke his spirit. I was thirteen when I hit the road and startin' doin' a man's work. But I tell you this, Mr. Jensen . . ."

"Smoke. Just Smoke, Davy."

Davy grinned. "Fine, Smoke. What I was gonna say is this: if I ever get Clint or Jud in gunsights, it's my swore intention to kill 'em. I want you to know that up front."

"Neither one of them are worth hanging over, Davy," Smoke cautioned the young man. "Putting a rope around your own neck won't bring your ma and pa back. Don't worry, though, I feel sure you'll get your shot at one or both of those men. How about you, Eli?"

"Clint raped my sister," the young puncher said. "Took her like an animal, he did. This was years ago. I was no more than five or six years old. I seen him ridin' off from where he done it. Sis made me swear never to tell 'cause she knew Pa would go after him and Clint or his hands would kill Pa. When she learned she was with child, she killed herself rather than face the disgrace. It broke Ma's heart. Pa, he just was never the same. Clint, he come ridin' over big as brass, grinnin' like the cat who licked the cream, and told pa he was gonna buy him out. That day. Pa knew it was over. He took the money, piddlin' sum that it was, and we pulled out. Injuns hit us down on the Ruby. I had gone off into the woods to play and they never knew I was about. Church people took me in. I run off when I was eleven and never looked back. But I intend to kill Clint Black."

Smoke looked at the two young man. Clint Black had to be one of the sorriest excuses for a human being he had ever run up against. He had never met a man who didn't have any redeeming qualities—until now. "You boys toss your kit in the bunkhouse and get ready for supper. My wife's cooking tonight, so it's gonna be good."

"Mr. Jensen . . . ah, Smoke," Eli said. "Did your wife really strap on a pistol and take up a rifle and ride with you to help you out of a jam some months back?"

Smoke chuckled in the fading light of day. "She sure did. She was born back east to a wealthy family, but that lady can ride and shoot as good as any man. Better than most. It isn't wise to cross her. Bear that in mind."

The young cowboys solemnly nodded their heads. Davy asking, "Can she cook as good as she shoots?"

Smoke patted him on the back. "Better, Davy."

"Lord have mercy," Davy said. "Eli, I think we done found us a home."

16

That same night, while the townspeople slept, the new First United Bank of Blackstown was robbed and the whole back of the building blown out with dynamite. But Smoke had suspected something like that might happen and had brought in other workmen from back East to build a second safe in the ground under the building, accessible by a trap door which was covered by a rug. The Circle 45 hands made a clean getaway and beat it back to the ranch, taking a round-about route.

When the Circle 45 hands ripped open the bank bags to count their loot, they found washers at the bottom of the sacks and stacks of worthless old Confederate money in place of greenbacks.

Clint was not amused.

"Burn all that crap," he ordered his men, pointing to the worthless money. "Save the washers, we might need them around the place. Two dollars worth of washers. Jesus!'"

Yukon Golden, who had absolutely no reason at all to like Smoke Jensen, found the whole thing funny. Back in the bunkhouse, he said, "This deck is stacked, boys. I felt it when

I first rode into town. This thing is windin' down to be a bloody mess, I'm thinkin'."

Bronco Ford cut hard eyes to the man. "You thinkin' about haulin' your ashes, Yukon?"

"No. I took the man's money, so I'll stay. But there ain't gonna be no good end to this. You mark my words."

"What do you mean?" Tex Mason asked.

"Well, I been hearin' talk that Clint has plans on treein' the town."

"There ain't nobody ever treed no Western town," Weldon Ball said. "And there ain't nobody ever gonna do it. That's a fool's game."

Grub Carson said, "I seen it tried a time or two. Man, them townspeople shot them ol' boys all to pieces. Most awfulest thing I ever seen."

Slim King looked over at him. "Look what happened when Jesse James tried to rob that town over in Minnesota back a few years. They shore got their comeuppance there."

"I ain't attemptin' to tree no whole town," Austin Charles said, summing up the feelings of all the newly hired guns, " 'Cause it can't be done." He finished rolling a cigarette and added, "And I agree with Yukon. I think this deck is stacked against us. It's one thing goin' in an' runnin' out nester trash or shootin' sheepmen. Used to be no one give a damn about them. But times is changin'."

The men in the bunkhouse had all fallen silent, listening to Austin.

"I ain't sayin' our day has come and gone," Austin continued. "But it ain't gonna be too many more years 'fore jobs like this one will be hard to come by. And when that day comes, we're gonna have to start doin' more thinkin' and less shootin'."

"What do you mean?" a hand asked.

"Plannin' things out, is what I mean. This night ridin' hell for leather and shootin' everything that moves is damn near a thing of the past. As long as the jobs is like this one, stuck out here in the middle of nowhere, we can get away with it. Telegraph wires is everywhere. And I seen a machine that lets people talk to one another from miles away. It's scary."

"You ain't neither seen no machine like that!" a Circle 45 hand sneered at him.

Austin cut his eyes. "Don't be callin' me no liar, boy. I seen it. It's called a telephone. Lots of cities has them."

"I heard of 'em," Cleon said. "How do they work?"

"I don't know. Spooky, I say," Austin replied. "We're gettin' away from what I was talkin' about. Now let's face facts, boys: we ain't gonna whip Jensen with guns. Not unless we back-shoot him and that ain't my style. We got to use our heads in this."

"You ain't runnin' this show," Fatso Ross reminded him. "Clint is. I don't take orders from you; I take orders from Clint."

"For a fact," Austin said, taking no umbrage at the words. "For a fact."

Smoke rode into town early in the morning. Most of the businesses were not yet open. He had awakened with a feeling that this day would be eventful; that this day would mark the turning point in this high country war. And Smoke had long ago learned to play his hunches. He had left the ranch before dawn, and his stomach was telling him he had missed breakfast. His eyes were busy, moving from side to side, but he could see nothing to give cause for alarm. He stabled his horse and entered the cafe. He was the only customer. Smoke ordered breakfast and a pot of coffee. He watched as Doc Garrett walked slowly up the boardwalk and stepped into the cafe. The man looked weary.

"Mind if I join you, Mr. Jensen?" the doctor inquired.

"The name is Smoke. Please sit down, Doctor You look like you're about ready to fall down from exhaustion."

The man smiled. "Twins, Smoke. It was a hard delivery.

But mother and babies are doing fine. No trouble last night from Clint?"

"No. But there will be today."

The doctor smiled as he poured himself a cup of coffee. "Can you predict the future, Smoke?"

"I play my hunches, Doctor. It's something I learned from mountain men. We're all born with that ability. You just have to work to develop it. It comes in very handy when danger is all around you."

"And what kind of trouble will be coming your way this day, Smoke?"

"Guns," he said softly. The sounds of hammering reached the cafe. The workmen were up early, repairing the rear of the new bank building.

The waitress took the doctor's order as more people entered the cafe, their faces still lumpy from sleep. They wanted no conversation until they'd had their coffee. They nodded at Smoke and the doctor, and the nods were returned.

The blacksmith came in and ordered a huge stack of flapjacks. "The sheriff and his deputies rode out early this morning," he told the waitress. "Seems like some fellers tried to rob the stage and they was headed this way. The news come in over the wires late last night."

"Set up," Smoke spoke very low. "Five will get you ten that one of Clint's men jumped the wires and sent that message to suck Harris and his deputies out of town."

"To attack this town?"

Smoke shook his head. "No. That would be very foolish. They're coming after me."

"You don't think they might attack the Double D?"

Again, Smoke shook his head. "No. That's coming. I'm certain of that. But not yet. Clint wants me out of this game first. And he wants people to see me go down. He thinks that will put the fear back in them. But he's wrong." He looked over at the smithy. "How far out of town did this attempted robbery take place?"

"Harris said they was goin' as far as Slater's Pass. That's a pretty fair piece out. I 'spect they'll be gone most of the day."

Smoke thanked him as the waitress put his plate in front of him and Smoke concentrated on eating his breakfast. The doctor did not attempt to engage him in conversation while eating. Eating was serious business for many a Western man. Soon the doctor was busy working on his own food.

"Well, bless Pete," a man said, looking up from his eggs. "Would you take a look at them two."

Smoke looked up and saw them. He silently cussed. He didn't know the two young men, but he was very familiar with the type. Young trouble-hunters out to make a reputation. They had heard he was in town, and here they came.

The smithy turned around, looked, and snorted. "Pearl-handled six-shooters, fancy rigs and boots. All decked out. Young toughs."

Smoke ate his breakfast, poured another cup of coffee, and waited. He watched as the trouble-hunters stepped up onto the boardwalk across the street and asked a man something. The citizen pointed to the cafe and Smoke sighed. It was down to minutes now.

"Am I missing something here?" Doc Garrett asked, looking at the expression on Smoke's face.

"A couple of young trouble-hunters heading this way. Probably looking for me."

The doctor turned and looked at them. "Not more that twenty-one or two at the most."

"But they're wearing guns," Smoke told him. "Out here, Doc, when you strap on a gun, that makes you a man."

"How will you handle this?"

"That all depends on those two would-be gunslicks. Try to talk my way out of it if they'll let me."

The door opened and the young men swaggered in, trying to look tough. They managed to look pathetic. But Smoke had noticed they had taken the hammer thongs off their guns. The pair looked around the large room, their eyes settling on Smoke. Smoke was sipping his coffee and seemingly not paying any attention to them.

"You boys take a seat," the waitress called from the kitchen. "I'll be with you in a minute."

"Shake a leg there, baby," one of them called. "You got the Shawnee Kid and Hawk Evans in here."

Smoke shook his head in disgust.

"The only thing that's gonna be shakin' around here is your butts when I kick you out of here," the cook said, stepping out of the kitchen. "You watch your mouths around my wife, you hear me?"

"Shawnee," his partner said. "I think that feller's threatenin' us."

"Sounds like it, don't it? Maybe we ought to pin his ears back some?"

Smoke sat the coffee cup on the table.

"Oh, my!" Evans said. "But we got the world-famous Smoke Jensen in here, Shawnee. The cook might be a friend of his. Don't that scare you?"

"Why . . . I'm tremblin' in my boots just at the thought of Mr. Smoke Jensen. Tell you what, Hawk, maybe we ought to ride out to the Circle 45 and tell Clint Black that we'll take care of his little problem with Jensen. That is, if we can get Jensen away from that coffee pot."

"If you boys have a problem," Smoke told them, finally turning his head to look at the pair, "I think it would be wise to carry it somewhere else. This is the wrong town to start trouble in."

"Because of you, Mr. Hotshot Gunfighter?" Hawk sneered at him.

"That's part of it," Smoke told him.

"What's the other part?" Shawnee asked.

"Actually there is more than one. They got the loneliest graveyard I have ever seen in any town. I'd hate to know I had to spend eternity on that hill."

"What's the other part?" Hawk asked.

"The cook has a double-barreled shotgun pointed right at your guts."

Both of their mouths dropped open and they jerked their heads toward the rear. Smoke left his chair like a striking snake and ran into the pair, knocking them sprawling. One jerked out a 45 and Smoke kicked it out of his hand. Whirling, he backhanded the other one just as he was crawling to his knees, the blow catching him on the side of the head and knocking him back to the floor. Smoke ripped the gun belts from them and hung them on a peg.

"Now stand up," he said in a very low and menacing voice. When they were slow in doing so, he shouted, "Stand up, damnit!"

They scrambled to their feet and faced him. Smoke stepped closer to the one called Shawnee. "Draw," he told him.

"Draw what?"

"Pretend you're drawing. Maybe this is the only way I can keep you alive and get you back home safely. Draw, damnit!"

Shawnee's elbow was just bending when Smoke's .44 leaped into the young man's face.

"Jesus Christ!" Evans said.

Sweat was pouring down Shawnee's face, even though the morning had dawned very cool for summer.

"You get the message, Shawnee?" Smoke asked.

"Yes . . . sir. I mean, *yes sir!*"

Smoke cut his eyes to Evans. "How about you?"

"Real plain, Mr. Jensen."

"Fine. Now you boys sit down and order you some breakfast. After you've eaten, ride back home, wherever home is, and forget about being gunfighters. The trails are long, the food is terrible, the company you keep is awful, the life expectancy is short, and the pay isn't worth a damn. Breakfast is on me, boys. Now sit down and eat."

"Yes, sir," they said in unison, and sat. Evans looked up at Jensen and smiled. "The cook ain't holdin' no shotgun, Mr. Jensen."

Smoke returned the smile. "I lied."

Smoke returned to his own table and the waitress brought him a fresh pot of coffee. She smiled and said in a whisper, "You could have killed them both and nobody would have blamed you."

"Ten years ago, I would have," Smoke told her.

"For a man of your size, you're devilishly quick, Smoke," the doctor said.

"It pays to be with the name I've got hung on me."

"Circle 45 riders coming in," a man called from a table by the window.

The doctor stared at Smoke. "I was planning on going home and getting a few hours' sleep this morning."

"I think it's going to get busy around here this morning," Smoke said, shoving back his chair. "You'd better plan on an afternoon's nap."

17

Smoke walked outside while some of the cafe's patrons exited by the back door, heading for home to make sure their wives and kids stayed off the streets. Hawk Evans and the Shawnee Kid sat at their table and stared out the window. Both of them knew that from this point on, they would never again strap on a gun. Dr. Garrett looked at the two young men, staring wide-eyed at Smoke, then turned his chair around so he could see what was taking place in the street.

Smoke knew only one of the men who had ridden in, a two-bit gunhandler who went by the name of Earl Cobb. He knew none of the others. He watched as they reined in and swung down, looping the reins on the hitchrail in front of the saloon. They turned and faced him.

The cork is out of the bottle now, Smoke thought. *They aren't even trying to conceal the reason they came to town. Clint must have upped the ante.*

The quartet of gunhands spread out.

Smoke backed up and entered the cafe. "They don't care that innocent people might be hit by a bullet," he said to Doc

Garrett. "I won't have it this way." He paused by the hat rack and took two of the guns belonging to the young men. "I'll return these in a few minutes," he said to the pair.

"Keep them," Evans said. "We won't be needing them no more."

Smoke walked through the kitchen, a borrowed pistol in each hand. The cook, who was the owner, said, "I've got a rifle here, Smoke."

"Stay out of this. I'm going to pull them away from your cafe and try to get them off the main street. People are all over the place opening up for business."

He went out the back door and ran two blocks down to the livery stable. He cut right and stepped out into the street. He was a good two hundred yards from the gunmen, who were standing in the middle of the street in front of the cafe.

"Hey!" Smoke called, stepping closer to the other side of the street where there were two abandoned buildings at the edge of town. "You jerks looking for me?"

Earl Cobb cussed at the distance between them. "Come on," he said to the others. "Jensen's tryin' to get us away from the main drag so's no citizen will take lead."

"Ain't he sweet?" another said.

"He's liable to take up preachin' 'fore long," another added.

Smoke was standing by the corner of what had once been a general store.

"Split up," Earl said. "Luddy, you come with me. Dick, Patton, you cut through that alley and come up behind him."

When he looked up again, Smoke had vanished.

Many of the townspeople had armed themselves. But since Smoke had pulled the action to the edge of town, where no businesses or houses stood, they could not leave their families unprotected. Most knew Smoke had done that deliberately.

"Jensen, you damn yellow cur," Dick called. "Step out here and fight."

"All right," Smoke said as he stepped out of a doorway behind the two men. "Here I am."

The men were lifting their guns as they turned to meet what their fates had long ago planned for them. The borrowed .45s in Smoke Jensen's hands roared and spat fire and lead and gunsmoke. Patton and Dick were down in the litter behind the old building.

"Nice action on these pistols," Smoke muttered, as he kicked the guns of the fallen men away from them and stepped back into the building. He had checked the pistols in the cafe and knew they had been loaded up full. He had fired four times and had put two slugs apiece in Patton and Dick.

Smoke had no illusions about fair fighting. The old mountain man Preacher had grilled that out of him. He never gave a damn for fair; he fought to win. "You always do your best to do right by the good folks of this world, boy," Preacher had told him repeatedly. "To hell with the bad folks. Man comes after you with intent to do you harm, you fight him any damn way you can . . . just win."

Luddy rounded a corner of the building and Smoke fired through a windowless frame. The slug hit the hired gun in the shoulder and knocked him down, the big shoulder joint smashed. Luddy lay on the ground and flopped and hollered in pain, his gun hand useless.

Smoke stepped out of the building just as Earl began pouring lead through the thin walls. He worked his way up the alley and stepped out to the edge of the street just as Earl was jerking out a spare gun he'd tucked behind his belt.

"You do like to waste ammo, don't you, Earl," Smoke called.

Earl cussed, spun around, and fired, the slug slammed into the building behind Smoke. Smoke drilled him clean and dropped him to his knees.

"Give it up, Earl," Smoke told him. "The party's over."

Earl tried to lift his .44. "You dirty son of . . ." He never finished it. The hired gun fell forward in the dirt.

Smoke walked around the building just as the boardwalks began filling with citizens. He stepped up and kicked the pistol out of Luddy's left hand.

"Damn fool," Smoke told him. "Give it up and live, man."

"You ruint me!" Luddy gasped through his pain.

"Maybe now you'll get a decent job and quit trying to kill people," Smoke replied, just as Doc Garrett rounded the corner.

"Go to hell! " Luddy said. "I don't need no damn sermon from the likes of you."

"Whatever," Smoke said, and turned his back to the man. He walked around to the rear of the building. Dick and Patton were still alive and moaning. They lay on the ground and glared hate up at Smoke. But they were smart enough not to try to reach their guns. They could still run their mouths, however, and they did, expelling a lot of wind cussing Smoke.

Smoke turned to the smithy. "Go get those two young men who wanted to brace me."

"They're gone, Smoke. Both of them left out pale as ghosts. I think they got the message. Their gun belts are still hangin' on the pegs."

"Somebody help me with these men," Doc Garrett said. "Pick them up and take them to my office."

"Hell with them," a man said. "They can get there under their own steam. I ain't helpin' nobody who works for Clint Black."

"Sorry bastard!" Luddy cussed the man.

"Look who is calling who sorry," the citizen said, then turned around and walked away. "My breakfast is gettin' cold."

Smoke waited around until Harris returned and told him what had happened, including the incident with the young men in the cafe.

"How many still alive?"

"Some gunslick called Luddy. The other three are dead."

"Luddy Chambers," Harris said. "He's a bad one. You going to press charges?"

"I didn't know you had any laws in this territory about calling a man out."

Harris sighed. "Well, we do, sort of."

"Doc Garrett said the bullet smashed his shoulder joint. He'll only have limited used of that arm for the rest of his life. And when word gets around that Luddy Chambers has a crippled gun arm, he'll either hunt him a hole and change his name, or get dead."

"You're right about that. There was no attempted stage-coach holdup, by the way."

"I figured Clint had one of his men tie into the line and send that message to get you out of town. But if he did, why not send Bronco or Austin or Yukon in after me? These ol' boys today were not the best he has on the payroll."

"What could he be up to?"

"You tell me. He's your brother."

"A fact I wish I could undo," Harris said with a grimace.

"I'm going back to the Double D. I'll see you in a couple of days."

"Smoke? Thanks for pulling those gunnies to the edge of town. I find myself respecting you more and more each day. And if the day comes when my brother braces you . . . put him down. He's stepped way over the line."

"Maybe it won't come to that."

"You know it will," Harris said, and then walked across to Doc Garrett's office.

"I'm afraid you're right," Smoke muttered.

The attack came that evening, about an hour after supper— a time that no one would expect any raid. Smoke was sitting on the front porch, drinking a cup of coffee and laughing as he sat watching two half-grown hounds play and mock-fight with each other, rolling and tumbling on the ground.

Suddenly the hounds stopped and tensed, the hair standing up on their backs. They started growling.

"Get to guns!" Smoke yelled, jumping out of the chair and overturning his cup of coffee. The sounds of pounding hooves reached him. "Take cover!"

He turned at his name and Sally tossed him his gun belt and then a Winchester. "Don't you worry about us in here," she calmly told him, then closed the door.

He wouldn't. Sally had been working with the twins and both of them had turned out to be pretty fair hands with a rifle. They weren't very good with short guns, but put a shotgun in their hands and watch out. He didn't have to check the rifle, he'd made it clear that if he found an empty weapon in the house—other than it being cleaned—he'd raise enough hell so it wouldn't happen again.

Raul was back home, staying in the main house, and Smoke could see him on the bed by the window; his aversion to guns was long gone after his beating and dragging. Smoke could see the muzzle of a Winchester sticking out of the bedroom window.

The cook was a frontier woman who wouldn't back up from a grizzly bear. Smoke had seen ol' Denver making calf eyes at her—and she returning them—and knew that Denver would be in the kitchen with her, both of them firing from there—the woman with rifle, pistol, or shotgun.

Then there was no more time for thinking. It was action now, as fifty or more riders came fogging into the front yard, circling the corral, the bunkhouse, and the main house, and bringing with them thick, choking clouds of dust.

Smoke knew then what they planned. They planned an all-out assault on the ground, on foot.

"Be careful in the house!" he yelled over the shooting. "They're going to take us on foot."

"We see them," Sally returned the yell. "You take care of your own business."

Smoke smiled. Hell of a woman, his Sally.

A shotgun roared from the side of the house and a terrible scream followed the blast. "My legs!" a man hollered hoarsely. "My legs are tore up. I think they's blowed plumb off. Help me. Oh, you damn Eastern hussy bitch you!"

The shotgun roared again. There was no more screaming.

Smoke arched an eyebrow as he searched for a target. He had a .44 in each hand. The man shouldn't have called the Duggan woman that. She sure took umbrage at the remark.

A man came running out of the dust and Smoke cut him down. He hit the ground, tried to lift himself up, then collapsed to the dirt. A slug whined off the stone of the house and went whistling wickedly off into the cooling air. Mask-and-duster-wearing riders continued to circle the grounds, dragging broken limbs behind them to keep the dust whirling. Smoke lined one up and shot him out of the saddle. He hit the ground, bounced, and then was still.

The hound pups had scampered under the porch, out of harm's way. They began barking furiously and Smoke turned in time to see a man swing one leg over the porch railing. The man looked up, his eyes wide with horror at the sight of Smoke, standing calmly, a .44 pointed right at the raider's head. That was the last thing he would see on this earth.

Raul's Winchester barked and a man slumped to the ground just outside the bedroom window. Raul called him a lot of very ugly names in the lilting Spanish language.

The boys in the bunkhouse were laying down a withering fire that was taking its toll. Through the dust, Smoke could see half a dozen bodies sprawled on the ground.

"That's it!" a man yelled. "To your horses. It ain't workin'."

"Hold your positions!" Smoke yelled. "Stay put until they're gone."

In half a minute, the sounds of hard-pounding hooves had faded into the waning light.

"Is everybody all right?" Smoke lifted his voice.

"Stony's got a scratch on his head and Joe's got a burn on his arm," Malvern called. "Everybody else is okay."

"In the house?"

"We're all right," Sally called.

Moaning could be clearly heard from all around the grounds. The dust had settled, coating everything and everybody.

"Reload before you step out," Smoke called. "Then we'll see to the wounded. Cletus, you hitch up a wagon. That old one that we were going to junk."

"Right, boss," Cletus said with a chuckle. "And I'll pitch a few forkfuls of hay in it."

"You do that. We want them to be comfortable on the ride back. And hitch up those two hammer-headed horses. The ones no one can ride."

Cletus laughed aloud. "They ain't harness-broke, boss."

"Yes," Smoke said. "I know."

He walked around the grounds. Seven dead and that many more wounded, two of them badly. They would not last another hour under the best of care. Smoke looked at each wounded man with cold contempt in his eyes. None of them would meet his gaze for more than a few seconds.

"Throw the dead in the wagon first, then the badly wounded on top of them," Smoke ordered. "The rest of you night-riding sorry sons can either find your horses or walk back."

"Say, now," a wounded Circle 45 rider mouthed. "I . . ."

"Shut up!" Smoke roared at him. He had jerked the masks off each one and every Double D rider had taken a look. "When you do get back to your range, pack your gear and get gone. If I see you again in this part of the country, you're dead on the spot. In a cafe, saloon, emporium, or church, I'll kill you, and I'll do it without warning. Now get up and get moving before I decide to end it right now."

Even the more seriously wounded moved mighty quick.

Eli tossed the reins to a leg-shot night rider sitting on the seat. "You take care now," he said with a chuckle. "This wagon's old and the road is mighty bumpy."

"You boys is cold," the night rider said. "Mighty cold. Tossin' the wounded in with the dead."

"You think you deserve any better?" he was asked.

The hired gun chose not to reply. He clucked at the reluctant team and the wagon lurched forward, the horses fighting the unfamiliar harnesses.

When the wagon was out of sight and sound, Smoke said, "Two men on guard tonight and every night. You work out the shifts, Stony. No riding alone. Ride in pairs at all times. Denver, give those hound dog pups something special from the kitchen. They saved our bacon this evening."

He walked back to the porch and righted the overturned chair, then took a rag and wiped the dust off of the porch furniture. The cook brought out a fresh pot of coffee and a tray of cups. Smoke sat down beside Sally. "There wasn't a known gunhand in the bunch. If there had of been, we would have knocked at least one of them out of the saddle. Clint sent his hands at us this night, keeping the best—in a manner of speaking—in reserve. Why?"

Denver and the twins had joined them on the darkened porch. A slight breeze had kicked up and it was pleasant. But the odor of blood and sweat still hung about the grounds.

"The only way he'll be able to get any more men in here will be to double the wages," Denver said. "One of them wounded told me that some of the gunfighters is talkin' about this bein' a stacked deck. He also said that Clint's talkin' about attackin' the town."

"That would be a very stupid thing to do," Smoke said.

"That's what the hired guns said."

"I've never met anyone like this Clint Black," Toni said.

"Sure you have," Sally spoke. "The East is full of them. They just operate in a different manner, that's all. There are ruthless industrialists who are like vultures, waiting to rip and tear at smaller businesses who are faltering. Bankers who pounce if a payment is one day late. Men like Clint Black are all over. They just use their powers differently, but the end result is the same. Smaller, less fortunate, less power-ful people—businessmen and ordinary people—are still ru-ined, homeless, and left penniless."

"I'd never thought of it like that," Jeanne said. "But you're right."

"The West is still raw, Missy," Denver said. "And it will be for years to come. Men like Clint Black come in here and tore the land loose from Injuns and outlaws. They fought blizzards and droughts and floods. The only law was their own. They ain't likely to change real swift."

"Only at the muzzle of a gun or at the end of a rope," Smoke said. He stood up and stared out at the night. "This is fine country up here. And it'll be a lot finer once the likes of Clint Black are out of the picture."

"Riders comin', boss," a lookout hollered.

"Here we go again," Smoke said, as the others on the porch scrambled for their guns.

18

"It's the sheriff and a posse," the lookout called. "Stand easy at the house."

"I'll make some more coffee," the cook said.

"I'll help you, Liz," Denver said. He did not see the smiles of the others.

Harris and a dozen townspeople and regular deputies swung down and crowded the porch. "A farmer came gallopin' into town and told me he saw a large group of men headin' this way. We met what was left of them a couple of miles back," he added, his tone dry. "They weren't in real good shape. Anybody hurt at this end?"

"A couple of scratches and burns," Smoke told him. "We were lucky. I was watching the dogs play. They warned me in time for us to get set."

"You going to press charges?"

"It isn't my property. You'll have to ask Toni and Jeanne."

"Ladies?" the sheriff asked.

The twins exchanged glances and Toni said, "Sheriff Harris, I think you are a good man . . . in your own peculiar way. But what would be the point in pressing charges? All your brother would do is blow up the jail again. That is, if the structure is even repaired at this time. Besides, I doubt seriously that any of those men whom we just sent on their way would testify against your brother. I've seen how Western justice works . . . when it does work. Those hoodlums would just claim they came over to . . . what is the word I'm looking for? Sort of like after a country wedding when the couple is . . . ah, shivareed by friends."

"Hoo-rahed, ma'am?" the sheriff asked.

"Yes. That's it. They would say that they were only having fun and that we opened fire on them. Oh, I'm learning, Sheriff. I'm learning."

"Yes," Harris said. "I can see that. But it might not work out that way. One of my deputies is escorting the men into town. I'll talk to them and see what develops from it. But don't count on much."

"We won't," Sally said.

Liz came out with a huge coffee pot and Sally had made doughnuts that day and the men all dug in. Smoke was conscious of the sheriff's eyes on him.

"You got something stuck in your craw, spit it out," he told the man.

"What is my brother up to? Those weren't top guns he sent over here this evening. Not a one of them has any kind of name. Least none that I saw. He's got something up his sleeve, but I don't know what it could be. Those gunnies who braced you in town—the same thing. It's puzzling to me. Mighty good doughnuts, ma'am. Mighty good."

"I don't know what your brother is up to," Smoke said, after finishing a doughnut. He reached out for another and pulled back his hand at Sally's warning look. He'd already eaten about twenty that day.

The sheriff caught the look in the lighted porch lamps and smiled. Doesn't make any difference if a man is the toughest gunslinger in the West—his wife could still back him up with just a glance. Sheriff Harris Black helped himself to another doughnut, and Smoke grabbed one when he thought Sally wasn't looking. Quickly.

Liz fixed a sackful of doughnuts for the men to eat on the ride back to town and the sheriff and posse mounted up. "After this raid," Harris said to Smoke, "I don't think there is any turning back for my brother. Personally, I'd rather see him go down in a hail of bullets than for me to have to put the noose around his neck, and I would have to be the one to do it. He's heading for a violent end, and I don't know of any way to stop him. See you folks."

Smoke left the ranch the next morning long before anyone else other than the guards were up. He rode back to the valley where the ambush had taken place. For a long time he sat near the flat where the men and boys were buried. He smoked a couple of cigarettes and thought about the lives that had been snuffed out in that murderous raid. Baylis would have told Clint about the young boys working the remuda . . . and Clint had not cared. Clint had callously ordered the deaths of three women with no more feeling than swatting at a bothersome fly. The law was unable to contain Clint and his raiders. It wasn't that the law wouldn't deal with him, the law *couldn't* deal with him. For whatever reasons, known only to Clint, the wealthy rancher was determined to drive the Duggan twins from their ranch and possess it.

Why?

Gold? Smoke didn't think so—even though there had been gold strikes in this area there was no evidence that any gold was buried in the earth of the Double D. No, it was just stubborn pride and ruthless greed and callousness on the man's part. Clint wanted everything he saw and would stop at nothing to get it.

Smoke walked among the lonely graves, pausing for a time at each rock headstone his men had carefully placed by each grave, the name and date carefully chiseled into the stone. Nate, Little Ben, Shorty, Davy, Duke, Matt, Harris, Eton, Johnson, Forrest. He paused for a longer time at the graves of the boys. Fourteen-year-old Rabbit and the fifteen-year-olds, Willie and Jake. Boys who wanted to earn some money and see some country and have a little fun.

They had found violent and senseless death.

Clint Black had ordered it, and his men had coldly and brutally wiped out half of Smoke's drovers. No Indian attack could have been any more savage.

Smoke knelt down by Rabbit's grave and let the coldness of the tomb wash over him and settle in his mind. When he stood up, he knew he was going to end this war. Clint wanted a fight, so be it. Clint was going to have a fight, but from now on, it would be a fight on Smoke Jensen's terms.

He headed back to the Double D.

Sally was sitting on the porch when Smoke rode back to the ranch compound. She looked for a moment at the way he sat his saddle and then stood up.

"What's wrong?" Jeanne asked.

"I'm going to fix a packet of food for Smoke."

"Is he going somewhere?" Toni asked.

"Yes," Sally replied mysteriously, and walked into the house.

"How strange," Jeanne remarked.

Toni watched as Smoke stepped down from the saddle and walked toward the house. "Maybe not," she said.

"What do you mean?"

"There is something quite different about Smoke. Look at him. He's moving like some great predator cat. See the difference in him?"

Jeanne looked. "I do believe you're right. There is a more, well, determined look about him."

The sisters looked at each other and smiled. Toni said, "I think Mr. Clint Black is about to discover that he has angered the wrong man."

None of the hands said anything to Smoke when he emerged from the house. There was a look about him that warned people away. He had changed clothes. He now wore earth tones that would blend in with his surroundings. He had selected a big rugged horse that was mountain bred, would not stand out, and who was a better sentry at night than a trained dog. Smoke had a packet of food, a small coffee pot, and a bedroll. He had put moccasins in the saddlebags. There was an extra rope on the saddle. He had shoved a Winchester .44-40 into the saddle boot and bandoleers of ammunition crisscrossed his chest with extra boxes in the saddlebags.

He had said his goodbyes to Sally while in the house. She knew her man and was stoic about their temporary parting.

When she had asked where he had been that morning, she knew even more what he was going to do when he replied, "Over in the valley, by the graves."

He held her for a moment, kissed her, and was gone. Sally busied herself baking pies.

"You boys hold it down," Smoke said to the hands that were gathered outside the barn. "I'll be back when you see me."

Smoke headed for Circle 45 range.

As the twins had suggested, Sheriff Harris Black got nothing out of the wounded raiders. Since no one was filing any charges, he could do nothing except let them go. Two of the raiders had died before reaching town and a third was not expected to live. Dr. Garrett's little clinic was jammed to overflowing, with pallets on the floor.

"They'll be more," one of the deputies warned him. "This situation ain't even built up a good head of steam yet."

"I'm running out of medicines," the Doctor complained.

"You better order some more," the deputy told him. " 'Cause when Smoke Jensen gets a gutful of this mess, he'll come a-foggin' like something out of Hell. Clint Black ain't seen nothin' yet. You mark my words, Doc."

The Circle 45 rider felt the loop settle around him, the rope tighten, and he was jerked out of the saddle before he could holler. Not that yelling would have done any good, since he was miles from the ranch house and riding alone.

The wind was knocked from him as he hit the ground. He managed to roll and shake the loop. He got to his feet spitting mad and cussing and reaching for his gun. Out of the corner of his eyes he caught a blur of motion and turned just in time to receive a big leather-gloved fist right in his mouth. The blow knocked him on his butt and addled him for a few seconds. He crawled to his feet and a combination of lefts and rights flattened him, bloodying his mouth, busting his nose, and watering his eyes. The blows came so fast he still was not sure who was throwing them. But he had him a pretty good idea. The Circle 45 hand tried to make a fight of it, but he never had a chance to get set.

The would-be tough felt himself picked up and hurled into a stand of trees. His head impacted against a tree and his world turned black. When he awakened, he had the world's worst headache, his face felt like someone had worked him over with a two-by-four, and to add insult to injury, he was hanging upside down from a tree limb.

Smoke Jensen was sitting on the ground, his back to a tree. He was chewing on a biscuit and staring at the puncher. The Circle 45 rider quickly decided the best thing he could do was to keep his mouth shut.

Smoke stared at him for several very long moments. He finished his biscuit, walked to his horse and took a drink from his canteen, returned to the tree, and sat down. "You have a home?" Smoke finally asked the upside-down man.

"Utah," the puncher said. "I'd like to see it again someday. Sir," he added.

Smoke reached down and pulled out a long-bladed knife. The bladder of the Circle 45 rider gave it up and a dark stain appeared on his jeans.

"How bad do you want to see Utah?" Smoke asked him.

"Real bad. Like I'd leave right now ifn I was able."

"I ought to just go on and split you wide open and be done with it."

"Oh, man!" the hired gun hollered. "Look . . . you cut me down and I'm gone. You won't never see me again. That's a promise, Mr. Jensen. Look here, I'll level with you. Clint's hirin' more men. He's payin' money can't nobody pass up. I'm tellin' you the truth."

Smoke stood up and walked over to the puncher. He cut him down and the man landed heavily. He lay on the ground and looked up at Smoke.

"You've got a bit of food in your saddlebags," Smoke told him. "I've taken your pistols and left you your rifle. If you think it's worth your life to ride back and collect what wages are due you, then do so. But I would advise against it. The best thing you can do is put some miles behind you."

"I'm gone, Mr. Jensen. I swear on the Bible, I'm gone like the breeze."

"Get up and get gone!"

Fifteen seconds later, the hand was in the saddle and riding. Montana would not see him again.

Smoke stayed on the fringe of Circle 45 range, whenever possible staying in timber and never skylining himself. The smell of food cooking drifted to him. He picketed his horse, slipped on moccasins. and taking the .44-40 from the boot, began stalking the source of the smells. He quietly walked to within a hundred feet of the camp. Four men sat drinking coffee and frying bacon. A pot of beans hung over the fire. Smoke injuned his way closer and smiled at the laxness of the men. They obviously believed that since they were on Circle 45 range they were in no danger. Rifles were in saddle boots and only one of the men was wearing a gun. The others had tossed their gun belts onto rumpled blankets. Smoke rose as silently as any Apache and stood for a moment, staring at the men. He knew one of them would spot him.

One did, his eyes taking in the rifle pointed right at him. His eyes widened and his mouth dropped open. "Morris," he finally said. "Boys. Don't none of you do nothin' itchy."

"What are you talkin' about, Granville?"

"Smoke Jensen."

"What about him?"

"He's standin' 'bout fifty feet behind you with a rifle in his hands."

"Sit right where you are," Smoke told the group. "Or die right where you are. The choice is yours."

"We're calm," Granville said.

Smoke walked into the camp site and placed the muzzle of the .44-40 against the head of the only one who was armed. He reached down and took the man's pistol. Smoke backed off a dozen feet and sat down. "Turn that bacon and stir those beans," he told the group. "Then dish me up a plate. I'm hungry. We'll talk while we eat and then you boys can saddle up and drift on out of the territory."

"Huh?" Morris said.

Smoke thumbed back the hammer on the .44-40 and the Circle 45 hands tensed. "You ride or you die," he said simply. "It's that easy. I'm tired of this war. I'm tired of the likes of Clint Black. And I'm tired of the likes of men such as you. I don't want to have to look at your ugly faces again."

"You ain't got no call to insult us," one said.

Smoke smiled. "There is nothing I could say about you that should insult you. You're murderers, thieves, and God only knows what else. But your lives are about to take a turn for the better. I think you boys are about to see the light."

"I don't think you'd shoot an unarmed man," one of them said.

"Then you're a fool," Smoke told him. "The only rules I play by are my own. I was raised by mountain men, boys.

Preacher and Nighthawk and Cherokee Jack and Dupre and Powder Pete and Lobo, just to name a few. I put my first man in the grave long before I had to shave. I'll shoot every damn one of you then sit amid your bodies while I eat your food and then I'll leave you for the buzzards and the critters. And don't you ever think for one second that I won't. You crap and crud killed my men and killed young boys and tried to kill my wife and me. Put yourself in my boots and think about that."

The four men were beginning to sweat as Smoke's words sank in. The one called Granville was pale, his eyes shining with fear. He said, "I can't talk for the others, but you let me, and I'll drift. You'll never see me again, Jensen."

"I won't," the one called Morris said. He looked at Smoke and his lips moved in an evil smile. "I'll hunt you down and kill you and then have my way with your wife. See how she likes a real man. What do you think about that, Jensen?"

Smoke shot him. The slug took the gunhand in the center of the chest and he was dead before he fell back on the ground.

"Dish up the food," Smoke said. "And then you boys can saddle up and ride out of here."

"You damn shore got that right," Granville said.

19

"We're short one hand," Jud reported to Clint. "He should have been in a long time ago. And that ain't all. Fatso rode out to the boys' camp this afternoon to see if they needed anything, what with them hidin' out after the jailbreak. The camp was deserted, except for Morris's dead body."

Clint came out of the chair. "What?"

"That's right. He was shot right through the heart." He held out the brass. "Forty-four-forty at close range. Didn't none of those boys carry a forty-four-forty."

"Jensen?"

"Has to be. Camp wasn't churned up with boot prints. Just the prints of the boys and one set of moccasin tracks. And one hell of a big man wearin' 'em."

"He is actually on *my* range, attacking *my* people?" That anyone would be so bold as to openly declare war on Clint Black was astonishing to the man. "Well . . . I won't have that. I will not tolerate it."

"Boss, don't order the boys out at night. That's what Jensen wants."

"What do you mean?"

"He'll attack the house if you pull the men away."

"One man will attack this house? Jud, you're turning into an old woman. Jensen isn't a fool. He's just stupid. He's up in the high country. Miles from here."

Actually, Smoke was standing by the front porch, listening to every word. Since Clint hated dogs, and shot everyone he saw, there were no dogs around to sound the warning. The corral was too far away for the horses to act as sentries. Smoke had been busy around the Circle 45 headquarters, having more fun than a half a dozen schoolboys. And more fun should start at any moment.

A scream came from one of the outhouses behind the bunkhouse. Smoke smiled, thinking: *let the fun begin.*

"What the hell's the matter over there?" Jud hollered.

"They's a goddamn rattlesnake in the shifter!" a hand bellered.

"Well, shoot the damn thing," Jud yelled. "Jesus! Act like a bunch of women sometimes."

Jud stalked off the porch and stepped on a rake that had just been placed on the path, placed in a manner that was tantamount to sabotage.

The handle flew up and smacked the foreman right in the face, almost knocking him down. Clint ran off the porch to see about his friend and foreman. "You all right, Jud? Jesus, your nose is busted. Come on back to the porch. I'll get a wet cloth." He started hollering for the cook.

Smoke ran around to the back of the house where he had placed a jug of kerosene he'd swiped from Clint's storeroom. He poured the kerosene all over the back porch and waited until it soaked into the dry boards.

A Circle 45 hand started hollering for someone to let him out of the outhouse, the door was jammed. It sure was. Just as soon as the hand had stepped inside and closed the door, Smoke had wedged a stick in tight.

Before leaving the house, Smoke had found a long string of old firecrackers someone had left behind. He had taken them along. He lit a match, started the porch burning from underneath and slipped to the bunkhouse. He lit the fuse to the firecrackers and tossed them through an open window. Then he decided he'd better get the hell gone from that immediate area.

"Let me out of this damn crapper!" the hired gun hollered.

"Fire!" another yelled.

The fuse burned down to the firecrackers and pandemonium took over as what appeared to be an attack on the bunkhouse opened up. The hand trapped in the outhouse was rocking the entire structure back and forth in his frantic attempts to get out. He turned it over. Backwards.

The hands in the bunkhouse began shooting all over the place at imaginary foes.

When the other hands reached the water barrels, they were all empty. Smoke had cut holes in them with his knife. Everybody began using blankets and coats and brooms to beat out the fire which by now was threatening the wooden part of the house.

Smoke was still laughing when he reached his well-chosen and hidden little camp.

"The sorry son actually was *here!*" Clint exclaimed. Come the dawning, he had looked at the few firecrackers that had not exploded in the bunkhouse, and at the bullet holes caused by nervous hired guns. Stared at the wedge in the door of the outhouse—the hand had finally succeeded in kicking out the bottom of the crapper. Clint had found the jug of kerosene, and looked at the cause of the water barrels being empty. "He violated my property, almost burned down my house, and sabotaged the water barrels. I can't believe it."

"It's almost like he was playin' a joke," Fatso Ross said. "Like he was havin' fun with us." Fatso looked at Jud's swollen face where the rake handle had popped him. "But I don't 'magine it was much of a joke, right, Jud?"

"I get that bastard in gunsights, the joke'll be on him," the foreman said.

For once it was Clint who had the level head. "We don't strike at the Double D. Not yet. We don't cause any trouble in town. Not yet. I want five men around the house at all times, the rest of you fan out, during the daylight hours only, and start searching my spread. Ride in pairs. No lone-wolfing it. The man is too dangerous for that. Take off. The offer still stands: five thousand dollars to the man who kills Smoke Jensen."

Smoke had risen before dawn and rode back to Double D range. He stripped the saddle from his horse and hid it, then wrote a short note to Sally, tying it in the mane. He slapped the horse on the rump, knowing it would head straight for the corral. He took his sack of food and his other gear, including the ropes, and headed back to his little camp, deep in Circle 45 territory.

Longman and Steve Tucker were riding together. Wyoming could not have produced any sorrier pair than these two. Both were wanted in at least five states and two territories. And both of them were thinking about that five thousand dollar bounty that Clint had placed on the head of Smoke Jensen. And they were not watching their backtrail.

Two seconds after they had passed along the narrow trail, Smoke stepped out and fireballed a fist-sized rock, then ducked back into the brush and slipped up the side of the trail. The stone hit Longman on the back of the head and knocked him slap out of the saddle and unconscious on the rocky ground. If he had not been wearing a hat, the blow might have killed him, which was what Smoke had in mind.

"What the hell . . . ?" Steve said, turning in the saddle at the sound of his buddy hitting the ground. There had been no shot and the rock lay among other stones on the trail. Steve couldn't figure out what had happened. He swung down from the saddle and knelt by his friend. Steve felt a blinding flash of pain and then he was stretched out beside his friend.

Smoke peeled them both down to their long-handles and took their clothing, boots, guns, and horses. They were a good ten miles from the bunkhouse and barefooted. It was going to be a long and painful hike back. Smoke threw the clothing away several miles from the still-unconscious men and unsaddled the horses, turning them loose.

He slipped back into the timber and brush.

The men of the Circle 45 hunted all that day for Smoke. The more fortunate of the hunters could not find a trace of him. Longman and Tucker staggered into the bunkhouse late that afternoon, their feet badly bruised and bleeding. Longman was seeing double and very nearly unable to speak. Bankston, Nelson, and Clements had not shown up by late afternoon.

"You better find them men 'fore dark," Bronco Ford told Clint. The gunman was not afraid of Smoke, but he did have a lot of respect for him. "You send search parties out after dark and none of 'em will come back. Smoke Jensen's like a puma in the woods."

"If I want your opinion," Clint told the man, "I'll ask for it."

Bronco shrugged his shoulders and walked off.

Bankston had become separated from his riding partner and was now tied to a tree, his own rope wound around him from ankles to neck and pulled tight. He was to spend a very uncomfortable night. Nelson and Clements were tied in the saddle, their hands behind their back, their horses wandering in a roundabout way back to the ranch. Smoke had gagged the men before tying them.

"There they are!" Grub Carson shouted, as the horses came ambling into the area. The gunslicks were untied and lowered to the ground. Neither man could feel anything in his hands.

The gags out of their mouths, Nelson croaked, "Man's like a damn ghost. He come out of nowhere. There wasn't no brush where we was. No place for him to hide. He's worser than a damn Apache."

"Nelson's right about that," Clements said. "Jensen was a-layin' right on the ground, right there in full open. And we didn't see him. You boys be careful. We're dealin' with an Injun here."

Clint was outwardly calm. Inside he was seething. He managed to ask, "Either of you men see Bankston?"

"No, sir," Nelson said. "But we seen his horse grazin', saddle and bridle was gone."

Clint turned to walk back to his house and his hat was blown off his head by a .44-40 slug. The man hit the ground belly down and got a mouth full of dirt.

Smoke had carried five Winchester .44 rifles to his position on a ridge near the big house—rifles taken from Circle 45 hands. They were loaded up full, giving him awesome firepower before he had to think about reloading. He laid down his .44-40 and picked up one of the .44s and began spraying the area below him with lead. He sent Circle 45 hands and hired gunslicks scrambling in all directions in the fading light of early evening. Smoke put ninety-five rounds of .44s into the house, the bunkhouses, and the outhouses before it was all over.

He put lead so close to sprawled Circle 45 men they could feel the heat of the bullets. He could have killed a dozen men that day, but chose not to kill or really injure anyone. But he made life miserable for those below the ridge.

He knocked out windows in the house and the bunkhouse. He perforated doors and stove pipes and punched holes in the roofs of buildings. His bullets smashed water buckets

and the fancy chandelier that hung in the dining room of
Clint Black's big house. The lead from his rifles clanged into
cook pots, off of the stove, and into the outbuildings of the
Circle 45. He poured lead into the gate posts of the corral
and knocked the gate loose, stampeding the horses. Several
of the panicked horses ran over men sprawled in the dirt,
putting them out of action for days.

When darkness covered the land, Smoke left the empty
rifles on the ridge and in a distance-covering run, vanished
into the night. Clint Black rose wearily from the ground and
walked to his house. He sank down to the steps and sat there,
looking at the hole in his expensive hat.

A gunfighter called L. J. McBride picked himself up from
the floor of the bunkhouse and began gathering his possi-
bles, stuffing them into a bag.

"You leavin'?" another gunny asked.

"You better believe it," L. J. said. "I read Jensen's message loud and clear."

"What message?" Cleon asked.

"Man, he could have killed twelve or fifteen men from up
there on that ridge. But he didn't. He tellin' us if we wanna
live, we better fly. I'm flyin'."

"You just hold on and I'll ride with you," another hired
gun said. "Smoke Jensen is a one-man war party. And this is
one party that I'm skippin'."

"You gonna turn your backs on that five thousand dollars?"

"Five thousand won't help you if you're in a grave, partner. I ain't never seen no armored bank wagon followin' a
hearse."

Sheriff Harris Black and one of his deputies made the
Double D in time for breakfast the next morning . . . just the
way they'd planned it.

Over coffee, Harris said, "Talked to three gunnies last

night. They stopped in town for a drink before riding on. Seems that some unknown rifleman's been doing all sorts of mischief out at the Circle 45." The sheriff had to smile. Then the smile changed to a chuckle. "Seems this feller burned down the back porch, tossed firecrackers into the bunkhouse, shot up some outhouses, and in general made life pretty mean for my brother and his hired guns. Is your husband around, Mrs. Jensen?"

"Why, no, Sheriff. He isn't. He's off on a business trip."

"Looks like it's a successful one," Harris replied. "Ammunition factories are going to be operating around the clock if this keeps up."

"Supply and demand, Sheriff," Sally said with a smile. "That's what keeps the economy strong."

Just as she was saying that, a horrified Bankston, still tied to the tree, watched as a passing parade of skunks paused a few feet from him, turned their backs to him, and lifted their tails.

"Oh, no!" the hired gun said, just as the skunks fired.

20

"We found Bankston," Jud told Clint. "We drew straws to see who'd cut him loose. Fatso lost."

"What are you talking about?"

Jud explained.

"Where is he now?"

"Down at the crick, washing, for all the good it'll do him. Them skunks scored direct hits, Clint. It was so bad Fatso got sick."

Clint pointed his cigar at his foreman. "Let me tell you something, Jud. I don't like jokes being played on me. Jensen thinks this is funny. But I'm not laughing. The man is not only making a fool out of me, but you and the men as well. You think about that and pass the word to the boys."

Clint watched his foreman's face and saw a scowl form amid the bruises from the rake handle. "I didn't look at it like that, Clint. But you're right. What do you want the boys to do?"

"That's the problem. I don't know. I feel like I'm a prisoner on my own land. Damn Smoke Jensen!"

* * *

Stony handed Sally the note from the horse's mane and she read it and smiled. "He's fine. And having fun."

"Fun?" the cowboy said. *"Fun?"*

"Yes. It's only a few lines, but I sense that he doesn't want to kill unless he's forced into it. He's trying to demoralize Clint's hands."

"I, ah, ain't real sure what that means, Miss Sally."

"He's trying to get them to quit."

"Oh. He ought to just plug everyone he sees. That's the best way I know of to get them to quit."

"It might come to that, Stony. But I hope not. There has been far too much bloodshed already."

"Clint ain't gonna quit, ma'am. I know the man. He'll fight to the bitter end."

"Then the man is a fool," Sally said.

"Yes, ma'am," the cowboy replied. "I reckon he is. But a dangerous fool. I hope your man ain't takin' him too lightly."

"Oh, I assure you, Stony. My husband is taking Mr. Black very seriously."

Smoke shifted his camp, moving much closer to the home of Clint. He lay on a ridge in heavy brush and watched the grounds through binoculars. Someone had rigged a tent about two hundred yards from the bunkhouse and Smoke couldn't figure out what in the world it was for. Only one man was staying in the tent and Smoke recognized him as the man he'd tied up in the woods. Every time he tried to leave the tent area, the others would curse and wave and shout him back.

"Strange," Smoke muttered. "Very odd behavior. Maybe the man has measles or something."

Taking a longer look, Smoke could see that few hands

had left the ranch grounds. They had rounded up their stampeded horses—most of them anyway— and the corral was full. Clint had called a halt to the search and was making plans. And he'd do it much more carefully than before. Smoke had stung the man and he'd be smarting from the sting. Smoke suddenly had a hunch that he had overstayed his welcome and it just might be time to get gone from Circle 45 range. The more he thought about it, the better that idea sounded to him. He gathered up his gear and headed back to friendlier territory.

He spent that night in a cold camp sleeping under the stars. He woke up just one time. But it was only a bear rooting and grunting around. Smoke stayed awake long enough to hear the bear's sounds fade away, and then he went back to sleep.

He was back at the Double D at noon the next day. He'd have to make a new pair of moccasins, for the ones he had on were nearly worn out.

After a bath and a shave and a change into fresh clothing, he told the others what he'd done.

Everyone got a kick out of it, especially about the hand trapped in the outhouse and about Smoke blowing Clint's hat off his head.

"But," Smoke told the group, "while I did have some fun at Clint's expense, he's not going to let it rest. He'll never forgive me for terrorizing his home and for making a fool of him. I don't know what he'll do next. But you can bet it won't be anything nice."

"We need to go into town for supplies," Sally told him. "We're running low on nearly everything."

"Make a list, get the wagons ready, and we'll go in tomorrow morning," Smoke said. "We'll take four men with us; the rest of you stay here and keep watch. We're not prisoners on the spread. If Clint or his men are in town and want trouble, I'll damn sure oblige them."

They were, and he did.

* * *

The Circle 45 hands were in no mood for fun and games; they were still smarting over the antics of Smoke Jensen. Tucker and Longman could not pull boots on over their mangled and swollen feet. A half a dozen Circle 45 riders had just disappeared without a trace. Several others had ridden back to the bunkhouse, collected their gear, and left, a couple without even staying around to get their pay. A man couldn't get within fifty feet of Bankston, he still smelled so bad. So it was a trouble-hunting bunch that waited in Blackstown that morning.

Sheriff Harris Black and all but one of his deputies had been called out of town to help to chase down two men who had robbed and murdered an elderly farmer and his wife the night before. It was a nervous deputy who watched the Double D people come in from one direction and the knot of Circle 45 hands ride in from the other. Lucas stepped back into the office and took a sawed-off from the rack, breaking it open and loading it up with buckshot—or what passed for buckshot in those days, usually nails and tacks and ball bearings and sometimes small rocks.

"Well now," Tex Mason said. "Would you just look who's ridin' in."

"I see them," Weldon Ball said. He stood by his horse, looking over the saddle. "We play this right and we got Jensen cold."

"Let's let them get all spread out. Some of them boys will stay with the women, guardin' them. John, you and Ballard go with Weldon. Art, you and Fatso stay with me. Austin, you take Cantrell and Miller. If we play this right, we can end it today and ride out with money in our pockets."

"Yeah," Austin said. "If we put Smoke Jensen down, we can name our price from here on out."

"We'll have a drink and let them get started doin' their

business," Weldon said. "Then we'll make our move. Stay loose and ready."

"I think it's gonna pop this day," Stony said, swinging down from the saddle in front of Hanlon's Emporium. They all, out of long habit, freed the hammers of their six-shooters. "That bunch of no-counts ain't taken their eyes off us."

"Check your guns," Smoke ordered the men. Stony, Malvern, Waymore, and Eli checked their guns and loaded up the empty chamber. "See how they're standing? There'll be three groups of them. Watch yourselves. Sally, you and the twins get inside the store and take your time shopping. Stay clear of the windows."

Smoke paused for a moment, standing by his horse. "Waymore, you and Malvern pull the wagons around to the rear of the store. Let's get our horses off the street while we're at it." Smoke walked down to the sheriff's office. He pushed open the door and told Lucas, "Pass the word to get the women and kids off the streets, Deputy. I think it's going to explode this day. Where's Harris?"

"Him and the others are out chasing a double murderer. And it's no joke this time."

"All right. Lucas, we're not going to open this ball. But when the music starts, we won't be wallflowers about hitting the dance floor."

"I understand. I'll start spreadin' the word."

Within minutes, the street was cleared of horseflesh and humans. The sun beat down; already it was a hot day. A wind devil spun around in the center of the street, then vanished, whirling like a dervish. Dr. Garrett began laying out bandages and instruments.

Smoke and the Double D hands had fanned out, all up and down the street. They stood in the shadows of buildings and alleyways and watched and waited. Inside the saloon, the Circle 45 hired guns were sipping rye, working up their courage to try to do what so many others had attempted and failed. To kill the legendary Smoke Jensen.

A drifting cowboy rode slowly into town. He stopped at the edge of town and took in the scene. Nothing was moving. Not a horse or man, woman, or kid in sight. Even the dogs had cleared the street. He turned into the livery and swung down.

"What's goin' on here?" he questioned the hostler.

"The Double D hands and the Circle 45 riders are gettin' ready to settle some old scores."

"Who's your money on?"

"Let's put it this way: the Double D is bein' bossed by Smoke Jensen."

"Smoke Jensen!" the cowboy exclaimed. "Here?"

"Durn sure is. In the flesh. You'd be showin' some smarts if you just stood right here 'til this is over."

"I ain't never been known to be real bright," the cowboy said. "I think I'll go find Mr. Jensen and ask for a job."

"Now?"

But the cowboy was gone, walking up the boardwalk. He stopped at an alleyway and grinned at Waymore.

"Git in here, Conny," Waymore said. "You damn fool. I thought you was lookin' at the rear end of cows down in Kansas?"

"I quit 'em after me and the foreman had a slight disagreement."

"You mean, you punched him in the mouth and he fired you."

Conny grinned. "Yeah. After he beat the stuffin's out of me."

"You never did have no sense. What happened?"

"He called me a bad name and I busted him on the nose. Your boss hirin'?"

"Now I know you ain't got no sense. You know who's ramrodin' this outfit?"

"Man down at the stable told me."

"And you still want to sign on?"

"Why not?"

"Now I'm sure you're crazy. Yeah, as a matter of fact, we could use another hand or two. You got a horse?"

"How the hell do you think I got here from Kansas—walked?"

Before he could reply, boots sounded on the boardwalk. "Yonder comes the boss," Waymore said.

Conny whistled softly. "He sure is a big'un, ain't he?"

"And hell on wheels with them guns." He waited until Smoke had calmly strolled up as if on a Sunday walk. "Boss, this here terrible-lookin' saddle bum is Conny. He ain't to be trusted around food nor whiskey, and he likes to fight—even though he don't never win—but he can ride anything with hair on it and he'll give you a good day's work. He needs a job."

Smoke smiled and shook hands with the man. "You're hired. Can you use that gun you're wearing?"

"I ain't no fast gun. But I generally hit what I'm shootin' at."

"You're stepping into the middle of a war. I want you to know that up front."

"If you're fightin' that damn Clint Black, I'd ride for nothin' but bunk and board."

"Don't hire him on them terms, Boss." Waymore said. "He can eat more'n any two men you ever seen."

Smoke chuckled. "You're a pretty good hand at the table yourself, Waymore. All right, Conny. Clint's hired a lot of gunhands. Some of them are pretty good. He's got nine men in town right now. Including Weldon Ball, Tex Mason, and Austin Charles. They're all over at the saloon. We wait for them to start the show."

"It's a good thing I ain't eat in a day," Conny said. "Eatin' makes me sleepy."

"If that was the truth you'd be asleep all the time," Waymore remarked. "You ridin' the line, Conny?"

"I ain't got a dime to my name."

Smoke handed the puncher a twenty-dollar gold piece. "That might make you feel better."

"Durn sure does, Boss," Conny said, pocketing the money. "Now if them bad'uns over there will just get this party goin', we can get it over with and I can get me something to eat 'fore I fall over from the hungries."

"You better get you some boots first," Waymore told him. "I can see your dirty socks on both feet."

"Conny," Smoke said, after looking at the cowboy for a moment. "You stay here with me for a moment. Waymore, use the alleys and tell the boys to move this thing to the edge of town. Up next to the bridge. I don't want a stray bullet to kill some innocent person."

"Right, boss."

"Conny. You follow Waymore and stop in at the general store and get you a hunk of cheese and a handful of crackers. You're staggering on your feet, man. How long's it been since you've eaten?"

Conny grinned. "Several days, boss. It just ain't in me to beg. And times is hard out here."

"All right. Go get something to eat and meet me behind the store in a few minutes."

Smoke gave Conny enough time to reach the store; then he rolled a cigarette and smoked it down, always keeping his eyes on the saloon batwings. There was no sign of the Circle 45 hands. Smoke ground out the butt with the toe of his boot and walked up the alley. Conny was sitting on the loading dock, wolfing down a huge sandwich and drinking a bottle of sarsaparilla. The puncher grinned at him. He was missing two front teeth, and Smoke suspected they'd been knocked out in a brawl.

"After three of these sandwiches, I could take on a mama bear with cubs," Conny said.

"Three!" Smoke said.

"I eat quick when they's shootin' to be done."

Sally appeared at the back. "I'm laying in extra supplies,"

she said with a smile. "Your new hand can put away the food."

Smoke shook his head and Conny brushed a few crumbs off his patched shirt and drained the sarsaparilla. He checked his Colt and loaded up the empty chamber. He hopped off the loading dock. "Now let's go see your varmint, boss."

As they walked, Smoke brought Conny up to date.

"I know Clint Black," Conny said. "He's as lowdown as they come. No mercy or feelin's for nobody in him. If you have to shoot a rabid animal, you're scared of it, but you can feel sorry for it. 'Cause he didn't want the disease. But I could shoot Clint Black or Jud Howes and not feel nothin'. I tried to work for them. Man, I can't harm no woman or child. Until farmers just got so many around here, there wasn't no stoppin' them, Clint burned out and killed many of them. I worked one week for him and then hauled my ashes. And don't feel sorry for no hand that hires on with the Circle 45. After they've been there a week, they know what's goin' on."

Smoke turned toward the street and the boys fell in with him.

"Are we goin' out in the street and face them gunhandlers, boss?" Malvern asked.

"No. You men aren't gunfighters. We're going to make them come to us and meet them around these shacks here. We'll step out into the street and then, at my word, dive for cover and start shooting."

"I like your style!" Conny said, just as one bootheel came off and he started limping along.

Waymore shook his head. "Make your shots count, Conny. With all that crowd up yonder in the saloon, they's got to be one with your size."

21

"They're all lined up across the street up yonder," Fatso said. "They got a sixth man with 'em."

"Who is it?"

"I can't tell from here. But it looks like one leg's shorter than the other."

Weldon pushed away from the bar. "All right, let's do it." He walked out of the saloon and into the light and heat of the street. He cussed as he realized Jensen and his men had their backs to the sun and were forcing the Circle 45 hands to walk east, into the morning sun.

"Slick," Austin Charles said. "I figured they'd be waitin' for us right outside the saloon."

"Thinkin' never was your strong point," Tex told him.

"They must think we're stupid," Eli said. "They really think we're gonna just stand here and get plugged?"

Stony and Waymore were to Smoke's right; Malvern, Eli, and Conny to his left. "Steady now," Smoke cautioned in a very low voice. "If they've got any sense at all, they'll have it in their minds to wait until there's about fifty feet between us before they pull. But that fat one is getting nervous already. See how stiff he's walking?"

"That's Fatso Ross," Stony said. "I want him."

"You can have him," Waymore said. "Bad as you shoot, you need a wide target."

"Art Long's had his eyes on me for a spell," Malvern said. "Me and him's had words more'n once. Even at this distance, I can see that he's got his eyes straight on me."

Behind the windows of stores and homes, the citizens of Blackstown were lined up, watching the slow walk toward death.

"Why, hell," Ballard said. "That's Conny Larsen. No-good saddle bum. He's mine."

"Ballard," Conny said in low tones. "He fancies himself a gunslick. He's in for a surprise. I always could outshoot, outfight, and outdrink that lowlife."

"Couple of more seconds," Smoke said. "Get ready. I've changed my mind. I'm going to open this dance and get it over with."

"Mason!" Smoke called over the ever-shortening distance. "It's a good day to die. Are you ready? Or have you lost your guts?"

Tex Mason's hands lifted and closed around the butts of his guns.

"Now!" Smoke yelled, and the street erupted in muzzle flashes and gunsmoke.

The Double D hands jerked iron, fired, and scrambled for cover. The move took the Circle 45 guns by surprise. They had not been expecting that and were caught flat-footed and in the open. Fatso Ross was down in the street and so were Tex Mason and Art Long. Nick Ballard was trying to hunt cover, dragging a busted leg as he scurried off to the side of the street and dropped down in a shallow ditch.

"Oh, Christ!" Fatso hollered. "It hurts!" His gun was in the dirt and both hands holding his bloody belly. He roared in pain and fell over on his face as the lead started whining and whistling all around him. Tex Mason was down but not out. Smoke's bullet was true, but the gunhand still had fight left in him. Sitting in the dust, he filled both hands with Colts and eared the hammers back and let them bang. Smoke, down on one knee, leveled a .44 and ended the bloody career of Tex with one shot. Tex fell over dead in the dirt.

Waymore coolly put a slug in John Wood and the hand doubled over, dropping his pistol. Waymore had a bullet burn on his left arm.

George Miller got a slug into the leg of Eli that knocked the puncher down. Cussing, Eli leveled his .45 and drilled George neat, right through the brisket.

Fatso staggered to his boots, cussing, both hands filled with guns. Conny plugged him and Fatso tumbled to the dirt of the wide street.

Art Long panicked and started to limp toward the board-walk. He got as far as the deserted building that once housed Nadine's Dress Shoppe before six-guns roared. Art was slammed against the old door. The door gave it up and Art died on the dusty and trashlittered floor.

Smoke's hat was blown off his head just as he turned his guns on Austin Charles. The gunfighter was snarling and shooting at Smoke as Smoke's bullets found him and turned him around, spinning like a top. Austin tried to lift his guns, but they were too heavy. The fancy engraved Colts fell from his numbed fingers and Austin collapsed to the street. The last words from his mouth were curses, directed at Smoke Jensen.

Ballard had dragged himself off behind Nadine's and was slowly staggering toward the saloon, hoping to get to his horse and get the hell gone.

He lurched past the rear of the leather shop just as the owner stepped out and conked him on the head with the butt of a shotgun. Ballard slumped to the ground, a swelling knot on his noggin.

Weldon Ball and Roy Cantrell made a dash for safety and

jumped into the saddles of the first horses they reached. They fogged it out of town on stolen horses.

Smoke and the Double D hands slowly stood up. Stony had a cut on his face, Waymore's arm was bleeding, Eli's leg was throbbing with pain and he was supported by the strong arm of Conny. No one else was hurt.

Smoke quickly reloaded and stepped over to view the carnage. Fatso was dead in the dirt. Tex Mason was dead. George Miller was alive, but not for long. Eli's bullet had punched right through him, high up, nicking a lung. Austin Charles was dead. John Wood was badly wounded.

"He'll probably make it," Dr. Garrett said, panting from his run up the street.

"I got one over here," the shop owner hollered. "Wounded in the leg. I busted his head for him."

"I want a posse formed up right now," Lucas said. "Weldon Ball and Roy Cantrell stole them horses in plain sight of everybody. You stay in town," he said to Smoke.

"I'll be right here," Smoke replied. He looked at his bullet-torn hat. "Shopping for a hat."

The dead were hauled off to be measured for a box, and the wounded escorted to Doc Garrett's office. The doctor worked on the Double D men first, while the Circle 45 hands hollered and complained about it.

Smoke went to the store for a new Stetson. He picked out one with a lower crown. "Presents less of a target," he told Sally and the Duggan twins. "Maybe this one will last me longer." He looked around as his men came in. Doc Garrett wanted to keep Eli for a day just for insurance.

"You boys get the supplies loaded up and escort the ladies back to the ranch. I'll wait around for the sheriff and give a statement. Get a few more boxes of ammo. After this, there is no telling what Clint Black might do. Stay close to the ranch and no riding alone with the herd."

* * *

Clint Black was furious when the deputy and the posse thundered into his front yard, but he had sense enough to know that to fight would be stupid.

"Get Weldon Ball and Roy Cantrell out here right now," Lucas told him. "They're under arrest for horse-stealin'."

"Deputy . . ." Clint started to bluster.

Lucas lifted the muzzle of the Winchester. The posse members had fanned out and circled so they could cover in all directions. Twenty rifles were lifted. The sound of hammers being eared back was very loud in the stillness of the morning.

"I said right now, Clint," Lucas told the rancher.

"Or you'll do what?" Clint said, anger taking over his mind.

"I'll place you under arrest for interfering with a peace officer and then kill you right where you stand."

"Lucas!" Jud called from the bunkhouse. "I'm bringin' the men out. Just calm down. Everybody calm down."

"Tell one of your men to saddle horses for them, Clint," Lucas said. "And bring out those horses they stole from town."

"Do it, Tom," Clint said, his voice heavy with rage and his big hands clenched into fists.

Jud walked up. Weldon Ball and Roy Cantrell were with him, shuffling along behind. Lucas stepped down and handcuffed the two men then waited until Tom brought up two horses. "Up," he ordered the Circle 45 men. Back in the saddle, he looked at Clint Black. "You won't break these two out. There's been some cell changes at the jail . . . while we were repairing the other damage. Be seein' you, *Mr.* Black."

The posse left in a cloud of dust. Weldon and Roy did not look happy at all.

"You boys get busy doin' something," Jud ordered the hands. "You might get together the gear of the men who ain't gonna be comin' back and see if they got clean clothes to get buried in." He turned to Clint. "We got to talk, boss. Right now."

"In the house," Clint said. Once inside and seated, with whiskey poured, he said, "Speak your piece, Jud. You know you can shoot straight with me."

"It's got to stop, Clint," the foreman implored. "This just can't go on. We gonna be buryin' six men tomorrow. Six more men. We . . ."

". . . Have had this talk before. I thought we settled it then." Clint drained his whiskey glass and slopped more booze in.

"We settled nothing, Clint. Clint? Did you see the looks on the faces of the men in that posse? Did you *really* see them? They're not going to ever bow and scrape for you. Not ever again. You've got to understand that. You've been the big bull in the woods for years and you're gonna have to settle for it being over. Cleon's got a newspaper from Helena; got it from the stage driver. This war is front-page news. Smoke Jensen's name is like bees to honey. There'll be reporters in here 'fore long, and they'll dig and pry to see what started all the ruckus and find out about the ambush and the kids gettin' killed and all of it. Then what kind of a light will you be under? I'll tell you what kind: a real bad light. We got to stop this and stop it right now!"

Clint had paused in the lifting of glass to his lips. He frowned and set the glass down on the table. "Go on, Jud. You're not through."

"Just like I said to you before, the last time we talked. We fire all these gunhands and get back to the raisin' of beef. We live and let live, and mind our own business."

"And live with the knowledge that a damn gunfighter and a bunch of weak-livered, two-bit ranchers and saloon keepers and storekeepers beat us? Not me, Jud. Not me."

Jud left his whiskey untouched. He stood up and plopped his hat on his head. "All right, Clint. If that's the way you want it." He turned and headed for the door. Clint's voice stopped him and turned him around.

"Is this it, Jud? It is over for you?"

"Yeah, Clint. For me, it's over. I won't stay in the game with a stacked deck. See you, Clint." He walked out.

Clint sat for a long time in his study. He did not drink. He'd been drinking far too much of late, and for him to come up with any sort of plan, he needed to be clear-headed. He heard the sounds of a horse trotting away and knew it was Jud. Jud! He and the man had been together for years. And now his foreman and best friend had lost his guts. He rose and walked to the front porch and waved to a hand.

"Yeah, boss?"

"Was that Jud riding out?"

"Yes, sir. He packed his duds, got him a packhorse, and was gone in fifteen minutes. I never thought Jud would turn his back to you."

"Neither did I," Clint said with a sigh. "Tell Bronco Ford I want to see him."

"Right away, boss."

Clint sat down on the porch. Bronco walked over and Clint waved him to a seat. "How many men do we have still around, Bronco?"

"Eighteen, last count. And that includes you and me and the cook."

Clint's laugh was short and bitter. "God, a month ago I had *fifty!*"

"Some just rode off and didn't look back, boss. I reckon Smoke Jensen read some scriptures to them that we busted out of the jail. They sure cut out. We got some with busted legs and busted arms and knotty heads. You want I should send out some wires and see what I can drag up?"

"Yes. Today. I don't care where you get them or what they've done in their past. The meaner, the better. You're now foreman of this ranch, Bronco. Move your gear into the foreman's house. You get rid of Smoke Jensen for me, and you'll have a job for the rest of your life. That's a personal promise—from me."

"Might be best if I flag down the stage and send them wires out of Helena."

"Good idea. Do that. Get packed to go. I'll have money for you when you're ready."

"Buckskin Deevers is around. He busted out of Yuma some months back. I know where he's hidin'."

"Get him. Get all you can find. I'll turn this country red with the blood of any who dare stand up to me."

"Sounds like my kind of war, boss. I'll be ready to go in fifteen minutes."

"I'll be here," Clint said grimly. "Right here. And I'll be here when all those who oppose me are buried!"

22

Jud Howes rode into Blackstown and stabled his horses. He planned to spend one night and then be on the trail come first light. He knew where he was going, and when he got there he was going to stay. He conducted his business at the bank, closing out his sizable account. Then he walked over to the sheriff's office. Harris had just ridden in and was talking over the morning's events with Smoke when Jud opened the door.

"I'm peaceful," the ex-foreman of the Circle 45 said quickly. "And I intend to stay that way. From now on. I want to talk to both of you."

"Fine," Harris said. "Have a cup of coffee and sit."

Jud poured his coffee and took a seat. He startled both men when he said, "I just quit the Circle 45."

When he found his voice, Harris said, "That's probably very good for you, and very bad for us."

"Yeah, that's the way I see it. That's why I come over to talk. Now if you think I'm here to confess to anything, you're wrong. Clint and me been friends for years and years, and I'll admit we both done some terrible things. But for me, that's past. This is now. I ain't here to talk against him. I got me a pretty good hunch he'll make that no-count Bronco Ford foreman. Which will be fine as long as Clint don't plan on runnin' no cattle, cause Bronco is a gunhandler and that's all he's been since he growed up.

"Now then, Bronco will be callin' in some salty ol' boys that he knows. And he knows plenty of them. Clint ain't gonna give up. Put that out of your heads. He's goin' to fight until he's either top man on the hill again, or he's dead. That's the way it's goin' to be." He looked at Smoke. "I don't like you, Jensen. But I ain't goin' to fight you. I seen men like you before. Not many, but a few. You really ain't no better than the men you fight . . . not when it comes down to the nut-cuttin'. 'Cause you still kill. You got bodies planted all over the West. But you kill for some sort of highfalutin' notion that otherwise decent folk find acceptable. That's always puzzled me. But I realize something else, too: men like you nearly always win. I don't know why that is, but it's true.

"You're goin' to have to kill Clint Black, Jensen." He cut his eyes. "Or you will, Harris. There ain't no other way. And I just don't want to be around to see that." He stood up. "I can't bring myself to wish you boys luck. I just can't do that. 'Cause I don't know whether I'd mean it or not. Men like Clint built this country. Oh, they're hard men, and they've done terrible things to others who come out later, when it was a lot easier and them others come in to squat on land that was settled by Clint and men like him." He waved his hand in a curt gesture. "Well, that's neither here nor there."

"You want to speak to Weldon or Cantrell?" Harris asked.

Jud shook his head. "I got nothin' to say to them two. You'll never seen me again, Harris. Nor will you ever hear of me. Jud Howes is not my real name. When I get to where I'm goin', I'll have a new name and paper to prove it. I'll ranch, and not do no harm to any man who don't come pushin' and shovin' and lookin' for it." He walked to the door and paused, looking around. "I was goin' to spend the night, but

I think I'll just ride on and get clear of this place." He looked at Harris. "You're a good man, Harris. I mean that. And when all this is over, you'll do well at the Circle 45. 'Cause it'll be yours. I just hope you change the brand." He cut his eyes to Smoke and stared at him for a moment. "You, now, I ain't got no use for. I just don't like you one goddamned bit." He stepped out and closed the door behind him.

"Strange man," Harris said, after a quiet moment had passed. "There goes a man who is just as vicious as my brother, who probably had a hand in planning the ambush against you and the Duggan twins, and who now says he's had enough. I never thought he'd leave my brother."

Smoke stood up and reached for his new hat. "We'll probably have about a week of peace around here, Harris. Until your brother can import a fresh crew of gunhands. Then I expect we'll face the problem and wrap it up."

"You act like it's just a job of work for you," Harris said, the words spoken much more sourly than he intended.

Smoke put his hat on his head. "How do you want me to behave, Harris?"

The sheriff shook his head. "Oh, hell, I didn't mean that the way it came out, Smoke. I'm certainly not defending my brother. This mess can be laid right at Clint's feet and I know it. But if you'll forgive me for saying it, I really wish you and my brother and all his hired guns would just go away and settle this somewhere else."

"I'll face your brother anywhere he picks. Guns or fists; doesn't make any difference to me."

"Yeah," Harris said, a weariness in his tone. "I know that, too. But he's not going to do that. Not yet. But Jud was right when he said that one of us will have to kill him."

"Could you?" Smoke asked softly.

Harris met his eyes. "If he braces me and pulls? You and me, Smoke, we're gunfighters. You know that reflex would take over. I wouldn't hesitate. I'd be sick afterward, but I wouldn't stand there and let him kill me."

"You through with me?"

"I wish," Harris said, softening that with a smile. "Oh, yeah. Someday there'll be laws out here against men settling arguments with guns. But that day is a long way off. Watch your back ridin' home, Smoke."

"I always do, Harris."

"Joe Owens seen Bronco Ford flaggin' down the stage this afternoon," Stony reported to Smoke after supper. "Headin' for Helena."

"He's gone to get more men. I expected it. Jud said that's what Clint would do."

"Jud's really gone?"

"He talked to the sheriff and me and then I watched him ride out, leading a packhorse. Said he didn't like me at all. But yes, he's gone for good."

Stony slowly shook his head. "I reckon stranger things has happened."

Conny asked, "So what do we do now?"

"Look after the herd, mend fences, and stay out of trouble. In about a week, we'll have all the trouble we can handle. I want one man in town at all times, starting tomorrow. By this time, Bronco has sent his wires and men will be coming in, some of them by stage. The last stage runs at three, so that'll give the men time to get back here for supper. I want to know who comes in and how many. The men Bronco will hire will be known gunfighters, easy to spot, and he'll probably hire at least one long-distance shooter, too."

"A lousy damn back-shooter," Conny said contemptuously.

"Yeah, you're right. I'm surprised Clint hasn't done that already."

"He just hasn't thought of it. But Bronco will. For sure, he'll pick up two or three or maybe more in Helena. And there'll be some hanging around Butte. It won't take long for them to get here. Tell the men who ride in not to brace any of these ol' boys. Bronco will be hiring professionals. And they'll be quick on the shoot."

"That back-shooter will be coming in for you, boss," Stony said.

"It's been tried before," Smoke told him. "I'm still around. You boys relax while you can. In a few days, it's going to get real tense around here."

The first of the hired guns arrived three days after Bronco sent the wires. Waymore described them to Smoke. "The first one is a bad hombre called Tall Mosley. He comes high. The redhead is a Irishman named Danny O'Brian. Danny came from a real nice family down in Southern Colorado. He went bad early. Killed his brother and left the country. He's left a lot of dead men behind him. I can't place the other one you described."

"I heard him called Ned in the saloon."

"Ned Burr. He'd make Sam Bass look like a Baptist preacher."

The following day, Conny reported back. He looked shaken. "Man, some bad ones come in this day. I seen Luke Jennings, Little John Perkins and Tom Wiley. Half a dozen more I didn't know, but they looked right capable."

"You catch any names?" Smoke asked, marveling at the man's ability with a knife and fork. His elbows never stopped working.

"Yeah. There was a Dan, a fellow called Rod, and one other name that sounded familiar: Morton."

"Might be Dan Hutton. Rod is short for Rodman; I don't know his first name. Morton is probably Henry Morton. They're all bad ones. Clint is hiring the best, or the worst, depending upon how you look at it."

The next day, Stony reported back shaking his head. "Boss, we got to hire some hands. Gunhands. You ain't never seen the like of what rode in this day. I heard 'em talkin'. Clint wired 'em money to ride the trains in and money to buy fine horses when they got to the gittin' off point. And they was all dressed up fancy." He began ticking them off on his fingers. "James Otis. Paul Stark. Ed Burke. Tom Lessing. Hal Bruner. Big Dan Barrington. Half a dozen more that I didn't know."

"Rider comin', boss," Jeff called.

Smoke stood on the porch and shielded his eyes. Then he smiled. "Well, I'll be double-damned."

"You know that feller, boss?" Tim asked.

"Huggie Charles."

"Huggie Charles!" Malvern almost shouted the name. "The Arizona gunfighter?"

"That's him."

Smoke stepped off the porch as Huggie swung down from the saddle and beat the dust from his clothing. The two men grinned and shook hands.

"You ol' warhoss, you!" Huggie said. "Damn, but you're lookin' fine, boy."

"You're looking fit and fine yourself, Huggie. Sally!" he called. "We've got company."

Sally came out on the porch and began smiling. She skipped down the steps and Huggie grabbed her. "Sally, girl. How you doin', Missy?"

"Now you boys see why he's called Huggie," Smoke said with a smile. "He never misses a chance to hug a woman. Slim or fat, tall or short, beautiful or so bad looking she'd stop an eagle in a dive, Huggie grabs them."

"It's been too many years since you stopped by the Sugarloaf, Huggie," Sally admonished the man. "Just too many years."

"Well, I got me a spread down on the Verde. I was up in Denver lookin' for stock to improve my herd—Herefords are the way to go now—and I heard about all the trouble up here. Why I just saddled up and took to ridin'. Here I am."

"In time for supper, too."

"If you cooked it, honey, that in itself is worth the ride."

"Huggie!" Denver bellered from the porch. "You ol' biscuit-stealin' outlaw!"

"My God, Smoke," Huggie said with a grin. "What ever possessed you to hire something as dis-reputable as that ol' coot? Me and him go back more years than either of us care to think about."

"Huggie's got to be sixty years old," Conny said to the hands gathered on the porch. "Or better. But I bet you he's still quick with them guns. Look at them Peacemakers. If he carved notches there wouldn't be no handles left."

Over supper, Huggie said, "Del Rovare is a day behind me. I told him what was happenin' up here and he quick started windin' up his business and he'll be along."

"I haven't laid eyes on Del since . . . why, it's got to be before Nicole was murdered."

Those around the table fell silent as everybody remembered how Smoke Jensen went after the men who had molested and murdered his wife and son.

"I come through that part of the country some years back, Smoke," Huggie said. "That land is bein' farmed by a real nice couple and they're doin' well. I told them the story of the graves. They musta come in right after you left. They been takin' care of Nicole and the baby's restin' place. Flowers all the time around the graves."

Smoke nodded his head. "Good," he said softly, then excused himself and walked out onto the porch.

Conny started to rise to join him and Sally touched his arm. "No. Let him alone. Nicole and Smoke had a special relationship. Part of him will always belong to her memory. And that's the way it should be. It was a terrible thing what those men did to her and a tiny baby."

"Did Smoke really stake one of them out over a big anthill and pour honey on him?" Ted asked.

"Yes, he did. He also gelded another and cauterized the wound with a hot running iron."

Several of the cowboys suppressed a shudder at just the thought of that.

"He must have been some riled up," Conny said.

"When my husband gets riled up, Conny," Sally said, "believe me, you'll know it."

By the end of the week, Smoke figured that all the new-hired gunslicks that was coming in, were in. And the names were impressive. One-eyed Shaw, Curly Bob Kennedy, Stew Lee, Purdy Wilson, Phil Dickinson. There were other lesser-known gunhands, but all were good at their trade.

Del Rovare had ridden in, looking about as old as God, but still rawhide tough, nimble, and very, very fast on the shoot. He owned a ranch down in Wyoming, the D/R brand. But when a friend was in trouble, Del buckled on his guns and saddled up for the ride.

And it was rumored that Buckskin Deevers was on Clint's payroll. If that was true, Clint had sunk to new lows, for Buckskin was just about as sorry as any man who ever lived. There was nothing he wouldn't do.

Smoke personally knew some of the gunhands that Clint had hired, and felt that if he could talk to them, a few might just pull out. With that thought in mind, Smoke rode into Blackstown one week after Jud Howes had pulled out and Bronco Ford had been named foreman at the Circle 45. The hitchrails in front of the saloon were lined with horses, some with brands Smoke had never seen, many wearing the Circle 45 brand. He paid a visit to Harris Black before heading for the saloon.

"I was hoping my eyes were deceiving me," the sheriff said. "But I might have known you couldn't stay away from a fight."

Smoke smiled at the man and took a seat. "Actually, Harris, I came to town to talk to some of those men over there. I know a few of them."

"So you convince two or three of them to ride out. My brother will just hire more. What will you have accomplished?"

"Why do I get the feeling that you are not in a real good mood?"

"I got fifteen hired guns belly up to the bar over at the saloon. The word I get is that they're under orders to shoot any Double D rider they see. I can't prove that, but that's the word I get from several sources, including the bartender, who is so scared of my brother he'd walk on fire before he'd testify to that in any court of law. Now you ride in just as bold as brass and tell me that you're going over to that saloon to *talk* to some of those tanked-up hired guns. You're right, Smoke. I'm not in a real good mood."

"Who's over there, Harris?"

"I don't know all of them. But I did see Tall Mosley, Little John Perkins, and Paul Stark. I spent half the morning sendin' out wires to sheriff's offices all over the west. There isn't a warrant out for any of them. Except for Buckskin Deevers and he isn't about to show his face in town."

"Sheriff, I don't want a lot of bullets flying around the main street of town. If you tell me to haul it out of here, I'll leave without a word."

Harris shook his head. "I can't do that. Hell, I *won't* do that. But I tell you what I will do. I'll walk over there with you. It's right at noon and a cold beer would taste good before I grab something to eat."

"Let's do it."

Harris stood up, checked another pistol for loads, and shoved it behind his belt. He checked his other Colt and then smiled thinly at Smoke. "I believe in insurance. You loaded up six and six?"

"I'm full."

"I think both of you are crazy!" Deputy Simpson said,

moving to the gun rack. "Sheriff, you want any of us to come with you totin' shotguns?"

"No. Just stay handy in case the lead starts flyin'."

The men stepped out to the boardwalk and stood for a moment. "What does it say in the Bible about Daniel in the lion's den?" Harris said.

"I don't know. But he made it out."

"Let's hope we'll be so lucky."

"I think God had something to do with Daniel getting out."

"I had a feeling a month ago I should start goin' to church more often."

Smoke chuckled and stepped off the boardwalk, the sheriff right beside him. Citizens and shoppers started ducking inside buildings. The wide main street suddenly became deserted.

23

The two men pushed open the batwings and stepped inside the saloon, walking shoulder to shoulder. Once inside, from long habit, they moved apart. The place was filled to overflowing with gawkers, ne'er-do-wells, gamblers, and hired guns. The hum of conversation died as the two men were noticed.

Smoke leaned against the wall and surveyed the situation through cool eyes, his gaze stopping at Tall Mosley. "Been a while, Tall."

"Several years, Smoke," the long, lanky gunfighter said. "Down around Boulder Creek, I think it was."

"That's right." He shifted his eyes to Little John Perkins. "John."

"Jensen," the little gunslick said. "You finally stuck your nose into something that you can't handle, didn't you?"

"Oh, I wouldn't say that, John. I'm still here."

Paul Stark turned and put his back to the bar. He stood smiling at Smoke. "Ain't seen you in two-three years, Jensen. You lookin' prosperous."

"I'm well."

"Your family?"

"They're fine."

"I heard your wife is here."

"Out at the Double D."

Paul's smile was not pretty. He straightened and dropped his hands to the butts of his guns. "I been lookin' forward to this. Ever since I first laid eyes on that wife of yours. When you're cold in the ground, Jensen, I'll lift the skirts of that pretty woman of yourn. I'll strip her nekked and see how she likes it rough."

Smoke shot him. He did not change expression, nor blink an eye. He just pulled, cocked, and fired before anyone could move a muscle. The bullet took the gunfighter in the center of the chest and Paul Stark was dead before his butt hit the floor. No one saw when he pulled his second gun.

"He had no right to say that about your wife," a Circle 45 hired gun said. "I might be shootin' at you 'fore long, Jensen. But I'll not say a word about a good woman."

"Paul raped a woman down in New Mexico a couple of years ago," another man said. "I never did have no use for him."

Smoke eased the hammers down on his .44s and a sigh could be heard from the crowd. A few of those who had witnessed the blinding speed and deadly accuracy of Smoke Jensen would finish their drinks and ride on. No amount of money was worth dying for.

Tall and Little John and the others now knew how fast Jensen was. And several of the smarter ones knew he had come to town to show them. If it hadn't been Paul Stark, it would have been one of them. The eyes of the hired guns widened as the batwings were pushed open and Huggie Charles and Del Rovare stepped in. These men were living legends in the West. Right up there with the old mountain man, Preacher. These two old gunhandlers rated up there with Smoke Jensen and Louis Longmont and Johnny North and Earl Sutcliffe and the Mexican gunfighters, Al Martine and Carbone. What the hell was this pair of ol' rattlesnakes doing here?

"We always miss out on the fun," Rovare said, his eyes on the stretched out Paul Stark.

"Well, maybe it's for the best," Huggie said, stepping around Smoke and the Sheriff. "Man gets to our advanced age, too much excitement ain't good for him." A Circle 45 hand stood in his way. Huggie gave him a shove that nearly put him to the floor. "Get the hell out of the way, boy. Ain't you got no respect for your elders?"

"Who you think you're shovin' around, you old son of a bitch!" the punk popped off.

Huggie slapped him. Huggie was not a young man, but he had worked hard all his life, and his arms and shoulders still were packed with muscle from spending years wrestling cattle. His hands were hard and callused and the blow rocked the young tough back on his bootheels and brought blood to his mouth. He reached for his guns.

"No, Will!" Tall shouted. "That's Huggie Charles."

"Who the hell is Huggie Charles?" the punk said, and dragged iron.

Huggie shot him twice before the would-be tough could clear leather. The kid rose up on the tips of his boots and gasped, then fell forward, landing on his face. He moaned and rolled over, staring up at Huggie.

"I'm Huggie Charles, boy," the old gunfighter told him. "A man ought to know who killed him."

"But I can't die," the young man said, both hands holding his shot-up belly.

"That's what you all think," Del said, looking around the room. "But me and Huggie know different. Like Jensen here. A month from now, not a soul in this town will remember this boy's name. Six months from now, the wooden cross will have begun to rot. A year from now, his grave site will be known only to God—or the devil."

"That's a hell of a thing to say to a dyin' man!" the punk said.

Del looked down at him. "What'd you want me to say, congratulations?" He walked to the bar, Huggie beside him. "Rye, with beer chasers, for me and my friend."

The barkeep was so scared he could hardly pour and pull.

Doc Garrett pushed in and knelt down beside the dying gunhand. He looked up at the sheriff. "Not a chance."

"But I can't die!" the man hollered. "They said I was fast."

"They lied," Smoke told him, then walked to the bar, stopped by Tall. "Get out of this one, Tall." He spoke quietly, his elbows on the bar. "Go on back to where you came from."

"You got a couple of old gunslicks, ten or so punchers, and you're tellin' me to pull out? You ain't got that many friends, Jensen."

The batwings were shoved open and heavy boots thudded against the floor, accompanied by jingling spurs.

"Aw, hell!" a Circle 45 hand said.

Al Martine and Carbone, the Chihuahua gunfighters, walked to the bar. Smoke smiled at the expression on Tall's face. "You think Bronco Ford is the only one who can send a telegram, Tall?"

Martine dropped a hand on Tall's shoulder and spun him around. "You and I, amigo, we have differences to settle between us, no?"

Tall stiffened. He didn't want to pull on Al Martine, even though he knew he was just as fast. But 'just as fast' won't get it. Both men would have lead in them. And standing one foot apart, the wounds would be hideous.

The batwings pushed open and two of the most disreputable-looking men anyone had seen in a long time walked in. They both looked older than dirt. They were dressed in buckskins, except for hat and boots. Both wore bright red sashes around their lean waists. Pistols tucked behind the sashes. They carried Winchester rifles, the '73 model.

"What the hell is *that?*" a Circle 45 hand asked.

"Puma Buck and Lee Staples," Smoke said. "You boys have heard of them, I suppose."

"Heard of them?" another gunny said from his chair, staring up at the old mountain men. "Hell, they been *dead* for years."

With no wasted motion, Puma laid the butt of his Winchester into the hand's face, busting his nose and knocking him out of the chair. "I'm a long way from dead, lad," Puma told him. "And you put a hand on that short gun and I'll kill you."

The hand cursed and came up with his fist wrapped around the butt of a .45. Puma pulled the trigger of the Winchester and punched the gunfighter's ticket for a long dark ride straight to hell.

"Whiskey!" Lee Staples hollered. "And plenty of it. It's been a dusty ride. Smoke, my boy!" He stepped up and pounded Smoke on the arms and shoulders. "It's been a long time."

Puma stepped over the man Huggie had left on the floor and walked to the bar, shaking hands with Smoke. He smiled at Tall, but there was no mirth in his eyes. "This one I helped raise. Me and a whole passel of other mountain men. Get out of my gawddamned way."

Tall's eyes widened in shock. No one talked to him like that. But he moved away, stepping lightly, his back still to the bar. This crazy wild-eyed old man scared him. Tall knew to leave old folks alone. For they had very little to lose and would kill you in a heartbeat.

"Another time, Tall," Martine said. He turned his back to the gunfighter and extended his hand to Puma. "I have heard of you for years, and I am honored to finally make your acquaintance. I am Al Martine, Mr. Buck, and this is my compadre, Carbone."

"Pleased, boys. I've heared of you. You come up to hep my boy, here?"

"Your . . . son?" Carbone was startled.

Puma cackled. "No. Not no blood kin. But a bunch of us mountain men sort of adopted him when he was a tadpole. Any man who is an enemy of Smoke's is an enemy of mine." He turned to face the crowded room. "And I'll kill any man who lifts a hand agin him. I'll shoot you in the back, I'll shoot you in the front. But I will kill you."

"Now just wait a minute," Harris said. "I'm the sheriff here, and I . . ."

"We don't give a damn who you are," Lee Staples said. "We don't believe in waitin' till a rabid skunk bites us 'fore we kill it. And don't even think about givin' me no lectures, I don't take kindly to them. Me and Puma there, we're somewheres around eighty years old. You think we really give a damn what you or anyone else says? Fifty years ago, I probably peed right here where this buildin' is standin'. Probably leanin' up agin a tree 'fore folks come in and cut 'em all down. Now you go run along and tend to lost dogs and treed cats. We'll handle this."

Harris stood speechless.

Puma looked at a young rider standing at the bar. "You work for the Circle 45, boy?"

"A . . . I, uh, yes, sir. I do. I hired on a couple of days ago."

Puma hit him a vicious blow in the belly with the butt of the Winchester, knocking the wind out of him. He doubled over, gagging, and fell to the floor. "Now you hear me, boy," Puma said. "Playtime is over. I talked with some Injuns over on the Divide a few days ago. They tole me that this here Clint Black who owns the Circle 45 had hired men to kill Smoke Jensen. Is that what you hired on to do, boy?"

"I reckon so," the young man gasped.

"Well . . . you a young man, you entitled to make a mistake. I did, a time or two. So I tell you what I'm gonna do. I'm not gonna kill you."

Lee Staples had turned around, facing the men in the saloon, his Winchester level, hammer back. Carbone and Martine stood with him, hands over their guns. Huggie and Del faced the crowded room, smiles on their faces. Not a Circle 45 hand moved a muscle. Most tried to not even breathe.

"Git up!" Puma snapped, and the young man rose painfully. "Walk out of here, get on your horse, and ride. Don't never let me see you within a hundred miles of this place whilst this little war is wagin'. 'Cause ifn I do, I'll kill you on the spot. You understand all that?"

"Yes, sir."

"Git!"

The young man got.

Puma turned around, facing the men in the room. "Anybody else here work for the Circle 45? If you do, make your peace with the Almighty, 'cause you're dyin' today."

"That son of a bitch is *crazy!*" a man whispered.

"Shut up," his buddy whispered.

Puma smiled. "Lee? You step on outside and get ready to shoot anyone who tries to mount a horse wearin' a Circle 45 brand."

Sheriff Black smiled grudgingly. These old boys were putting on the pressure and screwing it down tight. The pot might take the steam a while longer, but everything was coming to a head and it had to blow the lid off soon.

He cut his eyes to Jensen. The man was leaning up against the bar, a slight smile on his lips. In a strange way, he's enjoying this, Harris thought. Then he thought: well, why shouldn't he? He was halfway raised by the likes of these randy, uncurried, wild ol' mountain men. Their philosophy is his own.

None of the Circle 45 hands made any attempt to move toward the door. They did not doubt to a person that Lee Staples would shoot them down like a rabid animal if they went near any horse wearing Clint Black's brand.

Smoke cut his eyes to Tall Mosley. "See you around, Tall."

"Yeah," Tall said. "Bet on it."

Smoke walked out of the barroom, followed by Al Martine, Carbone, then Huggie and Del. Puma was the last one to leave, cautiously backing out, a wicked grin on his face.

Harris came out to the boardwalk a moment later.

"Think I won't shoot you if you interfere?" Puma asked the sheriff.

Harris slowly shook his head. "No, Puma. I don't doubt it for a second."

"That's good, Sheriff," the old mountain man said. " 'Cause me and Lee is gonna bring this here little pimple to a head." His grin turned into a smile. "And we got a few more surprises to spring on you."

"I can hardly wait," Harris said drily.

Puma cackled out laughter. "Course your no-count brother ain't gonna like it a bit."

"You gun my brother down, without it being a fair shooting, or any other man in my jurisdiction for that matter, and you'll face murder charges."

"Hee, hee, hee," Puma cackled. "And you think you be so keen with the high country you think you could find me out yonder in the lonesome?"

"No," Harris said honestly. "I imagine you could lose yourself back there and I'd never find you. I'm just telling you what the charges will be, that's all."

"I think you a good man, Sheriff," Puma told him. "Took you awhile to come to that, from all that I hear about you and your no-count brother, but you made a clean break. Now you ponder this bit of advice: don't confuse bravery and duty with foolhardiness. You just sit back and concentrate on catchin' chicken thieves and footpadders. Stay out of our way. And if you're thinkin' 'bout tryin' to 'rrest any of us, from Smoke Jensen to me, think agin. 'Cause it ain't gonna happen."

"I'll do my job," Harris said stiffly. "This is not eighteen-thirty, Puma. It's halfway civilized out here now."

Puma spat his contempt for that remark. "If it was civilized, men like your brother would be rottin' in the grave instead of hay-rassin' decent folk."

"You break the law, and I'll arrest you, Puma."

"You'll never do such of a thing."

Harris turned, stepped off the boardwalk, and walked to his office.

"What other surprises do you have in store, Puma?" Smoke asked.

"Hee, hee, hee," Puma cackled mysteriously.

24

Those few hired guns who had ridden their own horses into town rode back to the ranch to get any horse that didn't have a Circle 45 brand on it. They had taken Puma at his word, which was wise, for the old mountain man had meant what he said, Sheriff Black or no Sheriff Black.

"He *what?*" Bronco and Clint both screamed at the news.

Tall Mosley repeated what Puma had threatened, and added, "He meant it, Boss. That old man wasn't kiddin'. I got to get some horses for the boys back in town."

"Oh, go on, get them," Clint said, shaking his head. "I should have guessed something like this would happen. I'll be glad when those old coots are all dead. But Al Martine and Carbone? I can't figure that. They were *after* Jensen not that long ago."

"They switched sides," Tall said. "I know the story. Martine and Carbone stopped hirin' their guns and went to ranchin' down in Mexico. Got them a right nice spread, so I hear. Call it the M/C. And believe me, they don't have no trouble with rustlers or bandits."

"Get the horses for the men," Bronco said. When Tall had

left the room, he said to Clint, "You really think that crazy old coot will shoot anyone ridin' a Circle 45 horse?"

"Oh, yes," Clint said without hesitation. "But I've got horses with every kind of brand you can imagine. And I have bills of sale for them. That's no worry. Let's walk outside to the porch. Stuffy in here."

The rancher and foreman stepped out on the porch and a rifle barked, the slug howling off the stone of the house. Clint and Bronco hit the floor. Another slug, fired from a different direction, came screaming over their heads. A coyote yipped and a wolf replied in a howl.

"Those damned old coots brought friends with them," Bronco said. "That's no coyote or wolf."

Tall Mosley and a few others, caught in the corral, could do nothing except stay low in the dirt, crouched behind whatever cover they could find. Which was precious little.

"Crawl back toward the door," Clint said. "We can make the house."

A hand came galloping in from the range and he went galloping back out as long-barreled Springfield rifles, with a range of over three thousand yards, began barking. One knocked his saddle horn off—and another blew his hat off his head. He laid down on the horse's neck and got the hell gone from there.

The old mountain men on the ridges began making life miserable for those in the house and the hands in the bunkhouses. Stove pipes were knocked loose and windows were shattered. Doors were soon rendered useless as the lead knocked out great chunks of wood. Outhouses were riddled with heavy caliber lead and the horses in the corral screamed and reared and panicked and knocked down the gate. They went thundering out to open range, away from the frightening gunfire and the howling bullets.

Clint Black and Bronco Ford could do nothing except seek cover behind the stone of the house and cuss.

Back in town, the Circle 45 hands sat in the saloon and

wondered when in the hell Tall and the others would get back with horses they could ride out on. Not a one of them even remotely considered attempting to mount up on a horse wearing the Circle 45 brand.

Smoke, Martine, Carbone, Huggie, Del, Puma, and Lee waited across the street from the saloon. Waited and watched and smiled at the plight of the hired guns. Harris Black and his deputies sat on the edge of the high boardwalk in front of the sheriff's office.

And the citizens of the town, men, women, and kids, passed by the saloon in a never-ending stream, pointing and laughing at the grounded gunnies, while the hired guns drank whiskey and got madder by the minute.

"It's comin' to a head, Sheriff," a deputy said. "We ought to stop them people over there. They're gonna make them gunnies mad and they'll be a killin'."

"Not this day, there won't," Harris said, rolling a cigarette. "Those boys over there in the saloon aren't fools. They know that if they opened up on civilians, they'd be slaughtered in two minutes. Smoke and those mountain men and Mex gunslingers would shoot that place to splinters and pick their teeth with what's left."

Farmers and riders for other small spreads came into town, saw what was going on, and immediately turned around and beat it back to their places, telling others of the events taking place in Blackstown. By early afternoon, the town was filled up with onlookers.

Out on the Circle 45 range, old mountain men were rounding up the horses and driving them out of the country while others of their kind were having fun riddling the house and bunkhouses with rifle fire.

Up to now, no one had been hurt on either side. Then Clint gave the orders—by shouting—to start making a fight of it.

"Is he out of his mind?" Jim Otis questioned. "Those

sharpshooters are a good half mile off and on the ridges. Hell, we can't even see them."

"And I seen at least three riders makin' a gatherin' of the horses in the south range," another said. "There's something goin' on that I ain't too sure about."

Bullets slammed through broken windows and through the now doorless frame. One clanged into a potbellied stove and whined off, spending itself against a wall.

"I'm gettin' awful tired of this," Curly Bob Kennedy said. "There's a wash out back that I think we could make if we stay in the trees. How about it?"

"Let's go," another said. "Anything beats this."

Then the firing abruptly stopped. The hired guns looked at each other for a moment, then slowly began getting to their feet. Most of them veterans of dozens of range wars and shootings, they sensed the sniping was over, at least for this day. A Circle 45 hand walked his horse into the corral. One arm was hanging useless and his shirt was bloody. He was helped from the saddle just as Clint and Bronco walked up.

"Old men," he said. "Looked like they was all older than God. They rounded up the horses and drove them off. I tried to jerk iron on one of them and he shot me just as cold as could be. Told me to give you a message, Mr. Black. Told me to tell you that you wanted this war, you got it. Now what the hell are you goin' to do about it?"

Clint's face hardened. "Who were they, Tim?"

"Boss, I don't know. I never seen none of them before. They was all dressed in buckskins. And they was *old!* All of 'em old men. They looked like them drawin's of mountain men."

"That's what they are," Tall said. "They've come out of the caves and hidden cabins up in the high lonesome to help Jensen."

Clint Black did some fancy cussing. Scoundrel and murderer that he was, he was still a man of the West, and he knew what this development meant. There had never been a breed quite like the mountain man. They were, for the most part, solitary men who could go for months without seeing or speaking to anything other than their horses. They would brook no nonsense from any man, and if they were your friend, you had a friend for life. But if you were their enemy, they would shoot you on sight and do it without hesitation. Clint became aware that his hired guns had fallen silent and were all staring at him.

"They didn't get all the horses," Clint said. "Saddle them up and go into the east range and round up those over there. They haven't been ridden in awhile so they'll take some topping off. Cleon, you and Donovan hitch up a couple of wagons and go into town and get those men trapped in there."

"In a wagon, boss?"

Clint's hard eyes withered him silent. "You got a better idea, Cleon?"

"Ah . . . no, boss, I reckon not."

"Then get moving. The rest of you start picking up and repairing the damage. I've got to think."

"I think I'll ride in with the wagons," a newly hired gunhand said. "Get me a room at the hotel and take the mornin' stage out. That is, if you ain't got no objections. If you do, I'll walk in." He dug in his pocket and came up with greenbacks. "Here's your advance pay, Mr. Black. I ain't done nothin' to earn it."

Clint waved away the money. "You got shot at. That's enough. Ride in with the wagons and be damned." He turned and walked back to his shot-up house, Bronco walking beside him.

Hal Bruner looked at the gunny. "You think it's that bad, Teddy?"

"I think it's that bad. Man, Clint Black ain't got a friend in this world. The whole countryside is against him. Now these wild men done come out of their holes and is gunnin' for him and anyone who rides for him. I'm gone." He walked back to his bunkhouse to gather up his belongings.

"I think I'll tag along with Teddy," another newly hired gunslinger said. "I'm out of this party."

"Then git," Grub Carson said. "I don't want no man stayin' that I can't count on."

"Let's go get them horses," Yukon said. "Damned if I feel like walkin' into town."

"Who says we're goin' into town?" Slim King asked.

"We're goin'," Yukon maintained. "Clint ain't gonna stand for this. Beginnin' right now, boys, we start earnin' our money."

It was an embarrassed bunch of gunslingers who climbed into the bed of the wagons for the bumpy ride back to the Circle 45 range. None of them made any effort to retrieve whatever possessions they might have had in the saddlebags or to get their rifles in the boot. A townsperson talked briefly with Cleon and Donovan, and after the wagons had left he walked over to the sheriff.

"Somebody attacked the Circle 45 headquarters and run off all their horses. They really shot the place up bad. No one was killed, but a hand took a round in the shoulder."

Smoke, who was standing nearby, said, "Don't look at me, Sheriff. I don't know a thing about it and I'd swear on a Bible I had no knowledge of it."

"I believe you," Harris said. "But this little stunt just might be the final straw for my brother. You best brace yourself." He looked around. Puma and Lee had vanished. "Now where did those two old rowdies go?"

"I have no idea," Smoke told him. "I didn't send for them. They don't work for me or the Double D. They've lived a long, rich, full life, Harris. They'd rather go out in a blaze of glory. And they damn sure don't take orders from any man."

"Yeah," the sheriff said. "I noticed."

"You think Preacher sent them, Smoke?" Sally asked as they sat alone in a swing in the side yard that evening.

"I'm not even sure that Preacher is still alive, Sally. I think he is, and living in that home for old mountain men and gunfighters. No, I think these ol' boys just heard the news and couldn't wait to jump right in the middle of a good fight."

Sally looked around her in the dim light of gathering gloom. Mountains loomed all around them. "I wonder where they are right now?"

"The old mountain men? Oh, they're gathered around a little hat-sized fire, boiling coffee and searing fresh-killed deer or maybe one of the Double D's steers. They're laughing about what took place this day and figuring on how best to stir up some more trouble tomorrow. Don't worry about them. They've been taking care of themselves since long before you and I were born."

"But they're old men, honey. They're in their seventies and eighties."

Smoke chuckled. "And they're still tough as rawhide and mean as a just-woke grizzly. Sally, those ol' boys are having the time of their lives. They're giggling and cackling like a bunch of schoolboys right now. Oh, they've got aches and pains from rheumatism and the years of badly-set broken bones and the like. But this is fun to them. They've got something to do now. They feel a purpose to their lives. I hope none of them get hurt or killed. But if they do, they went into this with their eyes wide open. I lived with mountain men, Sally. I know the type of men they are; I'm a part of that breed. Don't worry about them."

From miles away, they both caught the very faint howl of a wolf echoing around the mountains. Another joined in, then another. Smoke chuckled. "That's them, isn't it?" Sally asked.

"Yes, that's Puma and Lee and their friends. But they're

not doing that for my ears. That's over on the Circle 45 range. They're letting Clint and his gunhands know they're still around. I'd like to be a fly on the wall of the bunkhouses right now.

"Old bastards!" Tall said, as he sat on his bunk, cleaning his guns.

Yukon Golden smiled. "I hear you had your chance at some of them this day. And Al Martine, too. What's the matter, Tall, you have a change of heart?"

Tall stared at the man. "It ain't over yet, Yukon. And was I you, I'd watch my mouth."

"Shut up! " Bronco said from the open door. It would be open for some time, since the mountain men had shot it off. "The both of you. We're riding tonight. We're gonna hit the town and burn it to the ground!"

25

"This is a dumb play," Yukon said. "Nobody ain't never treed no Western town and we're gonna get the crap shot out of us attemptin' it."

"We're not gonna treed it," Grub said. "Just burn it to the ground."

"How?"

"With fire!" Ed Burke said with a laugh.

"Clint's got all that worked out. Stop worryin' so much."

"Yeah?" Yukon looked at the man. "So you tell me this: we burn the town to the ground, where are we gonna get supplies and food and whiskey? Huh?"

That got everybody's attention. Slim King finally said, "I don't understand why we're burnin' the damn town noways."

" 'Cause the boss says to do it," another summed it all up.

"That's right," Bronco said from the doorway. "These folks are gettin' too uppity for Clint's tastes. We burn them out and then when they move on, we rebuild the town and fill it with folks who'll show some respect for Circle 45 hands. Get your dusters and your masks. Let's ride."

But Clint's plan wasn't a very good one. Had he halted

the thunderous drum of hooves a mile from town and sent men in in small teams, they could have easily burned down the town. Instead, the paid gunhands galloped up to the bridge, stopped, lit their torches, and then roared into town. By that time, the townspeople had armed themselves and were waiting. The Circle 45 men got the crap shot out of them.

They made only one pass through town and Bronco hollered at them to head for home range, taking the long way around to get there. There were six men dead in the dirt and four more wounded, their torches burning brightly on the ground beside them. Several buildings were set on fire, and that delayed the forming of a posse while the fires were extinguished.

"No point in going after them, Sheriff," Harris was told. "We all know who ordered it. They'll just alibi for each other like they've always done. Tomorrow we'll put signs up at both ends of town. No Circle 45 riders allowed in town. We're not going to sell your brother any more supplies."

"Do whatever you want to do, Felker. It's fine with me."

"And from now on, we all go armed, at all times. Swede over to the blacksmith's is gonna start sawing the barrels off of shotguns starting at first light. We've had all we're going to take, Harris. Any trouble starts, we're shooting."

The sheriff met the feed store owner's steady gaze. "All right, Felker. I guess it's way past time." *Past time for a lot of things,* Harris thought as he walked away. He turned up a darkened street toward his small house. Guns blossomed flame in the night and Harris Black fell forward on his face.

"Is he still alive?" Smoke asked Doc Garrett the next morning. A deputy had ridden out before dawn to tell them the news and Smoke had ridden back into town with him.

"He's hanging on," Garrett said. "I've done all that I can do. He took two slugs in the chest. Forty-fives, I think. One passed right through and the other lodged. I dug it out. He has not regained consciousness."

"He's a good man, Doc. The community would feel his loss."

"Yes. It took Harris a time to see his brother for what he really is, but he came around and then tried to do his best. They shot him down in the dark, from hiding. I doubt that he'll be able to add anything to that. If he ever regains consciousness."

"You're not from the West, are you, Doc?"

"No."

"I've seen men soak up half a dozen .45 slugs and stay on their feet and kill the man who put them there, and then go on to live to be old men. It's a tough breed out here, Doc."

"Well, Harris' breathing has evened out. He's got a chance. That's about all I can say."

"Tall Mosley hasn't."

"What on earth are you talking about? Has there been another shooting?"

"One is about a minute or so away. Al Martine rode in with me. And there's Tall stepping down at the saloon."

"What is it between those two?"

"They just don't like each other." Smoke walked out to the street and leaned up against an awning support post. He rolled a cigarette and waited.

Tall turned and faced Martine, who was standing on the boardwalk across the street. "What do you want, greaser?" Tall tossed the question out.

"Satisfacción, you son of a puta."

Doc Garrett stepped out. "I know what that means," the doctor said.

"Yeah. Very uncomplimentary," Smoke said, striking a match and touching the flame to his cigarette.

"I'll kill you for that," Tall said.

"Then try."

Tall grabbed and Al put two holes in him. Tall stumbled backward, dropping one gun into the dirt.

"I told him a long time ago that jerking both guns was gonna get him killed someday," Smoke said. "Cuts your speed down just a tad."

Tall lifted his right hand and tried to cock his pistol. Martine waited. Tall painfully eared the hammer back and pulled the trigger, blowing a hole in the dirt. He fell to his knees and dropped that Colt. Then he toppled over into the hoof-churned earth.

"One less," Smoke commented, as Al turned and went into the general store to buy some candy for his sweet tooth.

The two deputies who were in town had watched it all and they walked across the street to stand over the dying Tall Mosley.

"Sweet Baby Jesus!" Lucas said, looking up the street. "Look at that!"

Ten riders were walking their horses slowly into town. Smoke had already recognized Danny O'Brian and Yukon Golden. As they drew nearer, he could make out Slim King and Grub Carson. He was not familiar with the others.

"What do they want?" Doc Garrett asked.

"Me," Smoke told him.

"And you're going to do what about it?"

"Meet them."

"All *ten* of them?"

Smoke smiled. "Well . . . in a manner of speaking, yes."

Smoke looked across the street toward the general store. Al Martine had just stepped out and was standing in front of the store, sucking on a piece of peppermint candy. He pointed up the street and Smoke cut his eyes. Carbone was riding in and Smoke could tell by the tenseness of the man's body that he was quickly sizing things up. Smoke nodded.

"Get up to those deputies, Doc. And tell them to clear the street. Quick, now. Those gunslingers are hunting blood and they're liable to start shooting at any moment." He stepped back inside the doctor's office, and exited out the back way just as Martine was angling for a better position.

Smoke trotted down to the saloon and slipped in through the back door. He wanted as much of the shooting as possible off the street, for the town was unusually crowded this morning, and a lot of kids were in town with their parents.

The bartender saw him and nearly had a heart attack. This barkeep was about the most timid Smoke had ever seen. He put a finger to his lips, shushing the man, and moved to a corner of the room, near a table that was shrouded in shadows. He loosened his guns.

Donovan, and a hired gun from over Kansas way named Lessing, entered the bar. They failed to see Smoke standing in the shadows. Tom Clark, George Miller, and Ed Burke faced Al Martine. Carbone was walking up the center of the street toward Danny O'Brian and Yukon Golden. Slim King and Grub Carson had slipped down an alleyway, looking for Smoke.

"You, ah, boys want a drink?" the nervous barkeep asked.

"Shut up," Lessing told him. "If we want a drink we'll ask for one." He looked around him, his eyes finally picking out the shape of a man standing in the gloom. "Who the hell are you?"

"The grim reaper," Smoke told him.

"The what?" Donovan asked.

"The pale rider."

"Don't give me no lip, boy," Donovan said. "I want a straight answer." He stepped away from the bar and walked slowly toward Smoke. "Damn!" the word left his mouth as he finally recognized the man in the shadows. He jerked iron.

Smoke's .44 roared and spat flame and lead. Donovan doubled over and slumped to his knees, his belly on fire and his lips spewing painful screams. His six-gun slipped from his fingers. Lessing's guns roared just as Smoke dropped to one knee. The slugs went over his head and slammed into the wall. Smoke leveled his .44 and drilled Lessing clean, the lead taking him in the center of the chest.

Out on the street, guns were roaring and men were dying. Lessing cussed Smoke once and then fell forward, no longer able to stay on his feet. Donovan was out of it, stretched out full length on the floor, screaming in pain. Smoke picked up Donovan's gun and shoved it behind his belt. He walked toward Lessing as the man was fumbling to lift his six-shooter. Smoke took it away from him and tossed it on the bar. He loaded up his own .44 and then loaded up the gun he'd taken from Donovan. He sensed more than heard movement in the storage room. Smoke stepped back and waited. The barkeep was nowhere in sight. He had laid down on the floor behind the long bar.

Out on the street, Burke was down and dead with a bullet in his brain and Tom Clark was on his knees, both hands holding his bloody belly. George Miller had dashed down an alleyway.

Danny O'Brian was sprawled in the street and Yukon and Carbone had taken cover behind watering troughs and were exchanging shots.

Slim King pulled open the storage room door and cautiously stepped into the salon, both hands filled with guns. Grub was right behind him, holding a sawed-off shotgun. Both of them saw the bloody body of Lessing and looked around until their eyes found the source of the screaming. Donovan was jerking on the floor, just moments from death. Smoke gave no warning. He just lifted both .44s and started firing as fast as he could cock the hammer and pull the trigger.

One slug hit the shotgun just as Grub had turned and was lifting the weapon. Both barrels fired, the full charge taking Slim in the back at a distance of no more than two feet. The man was blown apart and dead instantly. Horror in his eyes at what he had done, and his fingers numbed from the unexpected discharge, Grub dropped the shotgun and clawed for his pistols.

Smoke let him clear leather and then shot the man twice, both .44 slugs striking him in the chest. Grub would no longer have to worry about his next meal. Reloading, Smoke carefully avoided the mess by the storage room door and walked out the rear door of the saloon.

A slug knocked out chips of wood by Smoke's head. He flattened against the wall, then edged back in the direction from which he'd come and slipped under the saloon, hoping he would not disturb any rattler who might be seeking shelter from the hot sun. He worked his way toward the front of the building and after carefully checking the rear of the alley, he slipped out near the mouth and stood for a few seconds, watching the action in the street. Yukon's back was to him.

"Hey, Yukon!" he called.

The gunfighter spun around and stood up. Smoke and Carbone fired as one. Yukon Golden lifted himself to his full height. He wore a very curious expression on his face. His guns clattered to the boardwalk and he pitched forward.

"How many left?" Martine called.

"Two, I think," Carbone shouted back.

"Clark and Miller," someone shouted from behind walls. "They're down near the smithy's shop."

The sound of galloping horses thundering out of town followed the shout.

"The bastards stole my horses!" a man yelled.

"That's it then," Smoke said, walking up to where Tom Clark lay in the street. Ed Burke lay dead a few feet away. Tom was still alive, but not by much. Smoke knelt down behind the mortally wounded gunhand.

"If you have anything to say, you'd better say it quick," Smoke told him.

"Go to hell," Tom gasped.

"I am thinking you will be there before us," Carbone said, punching out empties and reloading.

"You the one that shot me?" Tom asked.

"I did," Martine said. "I think."

"You go to hell, too!"

The Mexican gunfighter shrugged his shoulders philosophically. "All in due time, pistolero. But I have friends down there you might look up and say hello to."

Tom cussed them all and then closed his eyes. His fingers clawed at the dirt for a moment; then he relaxed.

The undertaker and his assistant ran up, both of them smiling. Business had never been this good. People began crowding the streets, eyeballing all the dead and congratulating the Double D men. But Smoke, Carbone, and Martine all knew the congratulations were hollow. They were welcome now, but whenever the shooting finally stopped and Clint Black was either dead, gone, or in jail, the welcoming would cease and the citizens would begin to drop hints that perhaps it was time for the gunfighters to leave. They had all been through it many times in the past.

"Somebody come in here and help me clean up all this mess!" the barkeep squalled. "I'm gettin' sick to my stomick. I never seen such a terrible sight."

The two deputies walked up, along with Dr. Garrett.

"Harris just opened his eyes," the doctor told them. "When all the shooting started," he said, 'Smoke Jensen must be in town.'"

26

Three of Clint Black's hands disappeared while out rounding up the last of the horses. Horses and riders just vanished. No trace of them was ever found.

"Them ol' men got them," Bronco opined. "They're camped all around the edge of the range. Brazen about it, too. They don't make no effort to hide their cookfires. They're darin' us to come get them."

"Hell with them," Clint said. "They're not our main problem." He was still shaken by the news that eight of his best gunhands had gone face down in town. Now it looked like his brother was going to live, and that irritated him. Everything was going sour. He'd lost two more of his hired guns. They had just saddled up and ridden out. Didn't even ask for any pay. They just left.

What made matters even worse was that not a single reply had been received on his latest bid to hire more men. No one wanted to tangle with a dozen or more living legends. Including the cook, he had twenty-six men. At one time, Clint had boasted he could field seventy-five of the toughest hands in the territory. Now he didn't have a single working cowboy left. Not that it mattered, for he personally had ridden his range and found that he didn't have a steer left. They had all been rustled, probably by the mountain men. His house and all the outbuildings were in a shambles from hundreds of rounds being pumped into them; the roofs all leaked. He could not find any workmen to repair the damage. No one would work for him. And he had even put ads in the Helena paper.

Clint sat in his den, his thoughts dark. The Double D was now in good shape, with a large herd and at least fifteen tough, seasoned hands to maintain it. Clint and his men had been banned from ever setting foot in Blackstown—the name of which had now been changed to Canyon City. His town no longer.

Clint was under no illusions about facing Smoke Jensen— the one person he blamed for all his misfortune. He wasn't as fast with guns as Smoke was and he didn't think he could take him in any type of stand-up fistfight.

Any reasonable man would have called it quits and tried to make peace. But Clint Black was not a reasonable man.

He rose from his chair and looked out a bullet-shattered window. He could almost smell the odor of defeat. It was not a smell he liked.

"God, I hate you, Jensen," Clint whispered. "I despise you."

He walked slowly back to his chair and sat down heavily. He did not know what to do next. But he did know this: he was going to kill Smoke Jensen. He just didn't know how he was going to accomplish that.

"I think you ladies are reasonably safe now," Smoke told the twins. "Unless I completely missed the mark, I believe Clint has shifted his hatred to me. Sending those ten gun-hands into town this morning tipped his hand."

"Then you feel we could safely ride our own range, Smoke?" Toni asked.

"As long as you have a couple of hands with you. I know some of those old mountain men are watching your range. I've seen their smoke."

"Their . . . smoke?" Jeanne said.

"Indian talk. They're out there. And remember this: you've got twelve pretty salty ol' boys on the payroll now, and that's plenty for a spread this size. And they're good men. Clint, on the other hand, has been losing men steadily. He can't have more than twenty-five men on his payroll right now. And none of them can tell the difference between a steer and a buffalo. I know gunhands. When they start sensing defeat, they'll pull out. And I'll bet that right now, it's pretty darn glum over on the Circle 45 spread."

"What do you think Clint will do next?" Toni asked.

Smoke shook his head. "I wish I knew."

Nelson, Clements, and Bankston (who was now free of the skunk odor) rode into town, their gunbelts hanging from the saddle horns. They stopped in front of the general store and were immediately met by a shotgun-toting deputy.

"Whoa!" Bankston said. "We don't work for the Forty-five no more. These are our horses. Look at the brands. All we want to do is provision up, have a hot meal at the café, and we're history, Deputy."

"All right. Suits me, boys. I'll pass the word to leave you be."

" 'Preciate it, Deputy," Nelson said.

The word quickly spread up and down the street, and the former Circle 45 riders were shocked when the townspeople actually spoke to them and were friendly. They certainly were not used to that from the citizens of the newly named town of Canyon City.

And true to their word, they bought supplies, had a drink

and a meal, and were gone within the hour. Harris Black lay in the bed at the doctor's office and watched them leave.

"My brother's little empire is falling apart," he said to the doctor. "It couldn't happen to a more deserving person. He fooled me for a long time, Doctor. He lied to me and I believed him. Then when I finally began to suspect him, I still believed him. I just couldn't, no, *wouldn't* believe that my own brother would lie to me. I was a fool."

"What do you think Clint will do next?"

"I don't know, Doc. But he'll go out with a bang. You can bet on that."

Clint had strapped on his guns and gathered his men on the grounds around the front porch. "From this day on, I'm paying triple wages for the men who stay with me to the end. And the five thousand dollar bounty still stands on Jensen's head. If you're going to leave me, do it now."

The gunslicks looked at one another and shuffled their feet and whispered among themselves. One-eyed Shaw finally spoke. "I reckon we'll stay, Boss. But we want a month's wages in advance. You might get killed and then we'd be stuck."

"That's fine with me. Line up and draw your advances."

As the men were being paid, Buckskin Deevers asked, "What's the plan, boss?"

"I don't have one," Clint replied truthfully. "And I'm sure open to suggestions."

Buckskin stepped to one side of the porch, allowing the other hired guns to be paid. When the last of them had drawn their pay and only Bronco remained, Buckskin said, "Whatever we do, we've got to leave the ranch on the quiet. Those old mountain men have ringed us."

"I still think we could take those old farts out," Bronco said.

Buckskin looked at him. "Ellis and Jones and Harden had that same idea. You seen them since they rode out?"

Bronco shook his head irritably. "Only their horses."

"That's right. Only their horses. Boss, I'm gonna say something that you ain't gonna like. But here it is. Those old men out yonder in the hills don't have no job of work they got to return to. They can stay here forever, and if Smoke wants them to, they will. Sooner or later, probably sooner, one of them will get a clean shot at you and it'll be over."

Clint slowly nodded his head and looked up at the murderer. "Go on," he said softly.

"We got twenty-three men able to sit a saddle and that includes you. We're not going to win this war, so you might as well put that out of your mind."

"I had already reached that conclusion," Clint said. There was no anger in his voice, just resignation.

"So you want . . . ?" He trailed that off, already knowing the answer.

"To kill my enemy."

"Smoke Jensen."

"Yes."

"The twin sisters?"

"Once Smoke is dead, they can be dealt with."

Buckskin suppressed a sigh. Clint just couldn't get it through his head that if harm came to Smoke Jensen, those old mountain men would wait until Hell froze over to get a shot at him. Buckskin was a murderer, thief, rapist, and was thoroughly worthless, but he wasn't stupid. Every fiber in his body told him to get clear of this fight. It was clearly over. There was no way that Clint could win, and to hang around was suicide. But Buckskin had taken the man's money and would stay. And he knew that the others would do the same.

"Thank you, Buckskin," Clint said, standing up. "I'll come up with a plan."

"Okay, Boss. Me and the boys will do whatever you say." Back in the bunkhouse, he said, "He has no plan. If we had any sense, we'd give the money back, tie a white handkerchief to our rifles, and ride out of this damn country."

A gunhand known only as Burt stood up and walked to the open doorway. "I want to see Smoke Jensen dead on the ground. That's what I want to see."

"I'm afraid Jensen will be walkin' around long after someone buries you, Burt," One-eyed Shaw said.

"Bull!" Burt said. He stepped outside, and a heavy rifle cracked from more than half a mile away. The big slug took the hired gun in the center of his chest and slammed him back against the outside wall. Burt slid down to the ground, dead on his butt.

After walking to the front door and seeing what had happened, Clint sat in his now heavily fortified study and cussed. All the windows had been boarded up and bookcases shoved against them. He was a prisoner in his own damn house. He cursed the old mountain men who had surrounded his home and he cursed Smoke Jensen. He cursed his brother and he cursed the Duggan twins. He cursed the citizens of Canyon City and when he couldn't think of anyone else to curse, he just sat and cussed. He was still cussing when Tom Clark and George Miller tied white pieces of cloth to the barrel of their rifles and rode away.

Puma Buck and Lee Staples stopped by the Double D late that afternoon and swung down from their saddles. They declined an invitation to come inside the house. Neither of them much liked houses. They sat on the porch and accepted coffee and doughnuts.

"Clint Black lost three more men this day," Lee said. "They buried one, and two rode out with white handkerchiefs tied to their rifles. We let them go."

"It's gettin' plumb borin' on them ridges," Puma said. "The boys want to attack the house and get done with it, Smoke."

"No," Toni said. "As much as I hate Clint Black, I want all the men to just go away and leave us alone."

"Let's ride over there and try to make peace with the man," Jeanne suggested.

"Bad move, Missy," Puma said. "No tellin' what Clint might do. Situation like it is, he ain't predictable no more. He just might shoot you both on sight. Me and the boys will stay just as long as it takes. We got no place to go and nothin' to do when we get there. We're living off Circle 45 beef. We rounded them up and moved them over into that valley where you-all was ambushed. He ain't got nary a steer left. All he's got is some mangy hired guns and a heart full of hate for Smoke. He can't get no supplies. We got the road watched all the time."

"I don't think he can hold out too much longer," Smoke said. "You boys keep up the sharpshooting, Puma. It's taking a toll on those guns of his. He's losing one or two every day. He's got to crack soon and then it'll be over." He smiled. "And I think I'll just heat up the fire a little bit."

Sally looked over at him. "Every time you get that look in your eyes, I start to worrying."

He reached over and patted her hand. "Don't worry. This isn't gun-talk, honey." He stood up. "Excuse me, folks. I have a letter to write."

Everyone looked at Sally. She shrugged her shoulders. "Don't ask me. I'm just his wife."

Smoke returned in ten minutes with a sheet of paper. He handed it to Sally. "Sally, how long would it take you and Toni and Jeanne to write out about fifty or sixty copies of this?"

She read the short letter and started laughing. "Not long. Come on, girls. Let's get busy."

Cleon Marsh found the note tacked to the gate, read it, and for a moment was stunned. Then he rode back to the ranch and handed the note to Clint.

Clint's face turned beet red when he read the letter. "It

says here he's posted this . . . thing all over the country. I'll be the laughing stock of the territory! The son of a bitch!" He threw the paper to the ground.

Bronco picked it up, read it, and said, "You sure will be if you ignore this. Did you read down at the bottom?"

"No!" Clint shouted.

"If you don't meet him, he's going to mail this to every paper in the territory."

Buckskin Deevers read the note. "He's callin' you out, Boss. You ain't got no choice in the matter. If you don't meet him and slug it out, you might as well ride on out of the country. You know as well as me how Western folks are."

Clint knew. Only too well. He took the letter and reread it.

THIS IS AN OPEN CHALLENGE FROM SMOKE JENSEN TO THE MURDERING, RAPING, AMBUSHING, NIGHT-RIDING, YELLOWBELLIED CLINT BLACK. I SAY YOU ARE AFRAID TO MEET ME IN A STAND-UP FISTFIGHT. YOU HIDE BEHIND HIRED GUNS AND DO NOT HAVE THE COURAGE TO MEET ME AND FIGHT IT OUT MAN TO MAN. I WILL BE WAITING IN THE MAIN STREET OF CANYON CITY AT NOON ON SATURDAY. IF YOU FAIL TO SHOW, THEN EVERYONE IN THE TERRITORY WILL KNOW EXACTLY WHAT KIND OF CRAVEN COWARD YOU REALLY ARE.

It was signed, "Smoke Jensen."

Clint lifted his eyes. All his men had gathered around the front porch. And he knew then that if he didn't meet Smoke Jensen, he would not have a hand left. They would ride out, showing their contempt for him. The rules were few in the West, but they were enforced rigidly. And if a man was called out by another man of approximately the same size and age, you went, or you got on your horse and rode out.

No one in the rugged, wide-shouldered west would tolerate a coward.

Clint was between a rock and a hard place and he knew it. He slowly folded the paper and stuck it in his pocket. "Well, boys, looks like we take a ride come this Saturday morning."

27

Of course Clint had far darker plans than just the fight on his mind. But those were quickly dashed when One-eyed Shaw told him the mountain men had left the Circle 45 range and had taken up positions all around the Double D ranch and grounds. Clint's plans of burning out the Duggan twins, while all the Double D hands were in town watching the fight, were tossed out the window with that news. Then he thought he might have a sniper shoot Jensen during the fight. But on this Saturday, all guns were to be banned in Canyon City. Every man would leave his guns at checkpoints at both ends of town. And Harris had ordered all able-bodied townsmen to be sworn in as special deputies and they would be heavily armed.

"Jensen don't fight by no rules," Bronco Ford told his boss. "He fights to win. And he'll offer no mercy nor give no quarter."

Clint nodded his head in agreement. Since he had made up his mind to fight, he had not taken a drink of anything stronger than coffee. He knew he was in excellent physical shape, for he had always been vain about that. He was strong as a bull and had knocked men unconscious with just one punch. But could he whip Smoke Jensen? He didn't know. He would have to rely on good footwork and lots of bobbing and weaving and ducking and try to wear the man down.

But he had to win. He had to. Everything was at stake. If he lost, he would be a humiliated and broken man in the eyes of all the people. He could not allow that to happen. One way or the other, by hook or by crook, he had to win.

"He's a bull of a man, Smoke," Waymore told him. "Strong and can punch like no man I ever seen. He'll gouge your eyes and use his boots on you if he gets the chance. I saw him cripple a man like that. He likes to hurt people, really likes it. He's a cruel brute."

Smoke nodded his understanding. "Thank you, Waymore." He wasn't particularly worried about Clint Black. He'd fought bigger and better men than Clint . . . and stomped them into the ground. During the time between the challenge and now, Smoke had cut out tanned leather and made himself a pair of gloves. They were almost double the thickness of ordinary gloves, and would enable him to hit harder and also protect his hands.

"Lots of bets on this fight, boss," Conny said, after returning from Canyon City. "Folks comin' in from seventy miles away to see it. The papers in Helena have sent reporters in. They wanted an interview with you. I told them I didn't have no authority to speak for you."

"The fight will be an interview that will speak for itself."

"You get a good night's sleep, boss. Tomorrow is a big day."

"I assure you, Conny, I will sleep like a baby."

"Don't nothin' bother you, boss?" Conny asked.

Smoke smiled at him. "No point in worrying about things a man can't change, Conny."

"I reckon not. Good night, boss."

Smoke ate only a light breakfast the morning of the fight. Sally and Toni and Jeanne had prepared baskets of lunches they would eat after the fight. Baked beans and huge sandwiches and fried chicken and jam and jellies.

"Aren't you worried?" Toni asked Sally. "I would be positively beside myself with dread."

"No. I've seen Smoke fight before. Oh, he'll have a busted lip and a black eye and some bruised ribs and various other abrasions and contusions, but he'll win and he'll be alive. Smoke fights coldly, you see. Never loses control. It will be very brutal, ladies. I doubt that you have ever witnessed anything like it before."

Although neither of the twins would admit it, they both were looking forward to the fight.

Canyon City had swelled to ten times its normal population, with people coming in from as far away as a hundred miles. Entire families had shown up, bringing picnic lunches and planning to make a day of it. Enterprising store owners along Main Street had rented out roof space for spectators. Bleachers had been hastily knocked together and Main Street was blocked off. Street vendors were peddling everything from beer to banners.

Boos and catcalls went up as Clint Black and his men rode into town and checked their guns under the watchful eyes of regular deputies and newly appointed special deputies. A special elevated bed frame had been built in the show window of the general store so Harris Black could look over the heads of spectators and watch the fight in comfort. The sheriff kept his pistols handy, for he suspected the fistfight would only be part of this day's events. His brother did not enjoy losing at anything.

Wild cheering erupted when Smoke and his party rode in. They stabled their horses and checked their guns.

"Keep the Double D people on one side of the roped-off area and the Circle 45 rowdies on the other side," Lucas told his men.

The arena was a simple one. Ropes had been stretched

from one side of the street to the other, so the men could have plenty of room to maneuver.

Smoke took off his spurs, handed them to Denver, and pulled on his leather gloves. He walked to his side of the ropes. There were no rules to this fight. It was kick, gouge, and stomp until one of the men was down and could not continue.

Smoke slipped between the pulled-tight ropes and walked to the center of the "ring."

"Come on, Clint," Lucas said, waving at the rancher. "Let's get this going." He stepped back and leaned against a hitchrail as Clint walked into the ring and up to Smoke Jensen.

"This one is for the boys you killed in that valley," Smoke told the rancher. "You child-killin' son of a bitch." Then he hit Clint in the mouth with a powerful and totally unexpected hard right fist that bloodied the man's lips and knocked Clint Black smack on his butt in the dirt.

The crowd roared and the fight was on.

Clint scrambled to his boots, his face dark with anger and his eyes blazing with wild hatred. He hadn't been knocked down since he was a boy. But he maintained a tight control on himself as he lifted his fists.

Clint jabbed and Smoke flicked the blow away from his face and drove a left straight in. The leather-covered fist impacted against Clint's mouth, and the blow snapped the big man's head back. Clint cursed and swung; his fist caught Smoke on the shoulder. Smoke ducked, weaved, and hammered at Clint's kidneys, forcing the man to give ground.

Smoke followed him, relentless in his pursuit. Smoke took a blow to the jaw that rattled his teeth. Clint could punch like a mule's kick, Smoke would give him that.

"I'll kill you," Clint said. "I'll beat you to death, Jensen."

"I doubt it," Smoke told him, then kicked the man on the kneecap.

Clint howled and jumped around, favoring the throbbing

leg. Smoke stepped in and busted the man's mouth with a left and a right. Off balance, Clint tumbled to the ground. Smoke made no attempt to use his boots on the fallen man. Unless Clint tried it dirty, Smoke would keep it as clean as brawling could be in those times.

Clint charged in, swinging wide. Smoke saw what the man had in mind and ducked. He grabbed the thick wrist with both hands and turned his body, throwing Clint to the dirt. Clint landed on his face and came up cussing, spitting dirt, and mad as hell.

The crowd was roaring and cheering, but neither man paid them any attention.

Clint bored in, smashing blows to Smoke's face and body. Smoke's mouth was bleeding and his side hurt where Clint had connected. Smoke stuck his fist into Clint's face and pawed. When Clint lifted his arm to brush away the gloved fist, Smoke blasted a right into Clint's belly. The man whooshed out air, dropped his guard, and Smoke hit him hard on the side of the jaw. Clint's knees buckled and he backed up. Smoke didn't let up. He stalked the man relentlessly, hammering at him with fists that seemed to be made of iron.

Clint recovered and connected with a solid left that hurt. Smoke backed up and Clint jumped at him, swinging both big fists. Smoke ducked and dove at the man, catching him in the belly with a shoulder. Smoke wrapped both strong arms around the man's waist and hurled him to the ground, knocking the wind from him.

Smoke grabbed the man by the hair, jerked his head back, and, standing over the fallen rancher, drove his right fist into the man's face half a dozen times. Clint's lips were pulped, his nose was spread all over his face, and one ear was nearly torn off.

Smoke released his hold on the man's hair, grabbed him by one arm and jerked him to his boots. Holding on to his arm, Smoke threw him across the street, with Clint spinning and staggering and flapping his arms, trying to halt the momentum. Clint slammed into a hitchrail and it shattered under his weight.

Clint crawled to his feet and ducked his head into a watering trough. Then he came up roaring like a maddened bull and charged across the street.

"Punch his head off!" Jeanne Duggan yelled, caught up in the excitement.

"Kick him in the parts!" Toni shouted.

Sally looked at them and smiled.

Clint connected with a wild swing and Smoke went down. He rolled and came to his boots. Clint bored in and Smoke stopped him cold with a right to the jaw. Clint backed up and Smoke came on, hitting him with both fists, belly and mouth. Clint went down and Smoke waited, both hands clenched into fists.

The rancher lurched to his feet and Smoke planted both boots and hit the man with everything he had, putting all two hundred-plus pounds into the blow. Those standing by the ropes heard the man's jaw shatter. Clint was poleaxed to the ground and did not move.

Smoke walked to the horse trough, stripping off his gloves and sticking them into a back pocket. He washed his face and dunked his head into the water. The crowd was yelling and hollering and cheering. Harris rose to his knees. He reached into a boot and came up with a knife. With blood pouring from his mouth, his nose, and one ear, he screamed curses at Smoke and ran toward him. Smoke could hear nothing over the roaring of the crowd. A pistol cracked, the slug taking Clint in the center of his forehead, stopping the man and flinging him backward into the churned up dirt of the street. He lay with arms outspread, the blade of the knife twinkling in the midday sun.

Harris Black had fired through the window of the general store.

The crowds fell silent, staring at the dead Clint Black.

The rancher had possessed everything any man could ever want. But Clint had wanted more. And all it got him in the end was a bullet in his brain. A ruthless man's reign of terror had ended. It was over.

28

The hired guns—now out of a job—stood and listened to Lucas's words. The words were familiar; they had all heard them before. The gunslingers were surrounded by fifty heavily armed and grim-faced men. "You got one minute to get clear of this town," the deputy said. "And don't you ever show your faces around here again. At one minute plus one second, we all start shooting. And no, you don't get your guns back. Now, *move!*"

Thirty seconds later, the pounding of hooves was fading into memory.

Harris Black motioned for Lucas to come into the general store. He handed him his sheriff's badge. "I'm through. When I get on my feet, I hope I never have to use a gun against another man as long as I live."

Smoke took a long hot bath behind the barber shop and dressed in fresh clothing. Before leaving the Double D that morning, they had packed for the ride back home. Smoke, Sally, and the three Sugarloaf hands stepped up into the saddles and looked at the crowd, watching them. The townspeople filled the street, standing in silence.

"We'll never forget you." Toni spoke for the twins and the town. The sisters had tears in their eyes as they watched the riders fade into the distance.

Harris, listening from his bed in the store front, muttered, "You can damn sure say that again." He lay his head back on the pillow and closed his eyes. He tried to work up some degree of sorrow and pity for his brother. He could not. "Hell with it," he said, and went to sleep.

The townspeople stood in the streets and on the boardwalks and cheered and applauded as the Sugarloaf riders headed south, back to Colorado.

Swede the blacksmith tossed a shovelful of dirt over the dark, bloody spot in the street where Clint Black had lain. He walked back to his shop and picked up his tongs. The undertaker's hammer could be heard, nailing the coffin lid shut on Clint Black. The old mountain men and the famed gunfighters slipped quietly back into history. Felker, at the feed store, hung a sign in his window: Open For Business.

The last depositor at Clint Black's bank withdrew his money and the manager shut the door, hanging a Closed sign in the window.

Denver and the former cook at the Double D, Liz, hunted up a preacher. They had a new life to begin.

Two traveling salesmen, riding in the stage, passed the five riders heading south. "Say," one of the drummers said. "That was Smoke Jensen!"

"That's balderdash," his companion replied. "Smoke Jensen is just a myth. He doesn't exist."

"Maybe you're right. There's Blackstown up ahead. Say, look at that sign. The name's been changed. Canyon City. Well, I'll be darned. I bet there's a story behind that."